THE BROOKFIELD DAUGHTER

The Brookfield Daughter

She's highly intelligent, very attractive, and almost human

Richard Douglas Taylor

Jer-Ben Publications, Inc.

Copyright 2015 by Richard Douglas Taylor

Published in the United States by: Jer-Ben Publications, Inc.

Library of Congress Cataloging-in-Publication Data

Taylor, Richard Douglas
The Brookfield Daughter/ Richard Douglas Taylor

ISBN-13:978-0-9789238-2-2 (trade pbk)
ISBN-10: 0-9789238-2-0 (trade pbk)

Printed in the United States

Email comments or queries to rdtaylor@mediacombb.net

10 9 8 7 6 5 4 3 2 1

Thanks, Jean Louise Taylor Newton:
The best editor I've ever worked with.

Prolog

Barely a stone's throw from Lake Macbride's dam and spillway, a small patch of defused bubbles broke the surface directly under the tail feathers of a dozen dozing mallards. Startled, the flock immediately webbed their way to less troubled waters, quacking in displeasure and indignation.

An object the size and shape of a bowling ball rose from the middle of the disturbance and hung suspended one foot above the water. Its lower hemisphere was raven black with white specks to match the night sky above, its top half a few shades lighter to blend with the shadowed earth below. After a quick, three-sixty radar scan showed no immediate threats, the probe shot to a height of three hundred feet and began a more complete, up-down-all-around infrared sweep in a two-mile radius.

Two raccoons waddling back into the woods glowed a warm pink on the submerged craft's monitor. The heat signatures of the twelve mallard ducks—now swimming even farther away and protesting louder—showed only a cool cyan, due to their thick, insulating feathers. The cold-blooded bullfrog—sticking halfway above the surface—registered nothing at all, his body temperature the same seventy degrees as the water.

The only red and orange returns to suggest the precautionary presence of warm-blooded humans came from a small tent at the far end of Macbride a mile away. But the two figures were horizontal and not moving, presumably fast asleep.

The length of a football field from goal post to goal post and half as wide, the Mejan ship slowly, quietly began to break the lake's gently-rippled surface. Sheets of water—trickling from its slick, arched hull—were barely audible above the buzz of a million noseeums in the summer night air. With most of it still submerged, the vehicle from another dimension held motionless, while the countershaded probe, hovering above, conducted one last scan. No other human signatures detected, it rejoined its craft through a hole in the hull just slightly larger than itself.

The night sky was perfect: both cloudless and moonless, just a blanket of blackness with a thousand pinpricks of light flickering through the thin haze. The extraterrestrials had been patiently waiting for these conditions for over two months. Any kind of a low ceiling would reflect back the city lights from Iowa City in the south and Cedar Rapids to the north, creating a lighted backdrop that would easily silhouette the rise and course of the enormous ship. Likewise, a clear night with any lunar phase from one quarter to full—bouncing moonbeams off its shiny skin—could catch even the casual eye.

Maximum concealment was a top priority with the Mejans, facilitated by their spacecraft's undetectability via any type of radar, laser beam, or sound wave. Yet, even sheathed in such stealth, it wasn't invisible. Some kind of cloaking device was still far off in the science fiction future, if even possible at all. And too many humans these nights were watching the skies with camera phones at the ready and overstimulated imaginations, while some media were always willing to inflate the fuzziest photo or slightest anomaly to the brink of hyperbole. So, the two remaining Mejans aboard needed the night to be as dark as possible, especially for this particular voyage.

June 24, 1994 was such a night. Twenty-one years ago.

To avoid creating a perceptible sucking sound when its flat undercarriage cleared the surface, the spacecraft—shaped like a sleek loaf of Italian bread with the back end sliced cleanly off—inched upward at a five-degree tilt until all twenty feet of its vertical girth were airborne. Once leveled off, it quickly and with only a token of turbulence ascended to an altitude of three thousand feet, leaving behind nothing more than a swirling cloud of silver mist.

Enough was enough. The dozen, unjustly maligned mallards took to the sky in a flurry of wing beats to find a nice, quiet puddle anywhere but here. The two raccoons couldn't care less, already snacking on some freshwater clams at the back of the northern inlet. The bullfrog's pea-sized brain had long forgotten about the disturbance, and resumed croaking for a mate.

Poised motionless high above Lake Macbride, a quick scan from its onboard radar confirmed no aircraft or other objects in their flight plan. Countershaded much like its probe, the daughter ship from Meja headed due west, gradually accelerating to a hushed and judicious fifty miles per hour. It would be over its objective in six minutes.

It would be *under* it in twelve.

Chapter 1

The 2015 silver Lexus SUV pulled over to the side of the gravel road, its twenty-inch mud and snow tires crackling against the larger stones on the narrow, less-traveled shoulder. Only two feet separated it from a sharp drop into the six-foot, grassy ditch, purposely dug that deep decades ago to hold the heaviest of a Midwest winter snow. But this was spring. The snow was gone. The ditch was dry.

Easing the gearshift into park, Jax reached over to the passenger seat and plucked his portable Galaxy S tablet from among the hodgepodge of organic energy bars, various plastic worms still in their unopened packs, and a half-full Dasani water bottle. There was also the never-worn Daiwa fishing cap he always brought along in case he ever convinced Jannie to join him on one of these fishing expeditions. Removing his pair of polarized sunglasses and tossing them on the dash, he dropped his gaze to the tablet for a more serious review of Google Earth's satellite image of the area.

"Right road. Right spot," he mused to himself, zooming in closer on the screen, showing a view about one mile in diameter. Satisfied, he twisted around in the black leather bucket seat to check his eight o'clock. There were the four blue Harvestores and the single gray silo, all five penetrating the skyline like an economy pack of dildos. Close by was the classic red barn with white trim and arched roof, plus many other outbuildings splayed out to the west. "Definitely the right farm," he concluded, dropping the tablet to his lap.

But when Jax Jackson visually scanned the area to his immediate left for the third time, he could only shake his head. "So where the hell is that pond?"

It was supposed to be to right there, about a hundred yards out, in that pasture. But there was only a weird hump, rising up from the otherwise flat terrain like some Indian burial mound. The only problem was that this particular Indian burial mound was large enough to entomb the entire Sioux nation. About two stories high and running parallel with the road, its south end tapered back to earth about three long casts from that red barn. The other end was way up to the north over a hundred yards, before also tapering back to ground level. Atop that north end stood a grove of trees, the only ones in the immediate pasture. Jax rechecked Google Earth, zooming in even farther. Sure enough, that weird farm pond—shaped like

11

a giant calcium pill—had trees capping the northern quarter. That's where the pond had to be: *On top of a weird knoll!*

Retrieving his pocket-sized binoculars from one of the console compartments, Patrick Bernard Jackson twisted around again, this time leaning out the window to scope the grounds around the farm buildings. No sign of anyone, just a couple dozen Black Angus cows grazing in that stretch between the barn and the foot of the hill. Ten minutes ago he had started to do the right thing by driving up to the farm house to ask permission. But he had stopped short. The foreboding, twelve-foot-high, black steel gate anchored by equally high brick stanchions—one of which sported a camera-intercom with a keypad—suggested the wealthy farmer didn't relish visitors. And Jax hated confrontations, even one as impersonal and nonthreatening as being told *No* by a disembodied voice over a crackling speaker.

But among this outdoor writer's most ardent passions was to someday find that virgin body of water where his beloved bass were big as beavers and ignorant of man and lure. Such was the stuff of his recurring night-dream, where he would crawl up on a ridge and peer down into a shallow inlet of crystal clear water twenty feet below. There, swimming around anxiously searching for food, were schools of monster fish: largemouths, smallmouths, walleyes, muskies, and channel cats. Quaking in anticipation, Jax would dangle a lure in the water and watch the fish fight over it in a feeding frenzy. A world record largemouth bass of over twenty-five pounds would capture the lure first and take off toward the main lake. That's when Jax usually woke up, still reeling fast and hard, his Persian silk sheets in disarray and soaked with sweat.

Of course, this pond was probably nothing like that virginal honey-hole of his subconscious adventures. But then again…the farmer had purposely built it on top of a hill for some reason. Logic would dictate he was hiding it from passersby on County Road 34. And why would he do that? Logic would dictate because the pond was full of fish and he wanted to keep them all for himself.

Conflicted, Jax now considered driving farther up that road to the end of the section, turning west, and parking where that very mound would block anyone at the farm from seeing his shiny-new vehicle. But according to Google Earth and his binoculars, that would have meant about a one mile, arduous hike back to the pond through a soil bank of waist-high American grasses dotted with shoulder-high Canadian thistles. No thanks. Besides, it was already ten a.m.; the moon and sun were in a good position for the fish to bite and it wouldn't last much longer. So he settled for easing the vehicle a quarter mile farther up CR 34, closer to the pond's north end. Once up there on the hill, with those trees, the angle, and by keeping low, he felt fairly certain the farmer couldn't see him fishing.

At the back of the vehicle, instead of using his fob to open the tailgate electronically, Jax eased it open with his hand. *No sense having that annoying, high-pitched beep-beep announce my presence to half of Johnson County,* he thought. He fetched his tan fishing vest—heavy with tackle and a few instruments—and slipped it on over his olive-green, poplin shirt from the Eddie Bauer spring catalog. He then collected two of the four rods-and-reels already rigged with his favorite mid-spring lures.

Sunglasses? Check. Smart phone? Check. Water bottle? Check. BassMaster cap? Check. *Testicles?* He took a deep breath.

Again to avoid those telltale beeps, Jax manually eased the tailgate closed and pocketed his fob without using it to lock his vehicle.

Feigning nonchalance, as if walking into a Taco Bell for lunch, the man—who many said looked like Josh Duhamel, only slightly taller and with a nose that curved the other direction, thanks to that touch of Navaho gracing the Jackson ancestry—casually crossed the gravel road. He clambered down into the six-foot ditch and up the other side to the waiting fence.

Left hand clutching the two fishing rods, right hand on the steel post, he two-stepped to the top, causing the tightly stretched barbwire to creak under his two hundred pounds. Careful not to snag his khaki Dockers, he dismounted to the other side with surprising agility for a man his size and a few years past his physical prime. But then, Jax was in excellent shape. And it was hardly the first time he had hopped a fence in the name of his self-proclaimed *fish and game research.*

It was, however, the first time he'd blatantly ignored a *No Trespassing* sign. Even worse, in this case there were a line of them, strategically spaced the right distance apart so the warning couldn't possible go unnoticed.

Continuing his overtly casual gait of innocence for the benefit of anyone watching, Jax and his thumping heart crossed the pasture, its mix of ryegrass and crabgrass just now turning emerald green in May's warming sun. He kept his eyes on the ground to avoid stepping in one of the many cow-pie landmines strewn hither and yon across a field still glistening with mid-morning dew.

In less than a minute the terrain changed abruptly from flat to a steep twenty-degree incline. Without breaking stride, Patrick Bernard Jackson trudged up the grassy hill to exit the world as he knew it.

And enter hers.

Chapter 2

Breaking the hill's crest at the north end by a mature sugar maple tree, Jax was amazed by what lay before him. The area was immaculate, like a well-manicured state park. The hilltop itself—smelling of the freshly-mowed Kentucky blue grass—was smooth and flat, serving as a twenty-foot buffer zone between the pond and the steep ridge on all sides. Beneath one of the many maple trees was a reasonably new, redwood picnic table. Ten feet away matching Adirondack chairs flanked a small fire pit.

The pond was indeed as symmetrical, oblong, and smooth-sided as Google Earth showed, about a hundred yards long and forty yards wide. The entire bank was professionally terraced with large slabs of smooth river stones in different shades of gray, probably purchased from some quarry specializing in exotic landscaping. This was quite an aesthetic twist from the concrete chunks hauled in from defunct highways and busted bridges he normally found rip-rapping the perimeter of most public waters.

And the pond's clarity? Unbelievable. When it rains in agricultural Iowa this time of year, the runoff into most bodies of water is so full of nitrates and phosphates that the resulting large blooms of plankton and algae lower the vertical clarity to only a foot or two. And with the fertile silt that builds up on the bottom over the years, all kinds of vegetation rings the shallows. Not this pond. It was almost tap water clear and completely void of the green stuff. But why not? This oversized bathtub was high on a hill with no watershed or feeder creek to cloud it up after a rain. So what *was* its source? Possibly an underwater spring, although aquifers are usually deep underground, not up inside a manmade mound. Maybe there was a pump somewhere feeding it from a well. That made the most sense, since there was no visible sign of an outlet. But still...

Jax shot another quick look toward the farm. From this angle he could see only the upper half of the four blue Harvestores and slightly more of the taller, light-gray concrete silo with an odd glass-like dome. So anybody on the ground couldn't see him either...just his eighty-thousand-dollar, silver Lexus parked down there on CR 34, sparkling in the sun like a diamond on a dirty rag.

His stomach started feeling queasy again. Maybe he should have driven it up around the section after all, and traipsed the mile back. Maybe he should just call the whole thing off and find some other pond to fish.

"Oh, well, what the hell," he breathed stoically to himself, resisting the creeping vision of a pickup full of war-whooping farmers with shotguns and two-by-fours running him down. "By law they can't do any more than ask me to leave."

Switching to exploratory mode, the piscatorial researcher eased down the stair steps of river stones to the edge of the pond and inserted his trusty darkroom chemical thermometer, capable of giving a quick and very accurate reading in just a few seconds. He repositioned his sunglasses to the roof of his cap to better read the needle on the round dial. It held at *53 degrees*. Jax found that odd for early May in southern Iowa. The pond he fished yesterday was ten degrees warmer. But if this one were fed from a deep well, that would explain the cooler discrepancy.

As Jax withdrew the thermometer, the southern breeze died for a moment, leaving the water's surface smooth as glass and just as transparent. Something under the water moved, catching his eye. Needing his polarized sunglasses to cut the glare, he ever so slowly brought them back down to their normal position on his nose. Unfortunately, that movement startled two...no three, maybe even four dark shadows, all flashing away. The fisherman's heart jumped into his throat and swelled to twice its size. He'd seen those apparitions many times before, in both his dreams and journeys. Those were largemouth bass. And at least one of them was *huge*!

Chapter 3

"Oh, my God! Oh, my God! Oh, my God!" Jax gasped, scrambling low and fast up the bank to grab one of his pre-rigged rods lying in the moist grass. He paused a frantic half second, trying to decide whether to go with the spinning outfit and its purple plastic worm or the baitcaster with the white spinnerbait. Choosing the former, he spun to the sitting position and fired the plastic worm rigged Texas-style in the direction the fish had headed.

The quarter-ounce bullet weight had pulled the bait no more than three feet under the surface when something smacked it and started running south, no doubt to keep it away from the competition. Jax's heart was back in his chest and thumping like a gas station's air compressor. He was tempted to just close the bail and haul back on the rod to set the hook. But, as his dad had taught him many years ago, his odds would increase considerably if he let the fish have a little more time and line to get the bait completely in his mouth.

Two seconds and four heartbeats later a little twitch in the monofilament signaled the bass had just done exactly that. Wasting no more time, Jax carefully stretched his arms as far forward as possible, and turned the reel's handle slowly to close the bail. Just as gingerly he began reeling up what little slack there was. Once the line was basically straight, he wrenched back on the stiff, six-foot, graphite rod with all his weight and strength.

"Holy shit!" he gasped maybe too loud, feeling the power and weight of a fish that had no intention of being reeled in. There was a momentary tug-of-war impasse, before the monofilament slowly began cutting a lazy wake to the right. Jax yanked back on the rod again. This signaled to the bass that something was amiss, and it decided to dig for the safety of the depths.

"Come on, big fella," exhaled Jax, his heels dug firmly into the grassy bank, his left hand reeling as hard as it could, but gaining very little line against the drag. From the powerful thrusts and thumping sensation being telegraphed up the line and down the spinning rod, Jax confirmed it was indeed a largemouth at the other end, trying to dislodge the single 3/0 Aberdeen hook from its jaw. It was also very possibly the largest bass he'd ever caught...provided he *did* catch it, of course. That prospect and the fear of losing it increased his heart rate to one-fifty, as he sucked in and held a deep breath. He prayed both his doubled-over rod and the twelve-pound-test monofilament line would withstand the strain.

Having the angle now, Jax was able to turn the fish toward him, and even more as he felt his quarry begin to weaken. After fifteen seconds of eternity, the tired bass weaved submissively to Jax's anxious hand at the shoreline. He jammed his left thumb between the bass's lips and locked his remaining fingers under its jaw to open its mouth wide and derrick the leviathan out of the water. Fish and fisherman looked at each other in utter amazement, both suddenly gasping for air.

As he crawled up the bank panting with his prize, the bass's size and weight surprised the seasoned angler…and even more so its strength, when a final, desperate kick of its tail launched the fish free from his grip. The characteristic tiny but sharp teeth lining its lower jaw raked the underside of Jax's thumb, cutting through the skin calloused from lipping many other bass the same way that spring. Small strands of blood appeared, one large enough to form a droplet. Picturing Jesse Ventura in *Predator*, Jax bravely told himself *I don't have time to bleed* and kept his focus on the unfolding situation. The largemouth had landed with a thud on the grass and commenced to thrashing wildly, flipping itself repeatedly two feet into the air. The hook easily popped free from the small hole that had been torn in the side of its jaw.

The dirty-blonde angler with a Methodist upbringing launched the F-bomb. Definitely too loudly.

Two hundred and fifty yards away, in the basement of the farmhouse, a three-quarters human watched and listened to all this tumult on one of four wide-screen monitors with Dolby surround sound. She was quite amused. She was also getting quite interested, because some of her internet data mining had already indicated this young angler may be more than just a ballsy trespasser.

Chapter 4

In sheer panic of losing the biggest bass of his life, Jax wildly flung his spinning rod to one side and flopped on top of the fish, gently pinning it to the earth with his vested abdomen. Keeping most of his weight on his elbows, he reached under, found the throbbing bass's huge lower jaw once again, and squeezed it tighter than ever. Ignoring the additional pain of those tiny teeth piercing his already-raw thumb, he rolled over onto his back, sat up, and hoisted the largemouth bass to eye-level, as much in victory as for a closer inspection.

The fish was magnificent! The belly—convex with a full stomach and plenty of spring eggs—had a rich, ivory color. Its back and tail were charcoal-black, its sides a deep Kelly green with a pronounced lateral line, also in solid black. All were signs of a healthy bass that had been in direct sunlight for at least five minutes. That wasn't surprising, considering the sharp clarity of the water and the cloudless sky.

Finally paralyzed again by having its mouth propped open to its fullest extent, the bass's black pupils seemed fixed on the hand that imprisoned it. Jax twisted the fish a quarter turn to check its girth. Its back was as broad as a football. The heartiest largemouth bass he'd ever seen.

With a shaking right hand, he fumbled for the small De-liar in one of his many vest pockets. Finding it, he placed the small, flat hook through the hole his Aberdeen hook had created in the soft side of the fish's mouth. Jax cautiously let go of the jaw, so the bass's full weight would come to bear on the mechanical scale. *Eight pounds even.* A full two pounds heavier than his personal best. And only about three pounds short of the Iowa state record for largemouths.

"Jesus H. Christ!" gasped Jax. "You great, big, beautiful thing!"

He was tempted to make a mad dash for Roger's Sporting Goods to show it off, and then have it mounted. But there was so much pressure on largemouth bass these days, he knew he should abide by the very Catch-and-Release method he had been preaching for years in his outdoors column. Plus there was the problem on getting back to his car without being seen, trying to hide a flopping fish under his vest, while also carrying all his gear. He didn't even have a cooler to keep it in for the drive into town. So, Jax opted to grab his smart phone and take about a dozen selfies-with-a-fishy.

Using another trick learned from his father, Jax slipped a fingernail under one of the scales on the bass's side and plucked it loose. Holding it firmly between thumb and forefinger, he slid down the bank, gave the fish an air kiss, and eased it back into the water. "Catch ya later," he said lovingly and hopefully. The magnificent creature gave a tired kick of its tail, and slowly disappeared into the darker depths. "Any more at home like you? *Bigger* sisters, maybe?"

Sitting back in the grass, Jax produced the old, magnifying glass on the end of a metal letter opener. It had been his great-grandmother's, he was told, when his dad bequeathed it to him ten years ago. He angled the fish scale and lens to get the best light and view, and counted the rings. Like its weight, there were eight rings, one for each year of growth.

"That's impossible," Jax said aloud, shaking his head. "That's a pound a year!" In Florida or Texas or California maybe…with their hybrids and year-round growing seasons. But not in four-seasons Iowa. A half pound a year is considered good in the Hawkeye State.

He slipped the magnifying glass and fish scale into a pocket, and turned his attention to finding the spinning outfit he had flung wildly to the side when the bass tried to jump ship.

Just as Jax located the rod and reel, he heard the sound of a vehicle accelerating. He quickly glanced behind him at the gravel road to the east where his SUV was parked. Nothing was moving in either direction. *Shit.* That had to mean someone was racing up the dirt lane from the farm. Jumping to his feet, Jax unconsciously jerked off his B.A.S.S. cap to make himself less obvious. He then negated that lame attempt by stretching his entire six-foot-two frame higher to better see a small plume of dust building up from the south.

His acidic stomach begged him to make a run for it. He could get to his car and drive away before the farmer could do anything but shake his fist and yell obscenities after him. But his heart said *stay.* This pond was a gold mine, a dream come true. He may never find another one like it again. As much as he dreaded facing whoever was coming up the hill— undoubtedly to boot his ass off their property and hopefully not shoot him—there was a chance it would be a nice guy who invites him to fish here anytime he wants. Okay, a very small chance. Okay, virtually no chance. But still worth the try.

"Man up, Jackson!" he whispered to himself, as he sat back down to nervously choreograph his upcoming tap dance.

Chapter 5

The white Silverado pickup popped the hill and continued toward the trespasser at an angry speed. It skidded up forty feet short of Jax. The driver's side door flew open. Out stepped the classic farmer: bib overalls, red-and white checkered shirt with rolled up sleeves revealing Popeye forearms. He was sweating like he'd just furrowed the north forty with a mule and a single bottom plow. What didn't fit the stereotype was the dark-brown, Indiana Jones fedora leveled just above his eyebrows. Whether the face under it was red from the sun or fury, Jax was in no hurry to find out.

"You got permission to be up here?" barked the farmer, striding purposefully and quickly toward the young interloper. Yep: *Fury*.

Jax put on his blameless face and rose to his feet. "Hi," he chimed, waving weakly, a wrinkled brow helping raise his bushy brown eyebrows in added innocence. "Aaa, isn't this Kent Park...open to the public?"

The irate farmer pulled up face to face, eye to eye, his shadowed, square jaw jutted well forward. The toes of his bright yellow overshoes—rimmed with smears of a brown substance of obvious barnyard origin—almost touched those of Jax's ankle-high, brown chukkas. His cracked lips seemed stuck halfway up on the straight enough teeth, which were grinding, not chewing, on what Jax assumed was a white piece of gum. As angry as the farmer seemed, it could have been a piece of calcified spittle.

If Jax hadn't been so intimidated, he may have noticed the reason for the fedora: the guy actually looked a lot like Harrison Ford in the Indiana Jones movies. And with those light-gray eyes dancing icily back and forth from one of the trespasser's azure irises to the other, he obviously enjoyed playing the part of a crotchety leading man.

"Does this look like Kent Park?" the farmer bristled, his Juicy Fruited breath pushing between Jax's half open mouth and into his nostrils. "Does this *one-acre* pond that I dug out with a bulldozer look like a *ninety-acre* county lake? *Huh? Does it?* Kent Park is two miles that way." He threw a hard fist with an extended index finger to the west.

Did we mention that Jax didn't care for confrontations? By those few people who had the privilege of observing him in action, he was, in fact, a pussy, especially for someone this tall, well-built, and athletic. In his twenty five years he'd never been in a fight, despite a couple occasions when a man with average self-assurance and dignity would have stood up

20

for himself and taken action, even at the risk of a bloodied lip or blackened eye.

One of the more indicative times was back in high school football. Jax was the tight-end and his quarterback had thrown a pass that sailed five feet over his head…completely uncatchable. Even so, this outside linebacker charged over and laid a late hit on Jax's kidneys. The fifteen yard penalty wasn't enough punishment to Jax's way of thinking. As the quarterback was barking out the signals for the next play, Jax's seething mind was seriously envisioning putting his helmet under that smaller linebacker's chin, and jamming him into the turf so hard he'd have to be pried out with garden spades and a tow rope. But then he suddenly let it slide, telling himself that would only get him suspended for the rest of the game…or even the season. The logic was impeccable and the profile conclusive: Jax was a clear-thinking wussy.

Then there was freshman year at the University of Iowa, when he wanted to deck Bruno Keller, the cocky, loudmouthed asshole on a full-ride wrestling scholarship. The guy was a bully. He'd been riding Jax's nerdy friend, Kyle, all semester, teasing him about his wall-eye and one leg being noticeable shorter than the other. Bruno finally went too far one day exaggerating Kyle's limp, as he walked behind him into French class, dragging a dead foot like Igor. A few students chuckled at the wrestler's mockery, but the room fell tensely silent when Jax suddenly stepped between them. With knotted fists, a twitching right knee, and a threatening tone, he told Bruno to stop riding his buddy. The smaller, 174-pound-class grappler got right up into Jax's face on tiptoes, and asked what he intended to do about it. Jax had him every which way physically…and absolutely no way mentally. The six-two, two hundred-pound journalism major just coughed into his fist, and sat back down to a chorus of groans. There was even one muted *chicken shit* lifted from the back of the room.

Now here he was nose-to-nose with an irate, overly-possessive, insensitive prick of a farmer, whose only goal in life was to crush Jax's life-long dream. So, for only the third time in his existence and for a completely novel reason, Patrick Jackson's fists clenched in preparation for mortal combat. His eyes pinched. His right knee began twitching. He sized up the opposition. They were the same height and probably once the same weight. But the farmer had twenty years and thirty pounds on him. Jax had youth on his side and probably quickness. The sodbuster looked rock-hard from doing chores all his life. The outdoor writer sat on his ass a lot, but he kept his still-well-defined physique in good shape, spending five hours a week in his basement exercise room, complete with treadmill, elliptical, a Bowflex Home Gym and tons of free weights.

Just as Jax's desire to bust the farmer in the nose was percolating to the visualization stage, the veil clouding his judgment predictably fell away to reveal the clear truth of the matter: Jax was in the wrong, flat out. This *was* the farmer's land and Jax *was* trespassing. The man in his face had every right to throw him off the property. And if he did, Jax had to submit willingly. That's what his dad—rest his soul—would want him to do.

But the superseding component of his sudden stand-down was the fact that no matter what it took—groveling, ass-kissing, an exchange of large sums—Jax absolutely *had* to fish this fabulous body of water again. An eight-pound largemouth bass was just hauled out. An *eight-pounder,* for crying out loud! God only knows what else might be under the surface. And even if that were the pond's biggest bass, give it a few more years and that leviathan could be a new state record. What that would do to his credentials! He could be written up in BassMaster Magazine. Hell, maybe the editors would even let him write the article. A few of those published pieces and he'd be on his way to qualifying for the elite Outdoor Writers Association of America. At the very least, people might actually start reading his local newspaper column.

"Hey, man, I'm sorry," offered Jax sincerely, unclenching his fists and sticking them into the front pockets of his Dockers. "I'd heard that Kent Park had some good fish in it, so I looked for it on Google Earth. I saw this pond and the trees and even the picnic table and thought this must be the park. I didn't bother to check how big the pond was. I should have."

With folded arms and one eye cocked, the Harrison Ford lookalike listened to Jax's explanation. He wasn't buying one grain of the bullshit.

Neither was the farmer's mostly-human wife back at the house. She had been watching and recording every word and deed since the young man pulled his silver SUV up to a stop on County Road 34.

Chapter 6

The twenty-by-thirty room looked like a compact version of the audio/visual department at Best Buy. On the north wall were four, fifty-five-inch, high-definition television screens, three of them tuned to a major cable news channel: CNN, Fox News, and MSNBC. The fourth screen continually rotated among CBS, ABC, NBC, and CSPAN, stopping when it found something interesting. It rarely stopped. In fact, it had been halfway through the *Fifty Shades of Grey* movie on a basic, commercial cable station before the room's technician suddenly became very busy.

Filling up the east wall were four more large screens, each of these a perfect square and not actual television sets. One was obviously a weather radar, spanning all of North America. There seemed to be a low pressure front moving up from the Gulf toward the Midwest, sparking some scattered thunderstorms along its leading edge. Both coasts were clear.

The other three had nothing to do with the weather. They would have been more at home gracing the walls of NASA or NORAD or the NSA. Two were live satellite feeds from space, with special access to the classified satellite USA-129. The first showed the current aerial view of the Brookfield Farm's immediate area, extending out one mile in all directions. The other was the same viewpoint, except in infrared imaging. It was showing heat signatures from the hood of a parked vehicle on the road northeast of the farm. It also showed the hood of another vehicle parked near the pond's northeast corner and two humanoid shapes standing very close together…the heat from one presently redder than the other.

The fourth square screen was connected to the farm's own radar angled forty-five degrees skyward in the top of the silo. Its constant rotation scanned all horizons and up to the heaven's zenith. With an effective range of some thousand miles, it could spot aircraft or birds or any solid object in the sky. But its main purpose was to detect unique, heat-seeking infrared rays from Regg scanners, which limited its range to only ten miles or so on a clear day. The screen's circular sweep over a green grid of concentric lines revealed no present activity. But there rarely was.

Turning another ninety degrees to the south wall brought into view the six computer work stations, replete with twenty-four-inch LCD monitors on short pedestals with their corresponding desktop towers, wireless keyboards and mice. All were lined up along a twenty-foot, beige-colored

Formica table, free-standing on the hardwood floor by steel frames and legs.

The far left monitor was displaying Google Earth's opening view of the planet Earth. Its unoccupied, swivel office chair on casters was tucked neatly in place under the table. The next monitor had the latest stock market and commodities reports. Its chair was also unoccupied and in place.

The third monitor was a split screen, the left half showing a close-up photograph of a silver Lexus SUV with its license plate clearly visible. Some data at the bottom of the screen said it was on *County Road 34* and exactly *656.7* feet from *Silo Cam 2*. The right half was a live action video and audio of two men discussing property rights at the northeast corner of the Brookfield Farm's private pond. They were averaging *589 feet* from *Silo Cam 1*.

The fourth PC had already hacked easily into the Iowa City Police Department's secure database. On its monitor was the same license plate number belonging to a 2015 Lexus LS 570, silver, registered to:
Patrick Bernard Jackson
100 Jackson Road, Iowa City, Iowa, 50442.
DL No. 025AA8310.
Expires 04/11/2016
Restrictions: None.
DOB: 04/11/1990.
Sex M. Hgt 74 in. Wgt 200. Eyes Blue.
Below was a mug shot of a square-faced, half-smiling, handsome young man with wavy, dirty-blonde hair, bushy eyebrows, and azure eyes, obviously taken from his driver's license at the DMV. Below the photo was scribed: *No warrants.*

The fifth PC had been trolling through the *Iowa City Tribune's* archives, finding a number of articles containing the name *Patrick Jackson*. Most were about his parents' tragic deaths in a fiery car crash off Interstate 35 near Ames on March 8, 2010, while Patrick was a junior at the local University of Iowa. He was an only child and therefore sole heir to his father's multi-million-dollar tire retreading company and their plush estate two miles south of Iowa City on Highway 6. Another article told of Patrick selling the company shortly thereafter for an estimated but unconfirmed forty-five million plus stocks. More current references uncovered a series of outdoor related articles in a weekly column named "Hawkeye Outdoors," all with the byline *Jax Jackson*.

The mouse of the sixth and final PC was being worked by a small, delicate hand with elongated ashen fingers and nails painted a blushing pink. The monitor was in the process of loading up all of Patrick Bernard

Jackson's 2014 tax forms from the IRS's super-secure, impenetrable databanks.

With no time to lose, the hacker went straight to Jax's 1040. The alien crossbreed almost gagged when she saw his gross income, most of it from capital gains on Schedule D. But it was when she got to his W-4 Personal Worksheet and saw he was single with no dependents that her sleek hand quickly reached for the smart phone and punched two keys.

"What's up?" asked the male voice on the other end.

"Darling, that guy is a strong prospect for Suzy," she replied excitedly. "Don't scare him away!"

Chapter 7

The crimson-faced farmer was preparing to launch another verbal onslaught at the dead-to-rights transgressor, when the mobile device in the front pocket of his bib overalls started singing, *Proud Mary keep on burnin'* from the classic Creedence Clearwater Revival song. He released the air in his lungs with a huff, pulled out the cell phone and stuck it to his ear. "What's up?"

The farmer's leathery face did a spontaneous fade from anger to surprise. He quickly turned his back on Jax and started walking away, obviously wanting to keep the conversation private. Unfortunately, he didn't allow for the southern breeze carrying his muted words right back to a very interested and very nosy outdoor writer with twenty-twenty hearing.

"Really?" he said softly though gritted teeth. "Are you sure?" He listened again, this time for a good five seconds, nodding a couple times. "How 'bout that." Pause. He nodded, "Okay, I suppose so." Pretending the dialog was still continuing when the other end had already clicked off, for the benefit of his trespasser he said louder, "Well, tell David to take care of it. He knows what to do. Bye, hon."

The black smart phone blinked out and eased back into his pocket. The farmer hesitated before turning around, gathering his thoughts. He didn't like this guy. But then he didn't like any swinging dick that may have designs on his precious daughter. And this one had blatantly trespassed on his land and lied to his face. Now he was supposed to keep the asshole from leaving? He was supposed to be nice to him? He was supposed to get a hair sample, if not some blood, because he may be a good match for his only daughter? *Christ!* thought the protective father. *Why not just bust him one in the back of the head and pick both the blood and hair samples off my knuckles?*

"Pig got out," he sighed matter-of-factly, turning and walking back to Jax at a more relaxed pace. "It's always something."

"I imagine so," nodded a still-nervous Jax. Yet he understood. Throughout his numerous outdoor adventures, to get permission to hunt their lands or fish their ponds, he'd had many an occasion to listen patiently to a farmer complain about too much rain, not enough rain, sheep in the meadow, cows in the corn. But all things considered, this particular bitching sounded superficial.

The farmer resumed his position in front of Jax, but a step back this time and in a less-threatening posture. With his head slight bowed and hands on hips, he took in a short lungful, let it out, and raised his eyes to no farther than Jax's broad chin. Like a kid being forced by his mother to apologize to a bratty little turd for calling him a *bratty little turd*, he said grudgingly, "Listen. Sorry for flying off the handle. I can get a little possessive sometimes."

Huh?

Jax took a moment to blink away his surprise. There wasn't much sincerity behind it, but it *was* an apology. Why the turnaround? "Oh, no reason to say that, sir," he offered, not too quickly. "I fully understand where you're coming from. I'd be the same way if it were my pond. You've done a great job with it. I should have asked permission."

"Well, no harm done," said the farmer with a half grin, softening a little. "I assume you didn't catch anything. Still too early for them to be biting, eh?"

"No, I didn't catch anything," Jax lied, unaware he had just taken the bait. "Didn't even get a line in the water. I was just rigging up when you came. But the truth is, it's not too early at all. Most fish should be trying to store up some food and energy for the rigors of spawning in a few weeks. Just yesterday I was…"

"I didn't know that," lied the farmer.

"Yup, they actually are biting real good the past few days."

"Well, I'll be. I was up here Tuesday and didn't even have a hit." That too was a fib: the farmer knew a lot about the fish in his pond and how to catch them. He should. He raised every one of them in a special aquarium twenty feet directly beneath his yellow boots.

Continuing the dumb act, he took off his brown fedora, and ran a hand over the thinning, chestnut hair. Now Jax notice the Harrison Ford resemblance. In fact, he thought the farmer looked like Harrison's Max Drummer character in *The Expendables 3*.

"You seem to know a lot about fish," he added, replacing the fedora.

"Done some of it," grinned Jax, turning his head to pay homage to the water. Then he added modestly, "Believe it or not, it's my job."

"No shit?" smirked the farmer. "What kind of a living can someone make fishing ponds without permission?" *Damn, that jab felt good!*

Jax gave a short laugh. "Yeah, I deserved that." Then he said quieter, almost as if apologizing for his chosen profession, "I'm a writer. An outdoor writer. I research and write about hunting and fishing around Iowa City and all of Johnson and Linn Counties."

If they made such a thing as a bogus light bulb, a sixty-watter just pretended to blink on over the farmer's head. "Say," he said, tapping a finger at Jax, "you're not the guy who writes that "Hawkeye Outdoors" column in the *Iowa City Tribune*, are you?" He silently thanked his wife back in the communications room for the background info.

"That's me," said the surprised columnist. Hardly anybody ever read his stuff, let alone knew the name of it.

"I read that now and then," he lied. Then lied again: "Interesting stuff."

"Thanks," replied Jax warily, his BS meter beginning to beep.

"Sorry, but I don't remember your name. I rarely look at who writes what."

"Patrick Jackson." He extended his right hand. "Better known as Jax."

Without a smile, the farmer slowly completed the formality, his heavily-calloused grip squeezing hard into Jax's, sending the message of who was in charge here. "Alan Brookfield."

"A pleasure to meet you. May I call you *Alan*."

"No."

Chapter 8

A tense, post-introductory pause hung heavily in the ether for a moment, with only the sounds of clanging hog feeder lids down on the farm and a distant crow announcing last night's road-kill. They both looked out over the rippled surface of the one-acre impoundment, wondering which of the two would break the uncomfortable silence. Alan Brookfield knew he should. He just didn't want to.

Jax knew the polite thing would be to apologize for trespassing one more time, thank the farmer for his understanding, and say he had to be going. But he still desperately wanted permission to fish this pond. And as long as Brookfield wasn't drop-kicking him over the fence, he wasn't about to leave voluntarily. Besides, with twitching lips Mr. Brookfield seemed to be pondering something.

"I imagine you'd like to fish this pond, huh?" Alan finally said. "Seeing how you went through all the trouble to hop my fence and ignore all the *No Trespassing* signs." *Another good dig.*

With all the calm he could muster, Jax's response was a pleasant yet moderate, "Yes, I'd like that, if you didn't mind." He didn't want to appear too anxious. It might give away the fact that he had already fished it and knew what was in there. Besides, Alan's question was just that: a question. He hadn't given permission yet. "I'd throw back anything I caught."

The hardened farmer turned to face the stiff young man. "Tell you what," he said, rubbing the back of his tanned neck, "you can fish it on three conditions. One, you always check with me first. Call. Don't come to the farm." Jax started to tremble. "Two, you promise to tell no one where this pond is." Jax feared losing control of his bladder. "And three, you give my daughter, Suzy, some fishing lessons. She loves to fish and I just don't have the time or know-how to teach her."

That last one almost stuck in Brookfield's craw. Here he was, with all the knowledge and experience of a fisheries biologist, pretending to know nothing about piscatorial pursuits. But far worse than that was the fact that he—the overprotective, loving father—was actually *pimping out* his daughter. And to a lying, trespassing, *outdoor writer*, no less!

Patrick Bernard Jackson's soul stepped outside its body and fist-pumped the air. *Yes! Yes! And yes!* He could see the headline on the

29

sports page of the *Iowa City Tribune* and every other major paper in the state: *Outdoor Writer Jax Jackson Lands State Record Largemouth Bass.*

"I could do that," he replied evenly, squelching the fervor from his voice. "I'll call you for permission first. I won't tell anyone where it is. And I'd love to teach your daughter how to fish. I've taught fishing classes before in town."

Was there even an ounce of truth in any of this dialog?

"Good," said Alan, the seasoned angler. "And if you have a moment, maybe you could give me a couple fishing tips." Again, his words had to crawl through the small opening of a tight throat.

"I'd be happy to," said Jax. "What would you like to know?"

"Well, show me what lure you would use here today."

"No problem. It's already rigged up." Jax bent down and picked up the spinning outfit. Opening the bail, he let the plastic worm fall into his upturned palm. He showed the farmer how the point of the 3/0 hook goes down through the head of the worm, turns, then sticks back into the worm's body, making it weedless. He had Alan try it for himself.

"Now show me how you work it," said Alan, handing the lure back.

Rather than cast into the pond, Jax flung the worm back toward the farmer's pickup in the grass. He certainly didn't want to hook into another bass…not with Brookfield right here. What if he caught a state record and the asshole made him throw it back? No way. The fish would need to be weighed and certified by a Department of Natural Resources official. So Jax worked the lure just as he would in the water.

It didn't matter. Alan Brookfield was no longer paying attention…at least not to the instruction. His focus had diverted to the back of Jax's head, and particularly the collar of the olive green poplin shirt poking above his tan fishing vest. Cocking his head and squinting to find the loose hair he was looking for, Alan surreptitiously plucked it off the collar and slipped it into the back pocket of his overalls.

For a brief moment of whimsical self-indulgence, he envisioned busting the trespasser in the back of the head to obtain the needed blood sample, as well. But Mary had already dictated that would be Suzy's job tomorrow. *Suzy's job!* And what if this guy's hair and blood reveals he is a viable candidate? Just the thought of what other *fluid* sample his darling daughter would then need to secure—and particularly the obvious method used—made Mr. Brookfield want to neuter Mr. Jackson on the spot. But that would lead to all kinds of problems, not the least of which was upsetting his wife…along with the strict Mejan protocol in these particular matters.

Chapter 9

"Always watch your line," coached Jax, "because some hits can be so slight you won't feel them. The only clue may be a twitch in the line or it starts moving to one side."

"Thanks," said Alan. "I'll have to try that next time."

"You could now, if you want," said Jax politely with no enthusiasm, short-arming his rod and reel to *Mr. Brookfield*. What if he, a dumb farmer, cast into the pond and pulled out a state record, stealing Jax's thunder and fame? The outdoor writer's dream would be shattered.

"I'd like to," said Alan, looking at his watch, "but I really need to get back to my chores. Thanks anyway."

Jax quickly retracted the rod and offer.

After exchanging cell phone numbers, Alan Brookfield stuck out his hand, a clear signal that this encounter was over and it was time to leave. Jax took the offering and immediately winched. Indiana Jones was again squeezing hard…real hard, making sure the trespasser understood who the king was on this particular hill. When he finally let go, he spun on his heel and headed back toward his white pickup. Jax flexed his fingers to make sure they still worked, and then gathered up his other rod.

"Mind if I stay and fish a while?" Jax suddenly called after him.

The backs of Alan's ears glowed redder. He turned around, but kept moving, back-stepping. "I'd rather you didn't today," he said as nicely as possible, when he wanted to run back and deck the presumptuous sonofabitch. "Come back tomorrow and show Suzy what you showed me. Come about nine in the morning."

Jax thought a moment, and then offered, "How about eleven? The moon will be in a better position and the fish will bite better."

Alan stopped his retreat to scan the sky with pretentious wonder. "The moon? Does that really have an effect on fish?" He was already well-versed on the solar-lunar influence. His largemouth brood bass usually timed spawning with the lunar cycles, plus were generally more active when the moon was overhead or underfoot.

"It really does," said Jax.

"Well, I'll be damned." Alan removed his hat and scratched his head. He started to turn away, but hesitated with an afterthought. "Say, you never asked what kind of fish are in my pond," he said with a contemptuous sneer in his tone.

Jax was getting this feeling that somehow *Mr. Brookfield* knew he'd already caught a nice bass. "Oh, yeah, I meant to ask. What *is* in there."

"Bass."

"Anything else?"

"Nope."

That had to be a falsehood. Jax knew no largemouth bass could grow to eight pounds in as many years without some kind of super-nutritious forage other than its own young. But this wasn't the time to push the point.

Jax waved and had started walking away from the pond, when he thought of one more thing. "Hey, how old is Suzy?" he called, as Alan was about to climb into the pickup.

Jesus Friggin' Christ! Alan's thoughts were seething. *What is this guy, some kind of child molester? I've got my Smith & Wesson in the glove box and a spade in the back. One shot and the world is a better place.*

"Why?" he asked, doing a poor job of keeping the suspicion out of his tone.

"Just want to know if I should bring a small Snoopy rod or not."

"That's not necessary," said Alan, standing on the running board, both hands on the top of the cab, fists slowly unclenching. "She's twenty. What you have there will work fine." He ducked inside, started the vehicle, and backed up along the narrow strip between the water and ridge.

As Jax shuffled down the hill toward the waiting Lexus, his imagination was already shifting into second gear. Here it was: the classic farmer's daughter premise, with a hundred potential punch lines. Will she be beautiful, virginal, and over-sexed, or big boned, ugly, and smell of lye soap.

"Put it out of your mind, dumb ass," he said aloud, climbing behind the wheel with an ear-to-ear grin. It didn't matter one whit what Suzy Brookfield looked like. He had a drop-dead-gorgeous girlfriend, a bloated bank account, and permission to fish perhaps the most prolific body of bass water he'd ever seen. Outside of losing his parents and family dog five years ago, life couldn't be any better.

Chapter 10

Night watchman Cleavon Washington slowly opened his eyes. With no sense of urgency he took in a deep, head-clearing lungful, and turned off the high-pitched beeping of the Timex alarm on his thick wrist. He didn't have to look at the dial. He knew it was two a.m., time to make his rounds again inside the huge Nebraska Furniture Mart in Omaha, Nebraska.

With the overhead lighting at one-tenth illumination and his own flashlight, the large mulatto wound his way through the labyrinth of Lazy Boy recliners, into the *Employees Only* lounge, and past the double swinging doors leading to the east side loading dock. He was just reaching to check the locks and security box when the lights went out. And it wasn't just the overhead lighting. His flashlight went dead, too. The little green and red LED lights on the security box and keypad were off. In the dark he groped for and found the handset of the wall phone. No dial tone. He checked the time on his watch with the built in *Indiglo* feature. No glow.

Starting to panic, Cleavon quickly fumbled for the Colibti Jet Flame cigarette lighter in his pants' front pocket and repeatedly thumbed the plunger. No fire. There wasn't even a spark from the electronic igniter.

Just when he thought he couldn't be any more frightened in the pitch blackness, the sixty-two-year-old heard what had to be the personnel door lock clicking off, followed by the unlatching of the two dead bolts. The rustle of the door swinging open sent his heart pounding. There was nothing to see in the entryway, because all the lights in the outside parking and delivery area were out as well.

When the gentle mist hit his face, it didn't matter anymore. Cleavon's fear was gone. He felt relaxed, serene. And when a scratchy voice in broken English lifted out of the dark, telling him to manually open the fifteen-foot-high, heavy, overhead sliding door on vertical rollers, he gladly obliged.

From the backend of the waiting moving van with no markings poured a half-dozen figures into the loading area, each about five feet tall, all wearing black jumpsuits and night-vision goggles. The store's overhead lighting came back on, but only at about five percent. For the next thirty minutes the hairy figures ransacked Nebraska Furniture Mart, loading the waiting capacious semi with bedroom sets, recliners, leather sofas, television sets, even a conference table with twelve matching black leather executive chairs. As ordered, Cleavon Washington stood wobbling stupidly at the door, happy to offer geographical advice when the leader with yellow eyes and a black nose asked where certain items could be found. Once his expertise was no longing needed, he was laid down on the floor, sprayed with another drug, and told to sleep.

Loaded to the brim, the moving van headed south out of Omaha on Highway 75 toward Plattsmouth, Nebraska. It turned west onto a country blacktop, and then south again onto a gravel road, before finally going north on a two-track lane into an abandoned strip mine. Having just arrived a moment earlier sat a stolen Piggly Wiggly eighteen-wheeler, idling patiently. The back end of something the size of a small town opened wide and a ramp extended out forty feet. Piggly Wiggly went first, followed by the overloaded moving van, both laboring heavily up the ramp. The door closed, and the pancake-shaped spaceship two miles across and three stories high silently disappeared upward into the dark sky.

Mr. Collison, the store manager, found his reliable, long-time night watchman flat on his back asleep on the cold, loading dock floor, the crotch of his pants wet and smelling of urine. The well-rested, slightly headachy Cleavon remembered nothing and had no explanation for the missing inventory. An investigation by the Omaha police could find nothing that implicated Cleavon, other than falling asleep on the job. Insurance covered almost all of the stolen products, including some items they probably could never have sold anyway…like that godawful painting of dogs playing poker. *Why would the thieves have possibly wanted that anyway?*

So Nebraska Furniture Mart didn't press charges. Of course, Cleavon Washington had to be let go, and that was okay with him. He started collecting his Social Security and unemployment and moved in with his sister just outside of Lincoln for a welcomed retirement…excluding the recurring nightmares of werewolves in jumpsuits.

Chapter 11

Jax clicked the *Send* button, leaned back in the black, posh-leather executive chair, and took a celebratory swig on his Dasani water bottle. He had just emailed the two best selfies-with-eight-pound-fishy to everyone in his "Friends" address book, most of whom were his fellow Hawkeye Bass Club members.

"Eat your hearts out guys!" he laughed. None of them had even come close to matching that bass. Ever. Well, Roger got that ten-pound Florida strain in Okeechobee two years ago, but that was Florida. A hybrid. On live shiners. With a guide. It didn't count in Iowa.

Speaking of Roger, after leaving the Brookfield farm pond, Jax had considered going straight to Roger's Sports Center and showing the pictures to anyone who'd care to see them and twisting the arms of those who didn't. But the small screen of a mobile device couldn't do justice to a bass this big and beautiful. So, he decided to head home, apply a little Photoshop where necessary, and email them. At least those friends with bigger, 2560 x 1600 resolution computer monitors could view them in all their glorious splendor. Maybe they would even go viral on YouTube.

Besides, Jax didn't really have time to hang out this afternoon. It had already been close to noon when he drove through town, and he needed to get home to his computer to log everything swirling in his head about that incredible fish and that incredible pond. Plus he couldn't wait to get started on his next column. He didn't know exactly what the topic would be, only that it would certainly revolve around his trophy largemouth. He hoped his managing editor, Angie, would allow some extra space for the digital photo. The more space the better. Everybody in Iowa City already knew who the rich Jax Jackson was. This would make him and his column credible.

He also wanted to get in a good workout before Jannie arrived. Her father's dental clinic closed at three o'clock on Friday afternoons, so she'd probably be coming through the door around three-twenty. They hadn't made any plans yet, but they usually had an early-evening dinner on Fridays, back here to "The Spread," (as she called his twenty acres) for wine and video games, and then into bed to bang their brains out.

A soft tapping at the closed door of his den snapped Jax's train of thought. He had been replaying the fight of that magnificent fish over and over in his mind, relishing the adrenalin rush and the personal feeling of man's superiority over the animal kingdom. He had yet to enter anything into his log or start on his column. Taking his feet off the desk and setting himself back upright in the office chair, he beckoned the person to enter. The one of many hand-carved, solid mahogany doors his folks had ordered from Italy when they built the house twenty years ago swung open and in shuffled Odett, his fifty-year-old, African-American, live-in housekeeper. She'd been taking care of the Jackson family since Jax was a toddler and had long since been considered one of their own. With his mom and dad now gone, she was the only family he had left. He loved Odett like a second mother. And she loved him.

"Yo had any lunch, Pee-Bee-Boy?" she asked suspiciously. "Didn't see no dishes in the sink."

"Oh, crap, I forgot!" moaned Jax, tapping his forehead with the tips of his fingers. "And it's PBJ day, too."

Patrick Bernard Jackson's second mother introduced him to the peanut butter and jelly sandwich when he was three, partly for the nutrition and partly because PBJ coincidentally were his initials. Odett got such a kick out of the way Jax scarfed down the fixings and wanted it almost every day, she started calling him *Pee-Bee-Boy*, and the love affair had been perpetuating ever since.

"Yo knows I'd gladly fix it for ya, if yo wants," she replied with a sigh, knowing the forthcoming answer all too well. Nobody but nobody made his PBJ for him. It had to be done with just the right ratio of creamy peanut butter to strawberry jam, all spread evenly to the very edge of the fresh wheat bread. But to her surprise, her young man spun around in his chair, revealing a thoughtful look.

"Hang onto your apron, Odett," he said, "but I just might let you today. I've got a lot of stuff to do, not much time, and I'm starving here."

Not bothering to verbalize the *Lord-a-mercy* she was thinking, the sweet-faced woman grinned ear-to-ear, flashing that gap between her two front teeth wide as a wooden spoon handle. Before he could change his mind, she spun her five-foot-four, rotund frame around and double-shuffled out the door toward the kitchen.

"Sixty percent peanut butter, forty percent strawberry jam," he called after her. "And plenty of Cheetos."

"I oughts to know hows to fix yo PBJ," she smiled, knowing no one else could hear her except Jesus. "Hell, I be the one what taught ya twenty year ago."

Chapter 12

Jax was just coming up the white carpeted stairs from his work-out room, when he heard Odett greeting Jannie at the double front doors. Their cordial chatter naturally grew louder on his approach, then ceased as Odett presumably headed back to her duties. He turned the corner at the top of the stairs and padded barefoot down the long, narrow hallway. On his left, through the virtually seamless series of plate-glass, thermal windows, a fox squirrel scampered down the trunk of the half-grown ash tree in the perfectly landscaped Japanese garden. He purposely let it hold his attention so he wouldn't have to see any of the family photos in polished, wooden frames on his right. He'd been avoiding looking at them lining the wall of dark granite slabs for the past four years. They only depressed him. But he couldn't bring himself to take them down.

Turning right again brought him onto the bright, warm marble of the cathedral like foyer. Suspended from the twenty-foot ceiling was that crystal chandelier his mom had insisted on having. It probably cost more than the guy who installed it made in a year.

"Well, look at you, stud," Jannie said approvingly, already halfway across the foyer to meet his advance. He was wearing nothing but white basketball shorts extending below his knees and a navy blue towel around his neck. His well-formed muscles looked even more defined. "Been working out?"

His respiratory rate still elevated from the two miles on the treadmill, Jax closed the distance to his girlfriend, arms spreading wide for a playful, sweaty hug. "Hi, babe."

"Stay back there, Conan," she said, holding him off with the very tips of her fingernails and a stiff arm. "You're slimy and probably smell like you look."

Jax honored her request and just leaned in to peck her lips. He swept an exaggerated sniff of her pink cashmere sweater and replied, "Hmm. Fluoride and gingivitis. Nice combination."

That was met with a pout and a slap to his bare, moist shoulder. "I don't either smell like that," she protested, wiping her fingers on her black skirt. "You know I stay at my desk all day. I've been back there maybe once in two years. Besides, I just dabbed on your favorite *Clive Christian* in the car."

Jax couldn't always tell if Jannie's indignation was real or not. But at this juncture he had no urge to find out. A much more important item was on his mind. "C'mon," he said, taking her by the hand and pulling her away. "I've got something great to show you."

A smile spread across her flawless, symmetrical features, her blue eyes blinking with intrigue. The last time he used this tone and gesture was three months ago on her birthday, when he led her out to the only empty stall of his six-car garage. It was no longer unoccupied. There sat her very own, brand new, 2-Series Beemer in Melbourne red. Last Christmas it was the four carat diamond stud earrings she had adorning each ear at this and most every waking moment. *Whatever could it be this time that couldn't wait until after they'd showered?*

Jax guided Jannie into his den and had her sit in his executive chair. He wiggled the mouse to kill the screen saver, and the selfie-with-fishy blossomed onto the screen.

"Whaddaya think?" he asked.

"It's you..." she said, as if answering the question of who's buried in Grant's tomb, "...holding up a fish."

"That's not just any fish," Jax said, grinning proudly. "It's a bass. An *eight-pound* largemouth. The biggest bass I've ever caught."

Jannie studied the photo again for a polite second, and then remarked unenthusiastically, "How nice. Did you catch it today?"

"Yep. Just this morning," he beamed with growing excitement. "On my one and only cast. Babe, you should see this pond. It's incredible. I think it's loaded with big bass. Hell, it could hold the next Iowa state record. If not right now, in a year or two. And I have permission to fish it."

Jannie lifted herself out of the chair. "That's great, Jax. I'm happy for you." She stood on her tiptoes to lightly peck his lips. "Now what say we both hop in the shower?"

That off-the-subject suggestion had the dual effect of throwing cold water on his great-white-angler ego, while firing up his always-ready libido. He willingly took the offered hand and followed her out of the den, into the foyer, up the left side curving staircase, along the hall's red carpeting and into the sprawling master bedroom. She immediately started undressing, throwing her pink sweater and black skirt on the circular bed's hand-woven, Pakistani spread in a linear pattern of dark blues and rust. Jax just stood there, still in his white basketball shorts, hands outward expressively. His eyes were locked intently on her baby-blues, not even noticing the svelte, five-foot-eleven body that could easily have graced any catwalk.

"I tell ya, Jannie," he said, dreamily replaying his battle with the bass, "if I could get you to come with me sometime, I could almost guarantee you hooking into a big bass. I think that's all it would take to get you interested in fishing."

Completely nude now, Jannie glided over to Jax and pulled down his shorts and jockstrap. "You know I don't like fish," she said for perhaps the twelfth time in their two-year relationship. "I don't like the smell." She turned him around and pushed him toward the shower room. "I don't like the slimy feel." She continued shepherding him past the cedar-paneled sauna door and dressing area, into the actual shower enclave. "I don't even particularly like to eat fish, except lobster. Or is that even a fish?" She punched a series of buttons on the wall and eight shower heads on the far wall and ceiling erupted with perfect one hundred and four-degree streams of pulsating water.

As they both stood beneath the relaxing, crisscrossing cascade, Jax's silence and distance gaze made Jannie realize she had once again deflated her boyfriend's wish to share his beloved fishing with her. As a consolation, with further and better restitution to come shortly, she began soaping his hairless back and broad shoulders in wide, sensuous strokes.

Chapter 13

The young valet with a Bieber haircut, white shirt and burgundy, sleeveless sweater moved quickly around to the driver's side of the yellow Lamborghini and waited for the gull-winged door to swing up. A second valet mirrored the formality on the passenger side.

"Evening, Mr. Jackson," smiled the first one, bowing with his hands remaining at his side. "Good to see you." Jax climbed out unassisted, as he always insisted.

"Hello, Miss Marin," grinned the second valet, offering his hand to bring Jannie to her feet.

Jax handed the keys to valet-one and walked around the back of the car to offer an arm to his waiting date. Jannie took it and the couple headed up the set of five stairs, with both valets pausing to watch. She looked stunning in the little black cocktail dress, cut low on top and high on the hem, barely concealing her assets. Jax wore tan slacks, a navy blue blazer and white shirt with open collar. But who cared?

Good evening, Mr. Jackson," chimed Richard, the maitre'd of Giovani's. "Your usual table is ready, or would you prefer a drink in the lounge beforehand?"

"The lounge would be nice, Richard. Thank you."

"You look ravishing as always, Miss Marin," bowed Richard, sweeping his hand in the direction of the Blue Moon Lounge.

Jax and Jannie were immediately given over to Marie, a refined bar hostess in her mid-thirties, stylishly dressed in a teal-green tight skirt and jacket. Following another chorus of formalities, Marie guided them to their usual booth, privately tucked at the far end in a little alcove. Instead of sending over a waitress, she personally took their drink preferences. Jax ordered a margarita, rocks, no salt for Jannie and a bottle of Pabst Blue Ribbon for himself. She thanked them, picked up the *Reserved* sign, said a waitress would be bringing their drinks in a moment, and drifted away.

The pair sat in silence, just occasionally looking around at what little else there was to see of the lounge from their limited viewpoint. In days past, they enjoyed the seclusion, wishing to observe nothing more than each other...play a little footsy under the table...among other things.

Times had changed.

When the drinks arrived, each took a couple of sips before either of them spoke.

"We got some sad news today at work," said Jannie, breaking the silence.

"What was that?" asked Jax politely, certain it would be anything except exciting. Jannie had a propensity for finding the mundane newsworthy.

"You know Donna, the older hygienist?"

"I guess you've mentioned her."

"Well, her grandmother died last night. Dropped over dead, probably from a stroke."

"How old was she?"

"They didn't say. But Donna's pushing forty, so her grandmother had to be at least eighty, maybe ninety. The family was shocked."

Jax had no further reply. There simply wasn't one. What do you say to someone who just told you about someone she doesn't know dropping dead from something she didn't know? At age ninety no less. *Maybe they should ask Marie for today's copy of the Iowa City Tribune, so they could peruse the obits and continue this fascinating conversation.*

Jannie saw the pained look on Jax's face. Jax in turn saw the apologetic look wash across Jannie's. He knew she was thinking she had just crossed into taboo territory with the subject of death…his folks dying in that crash and all. But that wasn't the cause of his expression, and he didn't want her to be burdened with a mistake she hadn't made. So, to quickly cover for his squirming girlfriend, Jax recalled a joke he'd read off the internet a few days ago. He'd been waiting ever since to spring it on someone. The timing and subject were perfect.

"Ever thought about how you'd prefer to die?" he asked leadingly.

Jannie was wide-eyed with surprise that the subject not only hadn't bothered him, but was now being prolonged by him. "No, not really," she replied, fidgeting.

"When I die," he said, turning philosophical, "I want to go peacefully in my sleep, like my uncle did…not screaming in terror like his passengers."

Jannie blinked a couple times. "I didn't know you had an uncle."

Jax's head dropped into his hands. Without looking up he said to the table, "I don't have an uncle. It was a joke."

Jannie reran it through her mind, giving it more careful analysis this time. "Oh, I get it," she said with a smile, but not a laugh. "That's cute. Did you just make it up?"

Chapter 14

Jax took his last bite of Gravlax salmon, leaned back in the banquet-style chair and wiped his mouth on the white cloth napkin. Jannie was still working on her Cobb salad with a side of baguettes and Brie cheese. When she finally finished, Jax was ready with another leading question. He'd already struck out again today with her sharing in his outdoor pursuits. And once more she'd revealed a very limited sense of humor. He also knew she didn't like going to movie theaters: God forbid having to sit in seats that hundreds of asses had occupied before, children wiping their hands and boogers on the arms, fat people farting into the cushions, those horrible sticky floors. So before even asking, he knew the answer. *But what the hell?* he thought. *Might as well go for the trifecta.*

"So, do you want to hit a movie after this?" he asked flatly.

"I don't care," Jannie sighed, making no attempt to hide the fact that she really didn't. "What's on, anyway?"

"The new DiCaprio flick is out at the Springdale," he said. "You like him."

"I do, but that movie seems awful violent. Isn't he some kind of slave owner or something in the south? Too much testosterone for me."

"You're thinking of *Django Unchained*, dear. That was two years ago. I have it on Blue Ray."

"Of course you do," snorted Jannie. "Between a wall full of Blue Rays, DVDs, and ancient Beta tapes…"

"VHS tapes," corrected Jax.

"VHS tapes then," she huffed. "Not to mention every conceivable movie channel offered by DirecTV, Comcast, Hula…"

"Hulu."

"…and Nutflux…"

"NetFlix."

…there aren't too many movies in this world you don't have."

"So, I like movies," smiled Jax, actually enjoying Jannie's uninformed, misquoted little rant. At least it showed some passion behind that blasé demeanor she usually exhibited about life in general. "They are a nice escape now and then."

Jannie took a long sip on her zinfandel, slowly closed one eye, and riveted the other on Jax. "I'm supposed to be your *nice escape*," she cooed. "Aren't I?"

"You are, babe." He reached across the table and squeezed her hand. "You know you are."

Jannie squeezed back. She licked her lips. Both blue eyes opened wide and then softened, like a puppy begging for a treat. Jax froze. He knew what was coming. He'd seen that look no less than four times before, three in just the last six months.

"So, when are you going to make an honest woman out of me?" she asked, now running her thumb up and down the washboard of Jax's fingers, which suddenly were squeezing his water glass to the breaking point. "We love each other. What else matters?"

"You know what else matters," he said impatiently, looking anywhere but at her.

Jannie withdrew her hand and drained her wine glass. She shook her blonde head and said flatly, "You know how I feel about having kids. I do want kids. Just not right now. Jesus, Jax! I'm only twenty-two. I'd like to keep this figure and lifestyle for a few more years."

"And how many more years is that?" he asked to the blinking green Heineken sign over this end of the bar. He couldn't face her.

"I've told you. Maybe till my mid-thirties."

"God, Jannie!" he groaned, turning his full attention to her. "Why do we have to keep going through this? I'll be in my late thirties or early forties by then. By the time my oldest kid is old enough to take on a weekend fishing trip, I could be pulling Social Security. I could be in a wheelchair. Or have muscular dystrophy. Or be...dead."

The reality of Jax's situation and his desires hit home once again for Jannie. She kept forgetting, or purposely denying how much the loss of his parents and particularly his father—his fishing and hunting buddy, his mentor, his idol—stabbed at his heart on a daily basis. Of course he wanted children soon. To rebuild his lost family, to have someone to pass along all that knowledge of the outdoors to. That would be his legacy. Not the family fortune. To Jax's way of thinking, no amount of money could come close to equaling the joy of sharing your life with your children. Doing things with them. Being there for them.

"I'm sorry," she said sincerely, looking hard into his eyes with the apology.

Jax nodded and looked away. He believed her. They'd been through this before. He knew she was apologizing as much for bringing up the subject of marriage and kids as she was for regurgitating the fact of their irreconcilable differences. They were on the fast track to nowhere. The gorgeous couple they made and their compatibility in bed were about the only things Patrick Jackson and Jannie Marin had in common. For two years they'd been kidding themselves it was true love. And in some ways it was: he truly loved her beauty and blow jobs, she truly loved his large member and money clip.

If it wasn't already evident, it became so when Jannie patted his white knuckles still on the water glass and said, "I'm sorry, baby. Let's go back to your place and let me make it up to you."

Chapter 15

With his fiber-filled, black coat still draped over one arm, Ned Wilson pushed open the double doors and stepped into the outdoor night. The thirty-degree rush of air slapped his face like an icy towel, and quickly turned his sweat-soaked, cotton shirt and denim pant legs to crispy stiff.

It felt good. So did the sudden drop in decibels of the Bee Gee's "Night Fever" behind him, being blasted throughout the college hang-out called *Sammy's on Highland*. Tonight was throw-back to the disco era, and four rounds of that song in five hours were enough already. Ned was about to stick his finger down his throat.

Highland Avenue in downtown Champaign, Illinois, was relatively quiet at one in the morning. The snow-packed curbs on both sides of the street were still end to end with cars as far as the eye could see. The brand new, 1992, candy apple red Corvette Stingray parked right in front of the club must have belonged to one of those privileged students inside with the white polyester suits, black silk shirts with butterfly collars, and high-topped Italian shoes with the pointed toes. Sad for them that disco was long dead. Even sadder was the fact that trying to look like Travolta didn't help them dance like Travolta.

Cooled off now, Ned donned his puffy waist coat and turned to look back at the door. Jean-Ann—the tall, cute blonde he's just met an hour ago—should be coming out any second. She'd gone to tell her roommate she had another ride home and to collect her coat. Ned could have been a gentleman and stayed inside to pay her three-dollar, coat-check ticket, but he really had to get out of there before he lost what was left of his hearing, sweat, and mind.

The handsome, five-foot-eight, nineteen-year-old farm boy hid his abnormally large cranium under a mop of brown, shoulder-length hair, and his equally enlarged eyes behind the dark-tinted, round-framed eyeglasses. He looked as intelligent as he was. Ned had come to town with one goal in mind: to find a mate. Not just any mate, but one with features matching a carefully designed index. She needed to be intelligent, too, which was a fair possibility considering this was a college town and she was a student. And of course she had to be pure human. At this point, those two were enough. Most of the other mandatory attributes would be determined later via the strand of blonde hair he had already lifted from the back of her dress, while slow dancing to *How Deep is Your Love*. So, for now anyway, Jean-Ann's good looks and wit were just pleasant pluses.

"Sorry," breathed Jean-Ann, coming out the door backwards, buttoning her knee-length, tan suede coat. "I couldn't find my roommate right away. She was in the powder room having a cigarette."

"No problem," said Ned, sending plumes of white, frosty carbon dioxide her way in the humid air. "It actually feels good out here."

Jean-Ann pulled a red scarf from her coat pocket and wrapped it around her neck, followed by matching red knitted mittens. "Oh, I know, she laughed, taking his offered left arm. "It's so hot and loud in there I couldn't hear myself going deaf."

The pair fell in step and hurried up the sidewalk toward Ned's car some five blocks away. With continued merriment they verified each one's first name, not certain they had heard correctly inside the noisy club.

"So, where do you want to go?" Jean-Ann asked, as they jaywalked against the red light, which hardly mattered, since no cars were in transit this late at night anyway. Such would not be the case in about an hour when Sammy's closed.

"Ever been out to Skelly's Diner on the interstate?" Ned asked, the tips of his ears starting to sting in the cold.

"The truck stop? Yes. Good food," she replied.

"Yeah, they make the greatest blueberry pancakes," he said. "I was thinking...."

A heavy buzzing in two short bursts vibrated against Ned's right thigh. He stopped dead in his tracks, causing his latched-on date to spin around, almost losing her balance. Wasting no time, he jerked a small, black instrument of some kind out of his jeans pocket and glanced down at the screen. It was glowing bright green in the night, illuminating his face with an eerie hue.

"What's that thing?" asked Jean-Ann, brushing the long blonde hair away from her brown eyes for a better look. She knew a little about cellular phones, but never saw one with a video screen or this small, about the size of an audio cassette. And no antenna.

"Oh, shit!" spat Ned. He shook loose from Jean-Ann, turned and sprinted away at full speed to the north. "Go back into Sammy's!" he yelled without turning or breaking stride. "Sorry. I'll call you."

The five-foot-ten blonde with beautiful facial features and killer body stood in the middle of the sidewalk dumbfounded. She wasn't used to being stood up by any man, much less abandoned in the night, in the cold, on an empty street.

"Don't bother, asshole," she yelled after the shortest date she'd ever had, both in stature and duration. She spun around and started back toward the disco music. "Prick doesn't even have my number…or know my last name!"

Jean-Ann was halfway back to the club door when two strange men wearing long, black wool coats, black stocking caps and dark glasses pounded by her heading north, leaving an odd smell in their wake. And it wasn't from the cigarette one of them had between the fingers of his gloved hand.

"I hope you catch the asshole," she called after them. "Whatever he did."

Chapter 16

Ned suddenly feared he may be running the wrong way, right into them. He slowed just enough so his eyes could focus on the numbered pad of his bouncing communicator. He poked the upper-right-hand corner twice. A small round bleep on the green grid showed the scanner beam had originated from the south, the direction he had just come from.

"Thank God!" he breathed, slowing a little more for a closer look. But just then the bleep dissolved. They'd shut off the scanner. He twisted his torso and head around to look behind him. Two dark figures in long coats were running after him…about a block away. *Oh, shit!*

Ned stabbed the 5 key three times, and resumed running as fast as his thirty-two-inch legs could carry him.

"What's up, dear?" squawked the communicator.

"Mom," he panted into the mouth piece, "whatever they are, I think they're after me. It could be them. Two of them. Right behind me about a hundred yards."

"Oh, my Leptos," gasped Judith Wilson. "Are you sure?"

"Well, my communicator lit up, showing I was being scanned by infrared."

His mother stopped breathing. This may be it: *direct contact.* But why did it have to be her son, Ned? "Can you outrun them, sweetheart?"

"I don't know. Maybe."

"Hold on," she said. There was a two second silence before she added with a hint of confidence, "Okay, I've got you on the satellite. You're just about to the corner. Turn left NOW!"

That was already in Ned's strategy. He didn't have to be told.

"Now where?" he panted, searching the area for another place to turn.

"Where's your car?" asked Judith.

"Three blocks straight north. I need to get there, but I'm running east."

"That's okay. Keep going and turn left again at the next corner. In fifty yards there's an alley. Duck in there and get behind something."

"Will do."

A few seconds later the two dark figures puffed past at three-quarter speed, one of them just giving a quick glance into the alley. They didn't see their quarry tucked into a narrow doorway.

"They've run past," whispered a gasping Ned into the communicator.

"Great," replied his mom, then she added thoughtfully, "Listen, Ned, if you can, hustle up and point your camera around the corner at them running away. Don't expose yourself, just the camera. I'll do the looking for you. *The Desert People* would love some video of what these things look like."

"Gotcha." Ned moved quickly and quietly back to the entrance of the alley. Leaning against the cold concrete wall, he poked the black box out just enough around the corner.

"A little more to the left," coached Judith. "Up a little. Hold it right there. Good. They're still running. Wait. Now they've stopped. They're looking around. Hands on their knees."

Ned's communicator vibrated again. "They're scanning again," he reported, keeping the camera on point.

"Uh-oh," said Judith. "They're starting back toward you. Oh, Leptos, Ned, they must have seen your scanner detector. They're running fast."

Ned quickly pulled the device back and checked the screen. Sure enough. The green light flooded his chest and face. He punched it off and put the phone back to his ear.

"I'm heading out of the alley," said Ned, now running. "Going west."

"Yes, get the hell out of there, Ned," said his mom with more urgency in her soft voice. "When you get to the other end of the alley, turn left and head north for your car." She had to grab her mask and tank for a couple breaths of extra nitrogen.

The seventy-five percent human reached the west end of the alley just as his box vibrated again. No need to check the grid. He knew where they were and that they knew where he was. It was another footrace. He cut to his left, almost spinning out on the refreeze of some ice that had been melting snow earlier in the day. With a hundred-yard lead, Ned felt he could cross the intersection ahead and get to the other side of the line of parked cars before his pursuers shot out of the alley. All he had to do to avoid their scanners was keep anything metal between him and them. But it would be tough maintaining his current speed, having to run while crouching down.

Three blocks later, bordering on exhaustion, Ned had no choice but to take a breather between two cars just one block from his own 1991 Buick LeSabre. He could only hope his pursuers were as tired as he was. Sucking the January air so hard his chest felt like it was going to shatter into ice shards, he raised up just enough to peek through the Pontiac's frosty front and back windshields. No sign of them. But his vision was quite limited. He crouched back down.

"I don't...see them," he whispered into the small microphone on his communicator.

"Please stay low, sweetheart," whispered Ned's mother. "We can't let them get you."

"No way," smiled Ned. "Even if they are closer now, I'm sure I can outrun them."

For two decades now the Mejan's advanced technology had been detecting heat-seeking, infrared scans coming from random places low in the skies all over the world. Since they were almost always under the cover of darkness or thick clouds, and from a static, dead-quiet holding pattern, it was assumed the scans were coming from another alien spacecraft with stealth and antigravity capabilities similar to their own. But that's all they knew at first. Then, as the scanning frequency began to intensify anywhere there were concentrations of Mejan-human crossbreeds—like here at the campus of the University of Illinois—the target seemed to be the crossbreeds themselves. If Ned Wilson's pursuers were indeed those extraterrestrials, it could become the first known physical encounter between the two races, neither one indigenous to Earth.

Chapter 17

Ned lifted up for another glance around the area. Still no sign of his pursuers. They were probably hunkered down behind some cars like he was, catching their breath, waiting for him to reveal himself. He pulled the car keys from his coat pocket and put the phone back to his ear. "I'm only a block from my car," he whispered. "I'm going to make a run for it. I think I can get inside and take off before they catch up to me."

"We know you can, Son." It was his dad on the other end now…his one hundred percent human father. It was good to hear his reassuring voice.

"Run like the track star you are, darling," added his half human, half Mejan mother. "They can't hurt you if they can't catch you."

"I will."

"And stay on the phone until you're back here safe, okay?" ordered his dad.

"Will do."

Feeling the lactic acid in his muscles starting to drain away and some breath coming back to his lungs, Ned adjusted his keys so the ignition key was front and center. He spun on the balls of his leather loafers to be facing northwest. With one last look over his shoulder, he sprang from his hiding place between the two cars and onto the glistening asphalt of Highland Avenue. With every ounce of energy left in his nineteen-year-old legs, the farm kid from the cornfields outside Champaign sprinted along the row of cars facing him. A quick glance back over his shoulder revealed only one of his dark pursuers. It wasn't directly to his six as he expected, more like to his four, popping up from behind a car on the other side of the street. He was a good fifty yards away and not yet moving. More than enough distance to get safely to the Buick.

His shoes skidding on the asphalt up to the driver's side of the white LeSabre, Ned was about to stick the key in the door lock when something thumped against the back of his right shoulder. He thought he'd been hit by a hard snowball or even a rock. Suddenly any attempt to raise his arm to unlock the door was futile. It just hung there, limp, paralyzed.

"What the…" he blurted.

"What's the matter, Ned?" queried an anxious mother.

Another ball of something whacked the back of his left thigh, buckling his knee. It too became numb and Ned went down hard on the asphalt.

"I...I can't move my arm or leg," he reported into the phone in his left hand. "I think they hit me with rocks or something."

Half paralyzed but still with all his faculties, Ned had the presence of mind to punch on the phone's video camera again with his thumb. He held it furtively tight to his left hip, while pointing it toward the rapidly approaching figure in the long, black overcoat. As it drew within a few feet, the dark humanoid figure stopped and bent down. It lifted its dark glasses and propped them up on the stocking cap for a better look at its prey. The alien didn't care it was exposing part of its face to Ned; it knew the human wouldn't be telling anybody. But it didn't know the digital reproduction of its beady, yellow, wolfen eyes was being relayed back to a farmhouse five miles away.

Judith Wilson drew in a breath in preparation for a scream of abject horror. Her husband quickly hit the mute button on the cord leading to her headset.

"We can't let them know we're watching," he said through his teeth, fighting back a scream of his own.

Two gloved hands of black leather grew enormous on the monitor, as they reached for the man behind the camera. Being jerked to his feet caused Ned to let go of his communicator to defend himself with his only good hand. The little black box clicking against the street, landing face up. Back at the farm, the computer's monitor showed a static image of a single overhead streetlight, star-bursting across the screen, as mom and dad listened in terror to the audio.

"Hello, Mejan halfbreed," said a raspy baritone. "You just what we looked for."

"Whoever you're looking for," pleaded the twenty-five percent Mejan, "you've got the wrong guy."

"Oh, my baby!" howled the frantic mother, grasping both sides of the monitor, tears flying from her huge, round eyes. Her husband wrapped his shaking arms around her petite frame and pressed his stubbly cheek against hers.

"And what this?" they heard the other Regg say, as it picked up the small device, renewing motion on the monitor. The distraught parents watched as it was turned this way and that, giving a brief flash of the other Regg holding up a struggling Ned. It then held steadily on a face with yellow eyes and a small, black, shiny nose. "A piece of your technology," spoke the mouth clearly into the phone, then widening into a hideous smile, exposing the distinctive teeth of a carnivore.

"That's something I just found on the street," lied Ned. "It won't do you any more good than I will."

There was a brief exchange in a dialect none of the Wilsons had ever heard before, followed by the universal language of laughter. Then the Regg holding the phone apparently stuck it in his coat pocket. "Oh, it do much good," came the now-muffled, barely audible words spoken in English for Ned's benefit. "You and Mejan race—as your satellite movies say— *now in deep shit!*"

Chapter 18

The silver, 2015 Lexus SUV was again parked on the shoulder of County Road 34. But this time it was lined up with the south end of the pond closer to the farm, rather than the north end with the maple trees. When Jax had called Alan Brookfield earlier this Saturday morning to verify the eleven o'clock fishing lesson with his daughter, he had again offered to pick her up at the house. But Mr. Brookfield repeated he should just park on the gravel road as before, and she would meet him on top of the hill at the pond. Although curious, Jax couldn't blame the father for being so protective. After all, Jax had hopped a fence to blatantly trespass on the Brookfield private land. Maybe once the family got to know him better, the caution flag would be lifted.

While waiting for his student to arrive, Jax walked around the one-acre pond in his usual exploratory mode. He found it very difficult not to fish, but he didn't want to risk catching a nice bass that the farmer's daughter could have caught. Getting her into some action would surely score points with the Brookfields. Besides, he had a feeling they were watching him…like they probably were yesterday.

A couple sideways glances into the maple trees didn't reveal any cameras, at least none that he could see. Same with the picnic table, but he wasn't about to crawl under it for a look-see. Maybe there was one mounted in that weird, glassy-looking dome on top of the silo two blocks to the south. That was a possibility. It was up high enough to have a clear shot to all parts of the pond.

Using a rubber practice plug with a pinched-on split-shot, the outdoor columnist just nonchalantly walked the bank, casting at regular intervals, using the count-down method to determine the water's depth. He was surprised to learn it was ten feet in all areas: both ends, sides, middle, everywhere. He knew an Iowa pond should be at least fifteen feet deep to provide enough oxygen for its fish to survive many months sealed off under ice during an exceptionally harsh Midwest winter. But if this one was fed by a spring or from a well, these ten feet may be enough. Besides, bass are a hardy lot. As he had written in one of his columns, *Salmonid Micropterus is one of the most adaptable freshwater species in North America. Like cockroaches, crows, carp and crabgrass, the largemouth bass would probably survive a nuclear holocaust.*

With Jax's polarized sunglasses and the high sun's angle at about ninety degrees to his side, he could see his dirty-gray practice plug an incredible five or six feet down. Yet there was little else to see. As far as he could tell, the pond had no underwater structures at all. No weeds, stumps, fallen trees, nothing. Just the high-priced rip-rap ringing the entire bank. This made no sense. There was no place for the young fry to hide from the adults. They'd get wiped out before they could grow to any size at all. And they probably already had, judging from what he could see...or more accurately, *didn't* see. Strange food pyramid. By all rights that bass he caught yesterday should have been shaped more like a malnourished snake than the plump football it was. The only possible answer was that Alan Brookfield was feeding them some kind of special fish-chow.

Jax's thoughts were interrupted when precisely at eleven o'clock a shiny burgundy Toyota Sienna popped the hill from the direction of the farm and pulled up twenty feet from where he was standing midway on the east side. Out bounded a petite young lady of twenty with a broad smile featuring two front teeth that were just a tad bigger than most...like Kristin Stewart's. She was wearing a green and white plaid shirt tucked into faded blue jeans. From under the short-brimmed, straw hat fell honey-blonde hair cut in a sleek bob just below her jawline. Dark, wrap-around sunglasses rested on a button nose. No shit-kicking boots from Farm Fleet like her dad, the footwear was stylish, white Nike runners with green trim and laces. Jax put her at five-foot-four and pleasantly elfin at about a hundred and ten pounds.

So endeth the fat and ugly farmer's daughter story line.

Chapter 19

"I'll bet you're Jax," she chimed, walking briskly up to him with right hand extended. "I'm Suzy Brookfield."

Jax took the tiny, soft hand in his meat-hook and tried to look into her eyes. But he saw only his own wide-angle reflection in the black lenses. He decided to keep his sunglasses in place as well.

"Jax Jackson," he said, returning her beaming smile. "Pleased to meet you, Miss Brookfield."

"Pleased to meet you, too, Mr. Jackson. And please, call me Suzy."

"Okay, and please, Suzy, call me Jax. *Please*."

If there had been any ice to break, that final and purposeful *please* in the string of five did it. Both young people found it pleasantly difficult to stop smiling or conclude the firm handshake. Once they had mutually separated, it was Suzy who took over, dispelling any chance of a post-introduction pregnant pause, like Jax had with her fart of a father the day before.

"I hear you're the outdoorsman extraordinaire," she teased.

Jax chuckled, a little embarrassed. "I don't know about that. I just do a lot of it. Sooner or later you're bound to learn something."

"Well, Jax," she said, whimsically spreading her arms wide in *take-me* fashion, "I'm ready to learn."

With that grin still plastered across his face, Jax led the eager student over to the picnic table where he had laid out three rod-and-reel outfits, his vest, and a small tackle box. He picked up the same spinning rig he had caught his eight-pounder on yesterday and handed it to Suzy.

"Ever fished with one of these?" he asked, using the opportunity to take a closer look at her dainty hands. They showed no sign of calluses or grime or anything one would expect from a farm girl. Even her fingernails were manicured and coated with a frosty-pearl kind of polish his girlfriend, Jannie, often wore. And there was just a whiff of a pleasant, sweet perfume he didn't recognize.

Suzy played with it a moment, then lied, "Nope. I've only used a reel that is shaped like a Butler bin with the line coming out of the small hole at the top."

Most folks in agricultural communities are familiar enough with the Butler bin, which is a large, squatty, silver, metal storage bin often topped with what looks like a huge bottle cap. Jax knew she meant a closed-face spinning reel...a favorite of most beginners, but generally not strong enough to haul in anything bigger than a one-pound crappie.

"Well, this is an open-faced spinning reel," he said, taking the outfit from her and walking back to the water's edge. Suzy followed on his heel like an eager puppy. Explaining each step, Jax hooked the tip of his index finger around the line just above the reel, opened the bail and made a smooth cast into the middle of the pond. He quickly reeled in and handed the rig back to Suzy. "Now you try it."

Her hands remained at her sides. She was peering up at him, seemingly lost in contemplation. "Anybody ever told you that you look like Josh Duhamel...'cept for the nose?"

For the next fifteen minutes and twice that many trials and errors, the deceptive little vixen pretended to finally get the hang of casting an open-faced spinning reel she already knew well, owning three of them herself. Out of necessity, but not without a degree of enjoyment to both parties, Jax had to stand right beside his student, slightly bent over, grazing her right shoulder with his chest, while offering hands-on guidance.

The lesson then advanced to the actual technique of working the bait in a seductive manner to entice a largemouth bass to strike. The lure in this case was still that hard rubber, hookless, practice plug, so there was no chance of catching anything just yet. He demonstrated the lift-and-pause, lift-and-pause method a few times, and then it was Suzy's turn. She pretended to catch onto it with some difficulty.

After the preplanned hour of practice, it was time. Jax's iPhone said it was almost high noon. And this being the day of a new moon, both the bright sun and the invisible moon would be directly overhead about now. The strong electromagnetic pull of those two celestial bodies in tandem should be inducing the bass to bite, and quite possibly influencing the two anglers, as well. Suzy was more than ready to try her luck for real. Jax clipped off the practice plug and retied the same super sharp Aberdeen hook buried into the six-inch, black plastic worm with a sliding bullet weight.

"Go get 'em, girl," he said, handing her the rod. "Just like I showed you."

Giggling with anticipation, Suzy took the rig, fingered the line, opened the bail, brought the rod back to the nine o'clock position, and threw it forward. The bait smacked hard onto the rocks three feet from the toes of her Nikes. Laughing at herself, she twisted around to look up into Jax's azure eyes. "Ooops," she said, curious to see her instructor's reaction.

"That's okay, said Jax, stifling a laugh, while lightly patting her shoulder. "You just need to let go of the line a half-second sooner. Try it again."

As instructed, Suzy let go of the line sooner this time. Too much sooner—accidentally on purpose—and the plastic worm flopped harmlessly behind both of them. Comically looking left and right, up and down for the lure, she then followed the limp line, turning around to come chest-to-stomach with Jax. She looked up into his face and said with the cutest little girl whine and crinkled nose, "You're never gonna want to take me fishing again, are you?"

Jax put a hand on each shoulder, smiled warmly, and said truthfully to her pouting face, "You're learning faster than anyone I've ever taught before. You're doing fine."

Chapter 20

By her fifth attempt the worm sailed faultlessly in the right direction with ample velocity to reach thirty feet out into the pond. That earned her a "Good job," from Jax and a pat on the back. Suzy was giddy. And not because of the cast. She had mastered that eight years ago.

"Now hold your rod tip high and steady and let the worm sink all the way to the bottom," coached Jax from behind with his mouth by her ear. He had a hand on each of her forearms, helping guide her movements. "Watch your line. Once it goes slack, you know you're on the bottom."

"Where's the line?" asked Suzy, feeling her knees go weak…that mild whiff of his virility grazing her nostrils. "I don't see it. There's too much glare on the water."

Jax could see it just fine with his sunglasses, which cut through glare like it wasn't there. "Don't you have polarized lenses?" Suzy just shrugged, like she didn't know what they were. "Well here, try mine," he said, handing his pair over her shoulder.

Purposely keeping her face away from him, Suzy took Jax's glasses, quickly slipping hers off and his on. "Whoa!" she chirped. "That's really cool."

Jax in turn put on Suzy's wrap-arounds. They had the feel of expensive and turned the vista to a pleasant, very dark-green. But they weren't Polaroids. He couldn't see her line either.

"Okay," he said, resuming the lesson, "slowly reel up the slack. Good. Then lift the rod tip to the one o'clock position. Good. Hold it there real steady. Good. Now watch the 'V' the line makes on the surface, as it comes toward you like a little water bug. See it?" Suzy nodded that she did. But her mind was slowly drifting elsewhere. Her dad taught her this lift-and-hold method with a plastic worm when she was twelve. But he hadn't taught her anything about the heat and pheromones emanating from a man like her instructor. "That's the worm swimming seductively back to the bottom," said Jax. "That's when a bass is most likely to strike."

That first cast having produced nothing, Jax helped his attentive pupil make another, this one much farther out and closer to river rocks lining the north shore.

"When will I know if a bass has taken the bait," she asked innocently, working it the way Jax had said, still relishing in the closeness of his firm chest and arms.

"You may feel a heavy tug or a slight tap," said Jax. "Sometimes nothing at all. The line may just move off to the side."

"Kind of like it is now?" she asked, watching the little 'V' cutting slowly to the right.

Jax couldn't see the line in the sun's reflection. So he quickly slid his right hand off of Suzy's and onto the sensitive graphite rod. He ever so gently lifted the rod tip a couple degrees higher, pinching the shaft with his thumb and forefinger. He detected the slightest thump, probably the bass getting a better grip on the worm. "Set the hook, Suzy!" he commanded.

In the annals of hook-setting there are powerful, moderate and weak. Suzy's hook-set initiated an entirely different level…purposely on the low side. Not wasting time with more verbal commands, Jax slapped his hands back on Suzy's, just as she hoped he would. He fully engulfed her arms and small torso, and hauled back on the rod, forcing her one hundred plus pounds to press hard against his two hundred, both barely maintaining their balance. At the same time his left hand cranked on the spinning reel as fast as he could, her left hand going along for the ride.

Knowing the hook was nowhere from being set in the bass's jaw, Jax pushed their combined weight far forward, and then rocked back again, this time so hard they tumbled backwards, his ass landing hard on the ground, hers landing pleasantly on the top of his left thigh. The natural motion of setting the hook had also brought Jax's forearms pressing into the softness of her bosom. Suzy's eyes rolled. Jax silently apologized by quickly moving his arms down to encircle her waist.

The fight was on. The bass knew something was wrong, and fought for its life. Suzy knew something was right, and it wasn't catching her fifteenth or twentieth bass this year from this pond. It was definitely from the sensation of being fondled by this man. And not just any man. This was a tall, handsome hunk, whose hair sample had already tested positive. As far as she was concerned, he was more than a strong prospect. But they needed the blood sample. She hoped beyond hope it proved positive as well.

"Don't lose him!" barked Jax, as much to himself as to her. "Keep the line tight."

He knew that was a ridiculous order to someone who was holding on for dear life, hoping the rod didn't snap in two or she didn't get pulled into the water herself. Jax managed to scramble back to his feet and pull Suzy up with him. He released her for the most part, but kept his hands locked around her narrow waist, as she battled the bass's every attempt to regain its freedom.

Chapter 21

It took another sixty seconds of runs and dives and Jax's coaching in her ear, but the fish finally weaved up to the shoreline, exhausted. Jax let go of his excited student to shinny down the rocks and lip the bass ashore.

"Oh, my Leptos!" said Suzy with an exaggerated gasp. "It's beautiful!"

"About three pounds," reported Jax, hefting it high for inspection, as he climbed back up the bank. He dislodged the hook and verified the fish's weight with his De-liar. "Congratulations. Three pounds two ounces."

With a chortle, Suzy bounded up and squeezed her instructor tightly around the waist. She then stood on her tiptoes to kiss the side of his jaw, the highest she could reach. "Thank you, thank you!" she grinned. "That goes down as one of the most exciting moments of my life. And I owe it all to you." She wasn't talking about the fish.

Blushing from the peck, as well as the stirrings it had started somewhere around his diaphragm, Jax smiled back at the darling pixie face. "I think I enjoyed that as much as you did." He gave her a return hug with one arm, then eased away to return the bass to the water.

"What are you doing?" Suzy suddenly challenged, an odd twinge of bewilderment in her voice. "We have to keep it."

Jax paused long enough to cover the high points of his Catch-and-Release policy. Suzy then countered that she was under orders from headquarters to bring home any fish they caught and have it for dinner. Not wanting to buck Farmer Alan, Jax sadly strung up the bass and set it back into the water, securing the sharp, metal end of the stringer between two rocks.

As he climbed back up, the pain of doing that to one of his beloved largemouths was overshadowed by the warmth building in his heart. Suzy had already straightened the plastic worm on the hook like a tournament pro and made another cast, all on her own. "I wanna get another one," she announced, her jaw set, determined. "An even bigger one."

"Alright, go for it," Jax coaxed, making a quick check of his thumb. It was showing a few reopened streaks of red from lipping the second big bass in as many days. Like his eight-pounder, that array of teeth ringing the upper and lower jaws were tiny, but very sharp.

"Oh, you're bleeding," said Suzy sympathetically, sticking the rod between her thighs to free her hands. She grabbed his thumb and pulled it toward her for a closer look. Despite his protest, she plucked a small hanky from a breast pocket and dabbed the minor wound, imprinting a minute stain of red on the white fabric. "There. All better," she announced, folding the piece of fabric and placing it back into the same pocket.

Silently relieved her main mission was accomplished, Suzy went right back to fishing. Lift-and-hold, lift-and-hold, watching the line slice slowly back towards her each time, while Jax watched her with head-shaking wonder. *What enthusiasm in this adorable little thing!* He may have found a new fishing buddy. He couldn't tell Jannie, of course. She'd never understand.

After one more cast, Suzy set the rod down and pulled the smart phone from her jean's pocket. She checked the time. *12:30 p.m.* "I need to call Mom," she announced, punching a couple keys. "She said she may have some chores for me to do."

Jax nodded, taking the opportunity to check his own iPhone for messages. Just a text from Jannie, saying she was going shopping with Olivia in Cedar Rapids and would see him later that afternoon at his house.

While Suzy connected with her mother and eased away toward the van, Jax decided to fetch his baitcasting rod-and-reel from the picnic table. From his vest he produced his favorite spinnerbait with a chartreuse skirt, chrome Colorado blades, and a white, four-inch grub for a trailer. He tied it on with his usual Palomar knot and walked back to the pond. It was about time he had a chance to make a couple casts himself. He didn't think Suzy—or anybody else who was probably watching—would mind.

Chapter 22

Inside the communication center, Mary Brookfield was just finishing her lunch. The world news on the north wall was mostly about ISIS pushing farther toward Baghdad, and the Russian rebels pushing farther into the Ukraine. On the national front, lame duck Obama was still trying to convince the country his affordable health care really was affordable. The local weather called for continued sunny skies with light winds and a high of sixty-four.

More importantly, the green screens on the east wall were showing no blips. As usual.

One of the computer monitors said corn was up to $5.23 per bushel, and beans had dropped a quarter. It was too early in the day for a report on pork bellies or October cattle.

The next two monitors had Google waiting patiently for something to search.

The fourth was a live camera shot of her daughter, Suzy, and Jax fishing up at the pond. But Mary was too busy finishing up with all the morning newspapers from around the state to pay much attention. The National Inquirer and Star should be arriving in today's mail. As the movie *Men in Black* had facetiously revealed, every once in a while these rags held a grain of truth to an alien abduction or UFO sighting. As clandestine as the Reggs were, any tidbit into their activities was helpful. The Mejans didn't know for sure what these other space travelers' ultimate goal was, but they could guess. And it was definitely not good. It had long been suspected they were behind the mysterious and unsolved disappearance of one Maggie Connors—a fifty percent Mejan—back in 1970. And it was a cold fact they had abducted Ned Wilson in 1992, because they had audio-visual proof.

Mary was startled when her communicator suddenly erupted with the classic tune, *Wake up, little Susie,* by the Everly Brothers. She put down the *Des Moines Register* and punched the *OK* key.

"Hi, sweetheart," she said, sliding her office chair down to the monitor spying on her daughter at the pond. "Any luck?"

"Yeah," chimed Suzy, loud enough for Jax to hear. "I caught a nice big bass. Three pounds, two ounces."

"That's nice, dear. Not your biggest by any means, but nice. Bring it home. How about the other thing? Did you get it yet?"

"Sure did," boasted Suzy, cryptically. "Am I good or what?"

"Really? Some blood?"

"Yep."

"Much?

"I think enough," she whispered

"On your hanky?"

"Yep."

Any chance Jax can hear us?"

"Nope."

"Good. So, is the hanky inside the plastic sandwich bag I gave you?"

"Soon."

"Just the same, honey, I think you'd better get it down here to the lab as soon as possible."

"Ah, Mom," whined Suzy, louder again. "Do I have to? I wanted to fish some more."

"Good acting, dear."

"Oh. Okay. I guess so."

"My, but we Brookfields are a deceptive lot, aren't we," replied Mary with a laugh.

"Okay. I will. Yes, right away. Bye."

Chapter 23

Suzy stuck the phone back in her jeans front pocket and walked over to Jax, who had just sent his colorful lure buzzing through the air and landing with a *splat* near the southern shore of the Brookfield pond. "Sorry, teach," she moaned, crinkling her nose, "but I have to head back to the house. Mom needs me to run those errands."

"Oh, that's too bad," said Jax, slow-rolling the spinnerbait just under the surface. "Well, at least you got yourself a nice bass."

Various smart phone photos were snapped of themselves with the bass, which was then placed on ice in a cooler Suzy had optimistically waiting in her van. As she opened the driver's side door, Jax asked if it would be okay for him to stay a little longer and fish.

"If it were up to me," sighed his student, turning to face him, "I'd say yes. But Dad told me he wants one of us to be with you when up here. I hope you understand. He's real possessive."

"I kind of got that feeling," said Jax, making little effort to hide his disappointment. "So, when do you think I could come back?"

"Well," mused Suzy with a sly grin, "if you could stand to give me another fishing lesson, I'm sure I could convince Dad to get you back up here real soon."

"That would be great," he said, a smile returning to his lips. "Call or text me anytime. Sooner the better."

The pair exchanged cell phone numbers, then shook hands goodbye. Suzy had turned to climb into the van, when she felt a large hand fall gently on her shoulder.

"Wait," said Jax.

Wait?

Suzy's heart skipped. The energy from this man's touch was tingling right through her shirt and down her arm to her fingertips. *What did he want? Was he going to spin her around and kiss her? Ask her for a date? Throw her down on the grass and ravish her?* She knew these were silly, schoolgirl thoughts, right out of some romance novel she must have read years ago in her early teens. But she couldn't help herself. Suzy had never been infatuated with someone before. And she certainly didn't know a lot about men...not *real* men, anyway. So much of her early carnal knowledge had come from those romance novels, plus R-rated satellite movies and series, the network sitcoms and dramas, magazines and the internet. But none of that was first-person flesh. Even worse, most of it was fiction: poorly written, directed, and edited fiction.

Her twenty-five-percent Mejan mother had blushed all through the anemic sex talk six years ago, ashamed to knowing little about the human male herself. And the only *man* Suzy did know something about wasn't about to give his beautiful, precious, vulnerable daughter tips on landing a man. Fish, yes. Men, never!

At age sixteen there had been Mel, her first boyfriend. And we do mean *boy*, also sixteen, pure human, the son of a transient hired-hand at the Brookfield farm. They did it in the haymow without knowing what they were doing. It was okay. Awkward. Painful. Messy. Interesting. Mel left soon after, as his family moved on to help with the harvest on another farm across the state.

And now her current beau, Jason, twenty-three, very smart, very shy. She had to practically rape him the two times they'd done it so far. His performance was adequate, at least the second time was. If nothing else, Suzy was totally convinced that making love with a real person was far more exciting than any of those fictitious alternatives.

But this Jax guy…this was another story altogether. She didn't know how to act or react around some incredibly handsome, big, strong, witty *man*, who just rang her chimes with his slightest touch and was making her stomach queasy with that single word, *Wait*. She had been hoping beyond hope that all the tests would come back positive and he would prove to be a viable candidate. But that was still unknown. Still in the future.

So, what should I do now if he tries to kiss me, asks me out, tries to jump my bones!?

The twenty-year-old farm girl took in a short breath and slowly turned to face the cause of her affliction.

"We have each other's sunglasses," reported Jax, tapping the bow of the pair he was wearing.

Suzy was caught in an uncompromising position. Outside of trying to hide the sinking feeling of disappointment and embarrassment, she couldn't remove his glasses in front of him in broad daylight. That would raise an issue she wasn't ready to explain to him…at least not yet. She had to think fast.

"Oh, I *love* these glasses," she whined, adjusting them tighter to her face. "Could I keep them? *Pleeeease*. I'd gladly pay you for them."

Jax thought about giving up his two-hundred-dollar pair of Revo Guide Extremes. He thought about the other five or six pairs he had scattered around his tackle boxes, cars and den…some even more expensive. He thought about how cute she looked in them, and how much he enjoyed teaching her to fish, and just being with her. He thought of how grateful she'd probably be and how that might help in getting an invitation to come back.

"Of course you can have them," he said. "Consider it a graduation present for passing your first bass class...with a first-class bass, no less." Jax had to grin at his own clever word construction. The third person observer back in the communications room concluded he was indeed a writer. But not necessarily a good one.

"Really?" she piped, stepping forward to give her teacher his second hug in less than fifteen minutes. "Thank you so much. I'll never go fishing without them."

"You're quite welcome," grinned Jax, removing her pair from his face and handing them to her. "Be sure to take yours, too. They're too dark for me."

Chapter 24

Joseph Saluni opened the door to the small, well-ventilated wooden shed and stepped inside. He felt for and found the six-volt Rayovac flashlight and clicked it on. Cursing himself for not doing this before sundown, he unscrewed the gas cap to the chugging generator and pointed the beam into the hole. Almost empty, as expected. He filled the tank from one of the half-dozen five-gallon gas cans, and replaced the cap. The tiny, private island would have electrical power for another day and a half.

The tired Samoan shuffled the final fifty feet to his three-room hut, turned off the forty-watt bulb over the sink, walked into the only bedroom and climbed into bed. A tentative, exploratory stroke with his right hand over the back of Emere's taut thigh resulted in no response or verbal recognition. She was obviously fast asleep and in no mood for making love this night. He couldn't blame his young wife. Mondays were always difficult and tomorrow would be only slightly better.

The *Island Dream* cruise ship had sailed away precisely at four o'clock that afternoon. Right on schedule, as always. Joseph and Emere had just two more days to make sure the beach was meticulous cleaned up and everything was prepared for the next ship's arrival at ten a.m. on Thursday. The two men from Puerto Rico twenty miles to the east would boat in tomorrow for a couple hours to resupply the small concession stand and haul away the refuse. Then the five-man crew would arrive mid-morning on Wednesday to rake the sand, scour the block-long dock, service the rental equipment in the dive shop, and clean every inch of all two hundred lounge chairs before motoring away again at sundown.

Other than those few daylight hours each week when workers and cruise ship tourists occupied the white sands of Solar Cay, Joseph and Emere Saluni were the island's only inhabitants.

The latch on the front door opened silently, and two hunched over figures entered. Both were wearing light-blue, polyester jumpsuits that zipped from crotch to neck with matching soft-soled sneakers, all stolen from a Sears warehouse three years earlier. The rosewood floorboards creaked under each footfall, as the hundred-pound intruders moved steadily through the open door into the bedroom.

Each taking a side of the bed, they bent down and sprayed a silvery mist into the faces of the sleeping couple, pausing a few seconds to allow the chemicals to take full effect. The pump spray bottles were then returned to their slots beside the other two spray bottles on the aliens' respective leather utility belts—also stolen from the Sears warehouse, hardware section.

The figure on Joseph's side bent down farther. With a course, muffled voice it said simply into Joseph's ear, "Sleep." The Samoan smiled and nestled himself deeper in the bedding. He would awaken the next morning fully rested with no memory and a slight headache. The one on Emere's side pulled back the single cotton sheet and ordered, "Come." The willing woman was guided out of the bed onto wobbling feet. She smiled, eyes half closed.

With one bulbous-headed, gray-faced, black-eyed, small-chinned alien on each arm, the petite, brown woman was led out of the cabin and around back. Waiting behind a grove of rum trees sat a spacecraft, somewhat resembling an Italian sports car in styling, but about ten times the size. As they approach, the eight-foot-high backend opened and a ramp extended to bid entrance.

Inside, Emere was stripped of her plain white nightshirt and laid naked on the cold, metal table in the middle of the cramped laboratory, her wrists and ankles secured with leather straps riveted to the table's silver surface. With systemic efficiency, eight electrodes were placed on precise parts of her head and body, instantly showing results on an array of monitors covering two walls. Blood was drawn separately from her carotid artery and jugular vein and run through a small hematological gas analyzer. Catheters were placed into her urethra and anus to draw out urine and feces samples, while a stomach pump brought up contents of her last meal. Eggs were taken from her ovaries, skin from the back of her hand, hair from her head and pubic region. With each prick, probe, and scrape, little Emere winced in pain, but quickly relaxed again with a dopey grin.

All testing results archived, the attachments and restraints were removed and Emere's nightshirt returned to cover her body. As she sat on the end of the table, a Q-Tip—stolen in bulk late-night from Walgreen's fourteen years ago—was dipped in a small vile of a greenish solution and dabbed inside her left nostril. Translated from Reggese, the compound was labeled *PR-1994*.

Emere was led back to the cabin and into bed beside a snoring Joseph. She was sprayed with the amnesia drug and told to sleep. Assured both humans were unconscious, the two Reggs removed the bulbous, full-headed, rubber masks, and tucked them into their utility belts. They walked over to the refrigerator and plucked out a couple cold Medalla Light beers. Kicking back at the kitchen table, one lit up a Merit cigarette from the half-empty pack on the table. He had his own Camels, but had never tried this brand. The other didn't care to smoke, as many of Earth's allergens had him coughing enough the way it was.

Being cooped up in their respective spaceships for days on end, it was not uncommon for Reggs to take advantage of any chance to spend a little time walking the actual earth. It was never condoned by the upper echelon, because obviously it increased the odds of being seen by humans or caught on security cameras. But in situations like this—in a low-populated area in the middle of the night miles from anywhere—who would know?

Break over, they walked back to their spaceship, taking the beer cans and cigarette butt with them; leaving any evidence of a visit *was* strictly verboten and punished severely. They climbed in the side doors to the cockpit, buckled up, and lifted off silently into the night.

Two weeks later, three Regg microbiologists sat in their daughter ship's recreation room, watching with mild interest a CNN breaking news report regarding another outbreak of Legionnaires' Disease. As many as fifty people onboard a cruise ship in the eastern Caribbean contracted the pneumonia-type illness. Since the Legionella bacteria was known to have an incubation period of two to fourteen days after contact, the CDC concluded it had originated on the fourteen-day cruise.

The Reggs were pleased that their new *PR-1994* appeared more effective than the previous amalgamations, especially the original *PH-1976* they had introduced at the 1976 American Legion convention in Philadelphia. But PR-1994 still wasn't measuring up to most of the flu and infectious diseases other Regg scientists had been injecting into Earth's human populous since 1930. So, these three microbiologists were ordered to scrap this avenue and concentrate their energies on something with a greater potential for creating a deadly, global pandemic.

Chapter 25

Jax woke with a start from a pleasant dream suddenly turning nightmarish. Still flat on his back, he rolled his head from side to side to reassure himself this was the real world, and not those huge, yellow cat eyes that had jumped out at him from behind a closet door.

To his left the first light of an orange dawn was bathing the otherwise white, floral lace curtains leading to the master bedroom's balcony. Overhead the globe light in the center of the ceiling fan still glowed dimly, as the five mesh blades rotated at the lowest setting. On his right Jannie was breathing heavily, her bare back turned to him, the silk sheet covering the rest of her. This was his true reality. Thank God.

It was Sunday. Yesterday was Saturday. What was this warm feeling suddenly replacing the nightmare, massaging his solar plexus and stimulating his thoughts? Jax took a deep breath and sent some oxygen to his brain. Oh, yeah. He had caught the biggest bass of his life on Friday. He had gone back to the pond to give the farmer's daughter a fishing lesson yesterday. *Suzy. Suzy Brookfield.* She loved to fish. She was cute as a water sprite and twice as bubbly. *Suzy.* A smile spread across Jax's face.

He reached for his iPhone on the nightstand and powered it up. It was ludicrous, but maybe Suzy or Alan Brookfield had called or texted during the night to say he could come back to fish today, or give Suzy another lesson. He checked his messages. Nothing. But why would there be during a Saturday night? It *was* ludicrous.

Jax put his smart phone back on the nightstand and picked up the remote. The sixty-inch Samsung flat screen ding-donged on and in faded Cinemax, the same channel when they switched it off last night. *Hot Shots* was on, one of his favorites. He propped up three of the goose down pillows and settled in to watch it for about the ninth or tenth time.

Jannie rolled over, flopping her warm right arm across his cool, hairless chest. She buried her face between the mattress and his ribs. "Whadda ya watching?" she mumbled into the bedding.

"*Hot Shots,*" he replied, jacking up the sound now that she was awake.

Jannie just groaned and snuggled up closer, bringing her face up to kiss his cheek. "I need orange juice," she slurred.

"Go ahead," said Jax half-mindedly. "Odett won't have breakfast ready for at least another two hours."

Jannie nuzzled his neck. "Wouldn't you just love to go down and get it for me?" she mewed, rubbing circles on his chest.

"I'm watching the movie."

"Again?" she said, now louder and not so lovingly. "You've seen that stupid thing a million times."

"It's not stupid," said Jax carefully, wanting to rebuke her, but afraid to piss her off. She could get testy over the slightest things. "It's a Jim Abrahams parody. Well-written, well-acted."

Jannie Marin's head crashed and burned on his shoulder. She stopped the massage. After a moment of contemplation, she expelled too much air too loudly. "Fine," she sniped, throwing back her side of the silver silk sheets and rolling out of bed completely naked.

Jax's attention left Charlie Sheen to watch Jannie walk over to the closet to fetch her robe. She did take care of her magnificent body. You could bounce a quarter off that ass. Maybe he should go get her the orange juice. She'd probably repay him in spades back here in bed. Wait. Here's the part when Toper Harley says to sexy Ramada, "I guess you've been with a man before." And she replies, "I'm a virgin. I'm just not very good at it." Jax mouthed the words right along with Ramada. He loved that part. And as for Jannie, her OJ, and a potential blow job…hell, they'd probably make love in the shower later anyway.

Odett's killer Sunday morning breakfast of scrambled eggs, soft bacon, hashbrowns, blueberry crepes stuffed with cream cheese, OJ and coffee was true to form. Jax ate it all. Jannie had a bite of eggs and the OJ. Jax gave Odett a big smooch on her cheek, as she loaded the dishwasher, then Iowa's City's best looking couple flopped on the top-grain leather sofa in the bright white sunroom to read the Sunday paper.

"So, what's on your schedule for today?" he asked, folding up the sports section.

"My aunt and uncle from Chicago are stopping by around noon on their way to visit my cousins in Denver," she said, thumbing through the colorful store ads. "Haven't seen them for a while. Then Olivia and I might go to Swimwear Essentials. We didn't find what we were looking for yesterday in Cedar Rapids. You?"

"Just working on my column," said Jax, reaching for the comics.

His iPhone suddenly chimed, signaling a text message had just come in. He lifted it off the arm of the sofa and scanned the message. He locked his lips so they didn't tattle his pleasure.

fishing lesson tues. same time same place. ok? pleeease! suzy

"Who's that from?" asked Jannie, her nose half buried in the paper and half in her boyfriend's business.

"Nothing," he said, closing it off.

"Well, it must be something," she poked, now more interested. It wasn't like Jax to be secretive about his phone calls.

"Just Roger, congratulating me on my big bass."

She studied his stone face a moment, found no clue, so went back to her paper.

Chapter 26

When Suzy Brookfield slipped out of her burgundy Sienna van and came floating toward Jax, he did a double take. Expecting a similar outfit as last time, he was pleasantly surprised, if not slightly aroused, to see his student dressed like the axiomatic, oversexed hill-Billy-Jean. The top two buttons of her sleeveless, red and white checkered shirt were undone to reveal a hint of cleavage, and the shirt tails were tied up in a square knot high around her ribcage. On her feet were blue canvass deck shoes and no socks. Between the shirt and the shoes the demure, lightly tanned body was completely nude…except for the skimpy pair of Daisy Dukes riding high in the crotch and low on the midriff.

Not that Jax took much notice, but she had the same bob cut sticking out from under the same straw hat. She was wearing his congratulatory Revo Guide Extreme sunglasses and that infectious Suzy Brookfield smile.

Typical, objectifying male, Jax couldn't help but compare. Jannie was the classic Sports Illustrated Swimsuit type of beauty with long legs, c-cups, and high cheek bones. She moved like a flamingo—proud and snooty. Suzy was more of a cute, Emma Watson type that made you smile with delight and want to squeeze the stuffing out of her. Yet seeing her glide toward him like a spring fawn, he had to admit his favorite apprentice was downright hot.

"What's the difference between a carp and a lawyer?" she queried on approach.

Jax knew he had heard this one before, but he couldn't take his focus off her long enough to remember the punch line. "I don't know," he said mindlessly, half grinning.

"One is a slimy, bottom-feeding scavenger," said Suzy, stopping almost toe-to-toe, looking sternly up into his face.

"The other is a fish," they said in unison, Jax snapping back to reality.

Suzy Brookfield just became even sexier. Jannie Marin had never told him a joke in her life.

For the next hour they practiced more casting with the spinning reel, and he introduced her to the spinnerbait. When things got serious, Suzy managed to derrick in a four-pound largemouth, with Jax's hugging help, of course. Jax himself fooled one just over five pounds with his basic plastic worm rig. He was pleased Suzy hadn't been ordered to bring any more bass home for dinner, so the fish were released right away.

Envious of her teacher's bass being bigger than hers, the pupil playfully demanded he let her switch to his spinning rod and bait. He agreed, on the condition that this time she do it all on her own...no help from him with the casting, lift-and-pause technique, hook-setting, cranking in, or even the landing. She agreed whole-heartedly right up until the landing part, and then she agreed only reluctantly.

Proud Mary keep on burnin' ...

Suzy quickly set down the rod, not even bothering to reel in the plastic worm. While walking away from Jax, she pulled the phone from her Daisy Dukes front pocket and punched *OK*.

"Hi, Mom. Sup?"

Jax surmised that Suzy's mom's name might be *Mary*. Nothing much got past this college graduate.

"I see you two haven't gone in to have *lunch* yet," Mary said, teasingly. "It's well past noon."

"I haven't forgotten," Suzy whispered emphatically. "I'm just a little....scared. What if he rejects me? God, Mom, he's so *sexy*!"

"I know. He won't. You'll do fine."

"Think so?" Suzy almost whined.

"We know so. We've seen how he *teaches* you to fish. He can't keep his hands off you. He's definitely into you."

"I hope so," Suzy signed, with a little more confidence.

"Now go have a nice lunch, sweetheart." Then Mary Brookfield added in sing-song fashion, "And don't forget the *dessert*!"

"*Leptos*, Mother!"

Suzy was already to the van, so she opened the side door and climbed in. After about a minute she stuck her head out and called for Jax to come have some lunch.

Chapter 27

Jax didn't want to quit fishing. The weather was a perfect seventy degrees, and a slight breeze and bright sun were warming the water. The moon was still in a pretty good phase and position. Everything was right for the bite. But he had to admit he was hungry. Odett's ham and cheese omelet five hours ago was wearing off. He reeled in his spinnerbait, and did the same to Suzy's abandoned outfit. If one of those hawg bass latched onto that plastic worm she left out there, it would have been sayonara three hundred-dollar rod and reel.

Ducking his seventy-four inches inside, Jax found Suzy sitting yoga-style on a heavy fleece, black and gold Hawkeye blanket that covered a good share of the van's folded-down rear section. To her left was an old-fashioned wicker picnic basket, and beside it a small white cooler with a blue lid.

"Come in, come in," she beckoned, still wearing the sunglasses for some reason. "Have a seat. I hope you like cold meat sandwiches and beer."

With a "What the…" Jax angled his hulk onto the blanket, interested to discover there was some kind of soft padding underneath. "This is quite unexpected," he said, settling in cross-legged, as well. He took off his B.A.S.S. cap and tossed it to one side. With the van's heavily-tinted windows, it was dark enough inside that his sunglasses were entirely unnecessary. He laid them beside his cap. Yet Suzy still kept hers on.

Jax was glad to see she at least had removed the straw hat, exposing the top half of her honey-blonde bob he had never seen before. It was a very cute hair style. He had no idea it was designed to make her head look smaller.

"Yeah," said Suzy, nervously rummaging through the basket, "it was Mom's idea. And I was so into fishing I had almost forgot about it. Until she called to remind me." Suzy produced two different sandwiches in plastic baggies and held them out toward Jax. "Shaved prime rib and Swiss on wheat," she said, jostling each lightly in turn, "or chicken breast and cedar on rye."

"Whichever you don't want," replied Jax politely, even though he wanted the former.

"I like them both," she said. "But we had this prime rib last night, so I should probably have the chicken." She handed the prime rib to Jax, who took it gratefully and began peeling back the wrapper.

"PBR?" she asked, handing him a long-neck bottle of Pabst Blue Ribbon from the cooler.

"My favorite," he smiled again. He twisted off the cap and took a long pull. He didn't care much for light beers. Too watered down. And PBR had been his dad's favorite.

It was hardly a coincidence all the fixings—right down to the Lay's lightly salted potato chips and Little Debbie oatmeal cookies—were some of his favorites. Compared to hacking into uber-secure places like the CIA, FBI, and IRS databanks, the private cash register records of the local restaurants Jax frequented and the grocery store Odett patronized on his behalf was child's play for Mary Brookfield. She had needed only a few hours before she knew more about Jax than he did himself. The same was true regarding his dead parents, Jannie Marin, and even his housekeeper, Odett.

When that data was combined with the results from his blood work and DNA analysis of his hair, then washed through a special compatibility software program devised by *The Desert*, it was determined that Patrick Bernard Jackson was an incredible *90.7 percent* match for Suzette Marie Brookfield. No one—male or female—in the Mejan's collective records had ever scored this high. Besides reaching the aspired level of *virtually humanoid* at 93.75 percent, Jax and Suzy's offspring would probably be exceptionally intelligent...not to mention quite comely.

And Jax had come along just in time. Suzy's current boyfriend, Jason Hubble, twenty-three, an agricultural sciences grad student at the University of Iowa, was on the cusp of being considered a viable father to Suzy's children. Jason's genes, blood, and semen were all sufficiently within the strict mating parameters, and Suzy liked him well enough. But other factors—such as his being only five-foot-ten and one hundred and fifty pounds—earned Jason a compatibility rating of 75.2. Good enough. But whenever possible the objective was to improve the physical portion of Mejan race significantly, while keeping the dilution of the superior Mejan intellect to a minimum.

The only thing that could possibly knock Jax out of the running now was if his little swimmers proved to be sterile. The tests on his DNA already showed that to be highly unlikely, but a sample of his semen was required to erase all doubts. It would also draw a fairly accurate profile of future children.

Chapter 28

"I've got to ask," prefaced Jax, wiping his mouth with the paper napkin," why you still have your sunglasses on. You real sensitive to light or something?" He hoped it wasn't to cover up a black eye or bruise. He wouldn't put it past that prick Alan Brookfield to be a child beater.

Well, the time had arrived for Suzy. Hopefully this handsome fellow liked her enough by now that what she was about to reveal to him would be sloughed off with the same ho-hum indifference as if she were uncovering an appendix scar or a small mole on the back of her heel. But how was a girl to know? He might be turned off by her deformity and say he suddenly had to be going. Maybe he'd laugh. Maybe degrade her. Pass out? She would find out shortly.

"My eyes are kind of weird looking," she forewarned. "Kind of big for my small face."

"Oh, come on," urged Jax, his writer's curiosity well piqued. "They can't be that bad. Show me."

With her head down, Suzy acquiesced, pulling the sunglasses free from her face. She inhaled and slowly raised her head, keeping her eyes downcast for one more moment. Blinking once, her eyes flashed up to fixate on Jax's reaction.

"What?" hooted Jax, studying the round, colorful orbs. His face was expressive, but noncommittal.

Suzy froze. Fear started to fill her heart, but she fought it off. *Don't read something into it that isn't there,* she thought. It was hardly clear what his reaction meant. It might have been good.

"You have beautiful eyes," Jax reported sincerely, leaning forward for a better look, seemingly captivated by the rich, copper-brown irises and large black pupils.

"You don't think they're too big...and round?" she asked bashfully.

"Not at all," said Jax pensively, cradling her chin to move her head left and right. "I like big eyes. Yours are like those Japanese anime drawings, only more realistic. And the color: gorgeous."

"You really like them?" she asked, like a blushing bride modeling her negligee on their wedding night.

"I do." Jax released her chin and leaned back a little, his eyes still locked on hers.

Just as intensely, Suzy studied her teacher's face for any indication he was lying. She couldn't find any. In fact, this man seemed quite intrigued. Half the tension in her torso relaxed. She exhaled.

Now it was time for boyfriend test number two. Would it go over just as well as test one?

Suzy ran the palms of her hands over her bobbed honey-blonde hair and locked her fingers behind her head. "And what about this?" she asked cautiously. *Might as well get it all out in the open at once.*

"What about what?"

"My head."

"What about it?"

"You don't mind that it's kind of big?"

Jax leaned even farther back to study one facet of Suzy he never had. "Looks normal to me. What makes you think it's big?"

Knowing she should just let it lie in its present banality, Suzy had to know for sure. She stretched far forward to fetch Jax's B.A.S.S. cap lying beside him on the blanket. Trying it on, it was obviously too small. "See?" she said self-consciously, letting the cap rest high atop her head.

"So, your head is bigger than mine," dismissed Jax, playfully retrieving his cap. "Big deal. Like something else I could mention, size doesn't matter." Then he added with a twinkle in his question, *"Does* it?"

Missing the sexual innuendo, carnal-ignorant Suzy broke in a broad smile of relief. Tears welled in both eyes. The big head issue was also hurdled. And with no explanation—or more accurately, *lies*—required. No doubt about it now: this Jax fellow was about to get a very nice reward.

"Ready for desert," she sniffled, a delicate finger wiping away a teardrop on her cheek.

Chapter 29

Propped up on one elbow, Jax was feeling comfortably sated, refreshed, and very much at ease. The conversation during lunch had been witty and fun, both sharing some of their favorite jokes and lines from movies. When she finally uncovered her eyes, he found them utterly fascinating. And so what if she has a big head? More room for brains. The girl was obviously sharp. Now with the offer of dessert and that gleam in both those copper orbs, the almost-engaged-to-another-woman, outdoor journalist wasn't sure what to expect. He wasn't even sure what he wanted *dessert* to mean.

To both his relief and disappointment, Suzy stayed on her side of the van, reaching into the cooler and producing a white bottle with a familiar shape.

"Ah, RumChata," smiled Jax, sounding like a commercial. "A great dessert liqueur straight up or in coffee." But of course she already knew he likes it. She seemed to know all his preferences. "Who you been talking to?" he asked with a droll smile, watching her pour six ounces-worth into a clear plastic cup and hand it to him.

"I guess that means you like it, too," she answered, pouring one for herself. "But then, who doesn't?"

Jax could only nod in agreement, as a good portion of the creamy liquid was already sliding over his tongue and warming his throat with a mild, exotic burn. By the time he had finished the rest, he was so tranquil he would have laughed at his new Lexus being t-boned by a Mack truck.

Suzy took his empty cup and stuck hers—untouched—inside his, and set them carefully inside a plastic litter bag. She shuffled slowly over to Jax on her hands and knees like a cat. By now he was flat on his back, defenseless, grinning at the van's soundproof ceiling. She placed a hand on his far shoulder.

"Now for the rest of your dessert," she cooed, gently urging him to roll over onto his stomach. "I'm going to give my favorite fishing instructor a well-deserved back rub."

There was no argument. It would be just a harmless massage. Jannie would never know.

Straddling him with her butt sitting firmly on his and two pairs of eyes rolling with pleasure, the twenty-year-old fox ran her hands under the twenty-five-year-old's white polo shirt and went straight for his broad shoulders. She squeezed his firm deltoids. Jax moaned. She kneaded his neck muscles. He purred. She bent down and kissed the back of his neck. Jax lost what little control he had left. He impulsively twisted his torso enough to get one arm around her waist and pulled her down beside him like a carnival teddy bear. Without reservation or consideration for the possible consequences, he kissed her hard on the lips. Suzy gasped with surprise and kissed him right back, harder, wetter.

Clothes went flying inside the van. A white polo shirt landed in the back, Daisy Dukes in the front. Khaki pants got caught on the driver's headrest. Pink panties graced the steering wheel. As one, the naked couple rolled and writhed on the Hawkeye blanket, groping and smashing mouths like long-lost lovers rejoined after years from opposite ends of the earth. The van's left and right side shocks took turns compressing and releasing. The interior temperature rose. The windows fogged.

When it came time, Jax had enough presence of mind to ask if Suzy had protection, because he didn't. She assured him she was covered, and the Toyota Sienna set back to rocking under the noon-day sun.

Horizontal in each other's arms, moaning and panting, Jax and Suzy slowly descended from Nirvana. Jax felt he should be racked with guilt for not only cheating on Jannie, but for breaking some kind of teacher-student code of conduct. But he wasn't. Suzy felt she should feel guilty for having lured him into her parlor and plying him with a spiked libation to have her way with him and get a sperm sample. But she didn't. She was long-gone in love with this guy and she felt he loved her, too. The end justified the means.

It was a good thirty minutes of cuddling and dozing before either one spoke. Jax was first.

"So, I guess you've been with a man before," he smiled, whimsically quoting Topper Harley from *Hot Shots*, which he had watched for the umpteenth time last Sunday morning in bed with an uninterested Jannie.

Suzy pulled her entire body up onto Jax and rested her chin on his chest. "I'm a virgin," she said with a mock accent of Ramada's, her big eyes blinking innocently. "I'm just not very good at it."

Jax's eyes got as wide as Suzy's. Suzy's mouth spread into a wide, knowing smile.

"*Hot Shots!*" they said in unison.

Jannie who?

Chapter 30

3:02 a.m., May 25, 2003. Two Reggs wearing light-blue jumpsuits and Roswell-type alien masks stepped up onto the wooden porch of the farmhouse ten miles southeast of Tallahassee, Florida. Behind them the German Shepherd lay quietly in the wet grass, having been stunned from a distance of two hundred feet with one sonic pulse to the head. It would wake up in the morning with no marks and a hell of a canine headache. After what only Lisa Travers believed was her previous close encounter of the anal kind, she had insisted her husband get the dog for protection. So much for that idea.

With the push of a button on the oval, hand-held device, the security system was disabled. A second button slid the dead bolt open with a soft clunk. The two aliens walked steadily up the familiar, creaking stairs to the bedroom and sprayed the faces of Lisa and Jonathan Travers. Jonathan went instantly catatonic. Tomorrow would greet him rested, but with confusion and that funny taste in his mouth he had experienced once before. Lisa became a woozy, willing captive once again, as they walked the small woman in her mid-fifties down the stairs, out the door, and into their waiting spacecraft, hiding behind the barn.

As during her first visit to that particular examination room, she was stripped of her nightclothes, laid face up and on a cold, silver metal table, and hooked up to a variety of probes and electrodes and catheters. Her ankles and wrists were strapped to the table as usual, but this time so were her waist, shoulders, and head.

After recording the usual data, a stick with a cotton swab was dabbed inside one nostril. The smiling Lisa suddenly began to convulse, shaking wildly, pulling at the constraints, eyes rolling to the backs of their sockets. Several monitors on the wall erupted with high-pitched beeps, showing spikes going off the grids. The two Reggs watched with much interest. In just a few more seconds, Lisa Travers gave a loud gasp and became deathly still.

Another complete diagnostic was mandated, after which both aliens trudged back to the farmhouse. They busied themselves fetching one of the Travers's Samsonite upright travel bags from the attic and filling it with some of Lisa's clothes, toiletries, and whatever an unhappy wife would hurriedly collect, as her lover came down the lane to whisk her away to a new and better life.

Everyone and everything were loaded aboard, and the charcoal-gray spacecraft—shaped like an Italian sports car but ten times as big—went straight up to an altitude of four thousand feet. It then took off on a heading of two hundred and ten degrees to the southwest. Being undetectable to all forms of electronic surveillance and appearing as nothing more than a temporary blur in the starry night, the craft casually accelerated to a speed of six hundred miles per hour, well below the sound barrier.

Ten minutes later it reached its destination eighty-six miles out in the Gulf of Mexico and descended to hover a few feet over the water. A circular metal object slightly larger than the waiting craft itself broke the surface and opened wide from rim to rim. The eighty-foot vessel settled in, and the portal closed behind it. The same colored daughter ship the size of a small islet sank slowly back to the bottom of the Gulf in one hundred and fifty feet of water.

Lisa was carried out of the craft into a large hangar bay, then through a pneumatic door, down a long, arcing hallway and into a small all-white room. Two other Reggs were waiting, also in all white from head to toe, excluding the Plexiglas shields over their hairy faces. The two kidnappers set her down on the floor by a large drain, said something in their native language, and exited the way they had come.

The larger of the small lab Reggs pulled down a pair of shackles from a pulley attached to a track in the ceiling and clamped one onto each ankle of the dead woman. The other pushed a button on the wall, and Lisa's body was unceremoniously elevated into the air, coming to dangle a couple feet above the drain. Her head and hands were severed with a hand-held laser, each landing on the drain, which automatically opened and sucked them away. As the body bled out, the torso was slashed open with the same laser and completely gutted with a shiny instrument the shape of a large spork. The drain ate those, as well, grinding everything to a fine pulp and jettisoning it out into the Gulf for fish food. The final step was to spray the carcass completely with a clear liquid disinfectant to neutralize any harmful bacteria or viruses, and particularly any residue from the Regg's latest and deadlier version of the black plague that may have worked its way into her muscle tissue.

A button on a panel by another door was pushed, and what was left of Lisa Travers was moved mechanically along the ceiling's track into the cold storage where frozen carcasses of a cow, two hogs, and one human of undeterminable gender hung quietly, waiting for future consumption.

Chapter 31

Jax Jackson sat out by his pool, taking advantage of the warm spell invading southeast Iowa over the last week of May. The maintenance man had been there earlier that morning to uncover the pool, fill it to a normal level, set in a new filter, add the right amount of chlorine, and do all that stuff Jax knew nothing about. It was his mom who had wanted the thing, shaped like a sock with a short waterfall at its toe. He didn't like swimming all that much.

Lying across his bare legs was today's Thursday edition of the *Iowa City Tribune*. He had just finished reading his own weekly column, this one entitled, *Texas Rig: The Deadliest Lure for Largemouth Bass*. He was tickled his managing editor, Angie, had allowed that photo of him with his eight-pounder to accompany the story. It had gotten him no less than three complimentary phone calls so far this morning from people outside of his fishing circle. His fellow bass clubbers had already paid tribute after he emailed the selfie-with-fishy to them last Saturday. They'd better. He covered everyone's club dues and tournament fees each year.

Every time the phone rang, he hoped it was Suzy. And every time it wasn't, he was relieved. The Josh Duhamel lookalike was in a quandary. He still wasn't sure how that little romp in the van had happened. It was like she had a spell on him. A spell that lowered all his defenses and opened him up like Christmas to anything Suzy wished to do to him. Maybe she'd drugged him with the RumChata. Maybe he wanted her so much he had drugged himself with lust.

But how could that be? He already had the finest looking woman in Iowa. Everybody said so. Jannie and he had an unspoken pact of exclusivity that had worked fine for the past two years. Despite Jannie forever getting hit on, and more than a few females throwing themselves at Jax, neither had met another person they wanted to sleep with, let alone date. It just seemed inevitable they would stay exclusive and eventually blend into marriage.

Then here came down-on-the-farm Suzy Brookfield straight out of a rerun of *The Beverly Hillbillies*. She and Jax shared a sense of humor, they both liked movies and especially the classics, and they loved fishing. Jannie struck out on all three.

But still…

"Yo shouldn't be sittin' out here in the hot sun so soon after yo workout, Pee-Bee-Boy," scolded Odett, setting another frosty, lemon-lime *Gatorade 02* beside him on the round, glass table and picking up the empty. "Heavens, boy, yo still sweatin'."

Jax was slow to come out of his thoughts. "I'm okay," he said, tossing the paper onto the table and sinking a little deeper into the soft cushion of the Mississippi chase lounge. "Just catching some rays."

Odett delayed her retreat a moment longer to study her young employer's profile. "Yo okay, Jax?" she asked with head cocked.

That got his attention. She hardly ever called him *Jax*. Only when she was concerned about him for some reason. He turned to look at his rotund, black, second mother through his back up pair of Revo sunglasses. "I'm fine," he said dismissively. Why?"

"Yo be actin' kinda quiet this mornin', is all," she said, putting hands on hips. "Yo and Jannie has a fight?"

Jax smiled. "No, we hasn't had no fight," he mocked, turning his head back to the front. "Just have a lot on my mind."

Odett knew that was her cue to butt out. She never liked interfering with Jackson business. She had all she could handle sticking with her own.

"Well, it almost lunchtime," she said, dabbing the sweat off his forehead with her terrycloth apron. "If yo wants, I'll make yo BPJ for ya agin."

"That would be nice," replied Jax, from someplace else.

Now Odett *knew* something was wrong. Only once before—last Saturday, in fact—had he ever let anybody make his peanut butter and jelly sandwich for him. And that was only because he was so busy with things he had forgotten to eat lunch, and was starving, and still had things to do. Now here he'd allowed it twice in less than a week.

Odett considered double checking, but then thought better of it. Jax seemed to be off to Neverland again. She shuffled back to the kitchen to make his lunch.

Chapter 32

When the smart phone between his legs suddenly erupted with Creedence Clearwater Revival singing the chorus, *Oh, Susy Q, I love you,* Jax almost knocked it into the pool in his haste to pick it up. He knew what the ring tone meant, because he had installed it soon after they exchanged numbers at the pond that first time. *Oh, Susy Q, I love you.* He didn't mean it literally then, he just liked the song. And Suzy Brookfield was indeed lovable. Now he wasn't so sure picking that chorus hadn't been prophetic. Besides, Suzy had never called him directly before. Only that one text requesting her second lesson. The way that little tryst yesterday turned out raised some serious questions about who had taught what to whom.

"Hey, Susy Q," he said, keeping the excitement out of his voice as much as possible. "You like the ringtone I gave you?"

"*Susy Q.* Yeah, I like that," she said. "From Credence, right?"

"Very good," he said, surprised. "How'd you know that?"

"I know most songs with my name in them," she said. "Particularly that one."

"Really?" he challenged. "Name some."

Well, there's *Wake Up Little Susie* by The Everly Brothers. Mom uses that one for me." There was a slight delay with some keyboard tapping in the background. "And there's *Run Around Sue* by Dion...

"You're cheating," said Jax. "You're on the internet."

"Busted."

"Thought so. And you missed one," said Jax, reading off his own internet connection via his iPhone. "*Susie Darlin'* by Robin Luke. A real oldie."

"Aw, am I your *Suzy Darling*?" she cooed.

"You're getting there," he smiled back. *God! Did I really say that?*

"Well, you just won yourself a free dinner at the Brookfield farm tomorrow night," announced Suzy.

"Really?" Jax said sarcastically. She was probably kidding. He knew Pappy Brookfield didn't like him and certainly wouldn't want to feed him.

"Yes, really," she replied sincerely. "Actually, that's why I called. The family wants to meet you."

It took Jax a moment to reply. This was a surprise, partly by a clear invitation from a girl to meet her parents, which usually signaled a serious step in the relationship. And partly by the chance to actually set foot on the hallowed, heretofore forbidden grounds of the Brookfield farm proper.

"You mean at your *house*," he asked pointedly, "and not at the picnic table by the pond or in your van?"

"Cute. Yes, at the house."

"Well, okay. Sounds good," he said still cautiously. Then he added, "We're not having bass, are we?"

"No bass, I promise," she laughed. "How about smoked pork chops? Our very own."

"Love 'em."

"About 6:00?"

"Perfect."

"See you then. Dress casual. Oh, and the code at the gate is *eight-three-five-star-star*. Got it?

"Got it."

"See ya soon."

Jax punched off and fell back in the chase lounge. He felt good all over. That was just a few seconds before his stomach tightened up and his face filled with blood. *Friday night?!* "That's date night with Jannie!" he groaned to the house sparrow preening itself on the privacy fence. They always go out for dinner…overture to other things, of course. What's he going to tell her? She won't be happy, that's for certain. For as long as he could remember he'd never broken a date with Jannie. Except that once when he got a migraine headache. *That's it! A migraine.* She won't come over to nurse him. She knows better. She gets migraines all the time and doesn't want anybody around. Just darkness and quiet.

The next afternoon at two o'clock Jax called Jannie at her father's dental clinic, and with his best impression of a dying man begged off tonight's dinner and ensuing activities. He then spent the next hour searching the web for anything about the Brookfields and especially Suzy. There was virtually nothing. He also used Google Earth again, this time to really study a close-up satellite view of the Brookfield spread. He was amazed by how many structures there actually were. The place looked more like a small town than a typical Iowa farmstead.

Chapter 33

8-3-5-*-* and the tall, black, double steel gate swung open, bidding Jax entry. He drove his freshly-waxed, silver Lexus SUV down the two hundred yards of smooth back asphalt canopied most of the way by beautiful old oak trees. There on his left was the Little League baseball diamond he had seen on Google Earth. It even had actual dugouts built into the ground and a six-foot-high home-run fence. On the right were the tennis and basketball courts, not unlike his own. Next was a large playground area with a two-story playhouse, swings, slides, monkey bars, you name it. Behind that high, good-neighbor cedar fence was probably the L-shaped Olympic-size pool with water slides and Jacuzzis.

He swung a hard left into a circle driveway and pulled up in front of the one-story, solid brick ranch that would have seemed normal were it not for Google's birds-eye view. The satellite photo revealed the house alone spread out over half an acre and was shaped like the number 3 in a block-style font. The asphalt driveway ran all the way around the structure, so Jax had assumed at least some of those wings in back were garages and storage rooms and whatever.

Not your typical Iowa farmhouse, indeed.

Jax had just climbed out of his vehicle and was looking around, when Suzy came bouncing down the flat stone walkway lined with waist-high, manicured evergreen bushes. She was draped in an airy, pink paisley, cotton sundress that hung from the spaghetti straps so free and loose that a good breeze could loft the whole thing over her head. On her feet were tan wedge sandals with wrap-around straps and two-inch heels. But Jax hardly noticed them, or the two white barrettes serving no purpose other than to add cuteness to her short, honey-blonde bob. But he couldn't miss those dazzling, copper eyes…big and round.

"Hi, teach," she grinned, closing in to give him a warm hug. "Welcome to my humble home."

"It's awesome," was all he could think to say, still scanning the periphery. "It's like a village."

"I know. Our last visitor got lost here three days ago," she deadpanned. "We're sending out the hounds tomorrow at first light."

"I believe it," he sighed, noticing the western horizon was blocked by buildings.

"Well, come on in," she twitted, taking his hand. "Supper's almost ready. I'll show you the lay of the land afterwards." Jax let that one go.

The inside was as rich and fashionable as his own abode, but without the cathedral look and spiraling double staircase. They had gone with a more rustic-western motif of knotty-pine paneling and vertical, load-bearing beams in shiny walnut that matched the floors. Jax felt he had walked into a Rodeo Drive version of a Texas Roadhouse restaurant. And the aroma of smoke pork chops did nothing to detract from the perception.

Suzy led him across the hardwood foyer into a carpeted family-recreation room to meet her two teenage brothers, presently engrossed in *The Hunger Games* for the third time on the large television flat screen. One of them hit *pause* on the DVR, and both jumped up from the black suede couch to meet their guest.

"Jax, this one is David," Suzy said, as the men bumped knuckles. "He's nineteen and quite the lady's man."

"Don't listen to her," smiled David. "Pleased to meet you, Jax."

"And this one is the baby of the family, Mike. He's seventeen and already a computer techie."

"Like his big sister," quipped Mike, also bumping fists. "How's it going?"

The four chatted cordially at first, a common interest being today's break-neck technology, particularly in computers and video games. But when the topic turned to movies, the conversation elevated to a louder, more enthusiastic level, with everyone expressing his or her favorite actors, actresses, directors, and sequels. So far this family seemed to be a bunch of staunch film buffs. He would find out why a little later.

Both teens were considerably smaller than Jax, being about five-ten and one-forty each. He found it interesting they had big eyes just like Suzy. He assumed they got them from their mother, because their father, Alan Brookfield—whose eyes he'd already had an opportunity to study in close proximity during their first meeting at the pond—had normal, nondescript eyes...even if he did look a little like Harrison Ford at his most pissed in *Cowboys and Aliens*.

As it turned out, Jax would have to keep assuming, since the mother, Mary—he was told by Suzy—wasn't feeling well tonight and would not be joining them. Then, after calling the gang to dinner by the ding-ding-ding of an authentic, chuck wagon triangle, Alan seconded the message, conveying his wife's regret in not getting to meet Suzy's *fishing mentor*.

The dinner was one hundred percent home-grown, from the smoked pork chops with a brown sugar glaze and red potatoes, to the garden-fresh green beans and home-made applesauce and cornbread. All the men forked it down like it was their last meal, while dainty Suzy darlin' ate like a bird. Everyone chipped in clearing the table, and then the boys disappeared back into the rec room to continue their movie. Suzy and Jax helped load the dishwasher and finish off the pots and pans. They were then quickly dismissed to go find something to do outside. Patriarch Alan had things to do.

Chapter 34

The evening was warm, and the humidity was just beginning to build toward its summer norms. Jax and Suzy walked hand-in-hand among the spans of outbuildings—most with white aluminum siding, those to the west reflecting a brilliant yellow from the setting sun. They were constantly serenaded by oinks, moos, baas, cackles, and the clanging of hog feeders, backed up with the hum of various air conditioner units, pumps, and battery chargers. Luckily, the gentle breeze was from the south, or it would have carried the corresponding, aromatic blend of pig, cow, sheep and chicken manure. As the farmers of those particular livestock were fond of saying, "Ah, the sweet smell of money."

By closing off the smells and sounds, the farm indeed had the look of a large resort or small village. Jax's sarcastic question of where the post office might be was immediately countered with Suzy's glib, "Coming, as soon as the application for our own zip code is approved."

Jax was shown no less than four large machine sheds full of combines and threshers and eight-bottom plows and cultivators and fertilizers and corn pickers. There were small barns and feed lots and about a hundred, eight-foot-diameter rolls of alfalfa. When he was told the big pump house supplied water from two wells to every area of the farm, including, *Aha! the pond*, he felt that mystery was solved. He didn't know the half of it.

The jagged circle tour eventually brought them back to about a hundred yards from the house. The pair stopped in front of the closest of three, two-story cottages, serving as housing for the hired hands. He was told they presently had two, both with families. When Suzy explained the Brookfields owned and operated over two thousand acres—ninety percent of which were tillable—he understood why so much manpower was needed. Suzy said the busy times were the planting in April and especially the massive harvest in late-October.

A Nerf football came wobbling up to Jax's feet. He picked it up and tossed a perfect spiral back to the bigger of the two young boys playing in the middle cottage's front yard. Suzy was impressed by her first indication of Jax's athleticism, while Jax didn't notice the larger than normal eyes embedded in the larger than normal skulls of both boys. They yelled their thanks and continued emulating Payton Manning throwing a touchdown pass to Demaryius Thomas.

"I don't think your dad likes me," understated Jax, watching the youngsters play catch, like he and his father used to. "He doesn't seem to think much of me…or that I'm an outdoor writer."

"Oh, don't let Dad get to you," said Suzy. "He'll come around. Give him time. If you think he's protective of his pond and land, that's nothing compared to his family. And I suppose he's especially protective of me, since I'm his only daughter."

"I can understand that," replied the orphaned Jax. "I just wish…"

"Hey," interrupted Suzy, bumping her shoulder against his arm "you should see how he treats Jason, this other guy I've been seeing. We'd gone out five times before he was invited over for dinner. No, wait. That was only for a barbeque lunch with the hired hands on a Saturday. And Dad spent most of the meal glaring at him. And if you think that's bad, before we left on our first date, Dad took Jason into the den and showed him his gun collection. Jason had me home half an hour early and didn't even kiss me goodnight."

Before Jax could pursue this sudden revelation of another suitor, little Suzy tugged him with a *C'mon* toward the enormous, two-hundred-foot-long greenhouse. She warned it was better not to go inside and possibly upset the delicate cross-breeding experiments, so they just peered in through the front door's glass panes. All Jax could see was a hodge-podge of various plants and colorful blooms from floor to ceiling, with rows of ultraviolet lights and automatic mist-sprayers. Suzy said they did a lot of their own experimentation with hybrids and high-protein foods. The green beans they had for dinner were examples of a new strain they developed that was high in the good fats and cholesterols and low in the bad ones. Jax had to admit they were exceptionally tasty.

Directly behind the greenhouse was the quaint, one-story brick guesthouse. In the fading sunlight it could almost have been the model for the cover of a fairytale book, with its cobblestone walkway, white picket fence and matching shutters. Even though there was a dim, yellow light in one of the two, small, front windows, he was told it was presently empty. *Then why the light?* he wondered.

The last stop on the tour was the huge red barn Jax could easily see from the pond, the road, or just about anywhere in a two-mile radius. Miss Brookfield led him through the classic up-and-down, double barn doors, and flipped on a light switch. The capacious interior was lined on both sides with stalls, most occupied by Holstein cows. Each bovine was serviced by its own high-tech, robot milking machine that allowed the cow to be milked on its own schedule. A couple of Morgan horses at the far end next to a locked tack room had feedbags on, eating their daily ration of oats.

The cement floor was swept clean, and there was virtually no smell at all. Twin air conditioners hummed from windows on opposite sides, keeping the air dry and pleasantly cool. Stretching the length of the barn on the east side was the upper level hayloft, half of it loaded to the edge with square bales of alfalfa.

Suzy expected Jax to comment on what the Brookfields considered the most modern barn in the county. But instead she got rabbit-punched with, "I didn't know you had a boyfriend."

Jax had been unable to shake the conversation left hanging back there at the greenhouse. And now that he had blurted it out, he found himself surprised by the twinge of green in his voice. *What's the matter with me?* he thought. *Why wouldn't she be dating other men? She's twenty and sexy and smart. Hell, I'm practically engaged to Jannie. There are no commitments here.*

"Who, *Jason?*" Suzy said offhandedly to a pigeon flapping around in the rafters of the barn's thirty-foot ceiling. "He's just a guy."

"Oh, yeah? Well, tell me about this *guy*," said Jax, pointedly. So much for the self-pep talk. He really was jealous.

"Not much to tell, really," said Suzy, forming an image of the man she hadn't thought about ever since meeting the one standing beside her. "Let's see. He's twenty-three, a grad student. Very smart. Drives an old Ford. Plays chess."

"How'd you meet him?"

"We were in the same agricultural class at Iowa."

"What's he look like?"

Still holding his hand as they remained standing just inside the door, Suzy suddenly spun into Jax and grabbed his other hand. She pressed her breasts against that hard six-pack under his azure golf shirt, looked up into his matching eyes with her big copper-brown orbs, and said with a playful grin, "Relax, teach. Jason and I are just dating. Play your cards right and he could be history."

Not only did the green-eyed monster disappear in a puff of smoke, Jax sensed the strong possibility they would be having sex again before this night was over.

Unfortunately, that brought on another disquieting wave of butterflies, this one of trepidation. If they did have sex tonight, *when?* *Now?* The last thing he needed was to have Father Brookfield walk in on them doing the deed. Jax envisioned himself waddling full speed across the yard toward his SUV, doing the penguin with his pants around his ankles, dodging loads of rock salt.

Too late. Since there was suddenly a pair of delicate but determined little hands squeezing his buttocks and a pup-tent rising in his Dockers, best guess said sex would indeed be soon.

That left the other question: Where? Her van again? His Lexus? Up at the pond? Surely not here in this barn. Well, it was surprisingly clean and almost odorless. In that locked room at the far end Suzy had called the tack room? And why was it locked, anyway?

How about the empty guesthouse? Yes. That one seemed to be the logical location. It would explain the light in the window. The little vixen had this well planned.

Surprisingly and without a word, the tour seemed to continue...not out the door toward the cottage, as he suspected, but up the worn wooden stairs to the barn's next level. They were immediately surrounded by six-foot-high stacks of hay bales awash in orange light from the setting sun, coming through the open haymow door. One more turn brought them to a small enclave in the straw section, where a red and green plaid blanket had already been spread over a soft cushion of loose straw. No explanation was requested for why the love nest was already prepared, and none was offered.

"And this is where...we keep the straw," said his tour guide, breathing heavily, licking her lips, turning full into her victim, "which is used as bedding...for the *animals*."

She threw her arms up and around Jax's neck, pulled herself up and kissed him hard on the mouth. One of his strong arms immediately coiled around her waist in a tight hold, the other drew up under her firm behind to help support her weight off the floor. He could tell she wasn't wearing anything under the sheer cotton dress. Bending at the waist, he set her back down, grabbed the hem of the dress, and in one smooth motion, said article of clothing was fluttering down beside the blanket.

All questions had been answered.

Chapter 35

"So, how long did your migraine last," asked Jannie, taking her first sip of the margarita just delivered.

"I was fine by this morning," Jax replied, bidding a silent *thank you* to the waitress as she placed his Pabst in front of him. "Slept like a baby."

"That's the only good thing about migraines," Jannie nodded. "I can usually fall asleep in an instant. I don't know how else I'd survive them."

End of conversation. They sat in silence for many minutes, both gazing out across the half-filled Blue Moon lounge of Giovani's. When Jannie finished her drink, she signaled for another. Jax mindlessly worked at the corner of his empty bottle's stubborn label.

"Anything bothering you?" she finally asked impatiently.

"No. Why do you ask?" He didn't look up.

"You've seemed distant lately...this past week...and especially tonight."

Jax couldn't reply. He was conflicted enough the way it was. He didn't need to add to it with the caustic dialogue he knew was inevitable. Regardless of how it ended, it would not be good for either of them. Yet ducking the issue was going to be next to impossible.

"Sorry," he said, glancing at her. "I didn't know I was."

"Well, you have been. In fact, ever since our fight right here in this booth a week ago. Is that what is bothering you?"

"What fight was that?"

"Oh, come on, Jax," she said, lowering her voice to argument mode, leaning forward on her elbows. "You know very well. The getting married, having kids thing. Our usual."

Well, there it was. Jannie had thrown down the gauntlet once again. No way out of this now. She thought it meant a spirited repartee, ending in the usual impasse, then back to his place for make-up sex: one of her favorite forms of foreplay. But if the truth came out, it would be more than the end to their relationship. It would be devastating to Jannie.

How could it not? How could he tell her that he'd found this cute little twenty-year-old sprite with big eyes and Daisy Mae persona, who doesn't know how sexy she is, who loves to fish and loves movies, who has the same sense of humor he does, and who he can't wait to see again? And while she hasn't come right out and said so, he thinks she loves him and is anxious to start a family, belonging to a happy and fairly large one herself.

And that family is certainly rich enough so there wouldn't be that doubt hanging over the union that she might be marrying him for his money.

All Jax could say for Jannie was she's beautiful, great in bed, and probably loves him in her own narcissistic way. As far as he knew, she hasn't stepped out on him...which is more than he can say for himself now. They have history, two years of it. Let's see, what else? Well, there is the fact that he does care for her, maybe even loves her. Enough anyway that he has to find another way out of this...a way to let her down easy. But how? Oh, God, not the old *we should take a time out and date other people* platitude! There has to something more creative.

Jax ordered another beer.

"Well?" pushed Jannie after a tension-filled minute.

Jax stretched one hand to mid-table and laid it gently on Jannie's. "You know I'm very fond of you," he said softly, sincerely, looking into her blue eyes.

"Oh, my God!" gasped Jannie, quickly removing her hand and falling back in the booth with arms folded across her chest. "You want to break up with me!"

"I-I didn't say that."

"But you do, don't you?"

Thankfully the arrival of the waitress with his next beer gave him time to think about what to say next. But it didn't really matter. He knew no matter what, it would be the wrong thing.

"Now that you mentioned it," he said cautiously, trying to run each carefully-chosen word through his brain before it left his lips, "maybe we should...you know, explore the possibility of, you know...seeing other people."

In the twenty four months they had been dating, Jax didn't know Jannie Marin could roll her eyes that far back in her head. The relatively small pupils actually disappeared for a moment like blueberries sinking in a bowl of cream.

"Okay, you win," she hissed, throwing her hands in the air...the gesture being too dramatic to take any way other than childish. "I'll have your kids. As many as you want. We can start tonight."

"You know that wouldn't work," said Jax softly, shifting uneasily in his seat, eyes back to downcast.

"Why not?" she hissed. "It's what you want."

"Yes, I want kids," he said softly, slowly spinning the beer bottle between his hands. "But not under duress."

"What you mean is *not with me*."

Jax took a long pull on the longneck. "Yeah, I guess that is what I mean. But not because I don't love you..."

"I thought you were only *fond* of me."

"It's simply because you don't *really* want children yet," he almost pleaded. "And forcing you to have them would not be good for anyone, would it?"

He had her there. Jannie went quiet, her face fell. Reality had come home to roost. Her good looks were still too precious to be ruined by bloated pregnancies and pushing babies through her sensually-tight vagina. Plus having a family means an end to any kind of social life…no more shopping with friends, lunch dates, parties, sleeping late on weekends, or sleeping at all for that matter.

Long silence.

"So, where do we go from here?" she asked, defeated.

Jax didn't have an immediate answer. His stomach was in knots. He didn't want to lose Jannie, yet he *couldn't* lose Suzy. When he had told her about Jannie, he could sense she was hurt, even more than he was when finding out about her other boyfriend, Jason. Suzy wasn't likely to settle for sharing him with another woman any more than Jannie would.

"We could still date," he suggested sheepishly, knowing it was about the stupidest thing he could say. "Maybe just not exclusively."

"Oh, sure," was Jannie's flippant reply. "Some Friday or Saturday night when you can't get a date, just call up ol' Jannie to come jump into bed with you."

"Well…"

"No thank you!" she spat, gathering her purse and sliding out of the booth.

"Where are you going?

"Home."

"Well, hold on," he offered, rising to join her. "I'll drive you."

"No thanks. I'll call a cab."

"Jannie, please," he said, reaching for her arm, but falling short, as she was already moving away.

"Fuck off, Jax!" she spat over her shoulder, stopping him dead in his tracks. "We're finished!"

And with that Jannie Marin walked out of the Blue Moon, out of Giovani's, and out of Jax's life.

Chapter 36

Patrick Bernard Jackson remained at the Blue Moon to finish his beer, mulling things over, taking stock of his feelings. There was no mistaking the hole in his heart and the queasiness in his stomach. He really was fond of Jannie. He hoped she'd be okay. He was missing her already. God, how he hated any kind of loss? But at least those unending, never-resolving confrontations with her were over and done with!

He pulled out his iPhone and tapped some keys.

The person on the other end answered, singing, *"I'm going to Jackson. I'm gonna mess around."*

Jax laughed out loud, the tension from the last hour evacuating his stomach like a covey of quail flushed from a slough.

"You made a ringtone for me," he grinned. "Johnny Cash and June Carter's *Jackson.*"

"Like it?" cooed Suzy.

"Love it! Absolutely *love* it," he said, not minding if she caught the double meaning. The hole in his heart was filling up quickly.

"And what might Jax Jackson be doing at six-thirty on a Saturday evening," Suzy asked, "still pulling straw out of his hair?"

"Among other places," he grinned. "What are you doing? Getting ready for a date with Jason?"

"Jason? Oh, Jason is history."

"I'm so sorry," replied Jax, feigning compassion, hoping his tone didn't give away his pleasure. "What happened?"

"Well, it seems this cardsharp stopped in at the farm last night and won me over with a stacked deck."

"So, I played my cards right, huh?"

"Let's just say my heart was trumped by the Jax of diamonds."

Jax groaned, unable to even force his laugh this time. "There's no way you just made up that corny thing," he chided.

"Yeah, I worked it up this afternoon," Suzy confessed sheepishly. "Figured I spring it on you, if the opportunity ever came up. Sorry. Pretty lame, huh?

"But cute, like you."

"So, what are *you* doing at six-thirty-two on a Saturday evening? Getting ready for a date with *Jannie?*"

"Jannie is sitting beside Jason in history class."

"Oh, I'm sorry," moaned Suzy with even less pseudo sympathy than Jax had offered her. "What happened?"

He almost said, *You is what happened*, but thought better of it. *Still too soon. Maybe.* "Let's just say we have different views of the future, different goals."

There was a slight pause. "I see," said Suzy, softer now, "and what *are* your goals for the future, if I may ask?"

Jax's heart rate quickened. He saw where this conversation was headed: basically down the same path he had just gone with Jannie. And that one ended with them parting ways...she literally walking out of his life. If this one with Suzy reached the same conclusion, it could be the end of their relationship as well. Two losses in one hour? He didn't know if he could take it.

"Nothing out of the ordinary," he sighed with a measure of ambivalence, hoping it would cover up the rising tension in his gut. "Get married, settle down, have kids." He held his breath.

There was a muffled silence at the other end. Jax wasn't sure, but he thought he heard Suzy sobbing softly. Shit, had he scared her off? Did he misread her? Was she a pedophobic, like Jannie?!

He had to ask. "Are you crying ?"

"I'm sorry," she whimpered, trying to collect herself. "It's just that you want the same things I do. I wasn't sure if you did. And hearing you say that you do, well, I just kind of lost it there."

"So, those are tears of happiness, right?"

"Y-yes..." was her tentative reply.

Jax had to fight back his own tears of elation. He was about one second away from jumping to his feet and announcing to the entire lounge he had found true love and the future mother of his children!

But there was just one more thing he had to know. And it could be a deal breaker.

"So...at what time of your life do you think...ah...would you like to start having children?" Then he continued leadingly, "Early thirties? Mid-twenties?"

His breath was still on hold.

"With someone I love..." she whispered, her tone soft and dead serious, "whenever he's ready."

"What if *he* said right away?" Oxygen depleting. Head getting fuzzy.

"I'd say, the sooner the better," replied the twenty-year-old. I can't wait to start a family."

Jackpot! For both Patrick Bernard Jackson and Suzette Marie Brookfield. That was all this orphan in his mid-twenties needed to hear.

He exhaled with a whoosh so loud it caught the attention of the bartender, twenty feet away.

"You need anything there, Mr. Jackson?"

Jax just smiled and shook his head. He was ready to start planting his seeds tonight.

Of course, Jax was not aware that Suzy may already be pregnant with his child. That was the main reason for inviting him over for dinner last night. His little swimmers had already checked out super strong, and Suzy was ovulating. Job-one of all Mejans and partial-Mejans women is to get impregnated by a *10*—a one hundred percent purebred human male. After that, it is always hoped that the man will stay around to be the child's father, like Alan Brookfield had. And if he loves his mate and they marry…well, nothing could be finer.

"You have one hour to get ready," said Jax definitively. "I'm coming to pick you up."

"Where we going?" her question was grinning ear-to-ear, her nose sniffling.

"Ever been to a drive-in?"

"Well, sure. Sonic, A&W, McDonalds…"

"No, I mean an old fashion movie drive-in."

"I didn't think those existed anymore."

"Believe it or not there is still one in Newton, just over an hour away. I've been wanting to go there, but Jannie never cared much for movies, even in a modern, multiplex cinema."

"Sounds great. What's playing?"

Jax had already pulled up the show times on his smart phone to see what they wouldn't be watching. "A double feature," he said. "The last two Bond movies: *Quantum of Solace* and *Skyfall*."

"*Dum da da dum dum*," Suzy hummed the 007 theme. "I love Bond, James Bond. And Daniel Craig is one of the best." Then she suddenly added with an odd hint of caution, "What car are we taking?"

"We could take my Lamborghini," he offered, curious why it mattered. "Or how about my Stingray convertible, since it's a nice evening. Or…"

"Let's take your Lexus," she said seductively, to cover up the real reason. "I'm sure it has more room."

"The Lexus it is, then," chimed Jax. "So, get ready, Suzy Q. I'm coming for ya."

"What should I wear?"

"Whatever covers the least and comes off the easiest."

Chapter 37

May faded into June, and emerald green life was busting out in all across the Iowa countryside. So possibly was Suzy. Just not in green. She had missed her last period and the secret Brookfield lab behind the kitchen refrigerator with its uber-sensitive ultrasound equipment was showing hints of a fetus. A little more time was needed to know for certain.

In the meantime Jax and Suzy couldn't stay away from each other for more than a few hours at a time. The very next day after the drive-in he gave her a tour of his house and grounds, and introduced her to Odett, who liked her immediately. "That's a keeper, Pee-Bee-Boy," she said later. 'Bout time yo wised up."

In turn, he asked to meet Suzy's mother. But she was still staying clear of people with a bad case of a very contagious flu. Or so he was told.

Jax also asked for Suzy and him to sleep together while at the farm, but her motherly father was still being Asshole Alan until Jax proved his complete devotion to Suzy. Jax assumed that meant buying her an engagement ring, so that's exactly what he did. To keep from being too ostentatious, he kept it down to a mere five-carat round for seventy-five thousand. Sometimes more is less. Or was it the other way around?

Even though that gesture had to improve his standing with Alan, the hard-nosed farmer still seemed to be keeping him at arm's length. Jax didn't understand why, and Suzy just kept saying to be patient. Her new fiancé didn't know all the Brookfields were waiting to see if he passed the final test…which was simply how he would react if and when it was determined Suzy was going to bear his child. Jax wouldn't be the first male to leave a cloud of dust and no good-bye after such news, even if already engaged. Humans could be a curious lot.

There was no reason whatsoever the fishing lessons could not continue. And hardly a day went by without the happily engaged couple hanging out up at the pond, casting, catching, making love, laughing, quoting lines from movies. He was even allowed to drive into the farm to pick her up, provided he always brought the Lexus. Its all-wheel-drive was the given reason, and it made sense. Again, he didn't know climbing that steep hill was only a very small part of the Lexus's virtues in the eyes of the Brookfields.

It was during one such hilltop excursion when a strange thing happened. Or perhaps *another* strange thing would be more appropriate, seeing how a degree of mystery surrounded this farm and its inhabitants on a daily basis. The pair were sitting on the bank soaking up the rays—Suzy in a skimpy cyan bikini with nothing else but her favorite sunglasses, Jax a pair of denim cut-offs, his B.A.S.S. cap and wrap-around Revos. She was slowly working the Texas-rigged plastic worm, while Jax was popping a floating stickbait to see if any bass were willing to hit topwater yet. Nothing much was biting.

Proud Mary keep on burnin' ...

It was the first cellular interruption since way back during their second fishing lesson…which was also their first lustful enjoyment in the ways of the carnal.

"Hi, Mom," she said, not quite as cordially as the last time. There was the slightest hint of concern in her voice.

"Honey," said her mom softly but emphatically, "we're picking up scanners over the Karl Jensen farm five miles northeast of here. They aren't pointed this way, but you'd better get inside the car right away just in case."

"Will do," replied Suzy, jumping to her feet and walking briskly toward the SUV only thirty feet away, the phone still to her ear.

"Even though they are probably hiding in one of those cumulus clouds in the sky today," continued Mary Brookfield, "it's strange for them to be scanning during daylight hours. And they haven't been in this area for years. It probably won't be long. Have the snack you brought. I'll buzz you when they've gone."

"Will do. Thanks, Mom."

Suzy quickly opened the door behind the driver's side. "Snack time!" she called back to Jax, as she climbed in and shut the door.

"What is there about these Brookfields and their goddamn privacy?" Jax mumbled to himself, reeling in both lures.

To demonstrate his annoyance, he sauntered slowly to his silver Lexus and took his time getting in the same door Suzy had. She had slid over to the other seat, a granola bar and lemon-lime Gatorade 2 already in her outstretched hands. She looked like someone trying too hard to look nonchalant.

Thirsty, Jax opened the sports drink first and took a long pull. When about a quarter of the sixteen ounces were gone, he screwed the cap back on, tore open the energy bar, took a bite and said through a mouthful of oatmeal and raisins, "What the hell's going on, Suzy?"

Chapter 38

It was less than one lane and not even a road. Just two ribbons of tire tracks winding through Henry Packart's four-hundred-acre stretch of timber eight miles northwest of Lake Cooper, Texas. It had been made by Henry himself going to and from his deer stand a dozen times each season in his 2009 Ford pickup with dually tires on the rear axle.

On this particular November night in 2013 there was a small buck in the back, a country-and-western song blaring on Henry's radio, and a bottle of Jim Beam between his legs. He'd spotted the young, four-point whitetail two weeks earlier, when it tripped his night-vision trail camera, while coming to investigate the hanging deer feeder he had set up the week before. He knew the buck would stay around a while, because there were no less than five does in the area, and estrus could start at any time. All it took this day was some scent and love calls, and the whitetail walked right up and waited for the three-blade, broadhead arrow to pierce its aorta three hours before dusk. That gave Henry time to track it the two-hundred yards before it succumbed, field dress it, and drag the carcass back to his pickup just after dark.

The short, one hundred and twenty-pound cattle rancher with child-like hands and a thyroid growth hormone problem was singing along with Mearl Haggart's *Okie From Muskogee* on his favorite station, 100.3 FM in Dallas. Suddenly, the radio went dead, along with every other electronic element of his pickup, including the engine. Sliding down the seat to stomp with his full weight on the rock-hard brake pedal and fighting the dead steering wheel, he managed to bring the vehicle to a stop, hopefully still on the trail. He knew there was a drop-off into a ravine not that far to his left.

Henry had to sit a spell for his eyes to adjust to the pitch blackness. In his blindness he found and replaced the cap to his Jim Beam bottle, set it in the cup holder between the seats, then fumbled for the flashlight in the glove box. By the time he heard the driver's side door open, it was too late. The spray instantly had him drunk as a sailor and purring like a kitten. With help, he willingly slid out of the truck and walked sleepily with his two escorts to the waiting spacecraft sitting on the trail in the dark, thirty feet behind the truck. A portal split open and a ramp extended. The three figures entered a small room dimly lit in a pink hue, and the portal closed behind them. One alien quickly pulled Henry's flannel shirt up and over his chest, but not off, while the other jerked his pants and shorts down to his ankles. Weaving to and fro on his feet, Henry just smiled.

With much effort, the hapless human was hoisted onto a silver metal table and hooked up to a variety of monitors on the wall behind his head, as well straps on each appendage. Along with his temperature, blood pressure, blood gases and a host of other readings, samples were taken of his semen, feces, urine, stomach contents, skin, and DNA via a swab of the roof of his mouth. A small tracking and monitoring device the size of a baby aspirin was inserted just under the scalp behind his left ear. Between relaxed winces of pain, Henry just hummed.

All data received and recorded, the efficient pair removed the probes, tubes and electrodes and redressed their lab rat. He was led back to his pickup and set gently down back in the driver's seat. His head was angled back and the tip of a slender applicator was dipped into a small vial, then applied to the back of his throat. It was a new and hopefully deadlier strain of the flu. The CDC would later label it H7N9, the next mutation of the Bird Flu. They would incorrectly designate its origin as southwest China.

Another mist was puffed in his face, and the small alien bipods dressed in pale blue jumpsuits walked spritely back to their ship. As they entered the portal, both systematically removed the latex masks covering their entire heads. Each disguise closely resembled the classic, adult-alien mask anyone could purchase from a costume store.

Suddenly, all the dash lights were back on and the engine was humming, as if it had never stopped. The flashlight and whiskey bottle were resting on the passenger's bucket seat and Willie Nelson was singing *Honeysuckle Rose*. Somehow the station had switched to 98 AM and the digital clock on the dash seemed to have jumped ahead three hours.

"Must've dosed off," said the dazed deerslayer, trying to shake the clouds out of his brain. He looked at the trail ahead in the high beams. "Damn lucky I didn't go off the road."

Feeling surprisingly chipper and rested, Henry Packart drove the final two miles to Road 3043, turned right with a squeal on the blacktop, and headed home to many nights of unpleasant dreams and an upcoming illness that was known to kill an infant or an elderly person in less than a week. As the aliens suspected, Henry's thyroid problem saved him from the same fate, and he would recover fully. So there would be no need for further adjustments to the molecular structure of the virus. Henry would survive the future pandemic and become a valued human in the Regg regime. He was a cattle rancher.

Chapter 39

Jax pulled into the circle driveway of the Brookfield farm and stopped in front of the sprawling, one-story, brick ranch, as always. He'd been invited to dinner for about the tenth time in the past two weeks, but this time Suzy had a giggle of anticipation in her tone, unlike any time before. He took it as good news or a celebration of some kind. But exactly what, he could only speculate. Suzy wouldn't say. Maybe he was to be awarded with free access to the pond from now on. But that was less important to him now. It wouldn't be half as much fun without his darling little fishing buddy.

He expected Suzy to come out and greet him as usual. But he was met only by McDoogle, the family Golden Retriever. As a matter of fact, there was no one around the farm proper, not even kids playing in the guesthouse yards or the playground or pool or tennis courts.

He checked his iPhone: *6:50 p.m.* He was ten minutes early. Maybe that was why. Maybe everyone was inside the house preparing for the something special. God, he hoped it wasn't going to be a surprise party. He hated those things. The poor slob would walk through the door and have a bunch of puppet people spring up from behind furniture and yell *Surprise!* And if he or she didn't go into immediate cardiac arrest or pee their pants, they'd die of embarrassment. The only thing worse than being a part of the surprise was being the victim. *But that, thank God, couldn't be for me. My birthday was months ago in April.*

Jax had an idea. With no one around, maybe he could a skip over to the barn and check out that tack room in the far corner Suzy pointed out in passing the night they did it in the haymow. It had a padlock on it, which seemed odd for what was supposed to house just some leather goods, like saddles and bridles. He could be back here in a couple minutes, no one the wiser.

He had to admit it was kind of eerie walking around the area unchaperoned for the first time. Even McDoogle had decided to go back to whatever dogs do on a late-June evening on a two thousand-acre farm in southeastern Iowa. Besides being protective, the Brookfields—and especially Alan, of course—were also secretive, even clandestine at times. Like that episode yesterday when Suzy practically ran to the Lexus because of a phone call from her supposedly sick mother. And when he asked what the hell was going on around here, she tried to placate him with yet another cautionary request to be patient, saying he'd have some answers soon. And when he asked for a definition of *soon,* the only response he got was a wet kiss and quickie in the back of his SUV. So, in that respect, patience was a virtue. And ignorance was indeed bliss.

Just as he expected, the combination Masterlock was secure. What he didn't expect was the wooden door being sealed so solidly to the frame it wouldn't open even a crack to allow a peek inside the twelve-by-six enclosure. It clearly was made of wood, but felt like solid steel. *Must be where they store their heroin, or TF2 rocket launchers*, he mused, half serious. Well, they *could* be drug or weapons dealers, couldn't they? Discouraged, he spun around and scanned the inside of the barn from this angle. Every Holstein dairy cow looked at him as if to say, *You were told it was locked, weren't you? But you had to come try it anyway, didn't you?*

As he exited the up-and-down barn door, his right side peripheral vision caught a movement in the adjacent greenhouse. When he looked straight on, he saw only plants and faint blue lights, no movement. Curious, Jax walked the fifty feet up to one of the many glass panels and peered in, using his cupped hands to shield out the evening sun in his face, still two hours from the western horizon.

His view was blocked by what appeared to be a small plot of short, green cornstalks, so he slid along until coming to a gap in the foliage. On the tray directly in front of him was some kind of clover plants, three inches high, in black soil, being misted by an automatic sprinkler system. Beyond, he could see a series of other plants on other tables running the width of the greenhouse, plus a symphony of multi-colored vegetation hanging from the grid of metal support rods.

He decided to slide down further yet, again being met by tall, leafy plants he couldn't see past. So he continued to the next gap, this time coming face-to-face with an alien.

Chapter 40

The shock knocked Jax backwards, causing him to lose his footing and fall on his butt in the grass. The creature continued to look at him through the window with a blank expression. Then, as if realizing Jax was someone it didn't know and maybe wasn't supposed to meet, it let out a muffled yell and disappeared.

Faster than any grass drill he had ever executed in high school football practice, the ex-tight end flipped over to his stomach, got his feet spinning under him and raced out from between the greenhouse and red barn, screaming like a little girl.

About the time he reached his vehicle—with every intention of jumping in and driving away at ninety miles an hour and never coming back—Suzy, Alan, David, Mike and three others he didn't know had already poured out the front door and headed him off as he rounded the back end of his Lexus. Alan and his two sons were quickly on the bug-eyed, frantic human, holding him firmly by his arms, demanding what was wrong.

"There's a fucking alien in the greenhouse," he yelled to them, fighting to free himself from his captors. "Get the hell out of here! Run!"

A chuckle began to rise from the group, building to laughter that was far more sympathetic than demeaning. Catching the odd tone of the others, the crazed look in Jax's eyes narrowed to a squint, as he began to study their faces. One of them was Suzy's, as she stepped closer to give him a reassuring hug.

"It's okay, honey," she smiled maternally. "That's not an alien, at least not in the sense you think. That was only Grandma. She takes care of the greenhouse."

Jax searched her eyes and mouth in disbelief. "Grandma?!" he howled. "No goddamn way! That was not human. It had big black eyes, a blue head with an orange outline, and, *oh yeah*, a tube coming out of the middle of its face!"

"Yep, that's Grandma," laughed David. Everyone nodded and verbalized in agreement, including Suzy.

Mike was sent scurrying in the direction of the greenhouse on an errand.

"What's going on here?" asked Jax, adding frustration to his fright. "Is this some kind of Area 51 or something?"

Suzy took over. She reached up and kissed Jax on his pursed, not-having-any lips. "Honey," she said calmly, "remember yesterday up at the pond when I told you to be patient and you'd soon have some explanations?"

Jax nodded weakly, his eyes still wildly flashing over the top of her head toward the greenhouse in case *the thing* were to suddenly emerge and eat his brains.

"Well, tonight's the night," smiled Suzy. "This dinner is to announce some very special news that you're going to love."

"What? Your plans for colonizing Earth?" Jax said sarcastically. "For terraforming the Midwest?" Then he quickly added with far more of a whimper than whimsy, "Dibs on being emperor of Iowa."

That brought a few laughs from the group and a bottle of Pabst for Jax. It was handed to Suzy, who offered it to her fiancée. Jax looked at it and then at Suzy, then back to the bottle. He refused to take it.

"It's okay, honey," she said soothingly, nudging the bottle to his chest. "Drink it. It will calm you down."

"How do I know it won't kill me, or paralyze me, or turn me into E.T.?"

"Do you love me, Jax?"

Jax hesitated, and then replied testily, "I thought I did."

"Do you love me?" she said again, more emphatically, her left hand firmly pinching his chin, forcing it downward.

Jax looked at her. That darling face with those big copper-brown eyes. That button nose. Those soft, rosebud lips. Of course he loved her. And he told her so with a feeble nod.

"Then trust me," she said, holding up the beer. "Just take a sip and you'll feel much better. I promise."

"Is it spiked?" he asked, still refusing to take the bottle from her.

"Yes, it is." she replied honestly. "There's a little bit of a drug like valium in there. It's harmless and fast-acting. It's what you need right now."

"I want to believe you, but...."

Alan stepped up, snatched the bottle from Suzy, took a big swig and shoved it back at Jax. "Drink it, you wuss," he said somewhere between disparaging and joking. "You can't trust your own fiancée?"

Well, there were two surprises in five minutes: a Martian inside the greenhouse and half a sense of humor inside Alan Brookfield.

About then Mike returned from the direction of the greenhouse with the third surprise. He held up the futuristic-looking gasmask for Jax's inspection. It was a cream-colored, full-faced rubber of some kind with two large, round, clear glass lenses and a short corrugated tube connecting to a small canister.

"Like Suzy said," panted Mike, "Grandma takes care of the greenhouse. Sometimes she has to wear this gasmask, because the pollen aggravates her allergies."

"But she had blue skin," argued Jax. "I saw it clearly."

Alan shook his head, sad for his future son-in-law's obliviousness. "That was from the blue light we use on some plants to help them grow. They run on timers."

The group murmured knowingly.

"And big black eyes..." Jax added, less assuredly.

"With the greenhouse lights and setting sun behind her," reasoned Mike, turning the back of the gasmask to the setting sun to demonstrate his point, "the lenses must have just looked dark."

Jax had to admit the lenses did seem to go dark. His expression changed from confusion to comprehension, before finally settling on sheepish. He looked at Suzy. She smiled and nodded. He took the bottle.

"I still get to be emperor of Iowa," he said flatly, and chugged four ounces in three gulps.

Chapter 41

In the same western motif as upstairs, but with darker pine paneling, the sprawling downstairs recreation room had wall-to-wall, off-white Berber carpeting and flat screen televisions everywhere. There were pinball machines, video arcade games, a pool table, ping pong table, two wet bars, and yes, that was a bowling lane with automatic pinsetter and ball return against the north wall.

The room was buzzing with all eight people from the outside excitement, the mood quite festive. Jax was sure they all knew something he didn't...namely the reason for this party. While he continued to hope it had nothing to do with him, from Suzy's preliminary overture about finally getting some answers, he suspected there was no chance of that. But more than being the center of the celebration was his fear of learning about his upcoming participation in Iowa's largest meth lab, or underground white slavery, or child pornography ring. Now that he was betrothed to Suzy Brookfield, how could he possibly back out from whatever dark dealings this family was into?

Still, with each passing moment, Jax was feeling less and less apprehensive, just as Suzy had promised. His mental faculties and reasoning seemed fully functional, maybe even more so. And as far as he could tell, he hadn't grown scales or another appendage. So, he was offered and gladly accepted a pure PBR in replace of the spiked one. Suzy was drinking the same, linking her right arm in his.

Jax was introduced to the other three people. Louis was a burly, redheaded hired hand about his age. His big-eyed wife, Karen, seemed the perfect match. Both were very good looking, as was the thirty-something woman, named Joyce, who was also a hired hand's wife. Her eyes were of normal size. Her husband, Larry, couldn't be here due to *his presence being required elsewhere*. He hoped to join them later. Jax stopped himself from trying to imagine what that *requirement* may entail.

Also glaringly absent once again was Mary Brookfield, Alan's wife, Suzy's mother. But she, too, was expected to join them soon. Her continued absence, along with even more people with big eyes and heads should have seemed odd to Jax. But thanks to chemistry, he didn't much care.

"Can I have everyone's attention," boomed Alan's voice over the PA system. He was standing on the small stage at the far end of the room with a cordless microphone in his hand. Behind him were a piano, drum set, chairs, and four large speakers, apparently in case One Direction decided to stop by for an impromptu concert. Everyone gathered around at the foot of the stage. "Suzy, Jax, would you two step up here, please?"

Jax jumped up on the stage and pulled Suzy up beside him. Since it also involved his wife-to-be, he had a pretty good idea what this was about. No big deal. He could handle a little congratulatory attention.

Alan moved in behind the couple and placed a hand on each one's shoulder. "As some of you already know," he said, "my little girl here just got engaged to Jax Jackson here." Just as Jax thought. "Congratulations to the happy couple." Applause and cheers.

Suzy showed off the five-carat diamond ring, and then she and Jax kissed and embraced. They were clearly the happiest couple on Earth.

Not waiting for the two to pry themselves apart, Alan continued, "But that's not all. We have even bigger news." The group fell silent.

Bigger news? thought Jax, his mind racing. He didn't know how much more he could take this evening. An alien who was really just an old woman with allergies, a beer laced with the fastest acting, funkiest valium he ever heard of, and just now their engagement announcement in front of people, most of whom—if not all—already knew about the ring. He prayed this next item on the entertainment docket didn't involve anything illegal or dangerous. Maybe it was something good, like they had discovered a cure for cancer or genital herpes or cluster warts.

"We just got the test back this morning," said Alan, softly into the microphone. He paused a moment for effect. The room fell silent. Jax could tell by the eyes glued on the Brookfield patriarch that no one knew what was coming. Then, at the peak of anticipation, Alan broke the news, almost in a whisper. "Suzy's pregnant. We're going to have a baby!"

The crowd erupted with cheers and high-fives. It was true: none of them did know beforehand. Jax stood frozen in place, the announcement bouncing around between his ears. *Did he say pregnant? Did he say Suzy? My Suzy?* With gaping mouth, he turned to his fiancée and whispered, "Really? Are you? Is it mine?"

"Of course, it's yours, silly," laughed Suzy. "You're going to be a father, Jax Jackson. Congratulations!"

Jax didn't realize that behind the clapping everyone was now watching intently to see his reaction. It didn't matter. He was in his own little world of dream-come-true, Jiminy Cricket, wish upon a star, fairytale euphoria. Hysterical blindness was scratching at his periphery, except this was the good kind of crazy. Suzy would tell him later that he threw his head back and both fists into the air in the victory salute. Tears rolled from the far corner of each eye and pooled up in his ears.

All others in the room—especially her father—cheered almost as hard and loud as he did. There was no doubt in anyone's mind that this *10*, this one hundred percent human, this outdoor writer, was elated by the news. He was undoubtedly here to stay.

The announcements morphed into flowing liquor and a buffet dinner of ribeye steaks with all the fixings. Sated, everyone started dancing to iTunes over the speaker system or challenging someone to the many choices of games. It concluded six hours later with Jax and Suzy finally being allowed to spend the night together in her bed. How much sleep they got was left open to speculation.

Chapter 42

Suzy awoke to a soft rubbing sensation on her stomach. She slowly rolled her head to the left to find exactly what she expected: her baby's father propped up on his right elbow, stroking her lower abdomen with the fingertips of his left hand.

"I just can't believe it," he smiled, shaking his head.

Suzy reached over to caress Jax's stubbly face. "Are you happy?"

"Happy?" he said, kissing her bellybutton, then sliding up to kiss between her breasts, ending at her soft lips. "I'm over the freakin' moon."

Suzy executed a half-turn roll to land face to face on top of Jax. "Have I told you lately how much I love you?" she said, pecking his lips, nose, and both cheeks.

Jax wrapped his arms around his naked fiancée and returned the maneuver to end up on top of her. "Let's make love again," he whispered. "Maybe that will give us twins."

Suzy started to quake with laughter, jostling Jax along with her. "If that were true," she said, trying to keep her breath with Jax's weight pressing down on her, "based on last night alone…we'd have quadruplets."

Things were just heating up again when a knock at the door and an announcement from David relayed that breakfast was ready: scrambled eggs and apple pancakes, his specialty. The newly-engaged, expectant parents in unison told him to buzz off, which immediately brought Father Alan's voice saying that if Jax wanted to learn some of Brookfield Farm's secrets, he'd better get his ass out of bed, eat breakfast and be in the upstairs rec room at oh-eight-hundred, twenty minutes from now.

At oh-seven-fifty-nine—with Suzy leading the way—Jax quick-stepped into the rec room, burping the last bite of breakfast, while wiping his mouth on a paper napkin. Obeying Alan's gesture, they plopped down on the over-stuffed, black suede sofa, holding hands and beaming bliss from both their auras. Suzy had already relieved any remaining qualms Jax had regarding the family secrets. There was nothing illegal going on at the farm—at least in the sense of ending up in jail, and he would—*for the most part anyway*—find the revelations exciting. He didn't know she had a pocketful of those calming pills at the ready.

"I suspect you have some questions about things around here," said Alan from the matching chair on the other side of the large, Persian rug.

"Questions?" huffed Jax sarcastically. "Oh, just five or ten dozen." He shifted forward on the couch cushion, his apprehension clearly edging toward excitement now. Even outdoor writers are basically news-people, which means nosy reporters, which means curious to a fault, which means sometimes you'd like to punch them in their nosy nose. He didn't know where to begin.

But before he could, Alan interjected, "Well, we are about to answer them as best we can. But we need something from you first."

"Anything. Name it. Money? I'm rich. Someone to run moonshine? I've two fast cars. A write-up in my column? I can talk to my editor. If she says *no*, I'll buy the paper."

The two Brookfields laughed. One of them wrapped her arms around his middle and kissed the back of his neck. She loved his dry sense of humor. The other waved him off with a crooked, Harrison Ford smile.

"All we need is your word," Alan said succinctly. "Your pledge that you will defend to the death the life and wellbeing of my only daughter, your unborn child, and any future children."

"Oh, you have it!" said Jax with no hesitation and more sincerity than he knew he had. "You don't even need to ask that. She's the best thing that has ever happened in my life, and my greatest wish to start a family is coming true. My word? You have it. I'll put it in writing if you want. I'll put it in blood."

"That won't be necessary," said Alan. "Paper crumbles with age and disappears in fire. A man's word can't be destroyed by anything but his own treachery. It is his bond."

Jax nodded in agreement. "You have my word."

"We also need your word not to reveal in whole or in part to anyone outside of this family anything we are about to tell you and show you." Without even thinking, Jax opened his mouth to agree, but Alan cut him off. "Don't be too anxious to comply, son." *Jesus, he called me son.* "Some of the things you are about to learn could be a little disconcerting for you, maybe even frightening."

"Worse than my seeing a Venusian in the greenhouse last night?" said Jax flippantly.

"I don't know," said Alan, stone-faced. "Maybe. Maybe not. It all depends on you." The smile faded from Jax's face. "I just want to forewarn you that your life as you've known it is about to rotate one hundred and eighty degrees."

Jax was taken aback, his brow narrowed. "Sounds ominous," he said more guarded now. Then he added, with a defensive tick of levity. "I suppose you're going to tell me that we are about to overthrow the government or something."

"I'm not going to tell you anything until I have your word," said the head of the Brookfield clan firmly.

A nervous silence fell over the room. Jax looked at Suzy, who smiled hopefully at him. She gave him another squeeze that didn't end quickly. He looked back at Alan, whose cold, gray eyes were riveted on his. He looked back at Suzy and thought of the life hiding there under her yellow terrycloth robe.

"With Suzy at my side and my children to come," he said, as if being sworn in as president of the United States, "I can take anything you throw at me. Yes. Again, you have my word."

Alan rose to his feet and walked over to Jax and Suzy. His open arms invited them to stand, and he embraced Suzy. Then Jax. "Welcome to the family," said Alan. The tone and embrace were not for a son, more like a distant cousin. But they were enough to make Jax's heart and eyes swell with nostalgia for his lost family and a sense of belonging to a new one. Alan could never replace his dad, and obviously had no intention of ever doing so. But it felt good, just the same.

"Okay, *son*," Alan said, returning to the padded suede chair and spreading his hands. "What would you like to know first?"

Chapter 43

Now Jax's heart was pounding like a trip hammer, excitement mixed with fear coursing through his veins so hard and fast he thought he might explode and pepper the room with red splatters. His mind swirled with a thousand disjointed words, trying desperately to coalesce them into some kind of intelligent syntax. It took a moment, but he was finally able to construct a coherent interrogative.

"What I saw in the greenhouse last night, was it really Grandma Brookfield or an alien?" Jax smirked at his own harebrained question. But he had to know for sure. There was still a slight shadow of doubt.

"Both," said Alan flatly, adding no further explanation.

Jax did the classic double take. "You mean *both*, both?" he repeated carefully.

"Yes, both," assured Alan. "It was Grandma and she is partly an alien…from the planet Meja."

Jax snorted. *The planet Meja. Good one.* Grinning, he looked back and forth between Alan and Suzy. Neither one was sharing in the joke. In fact Suzy was nodding, almost apologetically. Jax's stomach started churning. Suzy reached in her robe's pocket for a pill.

"But what you saw *was* a gasmask," added Alan. "That's not what Suzy's grandmother really looks like…not by any means."

He's kidding, right? The stunned young man from America's heartland didn't know whether to laugh along with them, cry for his lost soul, throw up in fear, or beat feet for the door. He hardly noticed Suzy ramming a pill into his mouth and his swallowing it in reflex.

Feeling he needed more information before deciding—in case this wasn't as *Spaceballs* as it appeared—he chose option number one: play along with the joke. "Well, that's a relief," Jax quipped sarcastically. Then his brow lowered in preparation, not sure he really wanted to hear the answer. "So, what *does* she look like?"

"She looks a lot like me," offered a mature, feminine voice. Jax turned to see it connected to small, beautiful woman in her late-thirties, gliding into the room, as if on cue. "Only older and shorter." She headed straight for Jax with her right hand extended. "Hi, Jax," she said pleasantly, "I'm Mary Brookfield, Suzy's mother."

With surprise plastered all over his face, Jax jumped to his feet, towering over the five-foot-two woman. He took her offered hand and kept his focus firmly there. It was even smaller than Suzy's and more delicate. She was wearing frosty pink nail polish. No rings or bracelets.

Almost afraid to do so, he eased his gaze from her hand slowly upward to her face. He was braced for it being different, because he had already had a quick glance as she walked into the room. Now here it was, in all its E. T. reality, looking back at him.

He stopped breathing. Mary's eyes were even bigger than Suzy's. The same copper-brown and the same round shape. But at least thirty percent larger. Her nose was small. The mouth was a fraction smaller than her daughter's, yet with a normal shape and symmetry. The chin was weak, cheekbones high. Her cranium may have been bigger than a normal human's, but it was difficult to tell with the mass of chestnut hair swirling all over it and cascading down around her narrow shoulders. All in all, she had an exotic beauty that human and alien alike would find intriguing.

Realizing Jax may need some time to find his tongue, Mary gently pried her hand from his, bent down to kiss her daughter good morning, and walked over to the padded chair to give her husband the same greeting formality. Jax noticed she had a pronounced swayback, which made her butt push out against the beige shift that covered her form from neck to ankles. Now that he thought about it, Suzy had a little bit of the same spinal configuration. But it only added to her many attributes.

That's when it hit him. Right between the eyes and smack in the stomach. *This really is about extraterrestrials! I'm sitting in a nest of them! And worst of all, my fiancé is one of them!*

If Greenhouse Granny is an alien, and Suzy's mother clearly is an alien, it had to follow genealogically that the woman sitting next to him, wearing his engagement ring, carrying his baby, smiling sheepishly up at him, is one, too.

This isn't about Suzy having six toes or a heart murmur or is just out of rehab for a heroin addiction. This is Outer Limits, Ridley Scott, little toothy, slimy bastards busting out of human chests, otherworldly alien shit!

Now Jax really wanted to run. He couldn't. His entire body was frozen in place, his mind completed disconnected from his body.

Chapter 44

The perplexed Mr. Jackson didn't look much like Josh Duhamel anymore...more like the poor soul in Edvard Munch's famous painting, *The Scream*. He couldn't look at Suzy. His imagination had distorted her eyes to the size of tennis balls, her head to pumpkin-like, beyond bulbous.

Suzy reached into the pocket of her bathrobe again, pulled out another well-anticipated pill and jammed it under Jax's tongue before he could even react. While it took effect, Mary casually fetched herself a cup of coffee from the kitchen, returned, and sat down beside Alan on the arm of the chair. Jax's face seemed more relaxed, but was still twisted up in consternation. He slowly, tentatively looked down at Suzy. She smiled weakly at him, and forgivingly laid her head against his shoulder. She found herself humming the Shirelles' *"Will You Still Love Me Tomorrow?"*

"Perhaps you're wondering about the Brookfield family tree," offered Mary. Jax didn't respond. A small drop of spittle had formed on the lower lip of his still-gaping mouth.

"Jax!" Mary almost shouted to break his stupor. "Snap out of it. Suzy is just as human as you are. Well, almost. And maybe more so, if you don't pull yourself together."

Jax started blinking. His tongue speared the ball of spit, and he turned in the direction of Mary's voice.

"If I can have your attention," Mary said like a third-grade teacher, "I'll explain our family tree. It will clear some things up. Would you like that, Jax?"

When Jax nodded stupidly, she began, "The *creature* you saw in the greenhouse is my mother. She's fifty percent Mejan, fifty percent human. I won't muddle your brain with where her home planet is or how she got here. We can do that later. For now, suffice it to say she mated with my grandfather, Lawrence. He was about a micron tall and lived in a test tube. He came from a sperm bank at the University Hospitals."

With mouth still open, Jax nodded, not sure at what.

"In case you are wondering," interjected Alan, "I'm one hundred percent human, just like you." That brought a weak smile of relief to Jax's lips. "I'm what we call a *10*. Mary here is 75 percent human, 25 percent Mejan. She's called an *8*. We like to round up. Greenhouse Grandma is a *5*, fifty-fifty. Her Earth name is Helen, by the way."

"Helen," mumbled Jax, like he'd just been lobotomized.

"So, if you do the math, you know that your darling fiancée there beside you is 87.5 percent human. We round up and label her a *9*. When your child is born, he or she will be 93.75 percent human, or a *94*. 94s are very special."

Mary paused to let Jax ask the obvious next question, on the outside chance he was following the Brookfield genealogy so far. It took a moment of lip movement, eye blinking, and the pill to continue dissolving under his tongue, but he finally gathered his thoughts.

"Why will...our child...be special?" he asked, the subject bringing hints of lucidity.

It was time for Suzy to step in. She put her hands on Jax's face and turned it toward her. "For one thing," she said, "the average body temperature of a 94 like our children will be is 98.2, very close to human's 98.6 degrees. This makes them indistinguishable from humans on the Regg scanners. Mine is 98.0. I can still be detected. So can Mom's at 97.1 and especially Grandma's at 95.5 degrees."

"What a minute," said Jax, the chill pill completely kicked in, coherency now replacing confusion. "What the hell is a...*Regg scanner*?"

"It's basically the same infrared instrument police use to pick up the heat signatures of criminals trying to hide at night," said Alan. "You can buy one anywhere. An object with a radiant temperature higher or lower than its ambient surroundings will show up on its monitor in various colors, depending on the degree of difference. But we believe the Regg's scanners are so sensitive they can detect half a degree difference in body heat...the difference between mine and Suzy's, for example."

Jax knew from his college biology classes that body temperatures can go up and down, depending on the person's current state of activity. When he mindlessly expressed that fact, Alan explained that the scanner's micro-circuitry probably takes that into consideration, plus it may be able to measure the size of the target's head. Even a one-eighth Mejan, like Suzy, has a cranium slightly larger than the average human.

Jax decided to pass on pursuing that subject any further. No sense having confirmed what was already obvious: Mejans were a lot smarter than humans. Or to put it another way, he was the dunce in the room.

"Can their scanners read through any substance?" he asked, hoping to redeem his little brain.

"Good question," said Alan. "We think theirs can still get an accurate reading through some things like cloth, wood, plastic, and so on, but not through high density material like metal and concrete."

Jax looked suspiciously at his future bride and fishing protégé. "Is that why you ran to my Lexus yesterday when your mom called? Was one of these *Regg scanners* around?"

Suzy nodded. "Sorry, honey. I couldn't tell you then."

"Jesus, Suzy! Were you in danger?"

"Not really," she said calmly. "Mom had said the scan was being conducted five miles away. My getting in the car was just a precaution. As far as we know, our farm hasn't been scanned in years."

Jax's skin crawled. He inhaled deeply and exhaled slowly, letting the prospect of his future wife and unborn baby being hunted by something sinister run its course through his system. But it only brought on another question, the obvious one.

"I'll bet *Regg* is not the brand name of their scanner, is it?"

Suzy got up from the couch and knelt down in front of Jax, putting her hands on his thighs. She looked up into his azure eyes and said quietly, so not to launch her baby's father into further discord, "The Reggs are our enemy, sweetheart, your enemy, the entire Earth's enemy. As far as we know, they have not, and cannot mate with humans. We don't know where they came from or how they got here. Information about them has been hard to come by. But we are certain they are hunting Mejans and any human who is part Mejan, with intent to learn more about us and then ultimately to keep us from blending into the human race. They also abduct humans; we suspect for experimentation and maybe worse."

Jax just stared cow-eyed at Suzy.

"Would you like another pill, sweetheart?" she smiled, reaching into her pocket.

"Yes, please."

Chapter 45

The foursome took a short recess, while Jax's third sedative of the morning kicked in. He was getting to like how they relaxed him and even made his mind seem clearer. Now with the triple dose, all this craziness didn't seem so crazy somehow…like it had always been his reality.

The break was used to move the Q & A session to the communications room, so Jax could start getting some hands-on indoctrination of what all occurs on—and under—Brookfield Farm. The four walked down the carpeted stairs to the rec room and followed Mary to behind one of the wet bars. She punched some keys on her burgundy smart phone and a section of the back wall pivoted on its left side axis, revealing a passageway. They walked down another flight of carpeted stairs and entered the buzzing, flickering room of televisions, computers and monitors. Young David Brookfield was currently on duty, but with nothing much to do, he was watching a movie recorded on the DVR.

"Hey, Jax," he grinned, getting a kick out of what his future brother-in-law was going through. "Welcome to the underbelly of Brookfield Farms."

After explaining what some of the machinery did and avoiding other aspects that Jax didn't need to know about—at least at this point in his crash course—they all sat in the rolling office chairs. Mary asked lightheartedly if he had any more questions.

"If you know so little about the Reggs," started Jax, feeling surprisingly calm, cool and back to his curious nature, "how do you know their name?"

"We don't," offered Suzy. "*Regg* is the Mejan word for *enemy*."

"How do you know they see you as *their* enemy?"

"At first it was mostly through logic," said Alan. "Only a malevolent race would do the things they were doing, namely scanning areas to locate us, and then actually setting foot in the area, wearing disguises, trying to capture any human with Mejan blood."

"I trust you have solid evidence of this."

"We didn't until 1992," said Mary, "when they actually captured an *8* near one of our sister farms in Illinois." She spun around toward David. "Run it, Son." She then turned back to Jax and warned, "You may want to brace yourself. This is pretty intense." Suzy reached over and squeezed his hand. Jax signaled with a confident smile and nod that he would be okay.

One of the four big television screens on the north wall that had been showing the movie David was watching switched to an opening title page reading: *Ned Wilson (8), January 10, 1992, Champaign, Illinois.*

Following was footage of two dark figures running along a sidewalk toward the camera, illuminated only by the city street lights. They appeared to be wearing long, woolen coats, stocking caps, sunglasses, gloves…all in black. It was determined they were, thin, about six feet tall with a general, humanoid shape, but slightly hunched over like Neanderthals.

"That's *it*?" asked a skeptical Jax.

"Keep watching," said Mary, as the video cut to a static shot of an overhead streetlight. "David, turn up the audio."

"Hello, Mejan half-breed," said someone off-screen with a raspy voice and a four-year-old's grasp of the English language. "You just what we looked for."

"Whoever you're looking for," pleaded Ned Wilson, "you've got the wrong guy."

"And what this?" croaked another disembodied voice, before picking up and looking straight into Ned's communicator/camera. "A piece of your technology."

Apparently unconcerned about revealing his face to his captive—since Ned wouldn't live long enough to tell anyone—the Regg had removed his dark glasses, and along with them came the attached human nose and mouth façade. Even in the limited backlight, it clearly revealed two beady, yellow eyes with horizontal, oval pupils, a stubby, black snout with forward-facing nostrils, and a narrow mouth that extended more forward than sideways. All the features were integrated in a sea of short, dark and darker-gray hair.

The shock of that image made Jax flinch. And when he saw the Regg's mouth widen into a hideous smile, showing wolf-like teeth, he had to look away. Thank God he had taken those valium-type pills or he would have been crawling under the table. The others in the room had seen it all before. But even they were upset by the image, not to mention the reminder of the Regg's malicious intentions toward the Mejan race.

The audio continued with Ned's voice. "That's something I just found on the street. It won't do you any more good than I will."

Mary asked David to pause the recording so she could explain to Jax that the Reggs didn't seem to know all the capabilities of Ned's communicator, or that it was transmitting both audio and video back to Ned's parents in a communications center similar to this one. So, one of the Reggs must have shoved it into a coat pocket at this point, probably to free up both hands to help load Ned into the car. Thus the reason why the following was only muffled audio with black screen video.

Jax nodded his understanding and David resumed the recording. What he heard was almost as bone-chilling as the previous video: a dialog in a strange alien language, followed by grotesque laughter. Then one of them said to Ned in poor English, "Oh, it do much good. You and Mejan race —as your satellite movies say— *now in deep shit!*"

Chapter 46

"So, we are at war with the Reggs," said Jax, more as a statement than a question. Everyone nodded. "But it seems more like a game where they are the hunters and we are the hunted. Don't we fight back? Don't we have the technology and the weaponry to blow their asses back to Mars?"

The other four were smiling, part by the wishful, humorous image, part by the questions, but mostly by the word, *we*. Jax was using the first-person plural pronoun without qualification or hesitation. He was definitely onboard. And it wasn't due to the pills he was popping like candy. They weren't that strong and only curtailed anxiety for about an hour. This display of camaraderie had to be fueled by the young man's powerful love for Suzy and their unborn child.

However, no one—not even Suzy—was yet aware of the less-than-virtuous aspect of Jax's psyche that his present bravado was covering up.

"I hear you," said Alan. "I felt and still feel the same way in many respects." He looked around at his alien wife, daughter, and son, all three nodding in acknowledgement of the difference between his human DNA and theirs. "But the Mejans are a peaceful race, probably far more advanced in that respect than us humans and certainly more than the Reggs. They bring to Earth a kind of divine respect for all life and tolerance of all things different. By mating with us humans, by blending our genes with theirs, the human race can only benefit. And we probably need it," he conceded. "Look at what course our so-called *civilization* has been on lately."

"Well, on the other side of things," interjected Mary, grabbing Alan's hand, "from the human DNA the Mejans pick up some backbone, some aggression, not to mention bigger and stronger bodies. Alan makes the Mejans sound like angels coming to save mankind from itself. But it works both ways."

"I understand," said Jax, purposely rising from his office chair, his pseudo-machismo level escalating. "But we can't just hide in a hole like rabbits, hoping the big bad hunter doesn't find us." He began moving around the room, gesturing. "We have to stop them, don't we? A good offense is the best defense."

There were some sideways glances and knowing smiles cast among Alan, Mary and David. Jax was beginning to overdo the bluster. This was, after all, the guy who ran screaming in terror like a five-year-old girl from

RICHARD DOUGLAS TAYLOR

greenhouse Grandma in a gasmask. Suzy refused to take part in the smirks, remaining loyal to her man. Anyone would have reacted that way. He had good reason to be frightened.

"You're right, Jax," said Alan, humoring him. "And we believe we do have the means to defeat them, or soon will have. The problem is intel. We simply don't know where they are. They could be hiding behind asteroids or deep in the oceans. We know their spacecraft have complete stealth, impervious to radar, sonar, laser, everything except visually."

"So, we can *see* their ships?" queried Jax with raised eyebrows.

"Of course," huffed Alan. "They aren't exactly Klingons with a cloaking device."

Jax appreciated the Star Trek reference—one of his favorite series—but not particularly the condescending tone. "So, we've seen one?"

"No, not in the flesh," admitted Mary.

"Then how do know they even have spaceships?" Jax knew it was a stupid question even before it left his lips.

"You mean outside of the fact they are clearly from outer space," Alan began with the list, "they don't resemble anything on Earth, they speak in an unknown dialect, and know exactly what a Mejan is, which is also from another world, which also has *spaceships*?"

"Well, ah…"

"Besides that," grinned Alan, like a basketball coach who had just slam-dunked one over the head of his tallest player, "every time they fire up their infrared scanners within ten miles of us, our own scanners pick it up. On that alone we can pinpoint their longitude, latitude, altitude, course, and speed." He pointed at the large green screen on the east wall, its grid and sweep hand current registering nothing. "So, unless they are only a foot tall and riding on the backs of buzzards, it's safe to assume they are in some kind of spacecraft similar to…" Alan caught himself before saying something he wasn't supposed to just yet. *But what the hell.* Jax was to be briefed eventually anyway. Besides, setting this match to the powder key of Jax's present mind, would be a hoot to watch.

"…similar to a spacecraft" he repeated "…*like ours*."

125

Chapter 47

"I knew it!" said Jax, with a short fist-pump. "How many saucers do we have? How big are they? Is there one here on the farm? Can I see it?"

"Calm down there, speed racer," smiled Alan. "There's plenty of time to learn about such things. But, yes, the Mejans have a few. And, yes, we have one here close by. And, yes, you can crawl around in it to your heart's content. But later. Right now we need to cover more important and immediate things, like getting you checked out on your own personal communicator."

Alan gestured to David, who scooped up the typical-looking mobile device off the table in front of him and tossed it to Alan, who handed it to Jax. It looked just like his iPhone, but lighter and with a leathery texture.

Mary, the communications expert, rolled her chair over to Jax. "First, let's program it to your touch and your voice." She held down a few keys and said, "Okay, say anything you want into it."

"Anything you want into it," quipped Jax. He was pumped.

Mary looked at Suzy, "Is he always a smart ass?"

Suzy just smiled maternally and shrugged one shoulder.

"Sorry," said Jax. "I always wanted to do that. Let's try it again. I'll be good."

"No need," said Mary. "That's all it needed." She handed the phone to him. "And that's all it needed for your touch, too. Bio-metrics. Please tap the SEND button."

Jax obliged.

"Now, if anyone else picks up your phone, it will appear dead and useless. We learned the need for that feature from Ned Wilson's abduction. In the meantime, it is always emitting a homing signal that we can track from this room or from any family member's phone. We will always know where you are."

Jax wasn't so sure he like that *Big Brother* feature. But he could see the benefit, now that he had joined a family of nice aliens who were being hunted by a race of not-so-nice aliens. "Cool," he said.

Mary took Jax's phone away from him, handed it to Suzy, and tapped some keys. "Now if Suzy needed to use your phone, it would work for her." Mary then handed Suzy's phone to Jax and tapped the same keys. "And now if you needed to use hers. Got it?"

"Got it."

"Okay," continued Mary. "You know the NSA can monitor any phone call they want, so it's a no-brainer that…"

"The Reggs can, too," said Jax.

"Exactly. Obviously they monitor many of Earth's broadcast signals, especially the television broadcasts. It's undoubtedly how they learned English and about our culture. It's how the Mejans did it at first, and Grandma Helen still does to some degree. But these days she finds most of it silly and mundane."

David piped in with a cocky, geeky smile, "We can monitor all cell and landline calls, too, and even pick out specific ones from specific phones." To prove his point, David turned and stroked his PC's keypad. A man's harried voice over an obvious cell phone filled the room, "…we need it here by four-thirty today or McKetchin is taking his account down the street." Another man replied, "Shit, Pete, how am I supposed to do that when I'm up to my ass in …" David cut off the dialog. "And that was from a month ago," he grinned.

Jax's stomach gurgled. Every phone call he had ever made over the course of his adult life was now possibly logged in the Brookfield archives for Alan or Suzy or any of them to peruse at their leisure. But before it got severe enough to require a Tums or another chill pill, Mary mercifully continued the indoctrination.

"So, any call you make with this unit to anyone of us individually or directly here to command central will automatically be encrypted. And there's no chance of it ever being decrypted, even if the Reggs have the most sophisticated software, because of the special algorithm Suzy programmed into it that changes the encryption code every two seconds. Plus, any device capable of picking up our own private frequency would hear only cracking dead air."

Jax turned to stare dumbfounded at his lover. She just shrugged and said, "No big deal. I had help."

Before he could pursue that or what other virtues may be hiding under that modest, hill-Billy-Jean exterior, Mary gently turned Jax's head and attention back to his new uber-smart phone. "To open the bar's back wall like I did to get down here, the code is *-0-*-9. To open the gate to the farm without using the keypad box out there, it's G-A, as in G-A-T-E."

"Easy enough to remember," said Jax.

"Oh, we're just getting warmed up," said Mary.

David snorted.

Chapter 48

Mary went on to show Jax the many functions of this definitely-not-just-another-smart phone. There was detecting the pulse of a Regg scanner within a mile, plus direction and distance. It even had an infrared scanner of its own. The camera had every feature found on typical three-thousand-dollar digital cameras today, including many that aren't, like the 200 megapixels, 100x power zoom lens with laser-lock-on, dead-still stabilization, Dolby surround sound, and super-sensitive night vision in full daylight color.

Everything recorded was automatically transmitted back here to HQ, but he could toggle that off with the touch of a couple keys. He could track any family member's cell phone, call HQ by hitting the 5 key three times, plus all the usual features of speed dialing, caller ID, etc. He also had access to every single App out there, for free. But they seemed vapid by comparison.

"I assume we can also do a video chat via Skype or whatever," said Jax.

That brought another snort from David.

"Yes and no," smiled Mary. "Just push the SEND key twice during a conversation and you'll see whatever the other person's camera lens is pointing at. But it won't be anything as low-tech as Skype. We have our own system and frequency. It never pixelates, you can zoom in, you can pan, you can have a conference call with any number of the family. No sign up, no monthly fee."

"Just a long-term agreement required," smiled Jax, winking at Suzy. This was one contract he was happy to sign.

If Jax thought his technology cup was overflowing, he was about to have it gushing like Mentos in a Diet Coke. It required going outside to the playground area behind the house. By now Mary had things to do, so she stayed back with David in the comm.

As Suzy looked on with an informed smile, Alan had Jax push #-#-0-0-7 on his key pad. There was a faint charging sound as the screen opened, showing what the camera was currently pointing at, plus crosshairs.

"Put the crosshairs on that soccer ball," said Alan.

He did.

"Now push the 7 key again."

He did. A barely audible beep sounded and a red dot appeared in the center of the ball.

"It's now locked on the ball. Push the 7 one more time."

Jax did as directed and the ball took off as if bent like Beckham, bouncing off the privacy fence by the pool a hundred feet away.

"Holy Mother of God!" laughed Jax in utter disbelief. "How the hell?"

"Sound," said Alan. "Plain old sound, concentrated along an invisible, high-powered laser-type beam. And, ironically, no noise. Not a peep. Just the percussion of the pulse hitting the ball."

"And no recoil, either," said Jax, the hunter and owner of an arsenal of pistols, shotguns and high-powered rifles that all have some degree of kick. He just kept shaking his head, staring down at the killer super phone in his hand. "This is the most incredible thing I've ever seen. How'd you ever come up with this?

Suzy snuggled up to the arm Jax wasn't using at the moment, and said, "You wouldn't believe it if we told you, honey."

"Try me," said Jax, zapping the soccer ball again, and howling again.

Suzy looked at her father for permission. He nodded.

"What we didn't play for you downstairs from the Ned Wilson 1992 file was the audio of his communication with his parents just before the Reggs captured him. He was saying that he had been hit in the shoulder and leg by something that felt like a hard snowball. It paralyzed him in those areas of his body."

"Permanently?" asked Jax, blasting the kids' swing, making it wrap around the high horizontal bar three times. He chuckled like a cartoon villain.

"We don't know, but probably not. Anyway, this made his family heavily suspect the Reggs had the same kind of sound technology that they themselves—with a little help—were close to constructing."

"Help? From Whom?" Clean over the privacy fence and into the pool went a plastic bucket from the sandbox. He hadn't had this much fun since his father took him and his brand new twenty-two rifle—along with a box of empty pop bottles—to outside the city limits fifteen years ago.

Suzy glanced at her dad again. He nodded again.

"You've heard about the famous Roswell incident, I'm sure."

"Who hasn't?" said Jax, searching for another helpless target. "Allegedly an alien space craft crashed in the New Mexico desert in 1947. All kinds of government cover-up and secrecy. A couple aliens aboard were killed."

"It wasn't true."

"I didn't think so, said Jax, placing the crosshairs on one end of the teeter totter.

"They *weren't* killed. They survived. And they were Mejans."

Chapter 49

Jax didn't fire. He let Suzy's words sink in, then did one of those Vaudeville head bob-and-scoops to end up facing her straight on. He didn't even know what to ask.

"That's right," smiled Suzy, amused at how high her future husband's bushy eyebrows had raised on his forehead. "A small, two-man Mejan scout vessel lost power and crashed. The rancher who found them wounded and dazed called the Air Force and they were taken to a secret base."

"Area 51," speculated Jax.

"Nope. I said a *secret* base. Area 51 is—for all intents and purposes— a decoy. They do some clandestine work there, like with stealth and prototype aircraft, but in terms of present-day technology, it's decades behind. And on purpose."

"So, you're saying Mejans have been working with the government ever since?"

"Well, most of the original Mejans have passed away. But their children and now grandchildren still are."

"Obviously they've mated with humans."

"Most did and do. Until an offspring is more human than Mejan, he or she needs to breathe five to ten percent more nitrogen than is found naturally in the Earth's atmosphere. So they need special equipment…"

"Like a gasmask?" interrupted Jax. "Like Greenhouse Granny?"

"Yes," conceded Suzy with a patient smile, "like *Greenhouse Granny.* May I continue?"

"Please do." Jax was feeling a little self-satisfaction. Allergies indeed!

"A few of the original Mejans chose to not mate with humans, sticking instead with their own kind in order to preserve the purity of the Mejan race. That was fine with everyone, because it also meant preserving their superior mental abilities. A pure Mejan's IQ is off the charts. They make Mensa look like a gaggle of geese."

"Wow."

"Where do you think all this technology in the past sixty years has come from?" posed Alan. "Nuclear power, the transistor, the computer, the integrated circuit, microchips, stealth, the internet, cell phones, stem cells, DNA double helix, vaccines…the list is endless."

"But a lot of that technology has come from other countries, not just the U. S." challenged Jax.

"It's a global community these days, sweetheart," said Suzy. "They shared the initial discoveries with our NATO allies like Great Britain and Germany, and we've worked together ever since."

"Does that mean there are other secret bases all over the world?"

"Of course."

"Jesus!" said Jax, running a hand through his flaxen, wavy hair. "How many of them…er..you…er…*us* are there on Earth these days?"

Suzy pulled out her own communicator and punched a few keys. "Let's see, counting you and me….three million, four hundred thousand, two hundred and eight. Wait, make that two hundred and nine. One of us just had a baby. Oops, there goes another one. Two hundred and ten."

"Man!" breathed Jax. "That means the odds are somebody I know in town is part Mejan." Jax's brain began profiling everyone he knew for an oversized head and big, round eyes.

"There are a few," said Alan, "plus those pure humans like us married or partnered with a hybrid. No need to list them now. You'll learn about them as needed. For now, suffice it to say Iowa City is one of two hubs in Iowa. The other is another farm north of Des Moines. We have a lot of key people in key places: judges, police, doctors, senators, professors, brick layers, heavy machine operators, you name it. And we are adding more each day."

"And now you have an *outdoor writer*," said Jax inanely, feeling like the ugly girl in the beauty pageant.

"And now we have the *best* outdoor writer in the world," corrected Suzy with a kiss. "And the handsomest."

Jax didn't feel vindicated. Alan Brookfield's face remained expressionless, but Jax could feel the disgust.

Chapter 50

The Reggs were getting nervous. They needed to get their hands on another Mejan of any degree, and soon. Their computer models revealed a strong probability that as of 2015 the number of Mejan-human crossbreeds and all their human mates had swelled to about three million world-wide and well over one million here in the United States alone. If left unchecked, that number would grow exponentially to a point where it would soon be almost impossible to reach their goal of colonizing Earth unopposed. They needed to find a way to start eradicating the Mejans en masse, or at the very least sterilizing them.

The Reggs didn't know the Mejans even existed until 1970, when one of the many human guinea pigs they were systematically plucking from isolated cars and homes turned out to be far different than any human they had abducted before. This female, aged twenty-two, named Maggie Connors, had huge blue eyes recessed into a bulbous head atop a ninety-pound body. With their usual probes, needles, tubes, and electrodes, plus a highly-effective truth potion the CIA would kill to get their hands on, the Reggs learned this human was half-Mejan, a race that had come to Earth in 1945.

While the Reggs were always searching out new planets to conquer and exploit, the Mejans had a far different agenda: survival. As their home planet, Meja, had been slowly widening its orbit around its sun over many millennia, each new generation of Mejan developed larger and larger pupils to compensate for the fading sunlight. During the final centuries they had gone underground for the geothermal heat in a desperate attempt to avoid extinction. But without adequate solar radiation to maintain their planet's food and resources, they knew their race would eventually die out in the dark tombs of their own making.

So, all their energies and intellect were put to finding new homes. Most ships were launched toward a neighboring solar system known to have planets with the potential to support life. But Maggie's parents and shipmates had worked on a different concept: inter-*dimensional* travel. They theorized that by changing anything's vibration to a different, highly-intensive and sustained frequency, it would instantly skip into any dimension operating at that same megahertz.

It worked, first with small objects, then with one brave Mejan himself, holding on for dear life to a hand-held prototype programmed to return him in ten seconds. So, without even leaving their underground facility on Meja, the enormous spacecraft with dozens of daughter ships onboard and over a thousand Mejan pilgrims, found themselves evaporating through the space time continuum and rematerializing at the bottom of the Atlantic Ocean on the planet Earth in 1945, twenty years after the Reggs had arrived.

Maggie Connor's disclosures proved a little disconcerting to the Reggs. Throughout their own history of bouncing from planet to planet within the Milky Way galaxy at half the speed of light, any civilizations they encountered were always far inferior in all aspects and easily conquered. The Reggs didn't want to annihilate them, just most of them, while controlling the rest. As lazy as they are barbaric, they needed the natives to do all the menial work, mainly of producing food and keeping the planet in good working order, while the Reggs feed on the produce and livestock at their leisure. Consequently, they've had no reason to upgrade their technology, including their weaponry. No planet ever had the potential to fight back. Until maybe now.

It was clear the average Mejan intellect was superior to the average Regg intellect, along the ratio of a dolphin to a carp. Equally clear, the Mejans were mating with the Earthlings, as a means of saving their race. With time and cross-breeding, they hoped to acclimate to the new atmosphere and environment, thereby living on the Earth in synergy...not off of it in hostility, like the Reggs.

They also learned from Maggie that she had been conceived in a test tube and raised on a farm hundreds of miles away in northern California. The farm setting was important, as it afforded growing food to be self-sufficient, while remaining reclusive until future generations could become human enough to blend into society.

Maggie didn't know where the mother ship was. She had never been told. She did reveal the presence of the block-long daughter ship buried on the farm. The Reggs scouted the area, but were unable to locate it. At that time they were a little afraid of the unknown potential of the Mejans and their craft, so they never really pushed the issue, opting to just keep an eye on that farm. A top priority was and still is to remain covert in all respects: the less the human race knew about them the better, until the time came. Besides, they already had a Mejan, who they kept for ongoing reference onboard their mothership...hiding at the bottom of the Pacific Ocean...five miles off the Oregon coast...in six hundred feet of water...at the eastern tip of the Astoria Canyon.

Chapter 51

Maggie Connors died just two years later. Her body was too frail and stringy to eat, so they sent it through the pulverizer and jettisoned the chum out into the ocean to join the food pyramid. Just another missing person that would never be found.

Perhaps the most helpful tidbit gleaned from Maggie back then in 1970 was that her body temperature averaged 95.5 degrees, a full three degrees below a typical human's. That wasn't surprising, seeing how her parents came from a cold, dying planet. That fact—plus the obviously large cranium—set the Regg scientists working on an infrared scanner that not only could detect those small differences in body temperature, but the head-to-body ratio, as well. The idea was to locate the Mejan hotspots, keep track of their numbers, plot, and correlate their movements and activities. In short, to learn all they could about the probable foe.

The plan worked well for a couple decades, until suddenly their scanners were no longer locating many Mejans. The conclusion was drawn that the Mejans had developed instrumentation that could detect their infrared scans from a distance and had gone *underground* to avoid further exposure. So, the Reggs needed to capture another Mejan for interrogation to see how much the race had advanced technologically and to get an update on their mission.

Before that mass disappearance, the Reggs had noticed a number of crossbreeds in the Champaign, Illinois, area, presumably looking for young, viable mates, which always ran in large quantities in college town environs. So, pairs of Regg scouts paroled downtown Champaign on foot with hand-held scanners. They hoped just short, random blasts at regular intervals would be enough to locate anyone with a slightly lower body temperature and a disproportionately bigger head. And if they were really fortunate, it would set off any infrared detector warning system the semi-Mejan may have on their person. That meant if a short scan sent someone suddenly running, there was an excellent chance he or she would be their sought-after Mejan subject.

Since a Regg's exterior looks quite different from a human's, heavy disguises were needed: long coats from neck to ankles, caps, dark glasses, gloves, all in black, plus masks with humanoid features. Such outerwear was not conducive to the streets of a college town, especially during daylight hours in warm weather, so their search was confined to winter nights. It took over a month of walking the streets in the winter of 1992, but it finally paid off when they flushed out Ned Wilson and brought him back to the ship.

Via their usual methods, they discovered he was seventy-five percent human. This was somewhat expected, as it had been more than a couple decades since securing their other Mejan captive, Maggie, who was fifty-fifty. Ned was obviously the next generation, and he had been searching for a human female with which to procreate.

They learned his intelligence quotient was a little less than Maggie's, which still made the Reggs mental midgets by comparison. Equally troubling was they couldn't get Ned's captured device to work. They had hoped to reverse engineer it, which would have provided a wealth of information about the Mejans' current technology. But apparently that technology included becoming dysfunctional if access was attempted by anyone except Ned, and it melted down completely when they tried to open it to explore its infrastructure.

Now here it was, 2015, twenty-three years later, and they had learned practically nothing more about the Mejans, their current technology, their actual numbers, their goals. Fear of the unknown had the Reggs mumbling. They needed to secure another Mejan crossbreed and fast.

Chapter 52

Jax was leaning forward in his high-back, executive chair, chin in palms, elbows on mahogany desk, staring at the blank Word page on the computer monitor. The little cursor in the upper left hand blinked monotonously, waiting for the start of his next weekly outdoor column. It would have to continue waiting. Writing about his beloved fishing and hunting seemed blasé after what he'd learned in the past eighteen hours.

He is going to be a *father*! He couldn't be happier. It still hadn't completely sunk in. His future wife is an alien. Well, only an eighth of her, so that's not so bad, is it? Hell, he himself is part German, part Irish, with a fair chunk of Navaho in there someplace. We can't all be purebreds. America is built on its diversity.

His new smart phone was so far beyond smart it was borderline genius. He'd been practicing with its features ever since he got home at noon. He hoped Odett didn't see him irrigate the flowerbed with about fifty gallons of displaced pool water. And he never did like that wooden wren house only sparrows ever occupied. It was now tinder.

He was a little apprehensive about its having a homing beacon. Now HQ could track him virtually anywhere, as long as he wasn't inside heavy metal or concrete. All things considered, probably not a bad idea. Still, just the thought that anyone at the farm—and especially his future father-in-law, Alan Brookfield—was capable of knowing that at this very moment he was at home, in his den, not doing anything requiring mobility and therefore presumably sitting on his ass, gave Jax the willies.

Thinking of which, Jax had also discovered that Brookfield Farm is just another Iowa farm about as much as Meryl Streep is just another actress. *Jesus!* It has its own spacecraft hidden around there somewhere. It has its own alien for a gardener. It has its own underground communication center that can hack into just about every conceivable data source in the world. It's a breeding ground for Mejans trying to integrate with humans. *And it may be Earth's only hope for salvation!*

"Sure, and my role is to tell a couple readers how to catch crappies," sighed Jax, slumping back in his chair and staring at the ceiling.

That had been weighing heavily on his mind for the past hour, but the seed was actually planted earlier this morning out at the farm's playground, when Alan and Suzy were explaining things to him. It seemed everyone else in the family has a special talent…is an expert in one field or another…serves a real purpose for the cause…is way out of his league.

So, what's *his* purpose. Where's *his* expertise? Well, let's see. If the Reggs ever invade the farm, he could quickly catch a bass and bitch-slap them to death with it. Better yet, he could run back here to his computer and write a column about them so scathing they'd jump in their ships red-faced and zoom back to where they came from, whining that Earth is too mean. How about…."

Oh, Suzy Q, I love you…

The ringtone wrenched him out of his thoughts and jump-started his heart. Recalling the video-activation sequence, he punched it and her cute face appeared on his small screen. "Hi, babe," he said. "I've missed you."

"Me, too," she replied, "What's it been…three hours?"

"Seems like days."

"I know. How you coming on your column?"

"Slow. After everything you guys dumped on me this morning, I can't think of anything interesting to write about…at least not in the world of the great outdoors. I feel like I should be doing a crossover piece like, *Using the Mejan Mind Meld to Locate Trophy Trout*."

"Well, actually," chuckled Suzy, "if you really want to know…"

"No! I don't want to know," interrupted Jax. "My little brain couldn't possibly absorb anything more." There was a two-second pause. "Besides," he said a little quieter in case someone was listening, "there isn't *really* a way to do that. *Is there?*"

"We can talk about it later, hon," said Suzy, quickly skirting the issue, for her lover's sake. "You need to get your article done and your rock-hard buns back here for supper. I'm going nuts without you."

"Tell me about it."

Jax could hear Alan saying something in the background. Suzy turned her head and replied to her dad with a muffled, "Really? Oh, he'll love that."

"I'll love what?" Jax asked before she was back facing him.

"Dad says he'll take you for a ride tonight after dark."

"A ride? Where? You've shown me most of the farm."

"Hardly," she laughed.

"There's more underground, isn't there? I thought so."

"Underground and above ground," replied Suzy with a smirk.

Only a one second pause this time. "You don't mean…" gasped Jax, "…a ride in the…"

"Dinner's at six," grinned his fiancée. Chicken ala Suzy." And she clicked off.

Chapter 53

As they crossed the clean cement floor, past the Holstein milk cows, to the locked tack room, Patrick Jackson walked a half step behind and to the left of Alan Brookfield. Expecting the farm's patriarch to work the padlock's combination to gain access, he was mildly surprised when Alan simply punched a few keys on his phony iPhone and the door popped open along a hidden seam. The padlock and latch were still in place, just window dressing.

"The code is T-A-C-K-#-# or if you prefer, 8-2-2-5-#-#," said Alan. Jax committed it to memory. But the possibility that he would ever have to use it on his own due to some alien emergency made his stomach churn.

The two men stepped inside and over to the far right corner. The door behind them automatically sealed itself tight. Alan took hold of Jax's arm to position themselves between two wooden sawhorses adorned with beautiful, polished leather saddles. Jax could get only a quick look around at the other leather goods hanging from hooks and some containers stacked in the corners before Alan nudged his attention to the iPhone.

"Just 8-3-6," he said, tapping the keys, and the floor began to drop out from under them. "If you can't remember that, just remember *U-F-O*."

Jax may have been going down, but his heart stayed up top. *They really were heading for the Brookfield Farm starship!*

The floor of the tack room above them closed quietly, as the three-second drop on the wooden platform with only the sawhorses and saddles for walls landed them at the start of an underground tunnel. Seven feet tall and twelve feet wide, the square, tubular cavern was concrete on all four sides and painted smooth with light-gray exterior latex. The reason the air was surprisingly dry for being fifteen feet under moist Iowa soil was evidenced by the slow turning fan blades of the exhaust fan in the ceiling directly above them.

A motion detector changed the row of LED lights running down the center of the ceiling from a dim-orange glow to a brighter white, revealing more exhaust fans. The pair settled into one of the two electric golf carts and began the journey of one hundred yards down the chute to true science fiction.

As they reached the end, Alan showed Jax that he was hitting just the *SEND* key, and a light-gray ramp dropped from the same colored ceiling. The gaping entryway lit up, and the golf cart drove right up the five-degree incline into the belly of the craft. The ramp closed behind them with a hydraulic hiss, as the white walls surrounding them glowed brighter.

"Welcome to an authentic Mejan spacecraft," announced a proud Alan. "We call her *Maude*."

Predictably, there was no response from the slack-jawed mouth of a mystified Jax.

"This is just a storage area," continued Alan, pointing at some square, shiny metal containers stacked along the walls. "That door back there leads to the sleeping quarters, dining area, recreation room…those kind of things where the original Mejans—Suzy's great-grandparents—stayed until landing here on the farm…or I should say *under* it. Beyond that is the engine room that runs everything."

"What's the… power source…" asked Jax, curious enough to find his voice, "nuclear fusion or something?"

"I would never understand it," said Alan, honestly, "even if someone around here knew enough to explain it to me, which no one does. Some translations of the Mejan chronicles we have on computer say it has something to do with drawing upon the invisible dark energy that makes up ninety-five percent of the Cosmos, and somehow generating matter-anti-matter in front and behind the craft to propel it at whatever speed and in whatever direction you want. The energy source seems to be unlimited and is literally astronomical."

"Could we go back there and look around?" queried Jax, not sure he really wanted to at the moment.

"Maybe some other time," said Alan. "More important things to see tonight."

"Yeah," grinned Jax, a twinge of excitement beginning to elbow in on his nerves, as he dared to envision them launching this incredible craft into the heavens and running circles around the moon.

Alan Brookfield bid his wide-eyed, future son-in-law to exit the cart and follow him hunched over toward another elevator platform. The ribbed metal ceiling was only six feet high, two inches shorter than both men.

"Remember," said Alan, climbing on the platform, "the Mejans who built this thing were only about five feet tall at the most."

They rode up to the craft's second and last level and stepped off the platform, still having to bend at the neck. Spread before them was a dimly-lighted room not much larger than the Brookfield's kitchen. Alan hit a light switch on a nearby panel and the textured walls glowed to a soft white. Into view came a console lined with inactive dials and screens and knobs, plus a few chartreuse, pinhead lights similar to those letting you know your PC's keyboard is ready when you are.

Two small, slate-blue captain's chairs on swiveling pedestals waited for their occupants. Forward of the console the entire wall appeared to be made of some dark, poly-carbonate glass, presumably a windshield, the exterior presently shielded by whatever retractable metal substance the ship was made of.

"This is the control center, the bridge," said Alan, stating the obvious. "Hasn't been used in over twenty years."

Jax's heart had finally caught up to him, but it was now lodged in his throat. "Do you actually know how to fly this thing?" he swallowed, still in awe.

"Oh, I could if I had to," surmised Alan, not with the most confidence in his voice. "Mary knows more about it than I do. She was taught by her mother, Helen. Then Mary taught me. Just simulation, of course."

"Then how are we going to take it out tonight?" Jax asked suspiciously, rubbing his fingers over the leathery texture of one of the captain's chairs. "Is Mary coming?"

"We're not taking it anywhere," said Alan curtly. "This craft is here to stay. Unless there was some kind of an emergency. In case you haven't figured it out, we're well underground."

"But I thought…"

"Relax," said Alan, stepping toward a door on the rear wall, which slid open with a quiet *whoosh* at his approach. He stepped through and motioned for Jax to join him. "Come on. *You*, especially, will get a kick out of this."

Chapter 54

The next bump on a light switch revealed just about the last thing Jax ever expected to see inside a vehicle from some distant planet. On a knee-high, brushed aluminum table sat an aquarium, about ten feet long, four feet tall and perhaps five feet in breadth. From a vibrating box the size and look of a toaster ran a one-inch-diameter, clear plastic tube up to the tank's black cover, through a hole and down to an aeration stone, spraying tiny bubbles back to the surface. A larger, corrugated tube siphoned water into a charcoal filter system beside the vibrating box, and a third one pumped the purified water back into the aquarium. There were a couple other tubes attached to apparatuses with no immediate indication of their purpose.

When Alan turned a rheostat knob on a control panel beside the tank, a series of blue, ultraviolet lamps running the length of its black hood brightened enough to reveal a largemouth bass of about three pounds hanging suspended in the middle, its pectoral fins barely moving to keep it in place. One black eye moved around, checking out the intruders in the new light of simulated dawn.

"What the f....?" was the only thing Jax's bewildered brain could come with.

"It's called a bass," mocked Alan. "Ever seen one before?"

Not taking the bait, the outdoor writer moved in for a closer look at his favorite quarry. "What is it doing in *here*?"

"Look closer," said Alan, "and you'll notice a cloud of bass fry just above momma."

"Obviously you're raising bass for your pond," said Jax, noting the bottom of the tank was covered with pea gravel along with an assortment of ceramic tree branches and plastic plants to make the bass feel more secure. "But why in the spaceship?"

"As you already know," explained Alan, "we eat the bass, as part of a well-rounded diet. We picked the largemouth for its adaptability, hardiness, its quality meat and good taste. And because of the special, controlled diet we feed them, they are extremely high in nutrition and low in fats and carbs. Everything on this farm falls into that category, from the corn and beans to the livestock. I don't need to tell you the benefits of eating healthy, do I?"

"No, but..."

"In this controlled environment," continued the farmer/rancher, who apparently also farmed and ranched *fish*, "we can better maintain and monitor the bass's diet and water conditions, and thereby its growth and health."

He pointed to the computer monitor beside the tank, which Jax slid over to inspect. It was showing the water temperature to be *72.2* F, O2 was *10.6 ppm*, pH at *6.9*, the bass's weight was *3 lbs, 1 oz*, the number of fry was *132* and averaging *1.1 inches* in length. At the bottom of the screen a timer showed the fry's next feeding of zoo- and phytoplankton would be in *1:35 hours* and the adult's feeding of *HN-283 pellets* was not for another *7.23 days*. Jax knew that fry eat almost continually, while a special hormone prevents the adult from wanting to feed while guarding its young. Otherwise, there would be no young.

"Amazing!" whispered Jax, his nose pressed against the glass. "So this is why your bass get so big so fast."

"And when the young ones are big enough to restock the pond, I push a couple buttons and they are easily transported upward through that apparatus there at the far end of the aquarium."

That took a moment to sink in. "You mean the pond is directly *above* us?" Jax's head jerked upward.

"I thought you'd have that figured out by now," said Alan contemptuously. "Oh, that's right. You're a college graduate. Let me explain it to you."

Chapter 55

Jax scanned the ceiling, looking for a clue that wasn't there. "Yeah, guess I am dumber than I look," he conceded humorlessly. Bringing his gaze back down, he fixated on the odd-looking vacuum-water-lock transport contraption Alan was pointing at. Upon closer inspection he saw how the bass would swim through a two-foot-diameter hole in the glass to enter the slightly larger, vertical cylinder that ran all the way up...*sure enough,* right through the ceiling. Alan explained that going through stages similar to the airlock system astronauts use for spacewalks, once the water pressure in the chute is equalized, the bass simply swim upward and into the pond at their leisure.

Jax was suddenly hit with a revelation he didn't much care for: obviously Alan wasn't the neophyte angler he pretended to be that day they met at the pond. In fact, he probably knew more about the largemouth bass and catching them than Jax did himself. It followed then that Suzy also knew a lot more about the piscatorial pursuits than she let on. When Jax called him on this, Alan verified Jax's suspicions: the whole reason Alan asked for fishing tips that day was to sneak one of Jax's hairs off his collar for DNA analysis. The same held true for his asking Jax to give Suzy a fishing lesson: she needed to somehow score a sample of his blood.

If Jax thought he couldn't feel any stupider in the company of the Brookfields, he was just proven wrong...*again.* They had played him like the rookie he was from day-one. Right down the line they were all good actors. Liars, actually. If he wasn't so in love with Suzy, and so excited about his soon-to-come child...well...who knows what he might do.

"Don't take it personally," placated Alan, giving Jax a playful bump on his shoulder. "Before letting you into the family, we had to know everything about you ...right down to your brand of toilet paper. It's not exactly a book club we're running here."

Jax's sneer turned to a wry smile. "That's for damn sure!" he hooted sarcastically. "More like black ops. Or a super-secret, underground branch of the CIA or NSA." Jax gave a snort. "Did I say, *Underground.* There's a laugh...considering we're in a Mejan spaceship under a block-long, ten-foot-deep pond in the middle of a cow pasture? Now that's *underground.*"

Alan waited patiently for the young Jackson to finish blowing. He couldn't blame him.

"And while on the subject," continued Jax without missing beat, "why in hell did you build the pond on top of a hill? I understand the hill: it's hiding a two-story spaceship. But why put a pond on top of the ship, the hill, for Christ's sake? Why not in a more practical location, like in the meadow on the other side of the hill? This brood aquarium could have been in, say, the barn. Then you could have easily transported the bass in a cooler or plastic bag and tossed them in the ground-level pond. But instead, I assume you cut an unnecessary hole in a spacecraft's perfectly good hull just to install an elaborate release system like this?"

"Well," said Alan, "besides hiding its presence from passersby, another advantage of being high on a hill is it saves the pond from any watershed runoff. So, very few impurities or chemicals can wash in after a rain. This keeps the water much cleaner and the bass much healthier." Alan edged past his incredulous tagalong toward the next door at the end of the room. "But you do have a point," he added. "If the pond were only for the fish, it would be kind of superfluous. But having Maude directly under the pond serves another purpose."

"And what might that be?"

"Easier to show you than tell you," said Harrison Ford in "*Sabrina*," as the door opened into the next room. "Get your nose back in joint and come on."

Chapter 56

Remember when Jax's heart was left back in the tack room elevator before finally catching up to him on the ship's bridge? It just went back to the tack room, hiding behind a stack of containers. He was introduced to the two-man Mejan scout vessel, similar to the one that crashed at Roswell sixty-eight years ago. Approximately forty feet long, ten feet wide, and similar to the low-slung styling of a DirecTV's remote control, the craft's exterior was seamless from fore to aft. The super-smooth surface was counter-shaded with a charcoal topside and sky blue underside. Its oblong, canopy bubble—running perpendicular across the chassis and only ten feet from the nose—was perfectly translucent, providing a clear, three-sixty view.

Jax ran a tentative finger along its hull to discover a slick feel with virtually no texture. He banged it hard with his knuckles; it made a dull, almost inaudible thump, like hitting an empty barrel with a Nerf football.

A smirking Alan suddenly and uncharacteristically craned his head sideways as far as he could, mimicking John Hurt's outer space, upside-down position when he offered an invitation to Jody Foster in the movie *Contact*. "Wanna take a ride?" he grinned sinisterly. It was becoming clearer that Alan—like his daughter and sons—was a movie buff, too. Jax figured it must be from all those dull, surveillance shifts each of the Brookfield have to take in the communications room with little else to do but watch HBO and Starz.

As the translucent canopy swung open on its hinges like a Venus flytrap, Jax backed away. Up until this point there had always been that safe element of *fantasy*... one of those *its-never-going-to-happen-anyway-so-no-harm-pretending* fantasies. But there was nothing imaginary about this spacecraft. It was as real as the twisting knot in his stomach.

As Alan ushered his uptight co-pilot around to the other side and helped him slide his big frame into the small cockpit, Jax almost screamed when he settled in. Just *seeing* the craft was bad enough, now actually feeling its interior wrap around him made this thing as terrifying as Alan's obvious intention to fly it. Oh, and there was another vessel—*Scout-Two*, he was told—resting thirty feet away. There couldn't be *two* of these things in his fantasy.

Alan hopped in the other side and poked a few buttons. The canopy closed over the pair and a large quantity of methane gas released from

Jax's rectum. Thankfully, some kind of air conditioning unit kicked on just in time. An array of low-light, colorful dials blinked on, including a television screen for each occupant. There was a barely audible hum, presumably the craft's engine powering up. Alan reached over and brought a double-shoulder harness around him and clicked it into the single buckle. He suggested Jax quickly find his and do the same.

"Look up," suggested Alan, pushing yet another button. As they began to lift quietly off the floor and toward the ceiling, a portal just slightly larger than their vessel opened without sound. The ship rose steadily into the dark hole until another portal opened revealing a sky full of stars.

When the ship had cleared the chute and drifted a few yards above and to one side, Alan announced he was turning on the night vision and that Jax should poke the bottom of his television screen to see from what they had just emerged. Jax's trembling finger ignited the image of the oblong chute that was sticking a few feet above the surface in the middle of the pond's southern half. The pilot pushed another button and the tube closed and descended back into the black water.

"Pretty slick, huh?" said Alan. "Now maybe you understand why we use the pond, rather than the ground. Water covers the launch portal right back up. Dirt, not so much. The original Mejans learned this the hard way. Their first daughter ships—like Maude down there—were about three feet underground, using natural grass and dirt to cover the scout ships launching portals. But with each opening and closing, crap easily got caught in the mechanism. Then there was the ongoing issue of rain and wind constantly eroding the natural cover. So Launching from ground required a lot of maintenance. The solution was to launch from at least ten feet of water. Easy in and easy out for the scout craft, plus that kind of depth was enough to deflect just about any kind of nosy scanner: electromagnetic, sonar, you name it."

Jax could only nod like a bobblehead. Below him—lit up in full color on the twelve-inch HD screen, as if it were daytime, when in reality it was the middle of a dark night—was the very pond where he had caught his eight-pound bass...the shoreline where he had met Suzy...where they had spent hours fishing and laughing...and other things. That one-acre pond certainly *was* more than a fish factory. It was a clever, well-disguised launching point for a spacecraft from another world. Who would have thought?

"Phone on," commanded Alan.

"Hello, Alan," replied a sultry, female voice.

"Call Mary."

"Calling Mary."

"Hi, honey," came Mary's voice, as clearly as if she were sitting right between them. "You boys having fun?"

"I am," laughed Alan. "Not so sure about my copilot at the moment."

"So, Jax, what do you think of our little toy spaceship?" she asked.

Speech was not on Jax's list of capabilities at the moment. He just blathered softly.

"He thinks it's great," translated Alan for him.

"Well, keep an eye on my husband for me, Jax," she said. "He tends to black out when he flies that thing."

Jax's eyes became wide and rotated to fix hard on Alan.

"She's just kidding," smiled Alan. "Tell him, hon, before he hits the ejection button and drowns."

"Just kidding, Jax," laughed Mary. "He's a great pilot."

Relief washed over Jax's face. He let out some air.

"Okay, hon," said Alan. "See you in a few hours."

"I'll be watching the grid," she replied. "Love ya."

Chapter 57

Alan nudged Jax to look over at what he was holding in his right hand. "I fly the ship from this little joystick," he said, "much like you do with your video games. Forward, back, left, right. And the more I push it in one direction, the faster it obeys. The upper part of this toggle switch on the front of the stick takes us up and the bottom half takes us down. Got it?"

Jax showed some improving mental acumen with a soft grunt.

"Hold on," warned Alan. "I'll take us up to one thousand feet."

The thrill Jax's stomach experienced was more intense than the Raging Bull roller coaster at Six Flag in Chicago his folks had taken him to when he was twelve. "Oh, my living Lord!" he gasped, rolling his eyes.

"It speaks," said the pilot.

"It might also throw up," said Jax taking a deep breath and swallowing back some chicken ala Suzy.

"If your eyes and brain are still functioning, flick that orange switch on the dash between us."

Jax did and another screen rotated into position at the center of the console. A green line swept around the grid like a fast second hand on a clock, showing a single, moving blip with numbers beside it at about two o'clock.

"Standard radar," said Alan. "Will pick up anything within a thousand-mile radius. That blip is a small plane just leaving the Cedar Rapids airport. It will probably go to twenty thousand feet. We'll stay well below that at about five thousand feet. That is our usual cruising altitude. It keeps us below most air traffic and above most birds and bugs. And even if something was in our path, the ship's collision-avoidance system would automatically steer us out of the way by many miles."

"You mean collision- *and* detection-avoidance, right?" mumbled Jax, his inquisitive mind beginning to function again.

"Very good. The less people know about something like this the better. They are convinced enough without us proving it to them."

Alan took the ship gradually up to five thousand feet, tapped more buttons, and the Mejan scout vessel took off to the west, slowly building speed.

"But aren't we detectable on radar, too?" asked Jax.

"Nope. Complete stealth, far better than even the B-1 Bomber."

"The Reggs have stealth, too, right?"

"Unfortunately, yes. And it seems to be just as good as ours."

"But we can still be seen visually," surmised Jax, "if someone were looking right at us, right?"

"True, but even if we were going only, say, fifty miles an hour and someone was looking up as we passed overhead, all they'd see is a moving black hole in the sky, temporarily blocking out the stars. And by the time they blinked, we'd be gone. Besides, UFO watchers are usually looking for funny lights doing funny things in the sky. Why? I have no idea."

"But I noticed the underside of this craft was a light blue," offered Jax. "Wouldn't that tend to show up at night, especially if it reflected city lights?"

"Excellent question, Luke Skywalker," said Alan. "That's why I flicked this little switch here just before we left. It changed the underside to midnight black. The light blue is only for daytime travel. And we do as little of that as possible, just to be safe."

"So, how fast does this thing go?" queried Jax, as he checked a round dial that read *110 mph* and increasing.

"I'm told it can do Mach-ten," chuckled Alan sinisterly, dying to test the theory. "But we are under strict orders to stay under Mach-one to avoid a sonic boom. Even this futuristic piece of hardware has to abide by the laws of physics. We could go up into the thinner ionosphere where the air displacement would be far less and the quieter boom wouldn't reach the ground, but that is also frowned upon. So we're going to stay at five thousand feet and cruise at seven hundred and fifty miles per hour, just below Mach-one. I'm increasing our speed gradually so the Gs don't shove us through our seats."

"We going anyplace in particular?" asked Jax, studying the various dials and gauges, getting a little more comfortable in the adventure."

"Yep," said Alan. "We're going to pick up a package of upgraded equipment, compliments once again of our Meja-Earth engineers in the desert.

"Cool. How often do you make these runs?"

"Not that often," said Alan. "Usually it's a software upgrade that we just download from *The Desert*, as we like to call it. But when it's a new piece of small equipment like tonight, we usually go get it. They don't exactly deliver via FedEx."

"How do you know where to go?"

"The exact coordinates have already been programmed into the ship's guidance system from our desert buddies, so all we have to do is sit back and ol' *Scout-One* here will do the rest. Besides, they don't want us to know where we are going."

"So, this isn't exactly the same scout vessel that came with Maude twenty years ago," proposed Jax. "It's been upgraded."

"Oh, yeah," nodded Alan. "More than once."

"How is that done? I mean, does an upgrade come with an instruction manual and you just slap it in?"

"Well, not by me," laughed Alan. "We have our own guru who knows all this technical crap. Name is Kevin."

"And what planet does *Kevin* come from?" asked Jax dryly.

"He's seventy-five percent human," said Alan. "He teaches at the university's College of Astrophysics. He looks a little Mejan with his big head and eyes, but what would you expect from an egghead college professor with hair down to his shoulders and coke-bottle glasses? Of course, he has to dumb-down his subject matter. The average physics grad student couldn't begin to comprehend much of what Kevin would like to teach."

Chapter 58

For multiple reasons—not the least of which was to stop his passenger from asking any more questions—Alan poked a series of keys on his communicator and "Star Trek, The Motion Picture" faded in on both their television monitors, and Dolby surround sound filled the cockpit. Jax was delighted, because he had seen that particular movie only five or six times, and not once in the past two years. A favorite of Alan's, too, this viewing being his fifth. It became obvious both men had more time on their hands than they were willing to admit.

The two-hour movie concluded just as Scout-One reached its destination, which turned out to be an isolated patch of sand adorned with a single ball of sagebrush in some unnamed desert in the middle of nowhere. The ship's speed had dropped to zero and descended from five thousand feet to just one foot, all on its own. So did Jax's stomach.

He watched with amusement as their individual television screens now showed a hatch on the ship's underside open, a dim flood light snap on, and a mechanical set of jaws like a giant doggy poop-scoop extend. It was heading for a gray plastic container about the size of a pet taxi for a Great Dane wrapped in twin, red nylon straps. It had an oversized barcode on its closest side and a fixed handle recessed into the top. With pure elegance of movement, the jaws engulfed the package and drew it into the ship's belly.

Alan pushed a series of keys on the dash and a soft beep followed. "There," he said. "I just disarmed the self-destruct mechanism."

"In case it fell into the wrong hands," surmised Jax.

"You got it," said Alan, starting Scout-One's slow ascent back to five thousand feet.

"Do you know what this new equipment is for?" asked Jax.

"Uh-huh."

When no other answer was forthcoming: "Well, are you going to tell me or make me guess?"

Alan thought a moment and said, "I'll tell you, but I don't want you getting all spooked again. I forgot to bring any of those anti-chicken shit pills you were popping like candy this morning."

"Let's see," mused Jax, "on top of everything else I learned today, the kicker was that these Reggs, who look like a Tim Burton remake of Teen Wolf, want to destroy all of us and take over the world. Would it be any scarier than that?"

"Well, based on that criterion," smiled Alan, "it actually would be good news."

"So, what *does* this new thing do?"

Alan activated the preset course for home and slumped a little in his captain's chair. He pulled out a pack of Juicy Fruit and offered a stick to his copilot. They both started chewing.

"We know the Reggs are increasing their activity," began Alan. "And by *we* I mean our brain trust, *The Desert People*, who confirm what we at the farm have been suspecting for a few weeks now. Our logic program says there is a sixty-five percent probability the Reggs will soon make a concerted effort to capture anyone with Mejan blood to get some updated intel on us, our numbers, our locations, our weaponry, our IQs, and so on."

"So, this new hardware does what?" asked Jax for the third time.

"You have to remember that the Mejans are a peaceful race," continued Alan, as if he didn't even hear the question. "They abhor violence. So, the weapons on these Scouts, on Maude, in the silo, in our communicators, all have limitations on the amount of damage they could do to someone, or something. You've seen what your communicator can do with its laser-guided acoustic pulse. And I guess I've neglected to tell you it is the same energy principle Maude used to bury herself under the ground twenty years ago: super high-frequency, high-intensity sound waves. Well, let's just say that we are now going to have the option to do more than push around some dirt or knock someone down..."

"We'll be able to blow his ass to Regg hell!" chimed Jax.

"Damn near," grinned Alan, with no attempt to hide his pernicious tone.

"Now that's what I'm talking about!" howled Jax, pounding the leather armrest with his fist.

"I feel the same way," confessed Alan, his enthusiasm rising along with his copilot's. "I guess it's our human nature, but just the thought of one of those hairy motherfuckers touching my wife or kids and..."

"Yes!" interrupted Jax, banging a fist again. "I know exactly what you're saying. Since finding out Suzy is pregnant, I've found myself thinking, *Just try messing with me and mine and I'll empty my Browning twelve gauge into your hideous faces!*"

For the next five minutes and sixty-two miles as the Scout flies, the two, one hundred-percent, testosterone-loaded, human males boisterously exchanged their pent up aggressions and primal urges to vanquish their enemies in the most permanent and bloody fashion allotted them through their combined arsenals of ten rifles, seven shotguns, eight pistols and one crossbow. And now they were being afforded weapons that could dispatch a Regg to ugly dust with the click of a button. *Yeah, Just try and mess with our family!*

It felt good for Alan to have this kind of discussion with a fellow, human male outside of his two teenage boys, even if the guy sitting beside him tonight had already shown he talked a far better game than he walked. But maybe he had changed.

"Tell you what," said Alan, when they'd pretty much run out of macho patter, "push that little button on the side of your right armrest."

Jax felt for it, found it, pushed it, and his own joystick popped up. "Really?" he grinned, his caution well overshadowed by his excitement.

"Really. You need to be schooled on this thing like I was more than a few years ago. Think you can handle it?

"No problemo," seethed Jax, dying to grab it, but waiting for permission. "I've got a Lamborghini, a Corvette Stingray, a twenty-foot Ranger bassboat with a two-hundred-fifty-horse Yamaha outboard, a Super Blackbird motorcycle, and every racing video game ever made."

"Then this will be so simple it will probably bore you."

"I seriously doubt that," said Jax. He took in a big breath. "Let's do it."

"Well, hold on a minute..." Alan opened a flip-top box between their seats and pulled a small, yellow lever. "Just as a precaution..."

"What the hell?" yelled Jax, trying to jump out of his seat in reflex, but finding it impossible to even move.

Chapter 59

Jax was completely engulfed in a pressurized spacesuit—helmet, gloves, boots, the works. And no matter which way he turned his head, the multi-colored, dimly-lit *Heads Up Display* (HUD) across the top of his helmet's face shield followed his eyes. He had instant access to every piece of flight data a pilot could want and need. He looked over at Alan, who had experienced the same puffed up phenomenon, suddenly looking like the Michelin man, except he was laughing while Jax was panicking.

"Talk about your child protection safety seat," Jax heard Alan chuckle clearly inside his helmet. "Our seats are a little more than seats, huh?"

"I feel like I'm thirty feet under water with the pressure pushing on me from all sides," said a frantic Jax. "Is it supposed to be like this? Is there oxygen in his suit? What's the purpose?"

"Yes and yes and it protects us from the G-forces during sharp turns and rapid changes in speed," replied Alan. "Not unlike your dad making sure your seat belt was snug the first time he taught you to drive in the Sears parking lot."

"Actually, it was K-Mart," mumbled Jax, before quickly getting back to the important point. "So, you want I should try running this flying contraption through its paces?"

"Sure," said Alan. "I promise it will be some of the most fun you'll ever have."

Jax's excitement suddenly switched back to caution mode. "But what if I crash into something, like the *ground*?"

"Can't happen. These scout ships have that avoidance system that makes it impossible to hit anything, even if you wanted to."

"Seriously?"

"Seriously. Go head, take the stick, Junior Birdman. Just don't go any faster than we are now. On second thought..." Alan reached forward to flip a switch and punch some keys. "I'm locking in the governor at seven-fifty, so you can't exceed Mach-One."

No, it wasn't like the first time he got to push that gas pedal of Dad's 1994 Cadillac in the K-Mart parking lot at ten-thirty on a chilly Sunday night in April. It was a hundred times better. Jax eased the stick gently to the left and the ship responded spontaneously and just as gently. He then pushed it to the right. Then up. Then down. With each change in direction the magnificent machine responded as if connected directly to his desire.

"Sweet!" breathed the rookie space pilot.

"Like silk, isn't it," said Alan. "Try some sharper turns now."

No need for the suggestion. Scout-One banked hard left and down. The altimeter reading on his HUD went from 5,000 feet to 4,000 in about a second. He pulled up quickly to level off at 3,550.

"Who-ee!" said Jax. "It didn't seem like we were even moving."

"It's the anti-G suit. Amazing, huh?"

"How's that work, anyway?" asked Jax, doing a barrel roll.

"Beats me, said Alan. "Besides the obvious cushioning the air pressure provides, it runs on the same mechanism that gives these spaceships their anti-gravity properties. In fact, I'm told our suits are somehow hooked directly into this vessel's anti-G engine."

"I'll be go to hell!" howled Jax, doing a hard right, then left.

For the next hour Scout-One headed home as the crow files…providing the crow intermittently crash dives to a thousand feet, then quickly climbs to five thousand, banks off a cumulus cloud, does four barrel rolls and two death spirals. And while Jax should have been throwing up, he was as comfortable as if sitting on his Italian leather sofa playing Xbox's Need for Speed 2015. He hated using overworked slang, but this thing indeed was *totally awesome*.

Chapter 60

With Alan back at the helm and their space suits retracted back into their seats, they came in from the east over the Coralville Reservoir just eight miles from the farm. Scout-One was only three hundred feet off the ground, and their cruising speed had dropped to a mere fifty mile per hour to avoid too much of a telltale whooshing sound at this low altitude. Having fished the Reservoir countless times, Jax was getting a kick out of viewing it through his night vision camera. It would be an hour before the sun came up, but again the HD screen made it seem to be high noon in full color.

As they approached the boat ramp by the dam, Jax noticed a pickup with a boat just pulling in.

"Can we hold it here a minute?" asked Jax. "I might know that guy. The rig looks familiar, even though I rarely see things from this angle."

"Well, let's find out," said Alan, coming to a complete stop short of the ramp, hovering quietly. He had his camera zoom in on the pickup's license plate. He then punched a few keys, and in three seconds received a read-out, stating it belonged to one Roger Morgan from Iowa City.

"Ha!" laughed Jax. "That's my best friend. He owns Roger's Sports Center. Yeah, he often comes out real early to get in a few casts before opening his store. He probably has Dan Kostner with him."

"Want to have a little fun with them?" asked Alan, an impish tone to his voice.

"What do you mean?" asked Jax cautiously. That *was* his best friend down there, after all.

"Oh, nothing serious," smoothed Alan. "Just a temporarily knock out of his vehicle's entire electrical system with an electromagnetic pulse. Then we'll start it right back up. Nothing will be hurt, I promise."

The prospect sounded fiendishly delightful. "Why not?"

Alan eased the craft more directly over the target at about one hundred feet up and waited until the moving pickup was in such a place that suddenly losing power wouldn't jeopardize the occupants' safety. He placed the screen's crosshairs dead center on the cab and pushed a button, sending a mild, negative EMP. Every light on the truck and trailer blinked out and the rig rolled to a slow, dark stop.

Giggling like two school boys with a frog, sneaking up behind an unsuspecting girl, they watched both men pile out of the cab and start checking under the hood.

"Want audio?" said Alan, flipping a switch and turning a dial.

"I don't know what the fuck's the matter," said Roger, slamming the hood. He walked back toward the boat, banging his fist on every part of everything along the way.

"It's gotta be the battery," said Dan.

"The battery is brand new," spat Roger.

The two delinquents watched a little longer, then Alan asked, "Ready to re-fire?"

"Go ahead," grinned Jax, zooming his screen in tighter on Roger, who was leaning against his pickup, hands behind his head, exasperated.

Simultaneously the engine and all the lights fired backed up. Both fishermen jumped a foot.

"What in the name of Christ is going on here?" yelled Dan.

Suddenly, Roger looked straight up at them. "Do you see something up there above us?" he asked, framing his eyes with his hands.

"I don't see anything," said Dan, now looking too, but in a different place.

Alan and Jax were laughing so hard tears were coming out of their eyes. "S'pose we should get out of here?" suggested Alan.

"Probably should," replied Jax. "But could we do it low and slow? Give them something to talk about?"

"That's kind of against the rules," warned Alan. Then he gave it more consideration. "But I don't see the harm. Just another couple of kooks who thought they saw a UFO."

"Can you keep the audio on?" asked Jax.

"Until we're over the trees, then we'll lose it."

Alan eased Scout-One forward at twenty miles per hour.

"There! See that?" yelled Roger. "Right there. Moving west."

"Where?" yelled a frustrated Dan. "I don't see anything."

"Not north, you dick! West. Over the trees."

"Where?"

"Aw, shit! It's gone now. It was like a black hole in the…"

Chapter 61

Things were rather busy around the Brookfield spread after that night. Kevin came by the very next day to install and program the new equipment Alan and Jax had picked up in the desert. By attaching an apparatus that looked like a silver sump pump to the silo's sonic cannon, it was turned into a blow-em-out-of-the-sky weapon with an instantaneous impact and effective killing range of one mile. The manual labeled it *Ultra Sonic Laser Accelerated Pulse (USLAP)*. Scout-One and Scout-Two received the same improvement with less power and range, but enough to earn them the new monikers of *Fighter-One* and *Fighter-Two*. And everybody's communicators got modifying chips that added a much more powerful punch, one that would actually burn a hole one millimeter wide through whatever its crosshairs locked on at a maximum range of two hundred yards. Everyone was warned to use this only in extreme cases.

Alan, Jax, David and Mike all took turns flying the fighters under the cover of darkness to get a feel for the new onboard firepower. Non-exploding skyrockets were launched out in the western meadow, and the target-locking system made it almost impossible to miss even such small, dark, flying objects. As for their hand-held mobile devices, Jax had to make a special run into Dick's Sporting Goods to replace all the playground's soccer balls, footballs and basketballs that lay scattered and flat with smoking holes.

Jax finally got to formally meet Grandma Helen from the greenhouse, when she reluctantly came to supper one evening. Her old gray eyes were big as golf balls and her balding head couldn't hide the fact it was shaped like a giant kettle gourd. At most she weighed eighty pounds and stood four-foot-ten. Helen--whose Mejan name was Ursalu—preferred fending for herself in her own cottage directly behind the greenhouse...the one with the dim light in the small window that Jax considered as a prospective location for making love that night a while back. He now understood why they chose the haymow instead.

Besides taking care of the plants, Helen mostly enjoyed listening to the library of audio books her parents had brought with them when they had crossed dimensions to end up in this one seventy years ago. She had watched American television enough to learn the language, but now found most of the programs silly and mundane. She did, however, like certain sitcoms, such as reruns of *The Neighbors, Mork and Mindy,* and *My Favorite Martian.* She also liked anything with Tom Cruise in it, especially *War of the Worlds.* But she couldn't understand why the killing machines roamed Earth on three legs. *Tripods? Stupid Martians,* she would say.

Helen was too much Mejan to ever completely acclimate to Earth's seventy-eight percent nitrogen and twenty-one percent oxygen atmosphere, so her gasmask afforded her the extra five percent nitrogen needed. Still, she was able to remove it for up to ten minutes before getting light-headed. Jax found her delightful. She spoke in forced English, mixed with an occasional Mejan word or phrase nobody knew the meaning of. But *Leptos* was one word everyone around the farm had picked up on, as it was the Mejan word for *God.* Jax remembered Suzy using it when she (supposedly) caught her first bass a few weeks ago: *Oh, my Leptos! It's beautiful!*

As Helen looked his towering frame up and down, the charismatic sweetheart of sixty-five immediately gave Jax the name, *Gimskoe,* which turned out to be a large mountain on her home planet. Jax threw the pet name, *Greenhouse Granny,* back at her, and the odd couple decided then and there the other was okay.

Concern over the increased possibility of the farm being scanned at any time by the Reggs, a practice drill was conducted one afternoon, mostly for Jax's benefit, since he had never participated in one. If the scanning was more than a mile away—which only the dish inside the top of the silo could detect—everyone's communicator would buzz at one second intervals for ten seconds. If the scan was closer, the beat would be more rapid and continuous. In either case, all people with Mejan blood and therefore detectable body temperatures and enlarged craniums were to head for shelter immediately. Meanwhile, the pure humans—e.g. Alan, Jax, the farm hand named Louis, and the other farm hand's wife, Joyce, were to stay in the open and act like they were doing normal chores on a normal farmstead. It was vital that Brookfield Farm held no interest to the Reggs.

Chapter 62

Ironically, on Independence Day, Jax and Suzy got married. It was just a small ceremony in the Brookfield pool and garden area. The guest list was quite lopsided, since all but three attendees on the bride's side had big eyes and heads, while those on the groom's side were normal and nonexistent. Jax wanted to invite some friends and Odett, but understood why that was not a good idea. It would be too hard to explain the pond on a hill, the justice of the peace looking like a barn owl, and the bride's big-headed, elfin grandmother wearing a gasmask.

Suzy's mother—Mary—was her maid of honor and Alan—Jax's about-to-be father-in-law—obliged to be his best man. Simple vows and beautiful gold rings were exchanged, then husband and wife kissed and groped each other so long and passionately, the embarrassed attendees began wandering around, pointing to birds in the trees, cool clouds in the sky, focusing on anything but them.

Suzy had no reason to throw her bouquet, because there were no single females present, just her two brothers. So in lieu of flowers, Suzy and Jax conspired to throw a tennis ball—wrapped with a note inside a zip-lock baggy—into the pool, explaining it was a coupon offering to do the recipient's chores for three evenings, while he went to town to find a bride of his own. Without hesitation or regard for their new tuxes, David and Mike hit the water at the same time and fought over the prize more ferociously than any two desperate old maids. David, the stronger nineteen-year-old, won, which was just as well, since he looked old enough to get into any of the night hotspots with his perfect, homemade, fake ID. Besides, he had already met a cute girl his own age whose hair sample had proven her a viable mate. At seventeen, the younger Mike had plenty of time for such mate-seeking endeavors.

All in all, the wedding went off—as Mike was fond of saying—*with* a hitch. As both families were wealthy, the newlyweds could have gone anywhere for their honeymoon. But for reasons ranging from wishing to stay close due to the Regg threat to simply needing nothing more than to be left alone and naked in each other's arms for a few days, they chose to stay around, splitting their time between the farm and Jax's estate.

Odett was, of course, hurt to learn her Pee-Bee-Boy and Suzy had run off and eloped like that without even telling her. But she understood the reasons they gave regarding the need for complete secrecy. The closest thing Iowa City had to a tabloid was the normally innocuous *Around Town* section of the *Tribune*. But the papers would still have been chocked full of the scandalous millionaire Patrick Jackson dumping his longtime girlfriend, Jannie Marin, for some destitute farm girl nobody knew anything about. She obviously was after his money, and the marriage had no hope of lasting more than a few months, at which time the gold-digging hayseed would take him for half his worth.

To make it up to Odett, the couple spent the majority of their honeymoon week at the Jackson estate, letting her do what she loves and does best: waiting on them like their own personal valet at Club Med, while whipping up her best meals from breakfast to lunches to dinners to late-night snacks.

That was Odett's wedding gift to them. In return, Jax's wedding favor to Odett was a check for half a million dollars and the promise that while he may not be around as much anymore, she could consider herself retired and continue living in the house as long as she wished. "You might as well," he told her. "It's always been in my will that you get it and all the acreage if I die before you." It wasn't often he saw his second mother cry.

One week later there would be more tears. But not from Odett. And not of happiness from anyone.

Chapter 63

As promised, Suzy and Jax were covering for David on a Saturday night, so he could take his new girlfriend, Missy, to a movie in Iowa City. Suzy took his night shift in the communications room, while Jax was finishing up shoveling manure from the stalls in the pig barn. That was normally David's afternoon chore, but on this hot, mid-July day he had purposely left it for his new bro-in-law to do.

Jax was lost in convoluted thoughts of how one week ago at this time he was curled up on cool, silk sheets in his round bed with his beautiful, soft, sweet-smelling bride, watching "Gravity" on Blu-Ray, and here he was now on a humid, eighty-degree Saturday night with a super-duper-pooper-scooper, shoveling stinking hog shit in a barn. *What a difference a week makes,* he thought. *But a deal is a deal.* And he had to be scoring points with the whole family, especially his new father-in-law, Alan, who was finally starting to treat him more like a real person.

Oh, Suzy Q, I love you...

"Speak of my angel," said Jax, gladly dropping the shovel and peeling off his yellow leather gloves to take the call.

"Wha.." is as far as he got.

"It's David. He's in trouble," blurted Suzy. "Get in here fast, everybody!"

Jax raced for the house, stopping only to kick off his smelly yellow boots on the porch. By only seconds he was beaten by Alan to the communications door behind the wet bar, and Mary was right behind.

"Are they chasing you, David?" were the first words they heard entering the comm. Suzy was asking as calmly as she could, watching the PC monitor in front of her. It showed David's face looking straight ahead from a belt-buckle view.

"No," he whispered. "Just walking, keeping pace."

Alan dropped into the empty chair next to Suzy and took over, per protocol. "It's Dad, David," he said calmly. "How close are they?"

"A good block back. They aren't gaining on us."

Everyone heard Missy off camera whining, "What's going on, David? Who's after us?"

"Oh, shit," whispered Mary, through welling tears. "Missy is with him. That's not good."

"What do they look like?" continued Alan.

David had put the phone to his ear so Missy couldn't hear the questions coming from the comm. "Not dressed all in black, like Ned Wilson described," he whispered. "But it *is* summer. Dark green shirts. Long sleeve. Tan pants. Long hair. Shiny faces, probably masks. Glasses. Dark lenses."

"Who are those guys?" whined Missy, louder now, getting more frightened.

With a shaking voice, Suzy quickly and quietly explained to Jax and her mom that David and Missy had come out of the theater on Clinton Street and were heading for his car to hit MacDonald's, when his communicator chirped the warning of a nearby scan. He looked around to see two men behind them fifty yards, slightly hunched over, about six-feet tall, walking at the same pace on the other side of the street. One was staring hard at them, while the other was looking down at what was obviously his mobile device.

""We have you on satellite and GPS, Son," said Alan. "How far to your car and in what direction?"

"Up one block and half a block over to the west."

"You're not in a parking ramp, are you?"

"Jesus, Dad, I'm not a complete idiot."

"And the bad guys are to your southeast, right?"

"Roger that."

"So, you can make it to the car."

"No problem. Easy peasy. And if they start running, I'm sure we can outrun them. Missy here has long legs. And nice ones, too."

"David, I'm scared," said the disembodied voice of his date.

"It's okay," soothed David. "These are just a couple farmers mad at my dad over a land dispute. They won't hurt *us*."

God, thought Jax. *The whole family are class-A liars.*

163

Chapter 64

"Are there other people around you?" asked Alan.

"One couple behind us. One in front about fifty feet."

"Good. As long as the *farmers* are just walking, do the same. They aren't likely to do anything with others around."

Jax stepped up and said softly in Alan's ear, "Think he could turn his camera toward them for a couple seconds?"

"David," said Alan, "kill the light on your phone and point it toward the assholes for a few seconds, okay? And zoom in a little."

"Roger that."

The resulting video was just as David had described them. The probability of these being Reggs was high and increasing by the minute.

Much to everyone's relief, David and Missy reached his 2014 dark-blue Tundra pickup without incident. The suspected Reggs just stopped on the corner and watched them drive away, one of them talking on his phone.

"They aren't running for a car or anything," reported David.

"Well, let's not take any chances," said Alan. "Get Missy home and you do the same, hear?"

"Ah, Dad…"

"You do what your father says," chided Mary, with her face right beside Alan's. "You hear me, David?!"

David set his phone on standby, and everybody relaxed a little. Except Alan. And Mary. And Suzy. And Jax. And Mike, who had now joined them. These *creatures* had all the earmarks of being Reggs, and the word coming down from The Desert People was the Reggs were desperate for a Mejan hostage. So why did they give up so easily on David?

They had their answer in less than sixty seconds.

"I think we're being followed," reported David, calmly for Missy's sake. "Every turn I've made, they've made. It's seems to be a black SUV. Can't make out the model or make."

"Go around a block," coached Alan.

A minute later David was back, "Still with us. No doubt about it now."

"Okay, you know what to do," said Alan, rising from his chair. "We'll meet you there."

"Roger dodger, Dad. Don't be late."

"You know the drill, ladies," called Alan back over his shoulder going out the door on the run. "Come on, Jax."

Jax didn't have to ask where they were going or what they were going to do. Even without the run-through two days ago, he could have guessed. In four minutes flat they were three hundred feet above the pond and completely encased in their pressurized flight suits. Alan punched *dot-dot-2* on the ship's keypad to activate the preset flight plan, and Fighter-One shot off due east, accelerating to two hundred miles per hour in just under one second.

They arrived at the designated rendezvous point five miles away in ninety seconds. It was the intersection of W66 and the private road leading into River Products, a sand and gravel quarry halfway between Iowa City and North Liberty. As expected, David hadn't arrived yet, but the GPS screen showed he was coming at eighty-five mile per hour, about thirty seconds away. Alan pulled the fighter to a dead stop, hovering just inside the quarry at an altitude of one hundred feet. With stealth and a moonless sky, it was virtually invisible.

Almost immediately the night vision showed not only the dark-blue Tundra pickup, but two black SUVs right on its tail tearing north on W66 just two seconds out. As practiced, David suddenly slammed on the brakes and took a hard left into the quarry. The SUVs followed, the first one almost missing the turn. The Tundra continued in for fifty yards, then left the gravel road to circle around a small mountain of washed river rock. The SUVs followed.

Jax already had the crosshairs locked on the first one.

"Hit it!" said Alan.

Jax pushed the orange button, sending out the negative EMP. The lead SUV's electrical system shut down completely, causing it to head straight into a large sand pile and roll onto its side.

"Hit it!" called Alan again, and the second vehicle lost all power as well. It missed the second pile and careened down into a shallow depression, coming to rest upright on the far bank.

Jax and Alan watched David and Missy complete their circle around the large mound of river rock and get back on the pavement to Iowa City. They were no longer followed.

Fighter-One rocked with war whoops. But the attempt at a high-five left much to be desired, seeing how both men were still in their inflated spacesuits and couldn't reach the other's hand. They had to settle for *knuckles*, which had all the manly impact of colliding marshmallows.

Chapter 65

"Everyone safe and sound," reported Alan to the womenfolk back at the farm.

"Way to go guys!" chimed Mary and Suzy in unison. They had been watching and listening to all transmissions from start to finish anyway, plus watching both David's and Fighter-One's homing blips on the GPS and USA-129 satellite monitors.

"Yeah, way to kick ass," added Mike. "Teach those mofos to mess with the Brookfields."

"Michael John!" rebuked his mother.

"We're going to follow them to Missy's, then stay over David until he's home," said Alan.

"Thanks, honey," breathed a relieved Mary. "Just keep an eye out. The Reggs have stealth, too, you know."

Even as they moved away from the quarry to stay with David, Jax kept his night vision camera zoomed in on the disabled SUVs as long as he could. He was hoping to get some video of the aliens getting out of the vehicles, but they never did.

"Don't you wish we could have tested our new USLAP cannon on them?" said Jax through his teeth.

"Yes, it was tempting," said Alan. "A few less Reggs to uglify our beautiful planet. But we had to follow protocol."

"I know," groaned Jax. "But just the thought of a cloud of Regg dust wafting into the sky…"

"Temper, Jax," teased Suzy inside his helmet. "The poor Reggs are just misunderstood."

That brought a laugh from all.

It violated his own standing orders, but Alan suddenly cut all outside communications, so only his copilot could hear what he said next: "Jax, you know, don't you, that there's a good possibility one of their scout ships was watching the whole thing back there."

"Huh?"

"Think about it. If their plan was to kidnap David, they would undoubtedly need to take him aboard a good-sized spacecraft to do their tests and interrogation. So, they would either have to drive to the ship, or one would have been following the SUVs all along the way."

"Yeah, I guess so," said Jax, trying to ignore the willies going up his spine. "But that would mean it's either back there picking up their crashed dummies or they are following us right now." Jax's willies turned into chills.

"Or there are two ships, one doing each." Alan immediately called David. "Son, don't go to Missy's or home. Go to MacDonald's or anyplace public and stay there until you hear from us."

"Roger that," replied David. "Anything I should know?"

"Nope, just playing it safe. We'll be in touch. Bye." Alan clicked off from David, then said to only his copilot. "Jax, start scanning with your camera above us and behind us. I'll take forward and down. If there's anything within a mile, the night vision should pick it up."

"Will do," said Jax, running his index finger over the screen to reposition the camera angle.

It didn't take long to see exactly what he never wanted to see. The Regg spacecraft filled the screen in full, daylight color like it was straight out of a sci-fi movie trailer. "Holy shit! he gasped. "It's right behind us."

Chapter 66

Jax's chills now had the willies…on top of goose bumps.

"How close?" demanded Alan, flipping his camera to rear view.

Jax checked the numeric scrawl at the bottom of the screen. "One hundred and ten feet."

"I show it's not getting closer," offered Alan. "Do you confirm?"

"Confirm. It's just waffling a little."

"Hold on!" Alan hit the brakes, coming instantly to a dead stop. The Regg craft almost rear-ended them, stopping just a few feet short. With a flick of his wrist Alan twisted the joystick counterclockwise and Fighter-One pivoted one hundred and eighty degrees on its axis, coming face to face with its alien counterpart.

Showdown.

Both vehicles just hung there three hundred feet in the air over W66 two miles north of Interstate 80, neither one moving an inch. The Regg ship was dark and angular, typical of older stealth. It seemed to be similar in size to Fighter-One, at least width- and height-wise. No telling its length at the moment. Their cockpit canopy was also angular, reflecting starlight off its surface like it was sunshine. It was impossible to see inside. Jax wished he had his polarized fishing glasses to cut through the glare. But the pilot or pilots would probably be wearing full helmets like they were.

"Think they have night vision, too?" asked Jax with what little breath was still in his lungs.

"Definitely," replied Alan, only a little less apprehensive. "That technology has been around since World War Two. It just may not be as good as ours."

"What are we gonna do?" asked a nervous Jax after fifteen seconds of farting. Again he deeply appreciated the adequate filtration and ventilation offered by his puffy spacesuit.

"Well, this isn't the time or place for a dogfight," said Alan, contemplating the situation. "Too close to town. Too much scattered carnage to explain. The Reggs probably don't want to be leaving artifacts all over the ground or escalate this cold war any more than we do. Job-one tonight is getting David home safe. Nothing more."

"Well, I trust our desert friends won't mind the video we're getting of a Regg spacecraft," chimed Jax proudly.

"Oh, crap!" hissed Alan. He just remembered taking the ship's onboard digital recorder out for a minor soldering job to a loose wire. That's what he was working on in the shop when David's predicament came up. And since he had cut off communications with the girls, they weren't recording anything either.

This presented Alan with a conundrum: stay incommunicado to keep Mary and Suzy from seeing what they are seeing; or reestablish contact and save this invaluable footage of a Regg spacecraft.

The girls are strong. He reasoned. *They're part Mejan. The Desert People would love this video...need this video. The Reggs don't seem to want a fight, so maybe the girls will stay relatively calm. I can downplay it.* "Hey, there ladies," chimed Alan, after flipping a switch. "Seems we lost you there for a few minutes."

"Jesus, Alan!" fumed Mary. "What the hell happened. You had us scared to death."

Before he could answer, Suzy screamed, "What the fuck is that?"

No doubt about it: the live video feed had been reestablished along with the audio. Jax and Alan looked at each other as if to say, *I didn't teach her that word, did you?*

"Calm down," said Jax, surprised by how tranquil his tone was, considering they were facing a possible departure to the afterlife and his insides were twisting in fear. "They obviously have no intention of doing anything. We're just looking at each other."

"Well, get your asses out of there!" one of the women yelled. It was too shrill to determine which one.

"Already in the plan," said Alan, sending Fighter-One to a thousand feet in a leisurely five seconds.

"The Regg craft stayed down there," reported Jax, relieved.

"Okay," said Alan, pushing the joystick gently forward. "We need them to follow us...away from David. See if they do."

Fighter-One accelerated to fifty miles per hour. The Reggs— suspecting the Mejans may be heading back to the quarry—not only followed up to the same altitude, they zoomed ahead. Once a good half mile in front, they pivoted to a complete stop, hanging there like a Rottweiler daring anyone to cross into his territory. Alan eased to a stop, as well, one hundred yards away.

Standoff number two.

Chapter 67

Not as close this time, the threat seemed less imminent. But it was still tense.

"Whadda ya think they're doing?" whispered Jax, after a solid minute, as if the girls couldn't hear, which of course they could.

"My guess is they're telling us to stay away from the quarry," said Alan.

"So, they can pick up their unbeautiful buddies and go home?" suggested Jax.

"Sure," broke in Mary. "They don't want conflict any more than we do. I'll bet they are saying they will leave our son alone if we will leave their stranded guys alone. So, please, hon, just back away and see what they do?"

"Will do," said Alan, pulling back gently on the stick.

The distance between the two crafts increased steadily in line with Fighter-One's reverse speed for about three seconds, then the gap grew wider in half the time.

"They're backing up, too," announced Jax.

"Keep your camera on them as I turn around," said Alan. "With a little luck they may show us some more of their ship's character."

But all the Reggs showed was its broad, tail end, as they slowly headed in the opposite direction. At that moment Alan stopped retreating and spun back around, hovering. "Just making sure they don't try coming back this way," he reported to everyone. He then called David.

"Sup, Dad?"

"Where are you?"

"We're at Micky-D's having cheeseburgers."

"How's Missy doing?"

"She's just coming out of the bathroom."

"Okay. When you're done there, take Missy home. Then call me when you're leaving her place. We'll be running interference the whole time."

"Roger that. Appreciate it."

"Missy to the truck yet?"

"About halfway. Seems in no real hurry."

"Think she'll be okay?"

"Yeah, she's strong. Doesn't seem to be shaking so much now."

"Think she'll still be your main squeeze?" smiled Alan.

"That's very nineties of you, Dad. And I guess I'll find out soon enough."

"Find out what?" asked Missy in the background, climbing inside the vehicle.

"If this is the year the Cubs win the World Series."

"Oh, that's not what your dad asked…"

"Later, Dad." David clicked off.

True to his word, Alan kept Fighter-One positioned directly between the gravel quarry and where the GPS said David was for the rest of the evening. Judging from the fact the homing *beep-beep* held steady in Missy's driveway for a good two hours before David's Tundra pickup finally headed home, love was still in bloom.

While maintaining vigilance on the night-vision monitor the whole time, Jax amused himself thinking about poor Missy and the prospect of watching some other uninformed schmuck go through the same Brookfield investigation, analysis, lab work, and overall scrutiny he did before acceptance. Jax could only hope she was treated better than he was by the uptight patriarch sitting beside him.

Chapter 68

At oh-ten-hundred sharp the next morning one of the large, HD television screens on the north wall of the communications room traded Fox News for a talking head named Joshua Middleton, a full-bird colonel in the United States Air Force. His craggy face with pointed, narrow jaw and bent nose was all smiles, as he gazed upon the entire Brookfield family. At least they assumed he was gazing at them. Under the slightly larger than normal head with a buzz-cut, the colonel always wore flight glasses, which all but screamed he was part Mejan. And based on his being in his mid-forties, that part was probably one quarter, like Mary Brookfield, making him an 8.

"I can't begin to tell you how pleased we are by that video," he began, motioning behind him at a large television screen replaying the footage of the Regg spacecraft. "In over twenty years of this cat-and-mouse game that's the first time we've ever seen one of their craft. Those sonsabitches are the sneakiest, most paranoid bastards in the Universe."

Judging by the colonel's frequent off-color language, it was also assumed that his father was pure human and a military lifer, making Joshua perhaps the Earth's first Mejan air force brat. No one at Brookfield was bold enough to ask.

"But they saw ours, too," said Alan. "And neither of us did anything to give anything away, so we're really back to square one, don't you think?"

"True, true," nodded Colonel Middleton, taking a sip of his coffee, revealing elongated fingers wrapped around the cup. "But we learned a bit of their new strategy in trying to snatch one of us."

"Roger that," piped David, who certainly should know. "I didn't expect them to be walking around Iowa City in the middle of summer like that. From the Ned Wilson file we thought they would always have to wear heavy clothes and stick to winter. But the lighter shirt and pants they wore last night did a decent job of hiding their bodies...at least under street lights. And I think they were wearing masks. Pretty good ones, actually. Like latex or something."

"So, why do you think they didn't try to box you in?" asked Joshua. "That had to be the idea behind using two vehicles."

"I can answer that one," said Alan. "We're pretty sure they initially hoped David would panic and lead them straight home to us. That would have been a major coup for them. So they stayed back a ways at first.

When it became apparent he knew he was being followed and was trying to lose them, their strategy shifted to getting him out on a quiet road somewhere and then box him in."

"Makes sense," said Joshua.

David piped up again. "That's why we have practice drills. Not two days earlier Dad, Jax and I ran through that same scenario at the quarry. In fact, it was the third time in two weeks." Then David added with a wry smile, "It's our *SOP*, Colonel, which is military for *standard operating procedure.*"

"I see you're raising a wise ass, Mary," said Joshua, hiding his mirth.

"Yes, and we just added another one to the family." Mary smiled and pointed at Jax. "I guess you haven't formally met my new son-in-law, have you?"

"No, I haven't," grinned Colonel Middleton, showing more bottom teeth than uppers. "An honor to meet you, son."

"And you," replied Jax. He got to his feet and offering a half salute.

"Well, congratulations to you and your darling wife there on your marriage," grinned Joshua. "Way to go, Suzy. Besides being quite big and handsome, you married a great videographer. Good job on the Regg footage, Jax."

Oh, goody, thought Jax, *I've found my niche: family photographer.* "Thank you, sir," he said half-heartedly, "but I didn't do anything more than push a few buttons."

"I guess we didn't tell you, Joshua," chimed in Suzy, "but we're going to have a baby."

"Well, I'll be damned. Super!" blurted the colonel. "Congratulations again, you two. He or she will be a 94, right?"

"Yep, 94."

"We need all of those we can get. Smart, too, I bet. And certainly good-looking."

Finishing up with the personal news and pleasantries, the group got down to more pressing business. And before it was to conclude, more people than Jax would be wanting one of those happy pills.

Chapter 69

"We're afraid this failed abduction attempt is only going to make the Reggs more determined, more aggressive," said Colonel Joshua Middleton, with no attempt to hide the seriousness in his tone. "And in turn, it puts you folks more in the crosshairs. They know you have a small spacecraft similar to theirs, which is no surprise, of course. But now they know David is young, part Mejan, and lives in or near Iowa City. So they will suspect he has a family nearby as well."

"The Reggs will be scanning the area more now," proposed Alan. He nodded to the echo of his own words, and drained the dregs of his second cup of coffee.

"That's what we would do in their boots," said Joshua, leaning back in his chair and folding his arms. "And we'd concentrate on the countryside, not the urban areas. They know you have to hide your spaceship somewhere close by, so that means farms, lakes, or even just an isolated house on a large acreage, preferably in a heavily wooded area. They'll scan them all, and probably in short, hit-and-run bursts, and not just at night. They know you can detect their scans. And they know you can launch a fighter in just minutes." The colonel leaned forward to make his point. "But all they need is to catch one of you in the open for one second to know you're there on your farm. So, you need to stay inside as much as possible. Sorry."

"We've already been doing that," said Mary. "But we'll double our efforts."

A short pause ensued, mostly because no one was sure what to say next. The concept of being attacked right there on their beautiful, peaceable home front was gut-wrenching. Unfathomable. Jax nudged Suzy for a pill. She took one, too. Then Mary.

"Is there anything else we can do for the cause?" asked Alan, coming back to his seat with a fresh cup of coffee.

"Not at this time," replied the colonel. "Unless you'd care to capture one of those Reggs. We'd dearly love to water-board the fucker."

"We'll get right on that," snorted Alan.

"We came close last night," piped Jax with his usual manufactured bravado. "I don't know if we could have captured any of them alive, but we sure could have blown one of their buggies out of the sky."

"It must have been tempting," nodded the colonel. "And we would love to know what damage the new USLAP firepower would have on a Regg ship. But you did the right thing. There is no way you could have salvaged the downed craft before the Iowa City police and half the town were out there ogling the wreckage. At best you may have got a couple dead Reggs onboard your fighter and brought them to the farm. And that would have made for an interesting and this time *true* alien autopsy. But we already know they are uglier than a bucket of hairy assholes. We need one alive."

"What *do* we know about the Reggs?" asked the newest member of the family. "I'm told it's basically nothing. Is that true?"

Joshua rose from his office chair and walked around behind it, the camera automatically zooming out to follow him. He placed both hands on the back of the chair, as if we were about to do a couple pushups. The camera zoomed back in on his face. "I'm afraid it is, Jax," sighed the colonel, his face trading its previous levity for frustration. "Your encounter with them last night and the footage was the first major breakthrough we've ever had regarding their spacecraft. But in all other respects: their numbers, their technology, their weaponry, where their spacecraft are hiding, especially a mothership, and their ultimate goal, we can only guess. As I always say, those sonsabitches are the sneakiest, most paranoid bastards in the Universe."

"So, you weren't kidding," speculated Jax. "We really do need to capture a live Regg."

"We really do," said Colonel Joshua Middleton, sitting sat back down and putting his hands behind his head. "G2 is working on it as we speak. They'll come up with something."

Chapter 70

The late-July sun felt good on Suzy's bare back. So did Jax's hands slowly rubbing the suntan oil over her shoulder blades and down her spine. The newly-weds were on the black and gold Hawkeye blanket, the same one they had first made love on inside her Toyota van some six weeks ago. But this time the blanket was on the grassy ridge of the pond, out in the open, exposed to the midday sun, the breeze, the birds, and anything else that may be hovering above them.

They both had their fishing gear with them, but no lures were in the water. For Jax anyway, catching the bass out of this pond had lost its appeal. It was more like a fish farm and the largemouths had become pets. Knowing they were spawned down there *under* the pond, in a Mejan spaceship named Maude, in an aquarium, and then pumped up through a chute, just took all the fun and challenge out of it. Besides, these days there seemed to be more important things to occupy his time and thoughts.

The 88.7 percent Mejan, with the honey-blonde hair in a pixie cut to deemphasize her outsized head, had her chin resting on stacked hands, her throat mewing with pleasure. "It's kind of weird in a way," she said, turning her head to the left and resting it on the beige surfer trunks encasing her husband's left thigh. "On the one hand I'm a little scared, lying out here like wolf bait, while on the other there's a strange sense of freedom." She rolled onto her side and propped up on one elbow. "For as long as I can remember, I've always had to be cautious. *Don't dawdle outside, Suzy. Stay close to the house, Suzy. Stay near the car, Suzy. Always keep your shoes on, Suzy.* Now suddenly it's *stay out in the open, Suzy. Let them scan you, Suzy. Don't run, Suzy.* Just seems weird."

"If you're frightened, sweetheart," said Jax, now applying the oil to the side of her left leg, "I could call one of your brothers to take over being *the bait*. I'm sure they wouldn't mind."

"No, no," she insisted, rolling back onto her stomach and reaching back to adjust the elastic of her yellow bikini bottom. "I don't get many chances to work on my tan. And I've just started on my back. If you hadn't molested me for an hour under the picnic table, I could have gotten started sooner." Restless, Suzy rolled onto her side again just enough to reach up and touch Jax's sweating face. "Besides, nothing is going to happen."

"Of course not," said Jax, putting one of his oily hands on hers and kissing her palm.

It *was* a longshot, after all. Foolhardy for sure, since they were virtually inviting the Reggs to come for tea. Not that it wasn't a good idea. It was. In fact, it seemed the only viable plan to capture a Regg or two and one of their vehicles. They felt The Desert would agree in theory, but they would never officially allow the Brookfields to put themselves in jeopardy like this. That's why they hadn't even discussed it with them. Besides, if the Reggs did come, they would be ready for them. They had a plan.

Suzy and Jax were right. Nothing did happen. For a good five minutes, anyway. Then both their communicators started buzzing at the same time. They weren't phone calls either. The continuous buzzing meant the scanner was in the immediate area. They both flinched. From years of programming, Suzy instinctively started pushing herself off the blanket, the first stage of getting to her feet and running for the Lexus SUV parked fifty feet away. But Jax caught her and pulled her down on top of him.

"It's okay, baby," he whispered, reassuringly in her ear, yet quavering himself. "It's okay. Just stay right here with me." He kissed her. "I love you. Nothing's going to hurt you. I promise."

It was debatable which of the two was the most frightened. Jax kept his arms firmly around his trembling wife until she slowly succumbed to his words and will. They kissed passionately, fearfully, excitedly, as if bombs were going off all around them in 1942 London and this may be the last moments of their lives.

Two thousand feet directly above, the Regg scout ship hung quietly, just a speck in the blue sky, virtually invisible to the human eye. A monitor connected to its onboard infrared scanner suddenly erupted with a series of unique beeps, signaling a biologic with the correct perimeters of body heat and head-to-body ratio had been located in the suspected area. The pilot immediately punched a button to mark the spot on his GPS, and the ship zipped off at high speed to its preprogramed destination.

Chapter 71

If the bastards were coming, Jax hoped it would be sooner rather than later. This waiting was playing havoc on his stomach acid and he was getting low on Tums. He could always take one of those valium-type pills Suzy had slipped in his pants pocket. But Jax was trying to convince himself that he didn't need that crutch anymore.

For the fourth time in thirty minutes, he rechecked the digital clock on his phony iPhone. It read *1:32 a.m.* He also rechecked the battery to make sure the newly installed laser was fully charged and ready to burn a hole in something or someone. Satisfied, he slipped it back into the breast pocket of his black, western-style shirt and snapped the fold-over flap shut. That left only to click on the night-vision scope atop his M16 rifle, also for the fourth time in half an hour. Under the farm's two yard lights, everything down there was lighted up in a bright, washed-out green hue.

He had to admit that despite the anxiety, it was getting tough to stay awake. He looked down at his wife, curled up against his chest in her dark jeans and equally dark blouse, breathing steadily. He couldn't blame her. Being in the haymow on a blanket on a soft pile of straw surrounded on three sides by hay bales stacked four high...well, it was sure more fun making a baby than waiting for Reggs. They had to stay vigilant. They couldn't even count on McDoogle, the family Golden Retriever, to bark a warning. He was staying in the mother-in-law cottage with Greenhouse Granny.

It was day-three since purposely letting Suzy be scanned by the Reggs, and—just as importantly—making certain she didn't scamper for cover. Hopefully that would make the Reggs believe she didn't know she was being scanned. After all, their infrared imagery would show she was mating with that human by that symmetrical pond, so she was probably too busy to notice if her scanner detector alarm went off. Consequently, if none of those farmers down there were aware of the scan, they probably would not be on guard. That opened the door wide for a surprise infiltration of the farm, probably some night, to kidnap one of the Mejans obviously living there.

That was the Brookfield's thinking of the Reggs' thinking, anyway. True, they were giving away their location. But, it was just a matter of time before the Reggs figured it out anyway. It was worth the gamble to capture one of them first, and maybe help put an end to this cold war with a mysterious enemy. The Desert didn't need to know. They were undoubtedly busy with their own plan to snag a Regg or two and one of their ships. Besides, they would have put the kibosh on this idea, most certainly.

Inside the house down in the communications room was Mary with Karen and Joyce—the wives of the two hire hands—taking turns sleeping and watching all the various monitors. No movies tonight. If the Reggs came by car, the Brookfield's own infrared scanner and radar would pick them up out at the main entrance. If they came by spaceship with their super stealth, the daylight-night-vision cameras in the silo could reveal their presence.

Upstairs, sitting in the dark on chairs behind the wall of the foyer were Alan and his youngest son, Mike. Alan had wanted Jax to be here instead of Mike, but Jax insisted he'd be more effective in the barn with a sniper rifle as a backup. He was a crack shot. Covering the back door were the two hired hands, Louis and Larry. Each of the four had on their person or immediate access to the following: his communicator with laser weaponry; a loaded pistol; night-vision goggles; a hand-towel soaked with chloroform inside a plastic bag; a large roll of duct tape.

Strategically placed a half mile away to the west in a grove of oak trees sat Fighter-One with David alone at the helm. He had strict orders to stay put unless absolutely necessary. Otherwise, his objective was to use the craft's night-vision cameras to help the silo scan the skies above the farm.

At precisely 1:45 a.m. something came into range. The alarm went off, and David spilled half of his Monster drink down his shirt.

Chapter 72

No doubt about it, it was a Regg scout ship, just like the one Alan and Jax confronted over two weeks ago. It apparently had dropped straight down, coming to a silent hover directly over the house. David immediately started to punch *star-star-star* to ring up everyone, which the silo was also doing automatically. But before either could complete the warning, the farm's two yard lights went out. Simultaneously, so did all the air conditioning units around the house and buildings, along with the dual water pumps in the pump house. Everything in the communications room, everyone's communicators, the night-vision cameras and radars and satellite feeds blinked out. Even Jax's night-vision scope on his M16 went dark.

The Regg's negative electromagnetic pulse had shut down everything and anything that relied on electrons. In, on, and under, within a hundred yard radius, the Brookfield farm was dark.

For Jax, just inside the large, open door of the hayloft, the sudden blackness was blinding and the silence deafening. His racing mind thought it could be a power failure somewhere along the Johnson County grid. That's not uncommon. But when his communicator and night scopes were dead, too, he feared the worse.

"Suzy," said his trembling whisper, "I..I think it's happening."

"What?" she moaned, squeezing her hubby, still half asleep.

"The Heggs are rear," spit Jax, although he had none.

"What?" she asked again, this time more receptive, looking up at the face her big pupils could barely make out in the blackness.

"The R-Reggs are here," he repeated a little better this time. "And they've shut down all our power."

"No surprise," whispered Suzy, now completely awake and thinking clearly. She got up to her knees and looked out the big window. "We go to plan B," she said cooly, studying the darkness. "You ready?"

Jax stuffed his useless communicator back in his shirt pocket and picked up the M16. "I guess so," he said, his hands shaking as he rested the rifle on the top of the hay bales stacked two-deep. From this vantage point he had a clear shot at anything from the lane to the playground, with the main house right in the center. *But how do you shoot something you can't see?* he thought.

Approximately fifteen seconds after the lights went out, the rustle of tires coming down the lane was clearly audible. So was the sound of the gate swinging open, the code for the keypad apparently no challenge. The unseen, lightless vehicle rolled the rest of the way down the lane, around the curve and stopped in front of the house, right where Jax usually parks. Jax was operating entirely by sound and the soft brushing of brake pads against the shoes. With her larger pupils, Suzy could actually see an outline of the vehicle.

"It's an SUV," she reported with the quietest of whispers into Jax's ear. "All four doors are opening. No interior lights. Four figures are getting out. Two are walking quickly to the front door. The other two are staying on the walkway. I see faint green lights around all their heads. Probably night-vision goggles."

Finding both the screen door and main door unlocked, the two Reggs thanked whatever demented god they pray to, and stepped inside.

They were about to discover they needed a more receptive deity.

Chapter 73

With the EMP having made their own night-vision goggles useless, Alan and Mike relied totally on their ears. That wasn't a problem, however, as the two Reggs shuffling across the tile floor purposely sprinkled with sand was as distinctive as fingernails on an emery board. And the faint green glow around the edges of their goggles as they walked into the trap was like a beacon, signaling the instant the Reggs crossed under the archway from the large foyer to the dining room.

Before either intruder could look left or right, Alan sprang from one side and Mike from the other. Coming in from slightly behind, each Brookfield slapped the chloroform-soaked towel around his respective Regg's mouth and held it in place with both hands as tightly as humanly possible. Alan was relieved to discover his bony Regg was not particularly strong, even before being weakened by the drug. Its furry hands pulled frantically at Alan's wrists, but they had no chance of succeeding. With Alan wrapped around him like a horny poodle on a dinner guest's leg, the Regg dropped to its knees from the weight, let out a muffled moan, and fell still.

Being almost one hundred pounds lighter than his dad, Mike was having trouble subduing his Regg of about equal weight and size, especially after not getting the towel completely over its extended nose and mouth. Mike was riding its back, trying desperately to get the chloroform in place. But in its frantic thrashing the Regg was able to fling him off, sending Mike crashing to the floor.

Yelling in its horrendous language, it repositioned its goggles and ran for the front door. It didn't make it. From the sitting position atop the passed out Regg, Alan drew his Glock G19 and fired at the speck of green light fading into the darkness. The bright flash from the muzzle blinded the farmer, and the next four shots were just in the general direction. The alien fell dead against the half-open main door, slamming it shut, causing a sixth *bang* to come from inside the ranch-style house in as many seconds.

The two Reggs standing outside on the walkway were having a few moments of disconcertion, followed by a few more of indecision. This apparently wasn't in their game plan. Should they go into the house to help their friends, or call for the ship to come get them, or make a run for it in their SUV?

The sound of the gunshots was Jax and Suzy's cue to take action. But it dismantled Jax. He slumped to the floor behind the hay bales and curled himself into the fetal position. "Not happening. Not happening," he kept whimpering, his lips barely moving. Seeing and hearing her husband revert to his second infancy was more than perplexing to Suzy. "Jax!" she shouted with a whisper, shaking his shoulder. "Jesus, Jax! Snap out of it. We need you!"

His mumbled reply, "I don't want to die. I don't want to die." sent a shiver down Suzy's spine. When all hell broke loose in the house—as they knew it might one way or the other—Jax was supposed to open up on any Reggs in sight, particularly any that were heading for the house; Alan and Mike may be in jeopardy and would need protection. Jax was the sharpshooter, having hunted with his dad many times before his death. He had said with no shortage of cockiness he could put a bullet between the eyes of any Regg, and everyone believed him. They didn't know his motivation sprung from not wanting to go hand-to-hand with any one, much less some creature not of this earth. And when it came time to do his job, they certainly didn't suspect he would crumble like a month-old sugar cookie.

With no time to waste on her lost cause of a husband, Suzy pried the M16 from his hands, laid it on the stack of bales, and peered through the scope. Her superior night vision enabled her to make out the Reggs' dark outlines against a slightly lighter background. One was easing cautiously up the stone walkway toward the house, the other even more slowly behind. Against everything in her nature, the passive, part Mejan female put the silhouette of the leader in the center of the scope and fired a three-round burst, just as Jax had taught her every day since being scanned by the Regg ship at the pond. There was a blood-curdling scream, a thud, and the sound of running footsteps. A car door opened and slammed shut. An engine started and tires squealed on the asphalt parkway.

Now framed against the downtown lights of Iowa City five miles away, Suzy could see the vehicle's outline quite well, as it slid around the curve and accelerated up the long lane to the south. She put the crosshairs on the back window and emptied the M16 magazine at the fleeting shadow. At that same time, Alan came running out of the house, firing his Glock at the sound of the retreating SUV. In seconds they heard the vehicle leave the asphalt lane and crash head-on into one of the mighty oak trees.

Jax just lay there in the fetal position, staring at nothing, trembling, wishing his mom was alive and there to hold him in her arms.

Chapter 74

In the next hectic seconds so many things happened so fast no one person knew them all in the aggregate. As the gunshots and car hitting the tree finished echoing off the outbuildings, there was heard a *whomp*, followed by a human groan and a body crashing through some shrubs. The alien craft had leveled Alan with a sonic pulse.

It started descending into the parkway, presumably in a desperate effort to retrieve its horizontal victim. But it was suddenly hit in the rear end by Fighter-One's laser cannon. Wobbling and smoking, it crawled back into the night sky and tried to flee to the west. David hit it again, this time in a critical part of the power source. There was a small explosion in the center of its undercarriage, and the gravity-defying Regg ship fell as dead weight from a hundred feet, crashing hard a few yards to the west of the pond in the open meadow.

Fairly certain it was out of commission, David maneuvered his fighter over the house, punched a couple buttons, and all electrical energy was restored. Everyone's communicator flashed on and was immediately abuzz with people walking all over each other. Except Suzy. Emotionally spent, she dropped the rifle beside Jax and sat down on a single hay bale. Lowering her face into her hands, she began to sob uncontrollably. The Mejan-human crossbreed was certain she had just killed another living being, maybe two. She turned her head away from the quivering man at her feet and threw up on the haymow floor.

The lights, the sounds, the smell of vomit...one or all three brought Jax out of his self-preservation stupor. He looked up at his retching wife. "You okay?" he asked like a five-year-old catching his mommy bent over the toilet. Suzy wiped her mouth on her sleeve and tried to explain what had just happened, but only disconnected words pushed out between sobs.

On rubber legs Jax got to his feet just high enough to pivot and drop down beside his quaking wife on the bale. He wasn't sure what all had happened, only that there had been very loud gunshots. He reached into his jean's pocket and popped a pill, gnashing it with his molars. Then a second one. He reached over and wrapped his arms around Suzy. "Baby?" She didn't respond.

David yelling her name over her communicator, slowly brought Suzy back to reality. The *whomp* and crashing sounds from a few seconds ago reverberated in her ears and mind. Ignoring Jax's continued questioning of her wellbeing and what was happening, she pushed away from him and leaned out of the open haymow door to scan the area. With the sodium yard lights blinking back on, the yard was again awash in brilliance. There in the front yard lay her father, flat on his back, his feet resting in a busted shrub, his hands clutching his chest.

When Jax' eyes followed hers to witness his supine father-in-law, he suspected something was wrong. And when his wife took off down the haymow steps without a word, he instinctively grabbed his M-16 and followed.

Out of the barn, and across the farmyard raced Suzy with Jax close behind. They hurdled the low shrubbery to land in the front lawn. Sliding on her knees up to Alan, Suzy found him still breathing and semi-conscious. "Dad! Dad!" she yelled in panic, lifting his head and placing it on her lap.

While she attended to her father, the valium was coursing well through Jax's bloodstream. He suddenly realized he was clutching the M16 white-knuckled like it was the staff of life.

"Check on the house, Jax!" demanded Suzy, not looking up from her father. "And goddammit shoot anything that's not us!"

Jax was almost semi-fearless. The fast-acting pills were also forcing him to recall the events of the past few minutes, including his crumbling under pressure. His mind ran the gamut from guilt and self-condemnation to hope no one finds out what he did…or more precisely, didn't do. One thing was certain in the moment: he had to do exactly what Suzy ordered.

Heading quickly toward the house, Jax found a Regg in a blue jumpsuit and matching boots belly up on the ground a few feet from the porch. There were two large exit wounds in its chest, still oozing a dark substance. Even with the double-dose of bravery, his knees started shaking again, just not as badly. He took a deep breath and swallowed hard before finally poking the body with the muzzle of the gun. The grotesque, wolf-faced creature appeared deader than dead. A dark, bloody tongue extended from its half-open mouth, the tip resting placidly on blades of grass. Jax stood petrified, staring at the first alien he had ever seen in person. He thanked God it was still wearing its night-vision goggles, so he didn't have to see those eerie yellow eyes with horizontal irises he'd seen on the Ned Wilson abduction video.

It all seemed so unreal.

Turning his head and blinking away the image, Jax remember Suzy's orders. He flipped the safety off his M16 and walked across the porch to the main front door. He had to push it open with all his weight. Inside he flipped on a ceiling light to find another dead Regg, this one face down, blocking the door with no less than three bullet holes in its back. Jax kicked it lightly with his foot. Also dead. Thank goodness.

The light and excited human chatter drew his attention and presence to the dining room. There he found Mike, Louis and Larry in the process of duct-taping the hands and feet of an inanimate alien.

"Holy shit!" gasped Jax, taking a step back. "Is that one *alive*?"

"Sure is," panted Mike, pulling the chloroform-soaked towel away from its face. "Just drugged."

"Alright!" shouted Jax, keeping his distance. "You got one. Way to go, guys!"

"Thank Dad," said Mike. "And he shot the one by the door, too."

While Jax gladly headed back out to spread the news and help Suzy with Alan, Mary was calling from the communications room, frantically trying to get someone to tell her what was happening. David was calling from the fighter, asking if everyone was alright, particularly his dad. By the time Jax reached Suzy, she had her woozy father sitting up and her phone to her ear. She looked emphatically up at Jax, her eyes asking if everyone in the house was okay. Jax gave her a hearty thumbs-up.

"Everyone is fine, Mom," she said with relief...a small white lie, considering Alan's present condition. "What about the Regg ship, David?"

"Down and done," he reported proudly.

"And we got a live Regg tied up in the house," blurted Jax.

"Hear that everyone?" chimed Suzy. "We got one, alive."

His ears still ringing and head swimming, Alan managed a feeble smile. David, Mary, and the other two ladies in the comm cheered. Then Suzy remembered the one running away in the black SUV.

"David," she said, "there still might be a Regg down the lane."

"Nope," her brother replied. "He didn't make it. I'm zoomed in on the Explorer right now off the side of the lane. The back window is shot out and he's slumped over the wheel. If you guys didn't get him, crashing into a tree did. I e-bombed the vehicle anyway, just to be safe."

Alan weakly reached over and took Suzy's phone. He punched a few keys and then held it a few inches from his mouth. "Good job, everyone," he said, still groggy. "Now we've got ...some cleaning up to do...before dawn. And then a phone call...to make."

Chapter 75

Larry and Louis took the green, John Deere Gator ATV around collecting the three Regg bodies and stacking them inside the meat locker at the back of the house. Jax and Mike were assigned the job of towing the shot-up, smashed-up, black Ford Explorer five miles out into the boonies by the Coralville Reservoir and setting it on fire, so no traces of the alien's abnormally dark red blood could be found.

Before doing so, they were to collect anything on the body, particularly the communicator, which was tucked in the utility belt along with three curious spray bottles. But the instant Mike touched the device, a thin stream of white smoke puffed out of the casing with a hiss. As a result, they decided to not take any chances with the three bottles, leaving them untouched on the utility belt. Everyone else reported the same self-destruction when they picked up a Regg communicator. No surprise.

In a dead-end, gravel parking lot Jax knew from his old duck hunting days with his dad, he and Mike flipped a coin to see who got the honor of burning a hole into the vehicle's gas tank with his laser from a hundred yards away. Mike won, but they both blasted it anyway. They were a little disappointed it didn't explode and send a ball of fire into the sky like it always does in the movies. But watching the expensive—and undoubtedly stolen—2015 Explorer become engulfed in flames from rear to front was pretty cool anyway. Plus, they decided the absence of an explosion waking up half of Johnson County was a good thing. The red glow it was creating in the night sky was beacon enough. They got the hell out of there.

Alan was rather stiff from being hit in the chest by that medicine ball of a sonic blast that launched him thirty feet through the hedge row. But after a few ibuprofens and a shot of Jacks, he felt good enough to accompany David on the Ford tractor to inspect the wreckage of the Regg ship a quarter of a mile out in the west pasture.

They were amazed when their flashlights revealed it was no longer a spacecraft with pilots, or even a recognizable vehicle of any kind. It was just a mass of smoldering metal—with presumably Regg hide and bones melted within. About a quarter its original size and glowing orange in the center, it produced a thin tail of pungent smoke winding into the night air. And most incredible of all, it wasn't even on the ground, but a good two feet *into* it, and getting deeper by the minute. This was producing a separate cloud of grayish smoke with an acrid smell. Apparently the alien craft was designed in its death throes to release a powerful acid for its final veil of secrecy. It wasn't presently covered in much dirt, but the sides of the hole were slowly melting in on the object, beginning the burial process.

"And we thought their communicators' self-destruct mechanism was being paranoid," said David. "These guys may be ugly and stupid looking, but they're pretty good at covering their asses."

"They should run for public office," wisecracked Alan, as he called for his two hired hands—Louis and Larry—to bring shovels and rakes. They needed to keep the mass of metal exposed as much as possible until the desert folks got there to see it. Being the first tangible piece of a Regg spacecraft, they would undoubtedly want to take it back to their secret hideout for analysis. Who knows what kind of intergalactic alloy it may reveal and what could be learned from it.

Of course, that smoldering chunk of spacecraft would pale in comparison to the real prize of the evening: the *Regg captive*! With enough Midazolam coursing through its circulatory system to keep it in dreamland for the duration, the wretched creature was presently wrapped in gray duct tape, lying on a plastic sheet, on the bed, in a spare bedroom, inside the main house. In light of the Regg's propensity for self-destruction, Alan Brookfield had ordered a thick bath towel to be folded and laid over this one's utility belt without touching the small tools, or the three little spray bottles, or its communicator. The towel then was secured with more duct tape. A Post-it Note placed on the Regg's chest read: *Touch nothing. Let The Desert deal with it.*

Everybody took a turn babysitting the alien to make sure it stayed comatose. The women especially found the thing hideous, what with its bent-over posture like a Neanderthal, its gray and black hairy face with yellow eyes and horizontal cat-like pupils. The head had an extended frontal lobe, lacked visible ears, and the mouth-nose combination fell somewhere between human and Lon Chaney's 1941 "The Wolf Man." The four incisors top and bottom were straight across, giving way to the extended canines, then typical molars. Thin, dark blue lips only partially covered the teeth, stretching into a naturally sinister smile while it slept. And it was the only one that did sleep that night, as everyone else was too wound up.

As dawn was breaking, Mary and the two hired hands' wives—Karen and Joyce—whipped up a huge breakfast served buffet style so people could eat in shifts. Besides the clean-up, no less than two people at a time had to be manning the communications room, watching for any signs of another attack from the air as well as the ground. It wasn't likely, but underestimating an enemy you know virtually nothing about is never a good strategy.

By eight-thirty a.m. all scans were negative, and Alan felt it was time to make the video call via the secured network to The Desert. He knew the man he was always supposed to report to—Colonel Joshua Middleton— usually rolled into HQ around eight Central Daylight Time. So, this would give the good colonel thirty minutes to dispatch with his jelly donut and black coffee in the conventional way, instead of all over his pressed desert fatigues upon hearing the news.

Chapter 76

"So, to what do I owe this early morning intrusion, Mr. Brookfield," asked Colonel Joshua Middleton, a little testy. Apparently the caffeine hadn't kicked in completely yet.

"Oh, just something we thought might interest you, " teased Alan. For effect, he took a slow draw on his own coffee mug, waiting to see if Joshua was awake enough to bite.

"Well...?" drawled the colonel.

"*Well*, we have a new friend here at the farm who wants to meet you." Alan punched the TV remote control in his hand and the live audio/visual feed from the spare bedroom was sent to the desert. The video camera, manned by Jax, showed the Regg mummy-wrapped in duct tape on the bed. "Zoom in on his face, Jax," said Alan.

Somewhere in a distant desert with no name, a coffee mug bounced off the floor and hit a table leg, flinging its contents into the air before splashing into brown puddles of various shapes and sizes on the gray tiles.

"Don't screw with me, Alan!" demanded Colonel Joshua Middleton, almost sticking his face through the monitor at his end. "Tell me it's real."

"It's real."

"Is it alive? Tell me it's alive."

"It's alive. In good shape. Just heavily sedated."

"Oh my God in Heaven and Holy Jesus mother of Joseph!" blithered the forty-something Air Force colonel, banging the table his laptop/camera was on so hard the screen at the Brookfield end pixelated for a moment. "How the hell did you...when did this...have you told...."

"You are the first to know, of course," smiled Alan. "And we have three more of them on ice. Dead, unfortunately."

The HD picture coming from The Desert was a super sharp 1080p resolution, so even though his watering eyes were not visible behind the flight classes, there was no hiding the moisture beginning to rim the colonel's nostrils. Embarrassed, the twenty-five percent Mejan had to turn and leave the field of view, using the pretense of, "Getting another cup of coffee." While away, he punched keys on his cell phone and emphatically whispered something into it.

"So tell me everything," he finally said, returning to view and sitting down in his chair before his shaking legs gave out. "I want every detail. Leave nothing out."

Purposely staying just off camera—but clearly announcing their presence by not being able to curtail their jubilance—a number of other Desert People gathered in the periphery to hear the report.

Alan, with Suzy and David by his side, spent the next half hour briefing Colonel Middleton on last night's events, from the Regg's electromagnetic pulse knocking out their power, and Alan chloroforming one that came in the house…to shooting the other as it tried to run away, and Alan himself getting turned into a lawn dart by the Reggs' equivalent of the Mejans' sonic-blaster.

It was hard for Suzy to describe shooting one of them to death with the M16 and probably the other one as it was driving away. But she had no choice. The EMP had knocked out all less-lethal means of stopping the Reggs. "And without the night-vision element of his rifle scope," she said, not wanting anyone to know the truth about her cowardly husband, "Jax couldn't see anything in the dark." As she spoke with quivering lips, Alan kept a fatherly arm around her shoulders. Jax sat still, looking blankly at the floor.

With plenty of bluster, David explain how he shot down the Regg ship with the new laser canon, so yes, it is effective. *Very* effective. That brought one loud clap from Joshua, basically high-fiving himself, and some exciting murmuring from the unknowns on the periphery. David also said it was no problem overriding the Reggs' negative electromagnetic pulse that knocked out everything electrical. He simply used Fighter-One's own EMP generator turned to the *positive* setting.

"The way it sounds," said Joshua, once all tales were told, "you not only knocked their dicks in the dirt, they came away with nothing, zip, nada. You probably downed their ship before it could even report it had been hit by the laser canon."

"We think so, yes," confirmed David. "It was getting ready to set down on our parkway and I caught him by complete surprise from behind. Staggered, it tried to run away, but I hit it with the fatal blow no more than three seconds later and it crashed and burned. Or should I say it crashed and melted into the ground?"

"Nowhere enough time to call home," said Alan. "Same with the one driving away in the SUV. No time. And even if there was, all that Regg knew about our weaponry was small arms." Alan pulled the Glock from its holster on his hip and blew across the muzzle. "Shucks, ma'am. We just be simple country folk."

Colonel Middleton clicked his mouse a few times. "You say their fighter *melted*?"

"Into a ball of unrecognizable metal," replied Alan.

191

With only a *hmm*, the Colonel ran the mouse's scroll wheel a couple times, then reported, "According to NOAA, your weather there in Iowa City tonight is to be hazy but clear. Dusk is about twenty-one-hundred and the three-quarter, waning moon rises about then. Not exactly ideal, so the transport will get there right at dark, about nine-thirty your time before the moon gets too high and bright. It will set down in your west meadow, if that works for you."

"We'll be ready," said Alan.

Chapter 77

While Larry and Louis herded the grazing Angus cattle over to the east side of the pond just before sunset, Jax and Suzy were busy marking off the landing area on the west side. Suzy drove the Gator ATV and Jax sat in the back, holding an open bag of lime under his arm, sprinkling a narrow line of white around the perimeter. He was still stewing over the embarrassing way he had acted last night. Pouring the lime did little to restore his sense of self-worth. But at least he was contributing. Suzy had been particularly quiet. He couldn't blame her.

When done, they had marked a two-hundred-foot diameter circle around the meadow, beginning just a few yards north of where the alien ship—or what was left of it—was embedded in the now five-foot-deep hole. This was all according to the specifications forwarded to them earlier in the day from The Desert.

Now, as zero hour approached, Alan, Jax and Suzy stood well back from the edge of the rough circle, watching the sky for the first sign of the promised transport. Mary and Mike were in the communications room monitoring—among other things, of course—the heavens from the night-vision camera mounted atop the silo. They would call them the moment something came into view.

David, meanwhile, was inside Maude, sitting in Fighter-One, ready to go up the chute and through the pond, just in case some Reggs tried another assault. He was almost hoping they would. Blasting that last one to alien perdition was *the bomb*, literally! He may have the same amount of Mejan blood as his sister, but he didn't share much of her passivity.

At nine-twenty-nine Mary called to say the transport was at five thousand feet directly above and descending. Then she added, "You won't believe it when you see it."

Alan immediately replied, "Ah, you forget we humans can't see shit out here in the dark."

"Oops, sorry," laughed Mary. "Okay, you won't believe it when Suzy describes it to you."

There was no sound, but Jax knew it was nearby, because he smelled something like ozone and the small hairs on his neck were bristling. But not from goose bumps. Those came when Suzy gasped, "My Leptos! The thing is huge. And it's shaped like...an *airplane*."

She was right. The converted C-17 Globemaster military cargo plane set down dead center inside the circle of lime with no sound other than the crunching of grass and soil under its tremendous one hundred and forty-ton weight distributed over forty large tires. Wasting no time the eighteen-foot-wide, twelve-foot-tall rear end yawned open from the bottom up, revealing the dimly lighted insides of the cavernous craft. A ramp had no sooner extended and settled than a man in desert fatigues and night-vision headgear scrambled down it with a flashlight and headed straight for the hole. He verified its contents visually and took readings with some apparatus resembling a Geiger counter. Satisfied, he flashed his light back at something inside the plane.

A twenty-ton boom truck with headlights off lumbered down the ramp and pulled up to where the man was painting the ground with his light. The thirty-foot boom dislodged from its latch and swung over the hole. A huge, open-mouthed claw dropped from the boom on steel cables and crashed into the hole. Its teeth worked their way under the mass of melted metal and shortly came up with the entire remnants of the Regg scout ship. It was carefully deposited on the flatbed and quickly strapped down by a crew of four. The truck then drove back up the ramp into the belly of the C-17 with the men following on foot.

Military precision.

A jeep was the next vehicle crapped out of the C-17's ass end. It picked up the man in fatigues, and drove over to meet their hosts. He jumped out, tossing three glowing light-sticks on the ground.

"Captain Wilowitz," the officer announced, a firm hand coming out of the dim, green background. Without removing his night-vision headgear, he located and shook the hand of each of the three, as their names were offered in return. He didn't bother to introduce the driver, which Jax figured meant he was either too low in rank or too high. The same headgear covered most of his face and he was wearing a nondescript jumpsuit, giving the nod to CIA. Probably Mejan. "Which way to our favorite Martian?" asked Captain Wilowitz.

"It's coming," said Alan, punching two numbers on his communicator and raising it to his ear. "Bring it on up, Larry."

Two hundred feet away the twin backup lights on Suzy's Toyota van blinked on and began bouncing along the meadow, growing larger and farther apart until stopping a few yards short of the jeep. Larry slid out and opened the tailgate manually. Inside were Louis and a silver mummy, the latter still very much unconscious. All four humans hauled the Regg out and set him upright in the back seat of the jeep. The one who now was definitely *not* military sat beside it with his arms wrapped firmly around, while Captain Wilowitz drove up the ramp into the bowels of the giant transport.

Military *and* Brookfield precision.

Chapter 78

Next came a military-grade, four-seat Gator ATV with desert camouflage and two first lieutenants wearing the matching fatigues and night-vision gear. They pulled up behind the van. "We hear you have three on ice," grinned the big African-American.

"Just follow the van," said Alan.

While that final chore was taking place, Captain Wilowitz rejoined the group on foot, no longer wearing his headgear. He now had his flashlight on and told the others it was okay to use theirs. Jax couldn't resist flashing his on the face of Wilowitz to see what the man looked like. He seemed to be about twenty-five—Jax's age—had beady eyes, teeth as bad as actor Steve Busemi, and undoubtedly one hundred percent human.

"You guys deserve the Presidential Medal of Freedom for this," he said sincerely, shaking each one's hand again. "Too bad you won't get it."

"Why not?" asked Jax.

"Because it has to be presented by the president," said the captain, "which means he has to know why he is presenting it."

"I take it that means Obama is in dark on all this," offered Alan.

Three of the four snickered, but decided to let the obvious jokes go.

"No president has ever been briefed on what we do in The Desert," said Wilowitz. "And none ever will be. Even the CIA and NSA know virtually nothing about us. Too many leaks. We just spear the best minds from each and tuck them away."

"So, what group *do* you belong to?" asked the ever-curious Jax. "Who do you answer to? Where does your funding come from?

The shorter Captain Wilowitz reached up, put a hand on Jax's shoulder, blasted his face with light, and said with a snide grin, "Stay young and dumb, my friend. What you don't know can't hurt you." He then tapped Jax's chest with his knuckles. "Kapish?"

Jax smiled weakly at the putdown. But unconsciously his hand was squeezing Suzy's a little too tightly and beginning to shake. Suzy wasn't sure what to make of it. Due to the newly-discovered, chicken shit nature of her husband, was he about to try resurrecting his manhood by taking a swing at the captain? As much as she would like to see him show some balls, the odds of that happening seemed very slim. A more likely action would be Jax entering into a verbal battle, which he *was* pretty good at…being a writer and all. But if that should progress to the verge of fisticuffs, Jax would probably back down…maybe even conducting another cowardly melt-down right there in front of everybody. Besides being downright embarrassing, it would expose what she had been keeping a tight secret since last night.

Feeling she needed to cover for her husband for the second time in less than twenty four hours, Suzy shouldered Jax off center from the captain and slipped in to take his place. "Tell me Captain," Suzy asked, purposely shining her flashlight in Wilowitz's face, "why was this transport a common C-17, and not something more space age, like the Mejan crafts?"

Blinking away the brightness, and slowly withdrawing his attention from the squinting Jax, Wilowitz replied, "It's always easier and cheaper to modify an existing plane like the C-17 than to build something new." He put his hand up to block the light, and Suzy lowered the beam. "Besides, the Mejan power source that also generates the anti-gravity system isn't all that big or difficult to install in just about anything."

"And as a bonus," speculated Alan, "no one thinks twice if they see a plane with wings and a tail cruising across the sky."

"Exactly," grinned the captain, shooting Alan with a finger bullet. "Most UFO fanatics are looking for odd shaped things with colored lights flying weird patterns in the sky. They never suspect most of the true alien spacecraft up there were made by Boeing."

"You said *most*," challenged Jax, making little attempt to stifle the disdain in his voice. "So, you must have other craft…more like *flying saucers?*"

Captain Wilowitz shined his flashlight up into Jax's face again. "You're curious, aren't you?" he stated with his own level of contempt. "I like that."

The timing of the Gator with the three Regg stiffs rolling by couldn't have been better, mostly for Jax's sake. Deep in the safety of his mind he was conjuring up a fantasy of straightening out a few of the patronizing little prick's teeth. But in his heart he knew that's all he would do. That pompous jerk was probably a black belt in karate or some other military hand-to-hand shit.

The captain quickly bid all a good evening and double-timed it up the ramp to disappear into the belly of the beast. The back end closed up, and the United States military's largest conventional plane went unconventionally straight up into the night sky with nary a sound.

Chapter 79

It was seven-thirty Friday morning, six days after the Regg raid. Jax and Suzy were taking their shift at manning the communications room, while the other Brookfields slept. Things had been so quiet around the farm lately, it was almost boring. So much so, in fact, Jax actually finished his *Hawkeye Outdoors* column for the *Tribune*...his first one in three weeks. His editor, Angie, didn't mind the missing pieces, and neither did anybody else apparently, since the only letter-to-the-editor on the subject asked what happened to the when-to-go-fishing moon table that normally punctuated the end of his column.

Jax emailed the column to Angie and pushed away from the computer keyboard with a sigh.

"What's the matter, hon?" asked Suzy, turning the page of the latest Enquirer. Not unexpectedly, there were no sightings—real or imaged—from this part of the country. The only item of mild interest was the Iowa City police report in the *Tribune* about the burned out stolen Ford Explorer found out by the Coralville Reservoir last Sunday by a couple of carp fishermen. Three weeks earlier the report listed the recovery of two slightly-damaged, stolen Chevy Suburbans at the River Products quarry. But there were no reports anywhere of objects in the sky. Good job, guys.

"Nothing," said Jax, placing his hands behind his head.

"Must be something," coaxed his wife, folding up the paper to give her full attention to Jax. "You've really been quiet this past week. I know something is bothering you." Of course she knew. And so did he. They both had been skating around it since the Regg raid. This elephant wasn't just in the room, it had been sitting between them, blocking any attempt to discuss the subject neither one really wanted to broach anyway. Suzy decided enough was enough. It was definitely time to kick this pachyderm right out the door.

Knowing it had to be handled gingerly, she and her office chair slid over to buddy up to the side of his, facing the opposite direction like a loveseat. She reached up and pulled his face toward hers. "Spill it, or incur my wrath, Pee-Bee-Boy."

That cracked his stone face, and brought a twinge in his heart. No one but Odett ever called him that. He missed her. And hearing it from Suzy was, well...heart-warming, especially after the burden he'd been carrying all week and the coolness between them it had caused. At the very least she deserved the explanation.

Jax shifted her hand from his chin to his mouth and kissed the palm. "I don't seem to be pulling my weight around here," he said just short of whining.

Suzy looked at him with a well-rehearsed, stunned silence before saying, "Whatever are you talking about? That's just plain nuts." In truth, it wasn't so far off. But this is not what she expected him to say. *Not pulling his weight? How about not pulling the* trigger?!

"Not so crazy, really," he said. "It's actually been bugging me ever since the day I was told about everything that goes on around here." Suzy searched his face for the answer she expected was coming. "You all are so smart and specialized," continued Jax, "What do I offer other than someone to help monitor the comm and go fishing with you?"

Suzy stared hard at her husband, cocking her head, questioning. He seemed sincere. He even looked depressed. She had to run this concept through the analytical portions of her left-brain a few times to even begin to understand where he was coming from. Maybe it was his way of building up to the main issue on both their minds.

"Jesus, Jax," she said, needling for more input, "you're a part of this family. Everybody likes you, loves you. You've done everything..." she had to stop and rephrase what she was about to say," ...you do *a lot* around here. You help with chores. You've learned to fly the fighters. Sitting here in the comm, monitoring all these screens is no small thing. And since you've been here to help, the rest of us have all gotten more sleep. We could use a couple more of you."

"Okay, sure I help in some menial ways," conceded Jax, "but it's a job anybody could do. I'm hardly gonna get my own action-figure."

Suzy found herself unconsciously nodding in agreement.

"Anybody?" she snorted. "Okay, what do you do when the infrared detector screen over there starts beeping?"

"I push star-star on the keypad," said Jax dully by rote.

"Right. And what's the code to the tack room?

"UFO or 836."

"Right. And what's..."

"Okay, I get it," said Jax with a forced half smile. "I've learned a few things and I have a good memory. But..." He paused, gathering his next words, wondering if he should even bring it up. Sure, why not? The waiting look on Suzy's face said that ship has already sailed. Before it sunk completely, he knew he had to reveal the secret he had been hiding from everyone for five years now.

Chapter 80

"The night during the Regg raid, while we were in the haymow," Jax said slowly, "my job was to take out any Reggs with my M-16."

Ah, thought Suzy. *At last we get down to it.*

"I'm a crack shot," moaned Jax. "I thought I could handle that job. But when it came right down to it, I couldn't do it. So, you took over. You, a gentle girl with Mejan blood, who hates violence, had to do what I, a man, who has killed many things in his life, couldn't do."

"Oh, come on, honey," said Suzy, grabbing his hand. "You couldn't see in the dark the way I can. You couldn't see where to shoot. The Reggs were easier for me to see. It was only common sense that I do the shooting." Suzy knew that excuse well. It's the one she had given to everyone, including herself. She had forced herself to ignore the image of Jax lying at her feet, hugging himself in fear.

Jax turned his head to look hard into Suzy's big eyes. "That's bullshit, Suzy, and you know it," he groaned, his face fallen about as far as a face can. "We both know I totally wimped out. I couldn't do it. I couldn't shoot them. The truth is, I haven't killed anything, even a squirrel, since my folks died. Jax Jackson, the great outdoor writer, who tells people how to shoot deer and filet fish hasn't killed another living thing for over five years. Not even a friggin' *spider*."

From deep inside that region of the subconscious that holds the truth—when all the other parts of the brain chose to ignore it—both parties knew Jax was using this non-violence defense to deflect what was really going on in his heart and mind that night. The grown man had been *terrified*, plain and simple. Whether he was afraid of killing, being killed, aliens, chaos, or whatever, it boiled down to blatant cowardice. And it had Suzy seriously questioning whether Jax could be counted to protect his *wife and children* in a crisis—supposedly one of the most deep-seated hallmarks of the human male.

But calling him on it, making him face and explain his shortcoming, could easily backfire and drive him away, or even deeper into his depression. After all, he was the father of her unborn child. So, Mrs. Jackson did what any good wife and expectant mother would do to protect her husband, her future children, and save their marriage. She rose from her chair, knocked it out of the way with a back-kick of her foot, and plopped her one hundred and fifteen-pound frame down on Jax's lap, straddling him face to face. She kissed him gently on the forehead, and said with all the deception she'd learned and inherited from the Brookfields, "I'm happy that you have such a respect for life, Jax."

The confused husband just sat there, blinking. It wasn't quite what he was expecting. *You lily-livered pansy* would have been more in line with the nature of his admission and how he was seeing himself these days.

Suzy put both hands on the side of his face and said, "Baby, that eleven-point-three percent Mejan blood in me commands a respect for all life. Big and small. Beautiful and ugly. Human and alien. To discover you share that same value can't be bad."

"But you took out those Reggs like you were playing Black Ops 4," said Jax, shaking his head.

"I was protecting my father, my mother, my brothers...*you*," she said, nodding with each loved one. "Family trumps all. If I had been down there in harm's way, you would have killed to protect me, wouldn't you?" *Wouldn't you?!*

That scenario tried to materialize in Jax's mind. "Of course I would," he said spontaneously. It made sense to him in the abstract. But when he tried to visualize his beautiful wife being threatened by a bunch of ugly, scary Reggs, the scene quickly faded to black. *How can anyone know what they would do in a situation that is too horrific to even imagine?* he thought.

"So, now do you see your value around here, big boy?" grinned Suzy. "Who else do I have that would not only *protect me with his life*, but kisses me with those soft lips, and gives me great back massages, and keeps me warm at night." She hugged Jax lightly. "And makes love to me (he hugged her back), and gave me this tiny life growing inside me." Suzy pushed back from Jax enough to allow both their hands to run gentle circles around her barely noticeable baby bump.

"You are needed a lot around here, Patrick Bernard Jackson," she said, more sternly than lovingly. "But your real duties begin in about seven months and will continue for many years thereafter. Our children need their father to teach them right from wrong, a reverence for life, how to fish using catch-and-release, how to shoot a jump shot, throw a curve ball, *not* play football...ever! There is no one around here or anywhere who can do that job but you, Patrick Jackson. No one. And you will be great!"

Suzy knew she had done the right thing, the smart thing. And it was the truth: Jax *was* needed. What she didn't know was how much she could still love this man she once thought was the center of her universe, when he couldn't even admit to himself the real reason for his melt-down under fire.

Not so the case with Mr. Jackson, who suddenly felt so good and so in love with his beautiful, *understanding* wife, he leaned up and planted a big wet one on her surprised mouth. When she instinctively kissed him back, the only two things that stopped Jax from tearing off clothes and entering her right then and there were: one, they were on duty in the communications room, and somebody could walk in any moment; and two, Colonel Joshua Middleton's mug had suddenly popped up on one of the east wall's flat screens.

Chapter 81

"Hope I'm not interrupting anything," said the talking head with flight sunglasses and a smirk.

"I was just getting something out of my husband's eye," said Suzy, chuckling at her own ridiculous excuse for straddling Jax.

"With your tongue?" retorted Joshua.

Suzy climbed off Jax and sat back in her own chair. "Haven't you ever been in love, Colonel?" she asked, red-faced and half-heartedly.

"Still am. I have a lovely wife. Almost as beautiful as you."

"Aw, ain't you sweet," tweeted Suzy. "So, what's up, Joshua?"

"Call in the troops for a pow-wow. Immediately." His tone had turned serious.

"Everyone is sleeping," said Jax, smoothing the creases in his Dockers.

"Wake 'em up. This is important. I haven't been to bed in forty-eight hours myself."

"Okay," said Suzy. "Can we tell them what this is about?"

"Sure," said the colonel. "I have the results of our preliminary interrogation with the captured Regg…around here affectionately known as *Reggie*. You're gonna want to hear some of it."

Forty-five minutes later all the Brookfields, some still in pajamas and robes, were gathered in the communications room, sipping coffee or orange juice. Mike was shoveling Honey Nut Cheerios from a bowl. David ate Honey Grahams right out of the box. Since there are always chores to do on a farm, the hired hands—Larry and Louis—were not present, to be filled in later. Neither were their wives, needing to stay with their children. And what the colonel was about to tell everyone was not for young ears anyway.

When all six were seated, Alan rang up the desert on the private and very secure wave length. "All here, Colonel," he said with a yawn. "Did our ugly friend talk?"

"Talk?" snorted Joshua. "We can't get him to shut up. It's like he thinks he's on some goddamn game show, and the more secrets he spills the more money he wins. "You know those three little spray bottles they all had on their utility belts? Well, we tested them on some volunteer corpsmen here."

"Any chance one of them was named Captain Wilowitz?" interjected Jax, thinking of the little prick with bad teeth who had demeaned him five nights ago in the west pasture.

"Who?"

Suzy smacked Jax on the shoulder.

"Never mind," grinned Jax, enjoying a little self-satisfaction.

"Anyway," continued Joshua, "the solution in the gray bottle, when sprayed in the face, makes the victim like a happy drunk. It's some kind of derivative of dopamine with parts similar to MDMA (Ecstasy), but not like anything our chemists have ever seen. Very effective. The recipient will follow you anywhere, do anything you say. He can answer questions, but he's kind of goofy, halfway in nadaville.

"The next bottle, the blue one...now here's a truth serum to end all truth serums. Its properties resemble sodium pentothal and amobarbital in some ways, but it's some five times more powerful and ten times as reliable. Used in combination with the happy drug, and you've never seen anyone so anxious to tell you his deepest darkest secrets, right down to how many times a day he whacks-off to doggy porn. Oops. Sorry ladies."

Some long draws were taken on some heavily caffeinated coffees. Young David and Mike made sideways glances at each other, stifling snickers. When adults weren't around, they both were on the web a lot. They knew.

"The third bottle, the white one, is just as amazing. It's an amnesia drug. One squirt and the victim forgets everything that's happened in the last couple hours. They usually apply this to the victim after they've put him or her back in bed or their car or wherever they had been abducted. They wake up thinking they just had a dream, but with no idea what it was about."

"So, did all these chemicals work the same on Reggie?" asked Mary.

"Sure did. The Reggs have pretty much the same respiratory and neurological systems we do. We did find that each spray was measured for someone weighing about one hundred pounds. This is because the Reggs always tried to abduct the smaller humans, in case they had to carry them somewhere. As you know, they aren't very big and strong themselves."

"Like when their experiments kill their captive," hissed Alan, "and they have to dispose of the body."

"I'm afraid so."

"Ugly *and* lazy," said Alan, recalling how easy it was to subdue Reggie with the chloroform.

"Okay, enough of how we got Reggie to talk," said Colonel Joshua Middleton. "Let's get down to what we've learned. Somebody there may want to take notes. It's quite a list. Of course, we'll be sending you the video and the written transcript of the entire interrogation so far, but it's lengthy, hours long. For now, for expedience sake, I'll give you the highlights."

Mary rolled her chair over to one of the computer stations and pulled up a blank page in Microsoft Word. "Ready," she said.

"Okay," here we go," said the colonel, squinting at his clipboard.

Chapter 82

"The Regg race is basically nomadic," said Joshua. "They originally are from our region of the Milky Way. Real close actually, only a couple light years away. They've been buzzing around from solar system to solar system at half the speed of light for eons, looking for planets like Earth to conquer and rule. Their mother ships have telescopes far more powerful than our Hubble or even the James Webb Space Telescope, so they can locate potential planets from light years away. They don't want to kill all the inhabitants, just most...the ones that serve no purpose to the Reggs' needs. They want to keep the farmers and ranchers and anyone vital to producing food and wares for their sustenance.

"They've been here on Earth since 1925, twenty years before our Mejan forefathers arrived. Reggie didn't know where their mothership is hiding, but his daughter ship, which is much like ours and your Maude, is...are you ready for this...hiding at the bottom of your very own Coralville Reservoir near the dam."

The women gasped. The men nodded, not surprised. They had to be somewhere close, and the 5,280-acre Corp of Engineers impoundment between Iowa City and Cedar Rapids was a perfect hiding place. Easy in, easy out for the scout ships.

"Holy shit," whispered Jax to Alan. "We went right over them the night we dropped the e-bomb on my friend, Roger."

"I know," he whispered back. "Christ!"

"And I can't tell you how many times I've fished along that dam."

"Did you have a question, Jax?" queried Joshua.

"Ah...just wondering if they have more scout ships like the one David shot down," Jax covered quickly. He was getting as good as any of the Brookfield at lying through his teeth.

"Yes, one more," said the colonel. "Reggie didn't know, but he said they would probably put in a request for a replacement. The higher-ups were usually pretty good about resupply."

"So, what's their immediate goal?" asked Mary.

"Okay, yes, I was just getting to that." Joshua checked his list. "Our unfriendly, neighborhood Reggs are determined—as we heavily suspected—to capture one of us with even a drop of Mejan blood in our veins. They want to know how many of us there are, where we are around the world, our technology and weaponry, and what *our* goals are. But aside from that, they want to run tests on us to see how they can kill Mejans en masse. Get us out of their hair, so they can get back to their original goal of finding a way to conduct selective genocide on the pure humans and take over the earth."

The communications room went eerily silent.

"They've been abducting humans for over three-quarters of a century now," continued the colonel, "and testing different drugs and viruses and bacteria on them. They thought they were onto something when they started the Asian flu labeled H2N2 in 1956, killing millions of people across the globe. But the human scientists—with considerable help from the Mejans, I might add—came up with an effective vaccine that stopped it cold. So, working from that basis, the Reggs introduced the H3N2 strain in 1968. It wasn't as devastating as the previous flu, and again our scientists developed a potent vaccine. So they switched gears and came up with the AIDS virus and more recently Ebola."

"Those goddamn motherfu....!" spat Alan, stomping his foot. Realizing the company he was in, he calmed himself with a deep breath and looked around the room. "Sorry, everybody."

"It's okay, honey," said Mary, patting his leg. "You said what all of us were thinking about those motherless cocksuckers."

That brought a round of stifled laughter and nods for some badly needed comic relief.

After seconding the sentiment, Colonel Middleton waved everyone to settle down, saying they had a lot to cover. When all attention was back on him, he continued. "It wasn't until they accidentally abducted their first Mejan, Maggie Connors, in 1970, that they even knew about the Mejan race being on Earth. Maggie was half Mejan, half human, like Helen, your mother." He nodded at Mary. "The Reggs were both flabbergasted and frightened by the Mejan intellect, which was far superior to theirs, even when diluted fifty percent by human DNA.

"From the same truth spray we used on our captive—Reggie—they learned all about how the Mejans had come to Earth via inter-dimensional travel, rather than the conventional running around the same dimension at sub-light speed. They would have loved to learn the technology for crossing into other dimensions, but Maggie, like most of us, had no idea how it worked.

"Of course, they learned the obvious: that Mejans were mating with humans, as their way of saving the race, since they can't acclimate to Earth's atmosphere and food sources without human genomes."

Alan interjected, "I suspect this is when the Reggs discovered that Mejans carry a lower body temperature than humans."

"Indeed," nodded the colonel. "And their infrared scanners were quickly developed."

Joshua paused to look down at his clipboard. He then slowly raised his eyes and said, "This may be a good time for a short break. Get some more coffee or whatever. And when we resume in a couple minutes, I would suggest you, Mary and Suzy, find something else to do. The next items we gleaned from Reggie are not very pleasant."

Chapter 83

The meeting resumed two minutes later with fresh coffee. All were present. When the colonel alluded to that fact, Mary replied, "We're all adults here, Joshua. We doubt there's anything you can tell us about the Reggs that would upset us *delicate womenfolk*."

"I thought as much," said Joshua proudly, with a half-smile.

The Air Force colonel proceeded to describe just what happens to most abductees when taken aboard a Regg ship. While under that drug of complete submission, but without the mercy of pain killers, they are stripped naked and strapped to an operating table of sorts. They are then hooked up to an array of probes, electrodes, needles and catheters. Every orifice is searched, with no concern for the discomfort or excruciating pain it may cause. Every piece of biological material is sampled and tested, from skin, hair, and eye fluid to feces, urine, blood, and reproductive elements. When all tests are complete, they may or may not be sprayed with the truth-inducing drug and interrogated thoroughly.

Once every possible piece of information has been extracted from the captive, they may be infected with whatever virus or bacteria the Reggs are testing at the moment. Previously, their prime directive was to eradicate a good portion of the Earth's population and gain control of the rest. But now being aware of Mejans, their sites are particularly set on annihilating us first.

When the colonel took a breath, Mary used the opportunity to ask what eventually happens to the abductees.

"I'll give you one more chance to leave the room," offered Joshua, as stern-faced as they had ever seen him.

Mary looked at her daughter. They both remained expressionless and seated. But Suzy did squeeze Jax's hand.

"Okay," said the colonel, setting his jaw. "After being infected, the pure humans are returned to their place of capture to resume their normal lives, most with no recollection whatsoever of what had happened to them, thanks to the amnesia spray in the white bottle. After all, the idea is to spread the disease among the populous. If, however, the subject dies while onboard, they are first tested for why, and then for anything harmful to the Reggs themselves. If clean, the victim is carted off to the daughter ship where he or she is hung upside down over a drain, decapitated and bled out. They are completely gutted, their innards sent to a lab for further tests.

The rest of the carcass is then pushed along a track in the ceiling to cold storage, where they are later consumed by the goddamn, meat-eating, soulless Reggs."

No one spoke. But no one fainted or started crying, either. Even Jax didn't ask for a happy pill. He just squeezed his wife's hand tighter, while throwing up in his mouth.

"What happened to Maggie Connors and Ned Wilson?" asked Alan softly, his head down.

"Reggie says the Maggie affair was before his time, but word was she was kept alive for another two years before dying on her own. She was too scrawny by then, plus they had plenty of other cattle and pigs and humans in the locker, so they just pulverized her and jettisoned her remains into the water for fish food."

Jax glanced sideways at Suzy. She was turning pallid. He already was.

"On the other hand, Reggie *was* involved with abducting Ned, and was, in fact, the very *ugly cocksucker* Ned's camera phone recorded."

A soft gasp lifted in the communications room. It was indeed a small world.

"They squeezed every bit of intel out of Ned, then saw no reason to keep him. So he was killed and—after a thorough autopsy which included his brain—eaten. The cannibalistic bastards seem to believe by eating their enemy, they acquire its strengths."

Chapter 84

"As I said," concluded Colonel Middleton, "you'll be getting the complete video plus written report shortly. "These are just the things we wanted you folks to know as soon as possible. I'll throw it up to Q&A, if you have any questions."

Most everyone asked at once, so Joshua picked the cutest. "Yes, Suzy."

"I'm just curious what the Regg race calls themselves. As you know, we've always called them *Reggs,* the Mejan word for *enemy.*"

"We wondered that too," said the colonel, flipping through his pile of notes. "Reggie says they are *Pin-shi-cals*, or something like that. His spelling, not mine. His own name is *Shash-Oceron*. But the drug had him so congenial, he said he liked *Reggie* better!"

"I trust we're going to learn their language," added Mary.

"By the time we're done with him," smirked Joshua, "we'll have their entire numeric system, alphabet, and vocabulary on software. As we speak, our engineers are helping him draw up a working manual for both their scout ships and their daughter ship at the bottom of Coralville. Might come in handy if we can ever steal one intact, huh?"

"Speaking of that," said Jax, "if we know that craft is just off the Coralville Dam, isn't there some way we can go down there and pull it out or something? I've fished there a lot. It's only about forty feet at its deepest."

"Well, the next time you're out there, Jax," deadpanned the colonel, "try and snag it for us, okay?"

"I'm serious," said Jax over the mild laughter. "Surely you desert people have some means of dredging it up. Or blowing it up, at least."

"I apologize for being facetious, son," said the colonel sincerely. "But the fact is what you suggest is almost impossible. First, we'd have to locate exactly where it is. Even around the dam area are some thousand acres of water, while that ship is only about one acre in size. We can't use a depth-finder like you do for fishing or any kind of radar or sonar. That thing has pure stealth, just like our crafts. All signals would just be absorbed with no return."

Jax's analytical mind was racing. "Wait a minute," he interrupted. "If the sonar signal from a depth-finder would return no signal, that alone would show up on the screen. You'd see a graphic line showing the lake's bottom, then suddenly nothing where the Regg ship was. That would tell us exactly where they are."

"Very good, young man," piped Joshua. "Always thinking. But we have to assume so are the Reggs. The second a depth-finder was scanning in their area, they'd know it. They could easily move laterally, playing cat-and-mouse, or even burrow deep into the lake bottom—just like your Maude did there on the farm—so the substrate covering the hull *would* return a signal. Thanks for the input though."

"Yeah," groaned Jax.

"So, the only way to find it," continued the colonel, "is by sending divers down or the Navy's Bluefin-21 submersible in water that has lateral visibility of about what, five or six feet under ideal conditions?"

"More like three or four feet at best," sighed angler Jax, who knew the murky lake well.

"There ya go," said Joshua with a flip of his hand. "It's a needle in a haystack, Jax. And again, surely the craft would have around-the-clock sonar and radar early-warning, plus a defense mechanism. It could easily outmaneuver our divers or submersible."

"Even though water is seven hundred and eighty-four times denser than air?" challenged the outdoor writer, who had used that fact in one of his columns a year ago.

"Well, let's see," mused the colonel, looking down and punching keys on his hand-held. "The speed of light is one hundred and eighty-six thousand miles per second divided by two then divided again by your seven hundred and eighty-four density of water. So, the Regg craft could move underwater at the reduced speed of only four hundred and twenty-seven thousand miles per hour."

"I'll shut up," conceded Jax.

"Say we did find it," continued Joshua, obviously on a roll he wasn't quite ready to abandon. "Then what? Blow it up? I'm sure the Corp of Engineers would love us blasting the shit out of their precious reservoir. Plus we'd have to invite every news network and UFO fanatical group in the world to come watch, because they'd be converging on the Iowa City area in droves soon enough anyway, once alien body parts and debris were floating all over the surface and washing up on the shores."

"Sorry," said Jax, totally deflated. "I thought maybe you guys had devised some type of tractor beam like in Star Trek and could just suck it out of the water."

"I'm sorry, too," said the colonel, now in condolence. "I wish we had such technology."

David raised his hand and Joshua pointed at him.

"Did Reggie mention if they knew anything about our USLAP cannon that shot down their scout ship?"

"Since he was chloroformed before it happened, Reggie knew nothing about that. We asked him if the Reggs knew *beforehand* that we have such a weapon and he said no. As far as Reggie knew, they think we have nothing more than the same sonic boomers they knocked your dad down with."

"So, they probably don't have anything like our weapon technology," concluded David hopefully.

"Reggie simply doesn't know either. He speculated that since they've never run into a race before that could fight back with spacecraft like theirs, there was no need to engineer stronger weapons. They'd probably like to now, but he doesn't know if they even have a prototype. Their engineers at HQ don't tell them much. It's something we would very much like to know, too."

"Having flown against them," said Alan, "they seem to have the same anti-gravity system we do. But any idea what their power source is?"

"Again, something we would like to know," said Colonel Middleton emphatically. "But Reggie had no idea. He's basically just a grunt."

Joshua leaned back in his chair, took a deep breath and said, "Listen folks. I'm about flagging here. Unless you have anything else that can't wait until you get the report, I need to sign off and catch some winks."

"Please, go," said Mary, echoed by Suzy. "And thank you so much, Colonel."

"Read the report," he added, just before punching out. "You'll find some more interesting stuff in it."

Chapter 85

Interesting was too mild a word. The report was *fascinating*. Reggie had provided detailed insights into everything from their favorite pastimes to how they make love...or in their case, how they copulate. Love and affection are concepts held in less reverence than by humans and Mejans. Death of a mate may spur some sense of loss, but it also can carry the benefit of moving up in rank.

And gender means less, too. The females of the species are generally only slightly smaller than their male counterparts and are just as fierce. In fact, two corpses from that night of the raid turned out to be females. With the exception of having vaginas, two rows of four small mammaries on each side of their chests, slightly shorter hair, and narrower snouts, there is little difference. They mostly do it doggy style. Of course.

They bathe every few days and most brush their teeth nightly. Many smoke cigarettes and do a lot of drugs. Just like us, they eat and defecate sitting down. The more intelligent Reggs are either chemists—working on the doomsday pandemic for humans and recreational drugs for themselves, or are strategists—planning when and where to raid the next grocery chain, furniture outlet, clothing store, electronics store, drug store—to keep resupplying all their ships and crews.

At first they hijacked delivery trucks, forcing them off the road with EMPs and neutralizing the drivers with sprays. But all too often they ended up with too many loaves of bread and not enough butter, or not enough milk and too many pumpkins. So they switched over to raiding the various stores after hours to better pick and choose what they needed. They would then completely disable the store's computer, so there was no way to tell how much inventory was missing. They rarely took meat, preferring it fresh from the variety of farm animals that were so easy to pluck out of open meadows at night.

So, most of the Reggs are just lackeys, carrying out the actual thievery, abductions, maintenance, kitchen duties, and so on. Even the busier ones have long hours of isolation in their cramped spaceships, with little to do until taking over the world. So, many hours are passed watching our television broadcasts, which is how they obtained a working knowledge of English long ago and try to keep up on the vernacular. Having long ago easily decoded all the satellite signals, including the Pay-per-Views, they particularly enjoy Hollywood's movies. Contests are often held to see who can name the movie a certain quote came from, like, "I'll have what she's having" from *When Harry Met Sally*. They think the Star Trek movies with Kirk and Spock are great, but their favorite is the Twilight series, as they root for the werewolves. They snicker at our love stories, don't understand our humor and Comedy Central, and they find humans fornicating on the Penthouse channels a howl, especially when it's done face-to-face.

Besides television and recreational drugs, another Regg pastime is losing themselves in their highly-advanced virtual reality technology. Reggie's favorite VR game had just been downloaded from headquarters a week ago. It is the sixth version of *Mejan Hunt*, where his game character can chase down an infinite number of Mejans, like a wolf would a fawn or jackrabbit through the pine forests and green plains of Minnesota's north woods. When a victim is caught, it is torn to pieces and eaten for extra speed and stamina.

Before the raid, Reggie's home ship at the bottom of the Coralville Reservoir housed fourteen of his fellow aliens. No kids. This was a working crew with the sole directive of capturing a Mejan. Doing the math, there are now only eight onboard, assuming the destroyed scout ship at Brookfield had a two-man crew. Would they be replaced? Reggie didn't know. They had never lost shipmates before. Usually when they need something, it is forthcoming.

As luck would have it, Reggie's main job was *maintenance technician*. He knows the layout of both the scout ships and the daughter ship like the back of his paw. He is also somewhat familiar with the navigation systems. So the floor plans and control panel layouts that he was happy to draw up for his new *Desert Masters* were detailed and hopefully accurate. The drugs did make him have to stop and think sometimes. Threats of castration and/or fang extraction usually stimulated his memory.

Intrigued, Jax eagerly took on the task of learning the daughter ship's floor plan, plus some of the functions of each button, knob, and switch on the central command's control panels. He discovered they were not all that different from the ones in Fighter One or any of his video games. Why would they be? Up is up and down is down, regardless of what part of the Milky Way you call home. It was more difficult to learn which switch switched which door or monitor or weapon or camera. But with Reggie's attempt to label everything in qualified English, Jax felt he had a reasonable grasp.

Suzy, meanwhile, found studying their religious philosophies, or lack thereof, quite absorbing. The Reggs generally and dispassionately believe in some sort of supreme being and an afterlife. But to no surprise their deity is an all-powerful, vengeful god, who rewards aggression and dying for the cause, while nirvana consists of a beautiful green planet where the human-like inhabitants wait on them hand and foot with choice cuts of raw, prime, tender meats and blood-red, sweet wines. There are no church services of any sort. No Regg has ever seen or heard their deity, so each one's specific beliefs are about as diverse as ours and perhaps only less so sincere. What little artwork or literature they have revolves more around conflict and conquest than spiritualism and beauty.

To Suzy, in some skewed aspects, she could almost feel sympathetic toward the Reggs, as in kindred space travelers from another part of the Universe trying to coexist on a peculiar, foreign planet. It had to be hard on them being sequestered inside their small spaceships day after day, unable to walk freely on Earth, as she could.

That tolerant and typical female Mejan perception, however, was set up for a quick and decisive demise.

Chapter 86

"Did you read that part about the masks the Reggs use sometimes when abducting people?" asked Suzy with a chuckle, spinning around on the barstool like an eight-year-old at Danny's Diner. Her bare legs and feet were tucked up under the pink chenille robe. She loved Jax's big kitchen with its piggy-back ovens, glass cabinets, double islands, a refrigerator that looked like the wall, and shiny black granite surfaces everywhere, even the heated floor.

"I guess I missed that part of the report," said Jax, setting two glasses of orange juice down on the breakfast bar. He planted himself on the padded leather stool next to her. He was wearing his favorite terrycloth robe in navy blue. Nothing else. "What about it?"

"Reggie said they used these fabricated alien masks to make themselves look far different than they are."

"What," said Jax, dropping a teaspoon of sugar into his coffee, "like the ones they wore in downtown Champaign when they kidnapped Ned Wilson? Trying to look like humans?"

"No, a completely different look. You know those classic alien, full-head masks you can buy at any costume store…with the enormous gray head, big black eyes, and teeny, tiny nose, mouth and chin?"

"Yeah, like Greenhouse Grandma," snickered Jax.

That earned him a slap on his shoulder. "She doesn't look anything like that, you jerk," Suzy retorted. Then she cocked a half smile. "But maybe a little like Grandma's father. I saw a picture of him once. He did have a big head and eyes. A real looker."

Jax snickered.

"Well, anyway," continued Suzy, getting serious again, "guess who originated that image?"

"Steven Spielberg?" That earned Jax another slap.

"No, funny boy, the Reggs. Once they started drugging and abducting humans, they discovered through repeat interrogations some of them would still remember the faces of their kidnappers…either via hypnosis or recalling vivid nightmares. So, the Reggs made these alien facades to hide what they really looked like and plant an entirely different image in their victims' minds."

Jax let that sink in, along with a couple bites of toaster strudel. "Pretty clever," he said wryly. "So if one of them ever did get exposed for what he

217

truly looks like, he could just drop down on all fours and bark like man's best friend."

"Will you be serious for one minute?" scolded his wife. "Sure, it sounds silly to us, but it's a testament to the lengths they will go through to keep their identity and existence secret. Besides, Reggie said they don't do it much anymore."

"That's because their sights now are entirely on capturing a Mejan," said Jax, no longer flippant. "And there's no way they would let one of us go. So, why hide their identity?"

They finished their breakfast in silence, both wondering why they were discussing the Regg report, when they were supposed to be enjoying each other away from the farm for a few days, staying here at his house. By all indications, the Reggs were not a threat, not in the short term at least. They were overmatched to begin with and were now undermanned. Plus they'd lost the element of surprise. With virtually no chance of another raid, Alan and Mary encouraged the newlyweds to go spend a few days away from the farm. And as long as they stayed under the solid metal roof of Jax's Lexus and the even more solid steel roof of his four-million-dollar mansion, Suzy Brookfield could not be detected by the Regg's infrared scanners.

As for their relationship…one eighth Mejan Suzy had typically pushed thoughts of Jax's cowardice to the back of her mind. He was, after all, her husband, the father of her unborn child. And despite his shortcomings, making love wasn't one of them. She had to admit that she still loved her big, handsome, Josh Duhamel look-alike, even if he was a wimp. Besides, she had already resigned herself to the fact that if it ever came right down to it, she would have to be the one to take on the role of protector of her family. After all, she'd already killed a Regg, maybe two, for the same cause. She wasn't exactly cast-iron hard now. But neither was she the same Mejan pacifist of just a few weeks ago.

Suzy slipped off the chair and moved behind Jax to wrap her arms around him and his soft robe. "Reggie also said they have no such thing as marriage," she hummed coyly, nibbling the back of his ear. "They just pair up and fight off any challengers." She slipped her hands inside his robe and rubbed his chest. "Would you fight for me, tiger?"

You could at least do that, couldn't you?

Without turning around, Jax reached up and pulled her head down for an upside down kiss on her cheek. "Nobody would dare mess with my woman," he said, adding a growl at the end.

Suddenly Suzy's entire robe was draped over his head, the sweet smell of her warm skin teasing his nostrils and face. This meant she was now naked, right down to her bare feet padding quickly over the flagstone floor on their way out of the kitchen.

"Then you'd better take me to bed or lose me forever, Goose," she shouted, her voice fading up the stairs.

"Meg Ryan to Anthony Edwards in *Top Gun*," he yelled, pulling the chenille robe off his head and running after her.

Chapter 87

That night, sleeping soundly on his back in his big round bed with Suzy breathing quietly against his chest, Jax was having a most pleasant dream. The two of them were lying on cushy, black and gold blankets in the sand at Megans Beach on St. Thomas in the Caribbean, enjoying the sun and sea and freedom. He'd been here a year ago with Jannie, but in this reenactment it was purely Suzy.

Circling low in the sky were three pelicans, each occasionally taking a headlong crash dive into the water to capture a colorful, sergeant major fish. A parade of people from many nations walked up and down the beach, enjoying the calm, turquoise water and temperate air.

To the distant musical pang of steel drums, two cabana boys approached, each with a pina colada on a tray. The boys separated to kneel beside their respective customer. But instead of serving the drinks in the normal fashion, they gently sprayed them in Jax and Suzy's faces. Our lovers didn't mind, because the sensation was very pleasant, very soothing. Bordering on euphoric.

The nice young men then helped the naked couple to their feet. They found Jax's dark-blue tracksuit somewhere on the periphery and helped him put it on, along with his cross-trainer Nikes. For Suzy they retrieved her yellow print sundress worn earlier in the day, draped over the valet. They slipped it on over her head, and placed the white strap wedges on her feet.

"Pick up communicators and put in pockets," one of the hairy cabana boys said. Jax and Suzy did as suggested. That was thoughtful of their escorts. They might have forgotten the devices otherwise.

"Where are we going?" asked Jax, although he really didn't care.

"Fishing," said the other one with a toothy grin. He was funny looking for a cabana boy.

Without turning on any lights and careful to not wake Odett in her bedroom down the hall, Jax and Suzy were led downstairs, through the kitchen, past the mud room, and into the six-stall garage. Jax was told to back his Lexus out and around to the trailer with his twenty-foot Ranger bassboat on it. He had done it so many times he could do it in his sleep.

His friends seemed to know nothing about hooking a boat trailer to a hitch on a car, so Jax had to do that, too. As he cranked the hitch cup down onto the ball and set the safety chains and tail lights, they sat Suzy in the back of the SUV and fastened her seat belt. She was delighted to be going fishing, too.

Jax offered to drive, but his friends insisted he sit in back with his lovely wife, while they sat up front. It was good they knew how to drive his big Lexus. No one except him ever had until now.

"Where are we going to fish?" asked Jax, looking out the window, watching the knee-high evergreen bushes and solar lights lining his long, brick drive way pass by. It seemed strange to sit in the backseat of his vehicle. He'd never done that before. Suzy leaned over and put her head on his shoulder. She seemed to be falling back to asleep.

"Coralville Reservoir," said the front seat passenger, lighting a cigarette.

"Oh, good," said Jax. He mildly wondered what happened to his pina colada. "I fish there a lot. I know it well."

It seemed odd they took such a round-about way to the lake, skirting Highway 6 that weaved between Iowa City and Coralville in favor of the back roads. But the folks up there seemed to know what they were doing. Jax wondered if they belonged to his bass club. Maybe they were friends of his friends, just in town for some fun. Maybe a dog show. He hoped he could get them into some nice bass. That would make him and them happy.

Suzy was leaning on him now as far as her constraints would allow. Definitely asleep. He stroked her short, honey-blonde hair. "Hey, this will be the first time Suzy fishes out of my boat," he announced with a whisper. "I've always wanted to take her, but it wasn't safe with the Reggs around."

The one riding shotgun turned to look back at the newlyweds. "It safe now," he said, smiling in a friendly sort of way. "No Reggs around here."

Just then a car came up fast from behind and passed them, its lights illuminated the shotgun man's profile. "Hey," chimed Jax, "you look kinda like McDoogle, our Golden Retriever."

The two dogs looked at each and smiled. "Woof. Woof," mocked the driver, glancing in the rearview mirror.

Chapter 88

The silver Lexus pulling the dark-blue Ranger bassboat made a hard left and eased down the steep asphalt road into the launching area by the Coralville dam. Besides the high-beam HID headlights, the only illumination came from the single sodium lamp on a high utility pole. It was ten p.m. The driver spent until ten-ten p.m. trying to back the boat down the ramp, but it kept jackknifing on him. He couldn't get it through his fuzzy head he had to turn the steering wheel in the opposite direction he wanted the boat to go. Exasperated, he told Jax to do it.

If the Reggs knew anything about running a bassboat, they could have helped out by backing it off the trailer into the water, then idling up to the dock and holding it there until Jax could park the SUV and trailer. But instead, they just sat there in the boat with Suzy, smoking, watching Jax systematically bounce from SUV to boat to dock to SUV to parking lot to dock and back into the boat. The only thing they were good at was directing him to the exact spot in the middle of the lake they wished to go.

"Do you want to fish *here*?" asked Jax, idling in one location as directed. "It's better closer to the dam."

"No," said one of the poodles in the front deck's pedestal seat. "We will not fish."

Jax was in a very passive mood. He hadn't felt this good since experimenting with various mind-bending chemicals in college after his parents' death. But something wasn't right. Why weren't they fishing? Why come all the way out here to his beloved reservoir with his beautiful bassboat and not fish? Sure, it was nighttime. But bass will hit at night. They have sensitive lateral lines that can detect even a plastic worm's water displacement as it swims silently along. Jax wanted to care, especially since this was Suzy's first time in his boat. But he couldn't bring himself to do anything more than smile.

Something in the dark water seemed to be happening all around them. At first, just a noise and mild swaying from churning water. Then against the city lights reflecting off the clouds and down to the water, he could see a dark wall rising and stopping about three feet above the surface. It seemed to be all around them. Then came a sucking sound and the sensation of slowly falling, like in an elevator. Either the round wall was rising high above them or they were sinking far below it into total blackness.

The next sensations involved a gushing, echoing sound of water being quickly extracted and the boat setting down on something solid, definitely not floating in water anymore. The two cabana coonhounds took each of the humans by the arm and helped them out of the boat and onto the black, corrugated deck of the ship's hangar. Just twenty feet away in the dim light sat a scout ship. It rang a bell with Jax. Where had he seen something like that before?

He didn't have time to ponder the question, as they were quickly led through a pneumatic door and down a long, curving hallway. The smell of an old butcher shop was not pleasant. But Jax didn't mind. He looked over at Suzy. She was awake and smiling, as she walked along with her upright Irish Setter escort. She didn't seem to care either. Life was good.

Another door hissed open and the pair were led into a white room with many pretty screens and lights on the walls, kind of like the communications room back at the farm. But instead of chairs, this room had two tall beds on silver frames and some moveable tables with trays full of shiny instruments.

"Put communicators here," said one of the Reggs, holding a silver tray in front of them. They didn't want to touch the units, fearing in the wrong hands they would become inoperable or possibly blow up. Suzy and Jax obeyed and the tray was placed on a nearby table.

A door at the other end of the small room opened and two more canines entered. They were wearing light-blue jumpsuits with orange gloves and matching rubber boots. *It's demeaning*, thought Jax, *to dress your pets in human clothes*. But he had to admit it was kind of cute.

Not so cute, however, was when one of them walked up to his smiling, half-asleep wife, reached down to take hold of the hem of her yellow print sundress and pulled it up and over her head, letting it float rudely to the cold floor. Sure, Suzy is pretty, and downright sexy when naked. But this was not right. They shouldn't be taking her clothes off in front of people in a pet store. And why were they now marching her over to lie down on one of those high-standing beds? And why were they strapping her to it? For that matter, why were his wrists being manacled at his sides to this cold, metallic wall?

Chapter 89

No, this most certainly was not right. Jax's euphoria was starting to drain away from his brain like water out of his boat's bilge. It was being replaced by small waves of clarity and the accompanying anxiety. His favorite verse from Jefferson Airplane's *White Rabbit* began swirling in his head: ...*when logic and proportion have fallen sloppy dead...*

The Reggs had made a serious miscalculation. Or perhaps oversight would be a better word. Their "happy, who-gives-a-damn" sprays were always geared for small humans, one hundred pounds or less. They didn't like abducting anyone larger in case they had to carry their carcass somewhere. Lazy bastards. Actually, the Reggs didn't weigh much more themselves. Jax, meanwhile, was twice that weight. They should have given him at least double the dose. They hadn't.

He looked down at his tethers. They were short, leather belts with buckles, riveted to the metal wall. There was a duplicate pair of them directly to his right, not occupied. He tested his. They held firm. He felt even more anxiety replacing his serenity. He heard Suzy moan. He looked over to see one of the lab technicians drawing blood from her arm, while the other scraped the instep of her right foot with a scalpel. Suzy was no longer smiling. Her head was twisting side to side.

Jax's heart rhythm began to increase to tango tempo. He could feel the adrenalin elevating throughout his entire muscular system. He tried the constraints again. The leather stretched and crackled, but held firm.

That's when reality suddenly snapped back in at full force. *Oh, my God!* He screamed inside his head. *We're in a Regg spaceship! We've been kidnapped. They have Suzy on a table poking and prodding her.* Jax bit his lip to keep from screaming out loud. He tasted his own blood. He tried the leather straps again. *Fuck!* Tears of fear and frustration started welling in his eyes.

Then one of the hairy, grotesque technicians pulled a syringe with a very long needle off a tray and started toward Suzy and her baby bump.

That was Regg mistake number two. And this one would prove fatal.

It's been well established Patrick Bernard Jackson is an easy-going guy. Okay, let's not sugarcoat it. Without a kinder, less description way to describe him, Jax is a chicken shit. He first proved it on the football field in high school when he didn't act on his desire to level that linebacker, who had blind-sided him smack in his kidneys. He did it again in French class freshman year in college, backing down from Bruno the wrestler after confronting him regarding his constant bullying of Jax's roommate. Just the other night, when Captain Wilowitz belittled him, he did nothing about it except punch him out in one of his signature fantasies. And of course the capper of them all, that night of the Regg raid, when he melted into a pool of pathetic fear rather than fight for his family.

But someone coming at his wife and unborn child with anything more threatening than an ultrasound transducer and plenty of Vaseline was not a good idea. Neither was designing their leather tethers to restrain only small, doped-up human beings. In the Reggs' defense, how were they to know they would be dealing with this larger-than-normal anthropoid, who could suddenly become so enraged that every fiber of his toned muscles was infused with nuclear strength, thermal-dynamic energy?

The metal rivets securing the leather straps tore from the wall like pieces of cheap tin. The lab technician with the long needle paused a foot from Suzy, turning at the waist to check out the source of the metallic sound. Its yellow eyes had time only to grow wide in surprise, as the raging bull with mayhem in his glare and a blood-curdling rebel yell from his gaping mouth lowered his right shoulder and caught the hapless hound mid-chest with all the force of a cannon ball. Ribs cracked, air left lungs with a voluminous *whoosh*, as one hundred pounds of lab tech—who in Jax's eyes strangely resembled that high school linebacker—crashed against the far wall so hard its scalp split open, rendering it instantly bloody and unconscious.

Still on his feet and seething like a mad bull, Jax quickly spun around to see what the other three Reggs were doing. Labrador number two—oddly with the face of one Captain Wilowitz—was coming at him with raised scalpel and bared teeth. Jax easily blocked the clumsy, downward thrust of the knife with his forearm, and countered with a haymaker to the snout, knocking three incisors and one fang into the back of its throat. If that didn't render the Regg catatonic, banging its head on the hard floor from the fall probably did.

Two down.

The Regg that had personally escorted Jax into the room was already latched onto Jax's back tighter than Quasimodo's hump. Jax instinctively spun around to locate the other Regg, while reaching back over his head to grab his attacker by the scruff of its shaggy neck. The other one was fumbling with its utility belt, ostensibly trying to dislodge one of the spray bottles. But before successfully completing the maneuver, that Regg was cross-bodied by its flying, wind-milling buddy (who seemed to look a lot like a University of Iowa wrestler named Bruno), sending them both against the wall where Jax had been shackled.

Dazed but both still conscious, the one on top got a Nike to the nose and went out like a light, while the one pinned under the first Regg lucked out, having the gray bottle ripped away from him and sprayed full into its bleeding nose and mouth. The escort immediately relaxed, its black lips spreading into a silly, hideous grin.

Chapter 90

Unbuckling his leather cuffs and tossing them to the floor, Jax wanted to head right over and attend to Suzy. But he'd seen too many movie clichés where that maneuver would only invite the supposedly dead villain to wake up and come at the hero from behind. *Not in this sci-fi thriller.* Thinking as clearly as he ever had in his twenty-five years, Jax's knew the more immediate concern was to retrieve his communicator in case some more Reggs came through the door. He picked it up from the tray on the nearby table and it woke right up in his hand. But no bars. No surprise. They were deep inside a Regg daughter ship under some forty feet of water in the Coralville Reservoir.

Jax knew he could put a hole through any oncoming Regg with its laser, so he programmed it to stun with a sonic punch instead. One of them might turn out to be the only Regg who knew how to operate this ship and get them the hell out of here.

Jax walked over to the two fallen lab technicians and sprayed their faces with the gray bottle. By now he was quite certain it was the same drug they used on him and Suzy to make them relaxed and easily controlled. So even if the Labradors woke up, they'd be too passive and suggestible to be a threat.

After spraying the unconscious Regg he had flung over his back and kicked in the face, Jax dropped to one knee and removed the utility belt of the conscious one he had already sent to funky-town. Hooking it to his own waist, he pulled out the Regg's communicator and watched it immediately self-destruct, as expected. Good. He then collected all three of the other communicators and watched their little melt-downs one by one. They were useless to Jax anyway. Now they were of no use to the Reggs either.

Finally at Suzy's side, Jax unbuckled the leather straps on her wrists and ankles. It was gut-wrenching to see her lying there so exposed in this godless, foul-smelling, bone-chilling hell hole. The new-born Hercules found himself in momentary remission, fighting back tears. But when his smiling wife sat up, put her arms around him, and said "Hi, honey," like nothing had happened, he quickly regained his composure. After all, Ironman never cried, did he?

"You're fine, Suzy Q," he stated firmly. "Everything's under control."

"Who was poking me?" she asked softly, confused. "It kinda hurt."

It was obvious Jax needed to somehow neutralize the chemical effects still working on his wife. His size and adrenalin had done it for him. But Suzy was tiny by comparison and completely mellow-yellow. His only choices were to spray her with one of the other bottles and see what happens, or wait for the effects to wear off—which the Reggie papers had said was about four hours, meaning at least two hours from now.

"Let's see, *gray to obey*," he said, quoting his own rhyme to remember the different sprays. "*Blue be true.*" And for the white bottle it was just, *remembers nothing,* because he never could come up with a way to rhyme *white* with *amnesia.*

Suzy was already goofy and obedient under the gray spray, so Jax debated between the last two, wondering which would be better: having his wife semi-alert, carefree, and emptying her soul with every question asked her; or dazed and confused, remembering nothing from the past two hours. He sprayed her with the *blue be true* one. He needed her to be totally aware of their critical situation past and present, even if she did continue to find it all somewhat amusing.

"What's going on?" smiled Suzy, looking around the room at the four incapacitated Reggs and her sweating, still-panting husband. Suddenly she remembered everything, even what she had seen from her supine position. Her usually milquetoast husband had turned into Captain America and made short work of the four aliens. "My goodness, Jax," she gasped with a half-smile of wonder and a new respect. "You were an animal!"

It took a minute for the concept to sink in. "Yes, I guess was," said Jax on reflection, while surveying the damage he had inflicted. He found the unique feeling of self-assurance rather pleasurable. But concern over their current situation was still paramount. Refocusing, he fetched Suzy's dress and shoes from the floor and helped her put them on. He then plucked her communicator from the tray and handed it to her. It fired right up.

"Program it to stun," he said, with all the command of his favorite starship captain. "We may need some expert advice from one of the Reggs on getting out of here."

Lastly, Jax told the conscious Regg to give up his utility belt, which he did with surprising sprightliness. Jax then handed it to Suzy and she buckled it around her narrow waist. It was a clashing accessory to her yellow print sundress, but Jax still found the *Victoria's Secret-Ace Hardware* combo kind of chic.

Together husband and wife lifted the two bleeding and unconscious lab technicians onto the two operating tables and strapped them in. Tight. They sat the passed out escort with the bloody mouth upright and raised his arms high enough to strap him in with the other pair of wall restraints. Real tight. They decided to take the fourth one with them, because he might come in handy. Under the influence, he was more than happy to accompany the two, nice humans.

"First, we have to neutralize all other Reggs on the ship," said Jax, taking Suzy's hand and leading her out the pneumatic door they had originally come through. The Regg followed, as ordered. "Reggie said there were fourteen onboard before the raid. So fourteen minus six at the farm, minus four here, leaves four." Jax stopped and turned to the spacey Regg walking behind them. "Is that right, four more onboard?"

"Yes, four more," he said with yellow eyes looking upward for the answer and counting on his short, fat fingers.

"By the way, what's your name?" asked Suzy.

"Beltztic. Beltztic Crunel."

"No," said Jax, "your name is Butt-Ugly. Got it?"

"Butt-Ugly," grinned the alien. "Beltztic like."

Chapter 91

In tow and half running to keep up, Suzy was so enamored with her suddenly courageous, virile husband, she just had to say it. "Have I told you how much I love you?"

"Yes, many times," said Jax over his shoulder, staying the course down the long, arcing hallway of dull pewter. "Why are you asking now?"

His question was a mistake. Under the control of the truth spray, Suzy started on a nonstop jabber about loving him the moment she saw him and how his azure eyes sent shivers down her spine, and while he had wimped out that night of the Regg raid, he had become fearless and foolhardy tonight, and how his new-found verve commanded attention and respect, and…"

Jax stopped in the middle of the dimly-lit hall and put both hands on his beautiful wife's face. He looked into those hero-worshiping, copper-brown eyes and said, "Babe, I love you, too. And it warms my heart to hear how much you love me and all that. But right now, please shut the fuck up."

Suzy had no choice but to obey. It didn't bother her though. All Jax had to do was ask and the flood gates would gladly reopen.

Recalling the layout Reggie had drawn up of the daughter ship, Jax was fairly certain the next door in the hallway led to the dining area. Butt-Ugly verified it, while inquisitively inspecting a large, blood-encrusted booger he had just extracted from his black nose. Staying clear enough to avoid triggering the motion-activated door, Mr. and Mrs. Jackson stood on each side like two detectives on any one of a hundred TV cop shows.

"If there are more than one," whispered Jax, "you take the ones on the left, I'll take the ones on the right." Suzy nodded. She liked this game. "We have the element of surprise, so take your time and let the laser sight lock on your target." Again she nodded, with a waggish smile of anticipation.

Jax waved his hand in front of the door to trigger the motion detector and rushed in, his laser phone leveled and ready to fire. Suzy followed right behind. Two red dots raced across the empty room's walls like berserk red bugs. No one there, just a long dining table of shiny silver metal with matching bench seats. What must have been the kitchen galley was at the far end. Jax half expected its counter to be lining with ceramic bowls of Purina Dog Chow.

The next door was a bathroom. Still in wisecracking mode, Jax started to say it should be a fenced-in backyard area, but decided to keep it to himself; the two goofballs with him would have laughed at any joke he made, funny or not. Besides, he could always put these little snippets of humor in the book he hoped to write someday about all this.

No one was using that facility either. Nor was anyone in the next room, the first of the sleeping quarters, its door wide open.

The next door was closed, signaling a strong potential to be occupied by a snoozing Regg. But to open the door from the hallway required a code punched into the small keypad on the wall.

"Do you remember, is there anything in Reggie's interrogation about getting into certain rooms?" he whispered to Suzy.

Ooops.

His darling wife started quoting chapter and verse of the Reggie Papers before Jax could tell her to stop and just answer the question.

"Yes," she said, nibbling on her lip to spur memory. "There is a universal, three button code for all of them. But I don't know it. It's not numbers, just strange symbols."

He decided to ask Butt-Ugly, who nodded stupidly. But when Jax told him to push the right sequence, the hairy, stubby finger just flew over the keypad haphazardly pushing buttons. He knew the code, he just didn't care enough to focus. Jax suggested that his testicles depended on it. On the very next try the door slid open.

Inside the darkened room was a snoring Regg, both legs twitching like he was chasing something in his dream. One spray in his face from the *gray to obey* bottle, followed by Jax's strict order to stay in bed, took care of that one. Suzy lifted its communicator from the night stand and it immediately self-destructed.

One down, three to go.

Chapter 92

"What's your job here?" Suzy asked their trailing Regg, as they moved on down the line.

"Pilot, cook," he replied.

"Pilot?" queried Jax. "Small craft or this big one?"

"Small craft."

"Do you know anything about flying this bigger one?"

"A little," he said. "But only go up to surface and back down. It not fly in sky long time."

"By the way," said Jax, "I've been wondering how you knew Suzy and I were at my house. There's no way you could have found us with your infrared scanners."

"Your car," smiled Butt-Ugly. "Saw it by pond when we scan her. Saw it go from farm to your house and not leave."

"Shit!" spat Jax. "How could we be so stupid to overlook that?"

"It's okay, honey," said Suzy, starting on the compulsive rant mandated by Jax's inadvertent question. "We've had a lot on our minds lately. We had to defend our farm and clean up after." Jax just shook his head, as Suzy kept rambling. "We had to bring in HQ with the C-17 cargo plane to take away the prisoner and melted Regg ship. We've been studying the Reggie Papers, we've been…" Jax's hand over her mouth and a quiet, loving order ended her answer.

The next two dorm rooms were open and vacant, bringing them to the recreation room, which had no door. Jax told the other two to hold back, while he peaked inside. There, stretched out on a light-gray, over-stuffed leather recliner with earphones and his back to them, was a Regg, dressed in the standard blue, jumpsuit uniform, watching a soundless, sixty-inch, flat screen TV. Butt-Ugly casually volunteered that all their jumpsuits were stolen from Sears, the recliner from Nebraska Furniture Mart, and the TV and sound system from Best Buy just last week. The Reggs liked to stay current with their entertainment systems.

"You're not going to believe this," he whispered to Suzy with a chuckle. "He's watching one of the Twilight movies."

"Oh, we watch Twilight much," offered their stoolie.

"Reggie did say it was their favorite," laughed Suzy. "They root for the werewolves."

That raised a question in Jax's ever-curious, calculating mind, which he directed to their Regg tag-along. "Is that movie in there straight off the airwaves or from a recording?"

"Recording," he said. "We have them all."

"How did you get them recorded in the first place?"

"From DirecTV satellite."

"But how? You can't get their signal down here under the water, can you?"

"At night when no humans around, ship go up to surface and extend dish. We check in with mothership, then download movies."

Jax looked hard at his wife. "Are you thinking what I'm thinking?"

"I don't know what you're thinking, honey," began another spiel, "but besides you being the most handsome, bravest man I've ever known, I think we need to get this ship topside to call HQ, or find a way to patch it through their dish. The Desert People have to be told what we've got here, so they can come and either take over this spacecraft or tow it away or...."

"Stop, Suzy. Thank you. Very good." Jax now knew he had made the right choice of sprays to use on Suzy. She was goofy and uninhibited, but her syllogistic skills were in good shape.

Just to see if Butt-Ugly would do it, Jax ordered him to slip in quietly behind the preoccupied Regg and spray the *gray to obey* chemical in his face. Without hesitation and with Jax right behind him with a cocked smart phone just in case, the first Regg gladly sprayed the second Regg. Jax took the bottle away from him, and told the newest member of the Jackson zombie squad to remain there watching his movie. One human finger on its communicator and it smoked itself to death.

Two doors down was the exercise room containing the next Regg. He was pumping iron on a bench press, wearing only red shorts and a matching headband. Since he was on his back facing the ceiling, he couldn't see the heads poking around the door frame. The Jacksons were informed this was a lieutenant, second in command, a male.

Since Butt-Ugly had done such a nice job spraying the last Regg, he was told to take care of this one, too...subtlety. As Butt came into view, the weightlifter apparently acknowledged his shipmate in their own language, and promptly received the gray spray right in his glistening kisser. Butt chuckled like a prankster, and Jax quickly followed up telling the now-congenial Regg to speak English and to remain in the room doing his exercises. Since this one seemed bigger than any of the others—a good one-fifty—Jax considered calling him *Big Dog*. But he also looked stupider than most, so Jax settled on *Scooby-Doo*. His communicator was dispatched in the usual fashion.

Three down, one to go.

Chapter 93

The last Regg aboard this foul-smelling daughter ship at the bottom of the Coralville Reservoir was in its control center. As the three marauders whispered out in the hallway, Butt-Ugly explained that was the captain and he was a she, although gender hardly mattered. While on the subject, he told Jax that the two lab technicians he had dispatched back there earlier were both females, too. That took a little swagger out of Jax's strut. When Butt confessed to being male along with the other kidnapper, Jax felt a little better, having knocked both their asses flat back there in the lab.

The female captain was slumped back in her gray, high-back chair, her hairy arms hanging loosely at her sides. She was either sleeping or watching one of the two bluish radar screens on the panel. Probably the former, because there was nothing showing up on the screens but flat lines. A few red and green lights were blinking weakly across the board, and many more showed no signs of life at all. Obviously this craft was ready to do little more than go up and down like an elevator, as Butt-Ugly had said.

"This is the one who can get us out of here," whispered Jax to Suzy. "Sneaking up behind and spraying her should be no problem. What worries me is which spray or sprays to use."

"What do you mean?" she asked, straightening a small lock of her husband's dirty-blond hair.

"Well, the *gray to obey* will make her putty in our hands, but how sharp will she be in getting this ship to the surface? If she turns out anything like Butt-Ugly here, she could end up driving us merrily sideways into the dam or flip us upside down or something. If we hit her with just the *blue be true*, she'll be forced to answer all our questions, but she certainly will not be on our side. She could easily trip us up at a critical point in our escape."

"Hit her with both," shrugged Suzy, spreading her hands, "like they did with Reggie and you did with me. Reggie happily spilled his guts, and you already know what I'll do."

"I know," nodded Jax impatiently. "It's just that both drugs close together could cause some unexpected effect, like knocking her out. That puts us up shit creek."

"What's the alternative?" asked Suzy with a maternal smile.

"We could leave all the sprays out of the equation and threaten her with our lasers." Jax turned around. "What do you think, Butt-Ugly, are you

Reggs afraid to die?" The question apparently threw him for a loop, his yellow eyes blinking and rolling. Before he could answer, he was told not to.

"I think hitting her with just the gray-to-obey spray is our best bet," said Suzy with drunken confidence. "If she doesn't seem lucid enough to operate the ship, then add the true-blue one. If that causes her to pass out, we can wait for Butt here to detox. He could at least get this rig to the surface where we could swim for it."

In agreement, Jax and Suzy both started to creep through the door toward the captain, leaving Butt-Ugly back in the hallway, still pondering the value and meaning of his life. Suzy was going to hit her from the left with the *gray to obey* spray, while Jax came in from the right, ready to introduce himself and make sure the captain was under his control and coherent.

They were halfway to the target, when Jax suddenly grabbed Suzy's arm and pulled her to an abrupt stop. With terror in his eyes, he frantically motioned for them both to get the hell out of there.

Chapter 94

As quickly as humanly possible without making a sound, Jax pulled his giddy wife back into the hallway and out of earshot of the captain.

"I want just a yes or no answer," he said emphatically, being very careful not to put anything in the form of a question. Suzy nodded. "When David shot down the Regg scout ship, it self-destructed. You read the Reggie Papers more thoroughly than I did. Did he say anything about a self-destruct device on this ship? Yes or no only, please."

"Yes," said Suzy, a little mirth glowing in her eyes.

"Did he say anything more about it, like where it was and how it was activated? Yes or no."

"No."

Jax thought a moment. "Then it's vital that you hit her with both drugs one right after the other. At the same time I'll pin down her arms and find out everything she knows about it. For all we know, before the drugs kick in she'd need only half a second to activate the self-destruct. It might be right in front of her."

Suzy nodded in full agreement. They quickly resumed the objective.

Finding the captain asleep, Suzy had no problem hitting her full in the face with the *gray to obey,* and then the *blue be true,* while Jax grabbed her hairy arms and pressed them hard against the arms of the chair. There was no adverse reaction, just a shift from a mild moaning to a pink tongue licking thin lips. The captain's pleasant dream of fornicating in the rec room with her second-in-command suddenly switched over to a subservient human unexpectedly bringing her a plate of raw pork ribs and rubbing her face with it. Yum.

Jax destroyed her communicator and took a moment to look over the control panel. He wondered if there was any possibility of him raising this thing to the surface without help. Recalling the layout with the labeled knobs and switches Reggie had sketched for them, Jax recognized some of the bells and whistles. The basic joystick would be easy enough: forward is forward, back is back, the toggle on the back takes you up and down. There was that round dial with two horizontal lines, the top one representing the surface of the reservoir, while the lower one the location of the ship, which was currently on the bottom of the lake. There was the switch to arm the sonic weapon. That red button fired up the main engine.

Jax had some recollection of what the other dozen or so would do, but not enough to operate it safely on his own.

He shook the dozing captain and she perked right up, saying something in Reggese, looking around, confused, but docile.

"Hi," said Jax, bending down to face her from the side. "I'm Jax. I'll be your master today. We will be speaking English. Do you understand? Yes or no only."

"Yes," she said, blinking and smiling at him.

With his keen eye on the captain's hands, in case she made a sudden move, Jax wasted no time in getting to the point. "Is there an autodestruct mechanism on this ship? Just yes or no."

"Yes."

"Is it armed now? Yes or no."

"Yes."

"What would set it off?"

"If ship in peril, crash to ground," she said, using her head to demonstrate that possible action. Then she grinned wide, "Or I throw the switch."

"If you threw the switch, would the ship blow up instantly or would there be a countdown?"

"A countdown. Twenty pactir.

"What is that in Earth minutes?"

"About six."

"Is that switch here on the control panel?"

"Yes," she smiled, starting to lean and trying to point. "It right over…"

"Wait!" said Jax, releasing her right arm. "Don't touch it. Just carefully show me where it is."

She did as told, one short finger with a thick, gray nail pointing off to the far right at a red, flip-top cap marked with a strange symbol.

"Is the switch under the cap? Yes or no."

"Yes."

"Do you know where the autodestruct mechanism is?"

"Yes, it under floor above main engine," she said almost laughing, pointing downward.

"Can you disarm it?"

"Yes. I hit sequence and pull out rod."

"You are doing very well, Captain," said Jax, patting her once on her bony shoulder. Your superiors are proud of you." She smiled. "Now they want you to disarm the autodestruct right away, and they will be even more proud of you. Do it now, please."

"Happy to do." She rose from the chair and wobbled to the back of the room. With both Jax and Suzy watching her like a hawk, she knelt down, flipped up an eyebolt and twisted it one half turn to the left. She used it to lift up the hard plastic, corrugated floor panel, and went right to work punching buttons on the newly-exposed keypad. The Jacksons held their collective breath, praying the *I-sure-love-my-new-Earth-masters-and-will-always-tell-the-truth* drugs were working one hundred percent and her senses were sharp enough to remember the code.

It took some heart-pounding trial and error, but she finally hit the right combination and a small door flipped open. The exact instant she pulled up a clear-glass cylinder encasing a glowing orange rod, it stopped glowing, and an overhead speaker system made an announcement in Reggese.

"What's it saying?" asked a curious Suzy.

"Ship no longer self-destruct," the captain said proudly. "Are superiors happy?"

"Indeed they are," said Jax, greatly relieved. "They now want us to call you *She-Wolf.* Congratulations. You've earned it."

"*She-Wolf,*" smiled the ship's captain. "Good title. Do I get second helpings now?"

Chapter 95

Jax checked his communicator for the time: it read *11:45 p.m.* Still dark up there in the real world. Trusting Captain She-Wolf completely now, he told her to sit back down in her chair and start the procedure for raising the ship to the surface. The captain explained that first they had to send up the tethered buoy to scan the area for human activity. Protocol dictated they surface only when no one was around. Jax said he understood and to launch the buoy right away. She pushed a couple buttons. There was a distant whooshing sound, followed by a beeping from a five-inch monitor on the control panel showing a green blip rising quickly.

While waiting for the scan report, Jax asked the best way for him to get topside into the night air. She-Wolf said he could either go through the reverse process on the elevator that brought them and the boat down in the first place, or climb up the ladder in the maintenance room to the hatch. If he chose the hatch, it had to be opened from here in the command center and only when the ship broke the surface.

"I'll get up there and call The Desert," he said quietly to Suzy. "They'll tell us how to best proceed." Jax knew under normal circumstances it would be better for him to stay and babysit all the Reggs and have Suzy go up to make the call. But the drugs had her mental faculties on the questionable side. She might start giggling and no one would take her seriously.

"Right," said Suzy. "Do you remember the calling code?"

"Three, three, star, star, star" he replied, without even having to think about it. "I've been repeating it to myself like the *one-two-cha-cha-cha* for the past fifteen minutes."

The full-perimeter scan from the buoy showed no humans or boats around, just Jax's SUV and boat trailer in the launch area. So Jax instructed She-Wolf to take the ship up just far enough to have the hatch high and dry. Expecting her to push the red button that started the main power source, instead it was an orange one on the other side of the control panel. The muffled, low frequency sound of numerous pumps filled the command center chamber.

"What's happening?" asked Jax, without thinking.

"Compressed air tanks fill ballasts," said the captain, like it was the most pleasant thing she had ever reported. "Make ship lighter than water and go up. Water displacement..."

"Stop talking, She-Wolf," Jax quickly interrupted, before he got the complete lecture of Archimedes' principle of buoyancy. "Thank you."

One of the Jacksons anxiously watched the screen showing the ship's progress toward the surface, while the smaller one found it delightfully entertaining. Judging by the rate, it would be only another couple minutes.

"While I'm up there," he said to his smiling wife, obviously enjoying all this more than he was, "stand in the hallway where you can keep an eye on She-Wolf and anybody down the hall that may wake up and come wondering up here. Have both your sonic weapon and the gray bottle at the ready."

"Will do, honey," she said, standing on tip toes to give her virile man a kiss.

"And make sure nobody goes closing the hatch on me, okay?"

"They wouldn't dare!" she said with mocked sternness, punching the air.

"I'll take Butt-Ugly with me to the maintenance room and have him stand guard while I'm topside."

A soft *beep-beep* from the control panel signaled the immediate top portion of the ship had emerged from the depths of the Coralville Reservoir. The captain poked another button and announced the hatch was now open. Jax gave Suzy and quick kiss and told Butt-Ugly to lead the way to the maintenance room.

After two threats to his malehood and three tries on the keypad, Butt got the right sequence to open the door to the maintenance room, and an impatient Jax pushed past him.

"Stand in the doorway," he commanded. "If any of your crew comes, yell up to me, and then stop them."

His flunky nodded stupidly. Hopefully the assignment wouldn't put too much responsibility on his medicated gray matter.

Jax wasted no time scampering up the twenty metal rungs welded into the wall of the round, dark shaft. When he popped into the warm, humid night air of Iowa, nothing ever smelled so sweet. He would have loved to take a moment to indulge in the wonderful ambience, but his heart was racing like the New York Philharmonic's version of *Sabre Dance*.

Three, three, star, star, star.

One ring. "Hello, Jax. What's up?" He didn't recognize the voice, but that didn't matter. It obviously belonged to someone at The Desert and well informed.

"I'm standing on top of a Regg daughter ship by the Coralville Dam," he almost yelled with excitement. "What should Suzy and I do?"

"Holy shit!" came the response. "Are you joking?"

"Not in the least," said Jax. "Your GPS satellite feed should show you exactly where I am: in the middle of the Coralville Reservoir and not in a boat!"

There was the sound of activity in the background, and then the man said calmly, "Yes, we have you on satellite, Jax. Are you in control of the alien ship?"

"Pretty much. We've drugged the entire crew. They should be under the influence for at least another few hours. Can you send somebody out here to help us, please?"

"It's already on the way," reported the man. "Be there in…thirty-two minutes, ten seconds, give or take."

"Super!" yelled Jax too loudly, fighting back tears of relief. His words echoed off the riprap of the dam two hundred feet away. An invisible flock of blue-winged teal took to the air.

"Can you hold out?"

"I think so. We can always spray the Reggs again."

"How many are there?"

"Eight," said Jax. "The captain, her backup, two lab techs, and whatever the other four flunkies are." Suddenly, the thought of his half-buzzed Suzy being down there alone in that temporarily suspended freakathon raised his anxiety to an uncomfortable level. "Listen, I should get back down there to help my wife. She's still under the influence of the gray and blue sprays."

"By all means go," said the man. "We'll contact you on the same frequency when we get there, in…thirty-one minutes, fifty-five seconds."

Roger that," said Jax, already working his way back down the rungs. "I may not be able to hear you unless I'm near the shaft leading up to the hatch. Can you still hear me now?"

"You…breaking up…"

Chapter 96

Good ol' Butt-Ugly was waiting faithfully right where Jax had left him. Asleep. After a soft kick in the hind quarters, like a good puppy he followed his master back to the command center. Jax's heart spilled over when Suzy jumped up and wrap her legs around his waist, planting a big wet one on his mouth.

"Everything okay?" he asked, having to pull his lips free long enough to get the words out.

"Oh, just fine," she chirped. "I have the best husband in the universe, my parents are wonderful, my brothers are…"

Again it was hard for Jax to interrupt her loving litany, but they'd be there all night, if he didn't. On his command she stopped immediately, smiling, no feelings hurt.

"Did you get through to the nice Desert People?" she asked, like a drunk trying to prove she wasn't.

"Yeah, they'll be here in twenty-five, thirty minutes. Until then, we need to go check on all the Reggs to make sure they are still under."

First stop was the good captain right there in the con. "She-Wolf," sang Jax, shaking her gently. "Wake up."

"Hello, human," she yawned.

"I just talked to your superiors and they say you are in line for a promotion," said Jax."

"Really? Wonderful."

"And they have another assignment for you. You are to stay here at the helm and not let anyone touch any of the controls but you. And you aren't to do anything with them unless I tell you to, or Suzy tells you to. This is Suzy."

Suzy stuck her face into She-Wolf's field of vision and said hello.

"Hello, Suzy," replied She-Wolf with a crooked, but pleasant smile. Her breath was horrendous.

"Good," said Jax. "Now, if any of your instruments show a spaceship coming close, you don't do anything. It's a good ship. If you understand, say you do."

"Understand."

The Jacksons and their pet Regg quick-stepped to the exercise room to find Scooby on the treadmill. Jax was about to spray him again for good measure, but Suzy's question of how would they know when the cavalry arrives distracted him. "They will call us on our communicators," said Jax, looking at the treadmill's panel and the funny labels, "but we will have to be topside. There's no reception down here."

"Then what do we do?" asked Suzy, again showing a little more lucidity. "Just jump onboard?"

"I don't know," said Jax, forgetting about Scooby and leading the way out of the weight room and down the hall. "We'll just have to wait and see what they say. I would imagine someone will come down to look over the ship. It will be a goldmine of technical information. As for all these Reggs, I don't know."

The one in the movie room and the one in his sleeping quarters both seemed dead to the world, but Jax sprayed them with the gray bottle again just in case. The two female Labradors in the examination room were still out cold and well strapped in. So was the escort manacled to the wall. No sense wasting any more drugs on them.

Jax checked the time. He reported to Suzy the cavalry would be here in twelve minutes, and they might as well head over to the maintenance room and wait for the call. He thought about his beautiful bassboat sitting back there in the hangar. But there probably wasn't enough time and Butt-Ugly probably didn't have enough mental acuity to operate the elevator, even though he said he could.

Once at the base of the shaft leading up to the surface, the newlyweds discovered they were in possession of something they hadn't had for hours. Time. A whole eleven minutes of it.

"What do you want to do while we wait" asked Suzy coyly, slowly lowering the zipper of her husband's dark-blue tracksuit.

"Oh, we'll think of something," he grinned, removing first his utility belt and then hers.

"Butt-Ugly," mumbled Jax from the crook of his wife's neck.

"Yes sir?"

"Close the door, please. From the outside. Good boy."

Chapter 97

With just one minute before the desert guys were due to arrive, Jax and Suzy scampered up the shaft to reestablish communications. She found the fresh, warm night air as pleasing as Jax did, especially after a couple hours of that putrid, tainted meat odor below. The singing of a dozen chorus frogs backed up by hundreds of tree frogs made them both temporarily forget the strange world they had found themselves in this evening.

Three, three, star, star, star.

"Hidey-ho, Jax," said a new voice from his smart phone's speaker. "We're right above you in the ionosphere. Coming down."

The Jacksons craned their necks upward, looking for any sign of the craft. But the overcast sky blocked any hope of seeing it until almost on top of them.

"Do you think it will be the C-17 again?" asked Suzy.

"Oh, I doubt they would send anything that big," said Jax, still scanning the cloudy heavens. "It's probably something about the size of our Maude. After all, I suppose it's just a few engineers to study the ship and some muscle to haul out the Reggs."

When the approaching spacecraft broke through the cloud ceiling, the combined city lights of Iowa City and Cedar Rapids reflecting off its underside revealed it was not the C-17 cargo plane. It was not something resembling Maude back home under the hill either. Remember that mothership that rolled in over Devil's Tower in the sci-fi classic, *Close Encounters of the Third Kind?* Or the one that blew up the Empire State Building, the White House, et al in *Independence Day?*

Toys. Children's toys.

This thing stretched from shore to shore at the widest end of the Coralville Reservoir...a good half mile. It seemed to span about the same distance upstream, too, making its overall shape somewhat circular. Despite its enormous size, its slowed descent was eerily quiet. Every hair on Jax's body was standing erect...whether from some electromagnetic energy emanating from the craft's antigravity power source or from simply being awestruck, he was too disconnected to know. It was the most incredible thing he had ever seen or probably ever would again in his lifetime. Or so he thought at the time.

Suzy, meanwhile, was just twittering.

Holding at about two hundred feet above, someone was talking to Jax again on his communicator. "You folks okay down there?"

It took Jax a moment to snap out of his mesmerized state and reply. "Ah, yeah, we're fine, I guess," he stammered. "May need some fresh underwear, if you have any."

"I'll see what we can find," laughed the voice.

"My God!" gasped Jax. "That thing is huge!"

"What? *Little Sister* here?" teased the voice. "You should see *Big Daddy.*"

Jax was speechless once again.

"I'm Major Henderson, by the way."

"Hello, Major," mumbled Jax, regaining his senses. "I'm Jax Jackson and this is my wife, Suzy."

"We know," chuckled the Major. "Your reputations around The Desert have preceded you both. And the way things seem to be going this evening, you're about to become *legends.*"

Jax could only nod, still overwhelmed by all this. Suzy just kept giggling.

"But let's get the ball rolling here," quickly added the Major. "It's zero thirty-two. About six hours till sunrise. Can you fly that thing?"

"Me? Oh, hell no," squirmed Jax. "But the Regg captain down there will do anything I tell her to." *I hope.*

"Super. Get down there and have her fly the craft right up here into our bomb bay."

"Are you *serious*?" challenged a gasping Jax. "I thought you would be sending some engineers and Blutos down here."

"Why do that," said the Major, "when we can have the whole kit and kaboodle in one fell swoop?"

"But this Regg ship is longer than a football field," warned Jax, waving his free hand from stem to stern.

"Our bomb bay is the size of *four* football fields," replied Henderson. "If you don't think that's big enough, we can go back and get Big Daddy."

Chapter 98

Feeling a little stupid, on top of apprehensive about going back down into that cold stink hole with a bunch of dog-faced aliens, Jax sucked it up and asked how they wanted him to proceed. Major Henderson relayed it would be best if they could first establish a communication link from the Regg command center directly to Little Sister, so the two of them could talk directly, while the Regg craft was being maneuvered into the bomb bay. Less chance of a fender-bender. He gave Jax a special megahertz setting for a secure channel that should work without falling on the ears of the FCC, NSA, or any of the other Regg ships around the world. Jax repeated it to himself a half dozen times.

Suzy stayed topside, while Jax made his less than enthusiastic descent back down the dark shaft into the smelly dog pound. Butt-Ugly was waiting. Again asleep by the door, but waiting. Jax had him *sit, stay* right beneath the shaft in case Suzy yelled something down to him. He was to obey whatever she told him to do. Butt nodded. Then he went right back to sleep as soon as Jax disappeared down the hallway in a full jog.

Rounding the corner into the ship's command center, he found She-Wolf right where he'd left her, also asleep. *These Reggs are easily bored*, thought Jax, shaking her awake. He asked if she could patch his communicator's signal through the ship's communications system and broadcast it topside via the same dish the Reggs used to download the DirecTV satellite feeds. She said that was quite doable, and proceeded to make it happen.

Patch completed, Jax was about to give her the special frequency setting, when a foot came up between his legs and crushed his left testicle. He went down hard.

Writhing in pain in the fetal position on the floor, Jax managed to crack open his pinched eyelids enough to see a Regg in red shorts and headband having undecipherable words with the captain. Scooby didn't seem to agree with what he was being told in his native language, and started reaching for the controls. Obeying her human master's orders, She-Wolf fought him off, snapping and snarling and biting. It seemed to be a stalemate, until Jax had recovered enough to climb to his feet and pull Scooby away from She-Wolf.

Surprised, the largest of all the Reggs let go of his captain's shoulders and tried to spin around to confront his human adversary. But Jax had quickly shifted his hold to a full-nelson from which Scooby had little recourse. He did try a backwards kick with his foot, but managed only to catch a half-turned Jax high on the outside of his thigh. Having a good fifty pounds on the smaller Regg, Jax used every ounce of it to run him into the closest wall headfirst. Scooby bounced hard off the light-weight metal, leaving a heart-shaped indentation a good inch deep. Jax let go and watched him crumble to the floor, becoming a pile of dark-gray hair with red trimming.

Still aching, Jax pulled the gray bottle out of his utility belt and bent down to spray the already dazed Scooby in the face for the second time. But the spray nozzle and uptake tube were missing, as were the bottle's contents. Apparently Jax had landed on it after being kicked in the stones, and the impact popped off the cap and spilled the chemical. *Damn!*

Scooby was semi-conscious, but not an immediate threat, groaning on the floor, a little blood oozing from where his ear probably was under all that hair. Jax searched his memory for where the nearest bottle of *gray to obey* might be. There were only two to begin with, one with each of the Reggs that escorted him and Suzy onto the ship. Jax had one and Suzy had the other. There might be more in the lab, but he wouldn't know what to look for or where.

Afraid to leave Scooby unattended, Jax grabbed him by one hairy ankle and dragged him down the hall to the maintenance room. As he pulled him through the open door, he told Butt-Ugly to wake up and sit on him, while he called up the shaft to Suzy.

"Hi, sweetheart," she echoed down. "Major Henderson wants to know what's taking so long down there. They've gone back up into the clouds until everything is set."

"Ran into a little delay with ol' Scooby," Jax yelled back, already halfway up the rungs. "I need your gray bottle. But don't drop it. I'm coming to get it."

"You alright?" she asked, stroking his head as he popped out of the hatch.

"I'm okay," panted Jax. "Bastard got me in the *boys*. Quick, give me your bottle. Tell the major we should have the radio hook-up in just a few more minutes."

He kissed his sympathizing wife, took another lungful of sweet Iowa air, and scooted back down the dark shaft. At the bottom he found both Reggs out in the hall, a loopy Scooby trying feebly to get out from under Butt-Ugly's bony butt, who was doing his best to obey his last order from his human master. Two measured sprays more than took care of Scooby and a half dose rewarded his pet with an extra sense of serenity.

Jax ordered them both to stay in the hall and stop any fellow Regg who came along. He had no idea who that could possibly be at this point, but after Scooby was able to shake off the effect—undoubtedly from all the exercising, plus being larger than most—no longer would anything be left to chance in this God forsaken kennel.

Back at the con he found She-Wolf licking the small wound on the back of her paw she had incurred during her tussle with Scooby—her heartthrob and second in command. Jax provided her with the megahertz setting, and the link with Little Sister was established without further travail.

"Are you ready for us?" Jax said into his communicator, relieved to be talking to a human again, and especially one who could get them out of there.

"Hold on, Jax," said Major Henderson. "We've run into a bit of a snag. We may need you to do something else first."

Christ! Now what?

Chapter 99

"The way I hear it from Suzy, between giggles anyway," said the major, "you folks got to the Regg ship in your bassboat, right?"

"Right."

"And where is it now?"

"Inside this ship. We were sucked off the water and down an elevator. It's sitting in the hanger next to their scout ship."

There was a short pause, while the Major consulted others. "Okay. Our cameras show a vehicle and boat trailer there in the launching area," he said. "I assume that's yours?"

"If it's the only one, yes."

Another short pause.

"Jax, we need to get your boat back up here topside and on the water."

"Hey, no need," said Jax amiably, "I don't mind if it goes with us to the desert. No matter where that might be, I'm sure we can find some lake to fish. I'll show you guys how to catch hawg bass. I can always buy another boat."

"Sorry, Jax," said the major, "but you and Suzy can't come with us."

"Why not," groused Jax.

"For one thing, we can't have your vehicle and trailer sitting there at the ramp. People will eventually realize Jax Jackson is missing and start looking for you. That will raise all kinds of questions and investigations. It will blow confidence all to hell. You aren't exactly unknown around Iowa City, Jax."

"But…"

"For another thing, your family must be worried sick about you two by now."

"They may not even know we're missing," said Jax. "It's the middle of the night and whoever is manning the comm thinks we are asleep at my place. I doubt they are even checking on us. Probably watching a movie. Otherwise they would have called us by now."

"Even so, they need you two at the farm."

"But…"

"No buts, Jax," said Major Henderson firmly. "As much as we would all love to have you and Suzy at our little secluded hideout…it's kind of a private club, you know. We let you in, the next thing Obama wants in, then the NSA, the CIA, Biden…"

"I see your point," said Jax, deflating. His innate writer's curiosity would have given anything to see what all goes on at The Desert...or just scout around inside Little Sister for that matter. But getting back home to some peace and relaxation with his wife and unborn child was looking pretty good about now, too. "So what do you want me to do?"

"I trust the elevator your boat is on can be raised from the control center."

"I'm sure it can."

"If so, do you think you can get the Regg captain to do it?"

"No problem," grinned Jax. "She loves me."

"Okay, then I'm going to tell Suzy to climb back down there," said the major. "You take her and put in the boat, then go back to the con and have your captain raise the elevator."

"Got it," said Jax. "Send her down. I'll meet her at the bottom of the shaft."

While Jax headed for the maintenance room, Major Henderson explained the rest of the plan to him. When done, Jax agreed, although it sounded a little more adventurous than he may have preferred. It would be from *two hundred friggin' feet* in the air, for the love of God!

Chapter 100

It was a mixed blessing for Suzy going back down into the Regg ship. The stink and chill seemed worse than before, but being wrapped in her man's arms again made everything okay. They stepped over the two sleeping Reggs and hustled the opposite way down the hallway to the hangar.

With Suzy bouncing in the driver's seat and turning the steering wheel left and right, Jax knelt beside her, giving her a crash course on running his bassboat. Even though currently in dry dock, he had her start up the two hundred-fifty-horse outboard, put it in forward gear, reverse, and back to neutral. He explained that doing so for just a few seconds out of the water wouldn't hurt the motor, but Suzy couldn't have cared less. Once certain she could handle it, he had her turn it off. She looked disappointed the noise and vibration had stopped. But she countered by buzzing her lips like a three-year-old's impression of a motor boat, while again working the steering wheel. He kissed her on the cheek, and ran back down the hall to the con.

He woke up She-Wolf and instructed her to raise the elevator to the surface. She did so by pushing a single button, no questions asked. When the green, rectangle dial showed it had reached its apex, she pushed another button and a quirky little animation on the same dial showed the double-hinged lid opening and folding back into the walls of the cylindrical shaft, which then receded back into the hull.

"You should see Suzy," reported Major Henderson over Jax's communicator, "there in a little boat that's high and dry on top of a huge spacecraft a block long."

"I'll bet she's not just sitting there, is she?" chuckled Jax.

"No, the little darlin' is turning the steering wheel back and forth and making the sound of the outboard," grinned the major. "That's about the cutest thing I've ever seen. Almost makes me want to try some of those sprays on my wife."

Getting back to it, Jax assumed the Regg ship now needed to submerge a few feet. His assumption was correct. She-Wolf conducted the maneuver precisely, closing the hatch and going down just enough to float the bassboat, while keeping most of the five-foot dish above the surface, so contact with Little Sister would not be broken. Once the major reported the Ranger boat was floating and the motor running with Suzy seemingly in control and well out of the way, Jax ordered the captain to bring the ship back to the surface and reopen the hatch.

Major Henderson said they were making one last reconnoiter of the area to make sure there were no eyes on the ground. At a little past one in the morning it wasn't likely. But Jax pointed out catfish are the most active at night in the summer, so it was entirely possible some night owl angler could be coming to the reservoir. Fortunately, nothing was moving at the moment, anyway.

"Let's kick this pig," said Major Henderson. "Bring her on up here."

As ordered, She-Wolf pushed the big red button and the ship's main power source fired up with a minor shudder and barely a whisper.

"Been long time," grinned the captain, obviously pleased to be doing what she was trained to do.

"I trust there are cameras with exterior views," said Jax,

"Twelve," she said. "Four on top, four on bottom, two on each end."

"Good. Turn them all on, please."

The front wall of the con exploded with an array of twelve screens: four across, three deep, each three foot square. In just seconds the four on top revealed water clearing from the lenses, followed by a vague, dark image of the massive underside of Little Sister.

"We could use a little light up there to guide us," said Jax into his smart phone.

The interior of the bomb bay suddenly glowed with a soft blue hue, while the square portal was ringed with pinprick LED lights in green.

"Good enough?" asked Henderson.

"Perfect," replied Jax. He then turned his attention to the Regg captain. "Take the ship slowly and carefully up into that hole."

"Breezy easy pie," said She-Wolf, happily working the joy stick.

The grammatically-anal outdoor writer started to correct her on the slaughtered colloquialism, but then changed his mind. "Close enough, sweetheart," he mumbled with a mirthful smile. "Just get us up there."

Chapter 101

It wasn't quite so easy after all. She-Wolf was enjoying herself and talking a good game, but the fact was the drugs had her focus a bit blurred and her perception somewhere left of center. Just when it appeared she was sticking the small pizza in a large oven, she jerked the joystick forward too hard and the ship started heading for a part of Little Sister that wasn't the bomb bay. Luckily the football field-sized craft was nowhere as cat-quick responsive as the smaller scout ships, so the sudden off course movement was more like a humpback whale coming up for air.

"Break off, break off!" shouted Lieutenant Gonzales, one of two men at the bomb bay who Major Henderson had assigned to visually guide the Regg ship into the hole. When a smiling She-Wolf made a sound that was probably the Regg equivalent of "*Whee*," Jax instinctively pushed the bony bitch out of her seat and took control of the joystick.

He pulled back hard, but it was too little too late and the two spaceships collided. Alarms went off in both, but for the half-mile wide Little Sister the impact was more the *thud* of running over a raccoon on the highway. Not so in the Regg craft, as Jax went sprawling forward over the console, pushing the joystick far forward once again, causing the Regg ship to rake along Little Sister's underside.

Red lights were flashing all over the board and another alarm sounded on top of the first. The Regg daughter ship hit something and caromed sideways. Jax had all he could do to keep himself upright in the chair and She-Wolf from landing in his lap. The ship's gyros must have been knocked off kilter, because Jax found it difficult to level off, as it went into a rocking motion, banging Little Sister's belly again and again.

"You need to take it down and back it up," yelled Gonzales. "You're a hundred feet too far forward.

"How can I stabilize this thing?" Jax yelled at She-Wolf.

Rocking back and forth on her feet, trying to maintain balance, the Regg captain leaned across Jax to push and hold one of the flashing red buttons on the panel. The craft slowly regained an even keel and at least a couple alarms and red lights turned off.

Getting himself composed and back into position, Jax eased off on the stick. Fortunately, he had both Lieutenant Gonzales's coaching from his phone's speaker and the four topside night-vision cameras to guide him along Little Sister's underside until the bomb bay came into view. It first showed up on the far left monitor, and systematically moved across the row. When all four were showing a light blue hue, his thumb pushed ever-so-slightly on the up-down button on the back of the joystick, and the ship floated gently up into the bomb bay.

"That's it," said the lieutenant. "Doing great. Easy. Easy. Okay, you're in. Level off. Now ease it forward until I tell you to stop, okay?"

"Okay," I'm all yours," replied Jax, still holding the same breath for the past five minutes.

"That's it. Two hundred more feet. One-fifty. One hundred. Fifty. Slow down. Twenty, ten, five, perfect. Hold there. Super. Now ease it down. You're only ten feet off the floor. Five feet. Gooood. Three, two, one. Splash down! Kill the power."

Jax was fairly certain what to do, but he asked She-Wolf just to be sure. No sense risking anything at this point. She confirmed, and Jax pushed the big red button, killing the main engine, alarms, and most of the flashing lights all at once.

"Great job, Mr. Jackson!" came the duet of a major and a lieutenant. Even She-Wolf applauded, although her action and expression looked more like that battery-operated toy monkey with cymbals.

For a moment, just a brief moment, Jax almost felt sorry for the drugged she-bitch. Little did she realize she and her shipmates were about to go where they had never gone before. And once their drugs wore off, the wretched Reggs would find the rest of their lives far from their great expectations of fresh meats on silver platters and red wines in golden goblets, all served up daily by obedient, but hard-to-look-at ugly human slaves.

Chapter 102

Some psychological studies report humans are capable of seventeen different emotions. When Patrick Bernard Jackson hoisted himself out of the Regg ship's hatch, he experienced nineteen or twenty of them. He was proud and relieved to have landed the Regg craft inside Little Sister with no further damage. He was elated to crawl out of that cold stink hole one last time and inhale that warm, humid air, sweeter than nectar, wafting up from that big hole he had just maneuvered through. He was surprised and embarrassed to be greeted by cheers and applause from about a dozen of Little Sister's crew members, all in regulation desert fatigues. He was worried about his wife down there all alone in the middle of his bassboat in the middle of night in the middle of the Coralville Reservoir. He was excited to be inside the belly of a UFO to end all UFOs. He was afraid that something could still go wrong. And he was mad that his testicles still ached from that sucker kick by Scooby. There were other emotions swirling inside his head and heart, to be sure. But at the moment he couldn't put a classification on them.

A red and white padded harness dangling from the eighty-foot arm of a mobile crane was swung over for him to slip into, and he was lowered the two stories to the floor. One by one those soldiers in the bay area stepped up to shake hands and give him a congratulatory pat on the back, the last one being Lieutenant Gonzales. Jax wasn't surprised to note the army officer's enlarged eyes and head were noticeably out of proportion to his five-foot-ten body.

"This is a dream come true for everyone at The Desert," chortled the lieutenant, pumping Jax's hand like he expected water to come gushing out of his mouth. "We've been trying to come up with a way to capture one of their scout ships before they can scuttle it like they did at your farm, and here you hand-deliver not only a scout ship, but a *daughter* ship and its whole blessed crew!"

"It wasn't exactly what Suzy and I had planned for the weekend," smiled Jax sardonically.

"But you did everything right," said a voice coming up behind him. Jax turned around to see a smiling army major also in desert fatigues approaching with his right hand extended. "Major Henderson, Mr. Jackson. It's an honor to shake your hand."

"Happy to meet you, too, Major," grinned Jax. "I couldn't have done much of it without your help."

The mutual admiration dialogue continued for few more minutes, then Jax was asked to provide a general summary of where all the Reggs were and their last known condition. He also offered the pet names he had given three of them: She-Wolf, Scooby, and Butt-Ugly. All this would help the six burly Marines who were preparing to enter the Regg spacecraft armed with pistols, zip cuffs, and what looked a lot like three different spray bottles on their belts. Jax knew the pistols would not be necessary, but the handcuffs might, since all three of the aforementioned pet Reggs down there had been ordered to obey only Jax or Suzy.

Jax didn't like the idea at all, but he felt he should ask. "Should I go back down there with the marines to get the Reggs to cooperate?"

"That shouldn't be necessary," said the major. "Our tests have shown any fresh dose of the gray-to-obey formula and the victim becomes subservient to whoever he sees or hears first."

As the major turned to go brief the Marines, Jax—the textbook, nosy writer—asked if it would be possible for him to tour Little Sister.

"I'll give you a choice," said the major. "You can have a tour, which will take about ten hours, or you can get down there to your darling wife, waiting in your bassboat, *in the dark*."

Jax didn't have to think long. "Get the hoist ready," he said, "I'm going down."

"Good choice," smiled Major Henderson, "because there's no way in hell any civilian—even a celeb like you—gets to see any more of this spacecraft than you already have."

Chapter 103

"How you doing down there, Suzy Q?" sympathized Jax into his communicator. "Everything okay?"

"Oh, hi, baby," she piped without a hint of distress. "Yes, it's kind of dark and I miss you and this motor keeps gurgling but I don't want to shut it off in case I can't get it started again and I think I heard a flock of ducks fly over when you crashed into the big ship and you should see…"

"Stop talking, Suzy," ordered Jax with a laugh. *Could he love her any more?!* "I'll be coming down to join you in just a minute. We have to get directly over you first."

"Okay. Be careful, sweetie. I'll be watching for you. Oh, there you are now in that big blue hole in the sky." She waved. "Hi, honey!" Jax waved back.

The same crane with the same red and white harness began lowering its two hundred pounds of payload the two hundred feet from spaceship to boat. The night was breezeless, so keeping him on target was easy, and within a minute he touched down in the middle of his Ranger bassboat. Before he could even slip out of the harness, Suzy's warm and passionate embrace had him engulfed, her mouth smashing his, her tongue cleaning his palette.

"Better let go," he breathed into her mouth," or we're both going to be hauled back into the sky."

"Sounds like fun," whispered Suzy, now reaming his ear.

"So does getting back to our place for a hot shower and some serious sack time," he replied, wiggling out of the harness the best he could with his wife still hanging on him.

Jax fished his communicator out of the utility belt next to the spray bottles—which they said he could keep for a *souvenir*—and rang up Major Henderson. "We're good to go," Jax reported, tugging three times on the harness. It immediately zipped up and out of sight.

"There for a minute," wisecracked the major, "it looked like by using you for bait, we were going to land us a keeper, and a real cute one, too. But she got away."

"From you, maybe," quipped Jax, pecking the lips of the female latched onto him like a koala on a eucalyptus tree.

"Well, listen," said the major, more serious now, "we're closing up shop here and taking off. Thanks again for everything you did, rock star.

We'll reverse-engineer this puppy, analyze all its computer data, and hopefully locate their mothership."

"And punt the entire Regg nation right out of the solar system," added Jax.

"Maybe so," hummed Henderson. "Maybe so. We'll be sending a full report of our findings to your farm. Might be a while, though. Lot to cover."

"We will look forward to it. Should be fascinating."

"Oh, by the way," said the major, "in the midst of all this, it seems some guy in a beat-up old pickup with rods in the back has pulled into the parking lot and was watching you being lowered into your boat from a big light in the sky. At the moment he's standing there like a two-year-old who just shit himself. Here, I'll feed you the live video."

Jax's iPhone screen lit up, revealing the close-up of a familiar face from a high angle. Jax then turned around to gaze back at the ramp area. Sure enough. "Ha, that's old Jeff Henniker," laughed Jax. "He came to do some night catfishing. He's harmless."

"If not mummified," said Henderson. "I trust you can handle this."

"No problem," said Jax, patting the bottles on his utility belt. "Have a safe trip, Major."

With Suzy determined to stay on his lap, Jax crammed their two bodies behind the wheel, and he pushed the throttle into forward gear.

Chapter 104

Jax pulled the twenty-foot bassboat up to the dock, keeping an eye on Jeff Henniker all the way, making sure he didn't bolt. The bent over man well into his eighties just remained frozen in place, silhouetted against the single overhead utility light. But when Jax jumped up onto the dock, secured the boat to a post, helped Suzy out, and started walking toward him, the poor old codger suddenly regained control of his muscular system and slowly began back-pedaling in fear.

"Hey, Jeff," called Jax, as friendly as he could, raising his hand in salutation, "it's me, Jax Jackson."

"Jax?" queried Jeff, slowing his retreat. "That you?"

"It's me and my wife," he smiled, walking into the light so Jeff could see their faces. "I haven't seen you since you brought that ten-pound channel cat into Roger's last summer. Beautiful fish."

"Yeah…" mumbled Jeff, glancing back and forth between Jax and the pretty woman clutching his arm.

"So, how you doing, Jeff?"

Old Jeff blinked a couple times, then said with less than certainty, "Not sure. Could've sworn I just seen you come out of the sky on a tether and drop plum into yer boat?"

"That you did," piped Jax proudly. "I was up there in a big spaceship owned by a secret organization out in some desert, and they lowered me right into my Ranger, slick as you please."

There was nothing Jeff Henniker could say to that statement. He just stood there, eyes blinking, breathing heavily through his mouth. And it was about to get worse.

"Yeah, it's a hell of a deal," continued Jax, having fun with the dumbfounded old human. Hey, after four months of not being able to tell anyone about anything of the incredible things he had learned about the Brookfield farm, it's buried spacecraft, its fantastic weaponry, their connection to The Desert, Mejans, crossbreeds, Reggs, *everything*…it felt good to tell the world all about it, even it was to only one old man, who wouldn't remember a word of it in a few minutes. "There are these aliens called *Reggs* who want to take over the earth and either kill us or make us their slaves. But we just captured a bunch of them along with their spaceship, so everything's gonna be okay."

Jax waited for Jeff to say something. But the old man—draped in his favorite tattered overalls and smelling of stink bait—seemed to be going deeper into delirious dumbness. His eyes had glazed up and a bit of drool was forming on his craggy, lower lip. Realizing he had gone too far with his blabbing about extraterrestrials and such, Jax felt he had to do something drastic and quick to jolt the man back to reality.

"Honey," he said to Suzy, "would you mind flashing this nice man?"

Without hesitation and still under the influence, a grinning Suzy grabbed the hem of her yellow print sundress and pulled it up high to expose every delightful feature of her frontal nudity. It worked. Old Jeff Henniker's eyes got bigger than Suzy's. He made some kind of unintelligible sound deep in his throat and almost swallowed his dentures.

"My wife's quite beautiful, don't you think?" grinned Jax, motioning for Suzy to lower her dress.

"Oh, sweet Jesus..." gasped Jeff, finally able to expel the air trapped in his lungs and--from the sounds of things—another orifice.

"Would you mind talking to her for a while?" asked Jax. "I have to go trailer my rig."

Jeff Henniker nodded stupidly. Jax had seen that expression more than once in the past few hours.

"Honey, Jeff wants to know all about the Mejan history. Will you tell him, please?"

"I'd love to," she beamed, walking over to take Jeff's dirty, calloused, arthritic hand in hers.

While Suzy offered a detailed dissertation that could possibly send the old catfisherman further into the land of the lost, Jax went through the one-man process of pulling his boat out of the lake. Once completed, he told Suzy to go sit in the Lexus, while he helped Jeff get his fishing gear out of the back of his beat up old pickup and head out onto the dock. Once he was settled on the aluminum bench with a line in the water, Jax asked his old friend if he was okay. When he mumbled that he wasn't sure, Jax took the white bottle out of his utility belt, hit Jeff in the face with one spritz, and quickly and quietly hustled off the dock, into the Lexus, and out of the launch area.

Jeff Henniker looked around, wondering how the hell he got out here on the end of the dock by the Coralville Reservoir dam. The last thing he remembered was working up his secret blend of Bowkers catfish bait with chicken livers and moldy, blue cheese in his kitchen sink some two hours ago. Maybe his wife was right. He needed to quit drinking that gawd-awful dandelion wine Pete Elkins keeps making in his root cellar.

Chapter 105

Jul Colcack, the Regg's supreme ruler, had gathered his staff for an emergency meeting aboard the mothership at the bottom of the Pacific Ocean, twelve miles off the Oregon coast near Astoria. Obviously something had gone wrong with their daughter ship in the Coralville Reservoir near Iowa City, Iowa two nights ago. A scout craft had been sent out to search the area, and had just reported a few moments ago the ship was no longer in its assigned location on the bottom of the lake near the dam. Since there was no order or other reason for it to relocate, it had to be classified as missing.

The last anyone knew, two of the Regg crew were on assignment to kidnap a part-Mejan female and her mate, and had been successful, reporting they were about to take them onboard the ship. That was the last communique until about an hour later when they received a short distress signal from an emergency buoy launched from the submerged ship. Since then there had been no follow-up, and all attempts at contact had been to no avail. Each daughter ship is under orders to report in every night, even if there is nothing new. The Coralville ship had failed to do so for forty-eight hours and counting.

"Fellows," said Colcack in Reggese from the head of the long, highly-polished mahogany table, appropriated decades ago from Nebraska Furniture Mart in Omaha, "we have virtually nothing to go on. But we can assume with considerable certainly our daughter is either experiencing a serious breakdown, has been destroyed, or…captured."

None of the ten Reggs lining the table spoke. A few fidgeted nervously in their leather office chairs—stolen from the same store the same night as the table—while others just stared down at their iPads, pinched from Best Buy two months ago.

All wore form-fitting, green jumpsuits—lifted from a JCPenney's warehouse in October of 2012—signifying their elevated status in the Regg hierarchy. The darker the green, the higher the rank. Each had a matching beanie on the back of his or her head, similar to a Jewish yarmulke. Since the hair back there tended to be course and stiff, the cap had to be held in place with a thin, cloth strap tied under the chin. To the Regg elite, this was considered both prestigious and debonair.

Jul Colcack's attire was the exception. He was dressed in a charcoal-gray, long-sleeved, two-piece of Asian silk, hanging comfortably on his body. It had gold piping around all four of the flared cuffs, the high short collar, and down the center of the pullover, which ended at mid-thigh. He wore no headgear. His silver and gray hair was combed back, resembling that of a border collie with his head out the car's window going thirty miles an hour down the road.

"Is there any chance they just took off on their own for some reason?" asked one of the officers.

"None," replied the supreme ruler, leaning forward in his high-back, black leather chair, stolen from Staples in oh-seven. "For them to do so, all their systems would have to be working in good order. And that would mean they had the means to communicate with us."

"Would they defect?" came another question.

"Defect?" scorned Colcack. "To whom? The Mejans? The humans? Perhaps the cattle."

Most everyone laughed. It indeed was a stupid question.

"Without more information," continued Colcack, "we would be foolish to plan a specific course of action at this time. We must obtain more data. What do we know about the Mejans in that area?"

Scanning the screen of his iPad, one of the officers offered, "We know a little, sir. We are fairly certain the Mejan female and her human mate spend much of their time at a farm about five miles northwest of Iowa City. Our infrared scan picked them up by the farm's pond in late-July. As you know, we ordered that raid on the house on August first, but results were unknown. The last report from our Coralville scout ship said that their four soldiers in a stolen SUV drove into the farm at three in the morning. Then nothing more was heard until Coralville reported the scout ship and none of the soldiers had returned, even many days later. That's when we ordered steady surveillance of the farm, looking for any evidence of our missing ship and men. They found nothing."

"But," chimed another officer with an index finger in the air, "we did have that one piece of good fortune. On August ninth we tracked the movement of this particular silver SUV we knew associated with the farm and possibly that female we had earlier caught on our scanner. It drove to a large estate three miles south of Iowa City, and was still there late the next night. So, our tactical staff here at headquarters felt it was worth the chance, and ordered the remaining Coralville scout ship to drop off two soldiers in the back of that house. The craft was to exit quickly before it could be located by what we suspect might be the Mejan's superior surveillance system and possibly even destroyed by their superior weaponry. The men were successful in capturing the female and male and covertly driving them to the daughter ship in the human's own vehicle pulling a water craft. They were not spotted. Pretty clever of us, really. You know the rest, sir."

Colcack spun the back of his chair on the group, and took a moment to absorb the report. His officers waited patiently. One female started running her foot up the pant leg of the male across from her.

"What is the status of our other outposts in the Midwest?" he asked without turning around.

The logistics officer didn't have to look at his screen. "All in full force, sir. And ready to go."

The general turned slowly back to face his cadre. "Then we know what we must do."

Chapter 106

At three o'clock in the afternoon on August 14, four days after Jax and Suzy had escaped their kidnappers, a semi-emergency video conference was called by Colonel Joshua Middleton. As all of the Brookfields and Jacksons assembled in front of the fifty-five-inch flat screen like patrons of the arts waiting for the second act, the major was perusing his notes with head down and a knuckle rubbing his cheek.

"Needless to say," he began, finally looking up at his attentive audience, "we've only just begun to reverse engineer the Regg daughter ship—which we've code-named *Regina*—and comb through her computer data and logs. Even though we have a working knowledge of their language and our new software program can translate fairly effectively, the process is still quite slow and painstaking. A lot can get lost in translation."

Joshua took a breath and set his notes down on an off-camera table. "But we have deciphered enough at this point in time," he continued, with a look of concern, "to believe we—and especially you nice folks at Brookfield—need to go back on Defcon 3."

"What's up, Joshua?" asked Alan, voicing the question on everyone's mind.

"It turns out one of the Reggs somehow managed to send a mayday signal from the control center that night the two of you were kidnapped."

"That's not possible," protested Jax, with his newfound confidence, hands behind his head, leaning back in his chair. "We were extra careful to secure every one of the Reggs onboard by physically strapping them down or dosing them with the *gray to obey* spray...or both."

"How many of them had access to the con while you were there?" asked the colonel.

"Just two: She-Wolf—who is the captain—and Scooby—the second in command. But the captain was always well under my control, and Scooby..." Jax paused, recalling the events.

"What about Scooby?" prodded Joshua.

"As I said in my report, he sneaked up behind me and kicked me in the nads (Suzy winced), then tried to take control of the con. But I thought She-Wolf held him off until I could get him in a full- nelson and restructure the wall with his head."

"But it *is* possible," said Joshua, "that while you were recovering on the floor from what had to be excruciating pain, Scooby could have punched the distress button before She-Wolf could stop him?"

Jax shook his head, "I guess it's possible. I just didn't see him do it or hear any kind of an alarm go off."

"According to your report," said Colonel Middleton, rechecking his notes, "you think the time was about zero thirty-five—that's twelve-thirty-five in the morning for you civilians—when you and Scooby were fighting, correct?"

"Yes, that was my best guess, give or take a couple minutes."

"Well, the ship's log shows the mayday buoy and signal went out right then, and lasted only for a second."

"Shit!" hissed Jax, sitting upright. "Then I guess that hairy bastard did manage to pull it off. *Shit!*"

"Take it easy, son," said Alan, coming around behind Jax and laying a hand on his shoulder. "You did everything you could, and more." The group nodded and buzzed in strong agreement, followed by a patented Suzy hug.

"That's right, Jax" added the colonel. "If it weren't for you, we wouldn't have the Regg ships and a whole Christmas morning full of intel. So, can that self-pity shit, and let's get on with the briefing, okay?"

Jax smiled weakly and leaned back again. Suzy used the opportunity to slip onto his lap and pay far more attention to him than to the colonel. People had been wondering if she were under some residual influence from the Regg drugs. But she kept insisting she was simply in love with her brave, *protective* husband, more than ever. None were aware of Jax's self-preservation melt-down in the haymow the night of the Regg raid. They thought—as Suzy had told them—he simply could not see well enough in the dark to shoot, so she had grabbed the M16 and killed the intruders. Suzy knew better, of course. And now that her husband was born-again-hard, she was truly ecstatic.

"The brain trust here at The Desert," continued Joshua, "feel there is a strong probability the Reggs will hit your farm again."

Mary groaned. The brows of Jax, David and Mike scrunched simultaneously. Suzy was too involved with Jax's hair to hear the warning. Stone-faced Alan asked why.

"It's logical, mostly," said the colonel, picking up his notes again and adjusting his prescription dark glasses. "Let's look at all the factors we know are true, based on the ship's log we have translated so far." He took a pen from his breast pocket and pointed it at his list.

"*One*, to bait them into raiding your farm—and *without clearing it through us*, I might add—you let them scan one of you with Mejan blood…in this case it happened to be Suzy; so they learned she is part Mejan and connected to the Brookfield farm. *Two*, they surmised their raid on the farm was unsuccessful, because there was no communication after the Reggs entered your house and no sign of their scout ship or Regg raiders anytime thereafter. *Three*, desperate to find out what happened during that raid, they kept a close watch on the farm, and followed Jax's Lexus to locate and abduct you two at his house. *Four*, they were in contact with their HQ right up until Jax interrupted their little experiments and took over the ship. *Five*, Scooby managed to send that distress signal, and we can assume it was received. *Six*, we can also assume there was no follow up or communication thereafter from daughter ship to mothership, since we had Regina well sequestered in an electronic net and inside Little Sister.

"Their headquarters can't know for sure what has happened to their equipment and men," continued the colonel, "but logic dictates they are compelled to find out. We sure would in their shoes. The answer could be instrumental in their strategy going forward, especially if they discover we have their ship and its crew. They are going to want them back, and as soon as possible."

"So, they are likely to hit our farm again," surmised Alan, "the one place they know for sure houses at least one Mejan and probably more."

"That's the thinking, yes. But not just Mejans," cautioned Joshua. "They would want to capture anyone who could provide them with answers."

"Well, bring 'em on," said David. "We kicked their ass the first time, we'll do it again."

"Easy, son," warned the colonel. "We doubt they would try the same tactics as before."

"So, what might they do different?" asked Jax.

"We can only guess," said Joshua, shaking his head. "We just need you folks to be ready for anything."

Chapter 107

They didn't have to wait long. That very night Jax was on duty alone at the helm of Fighter-One, hunkered down just a few feet inside the grove of trees west of the pond. David was in Fighter-Two in the same grove a hundred yards to the north. Night vision cameras were trained on the farm and high into its air space. Whether from the ground or air, they would see an assault coming.

Alan and Mike were sleeping before relieving Jax and David in the fighters at midnight. Suzy and her mother Mary were manning the communications room. They would also be relieved at the bewitching hour by farmhands Larry and Louis.

At eleven-thirty-two, all six night-vision cameras—two in the silo and two in each of the fighters— simultaneously picked up the Regg scout craft flying in from the southeast at an exceptionally high speed and coming to an abrupt halt a hundred feet above some Angus cattle resting in the pasture. Before anyone could react to the alarms and visuals, it hit the silo with three powerful sonic blasts, exploding the top half of the structure as if hit by a ten-ton wreaking ball. Silo Camera One and Two instantly went out of commission along with the two radars, parabolic reflector, and the USLAP cannon.

"My, God, they've just destroyed the silo," came Suzy's frantic words in Jax's helmet. "We've lost visuals from the cameras, along with radars. Keep your ship's cameras on so we can see what's happening."

"On it," said Jax, already above the grove and accelerating toward the cloud of dust and debris rising from the still-crumbling silo.

As Jax approached, he saw the Regg fighter turn a quick ten degrees to the right and fire a double burst at the closest blue Harvestore bin. With nothing inside, it only imploded like a lumberjack crushing an emptied beer can.

The Regg didn't have time for any more blasts, as Fighter-One fired a pulse across its bow, just missing by a foot. Jax hadn't taken the time to lock in on the target; he had fired in the general direction, wanting first and foremost to stop it from doing any more damage to the farm. Unfortunately, the wild shot took out a small utility shed just south of the house.

His next shot, however, was locked on. As the Regg spun to face its attacker, it was met with a hole burned through its nose, knocking out vital control software and mechanisms. The large, angular, sports car-like vehicle went into a death spiral, crashing hard on the pasture equidistant between the barn and the pond, just missing some cattle, aroused by all the unusual commotion and noise. Jax and David immediately hovered directly overhead, watching it for the slightest tick. It held motionless and upright, a little smoke trickling up from its nose.

"It should self-destruct any minute now," said David, "like the last one did."

But it didn't.

"Wake up your dad," said Jax. "We have an issue here."

"So I see," Suzy replied. "Dad and Mike are already on the way down here."

"Fill them in on the situation and see what Alan wants us to do with the dead craft."

Just then Jax, David, Suzy and Mary heard something over their secure wavelength they certainly didn't expect.

Chapter 108

"Hola, Brookfield Farm. This is Major Ramirez in the C-17 directly above you at one thousand feet. We will be setting down in the same place as last time in thirty seconds. Please stay clear of the area. Do not attempt any contact with the downed Regg craft. We will take it from here."

"Roger that," said David, excitedly, backing off.

"Roger," said Jax. "We will stay airborne and maintain surveillance of the area."

"Excellent," replied Major Ramirez. "Touching down in ten seconds."

"Did you hear all that, Suzy?" Jax asked.

"Got it, and so did Dad. He and Mike are already on their way to the area."

Before Alan and Mike could get near the smoking craft, they were halted by a lieutenant, asking them to stay back for their own safety. It still could blow at any minute. Behind him they could see two men in the obligatory desert fatigues, applying the Jaws-of-Life to its windshield. Popping it free, their flashlights revealed only one Regg, and he wasn't moving.

"No pulse," announced one of the sergeants. "And no blood. Just white foam around the mouth. He might have committed suicide."

"How damaged is its front panel?" called the lieutenant.

The other sergeant leaned in to inspect the cockpit. "Pretty messed up," he yelled back. "A few lights are on, but most are off and smoking."

"We must have hit the auto-destruct mechanism," said the lieutenant to Alan and Mike. "We'd consider that a big break, if we didn't already have one of their fighters in A-One condition. But, it never hurts to have a second one, even if it is a little banged up." He punched a few buttons on his phone, put it to his ear and said, "Bring it over."

The same twenty-ton boom truck rolled out of the C-17's monstrous backend and made its way to the Regg fighter. As if doing it every day, the giant claw easily and quickly grasped the forty-foot ship, lifted it off the ground and swung it onto the forty-foot flatbed, creaking and straining under the weight. It was quickly and expertly strapped down, then the truck lumbered over the bumpy ground back to the plane.

"I'm Lieutenant Persons, by the way," said the officer, offering his hand.

"It would seem," said Alan, shaking his hand, "you folks were up there the whole time, keeping an eye on things."

"Actually, we've had your six since last night," smiled the lieutenant.

"Even before we were notified by Colonel Middleton that we might be in danger," nodded Alan knowingly, doing the easy math.

"We came the minute G2 spit out the probability. We weren't about to leave our favorite civilians unprotected."

"Well, we certainly appreciate that, lieutenant," said Alan sincerely. "But as you can see, we have a couple of sharp-shooting, Wyatt Earps here, who don't seem to like Regg fighters coming into Tombstone."

"We could use a dozen more just like them," laughed Persons.

He shook hands with Alan and Mike, then begged off. "Gotta get this load back to The Desert. We'll be *airmailing* you all the equipment you lost in your silo, plus some extra things we think you'll like. Should be here in about an hour. Meanwhile, you all keep vigilant," he cautioned, walking spritely away. "There could be more to come. This so-called raid seems a little anemic."

"I trust we have other eyes in sky, even when you leave," called Alan after him.

Lieutenant Parsons stopped and gave a quick glance up at the star-sprinkled night. "Oh, yeah," he said with a sinister smile. He then double-timed it into the backend of the C-17.

Chapter 109

Almost exactly one hour later, true to their word, the quietest helicopter in the world set down just long enough to deposit four large crates of equipment beside the still-smoldering silo. It took Jax and David in tandem to lug each one into the barn and stack just inside the huge north door. Meanwhile, Alan and Mike—now taking their shifts in the two fighters—escorted the chopper in and out, then hung close by to protect the shipment.

"I'll get *the crew* out here first thing in the morning," Alan relayed to everyone over the special Brookfield channel, "to start rebuilding the silo and install the new equipment."

Mike chimed in excitedly, "Plus, the lieutenant said there would be some extras we would really like."

"A big dome over us would be nice," suggested Suzy from the comm, "so we could get some sleep around here."

David went into the kitchen for a snack, and Jax headed down to the communications room to reunite with his wife. She greeted her sharp-shooting, brave, conquering hero in the usual Suzy way. She, Mary, and Jax himself should have gone to bed, but everyone was too wound up to sleep. It was getting to be a habit these nights.

"Something doesn't seem right about the raid," said Jax, pouring himself some coffee, black. He offered the insulated mug to Suzy, who waved it off, saying she'd had too much already. "It was more like a suicide mission," he said, pulling up an office chair between Suzy and Mary.

"What are you thinking, Jax?" asked Mary, sitting forward with interest. She had been thinking the same thing. "Suicide mission?"

"First of all," he began, leaning back in the chair, formulating his logic with an index finger tracing the rim of his coffee mug, "they send only one ship with one guy in it. He seems determined to do nothing more than blow the hell out of a few buildings. The fact that he took out our best surveillance equipment was probably just dumb luck...or at best an educated guess, since it is the tallest structure on the farm. Whatever, we knock him out of the sky with one shot. And instead of self-destructing like the Reggs are so fond of doing if you even look at them sideways, the craft just sits there, begging to be captured. And so we can't get any intel out of him, the Regg bites the big one and croaks. All too pat."

"Go on, honey?" said Suzy, beginning to see the anomaly.

"I'm not sure," Jax said, rising to his feet and walking slowly around in a tight, pensive circle. "But I wouldn't be surprised if they purposely sacrificed this pilot and craft for some reason, possibly to learn about our firepower capability."

"That could be," agreed Mary. "Up until this point in time, they didn't know how we shot down the first scout ship two weeks ago."

"That was one reason why they kidnapped us," added Suzy, "to learn how we did it."

"Right," said Jax. "But they never got around to interrogating either one of us. They were too anxious to study my beautiful Suzy darlin' first." Jax bent down and kissed the top of her head. She smiled widely at her mother, who smiled right back. Her daughter was so happy in love these days, nothing seemed to bother her, even such reminders of the abduction and examination. But then, she was so heavily drugged throughout the episode, there actually were no horrible parts as far as her memory was concerned. For Suzy, it all seemed like being in a primetime sitcom.

"Now they know about our weapons," continued Jax. "The pilot undoubtedly was in constant communications with his HQ, and chances are he was able to describe my USLAP blowing right through his control panel. And even if he didn't, they probably had the ship rigged with auto-diagnostics being continuously radioed back to HQ."

"It makes sense," nodded Suzy, recalling her study of the Reggie papers regarding their philosophies of a deity and the afterlife. "The Reggs don't hold life nearly as sacred as we do. They are like our terrorists, who believe death from a jihad is the fast-track to Heaven. And for those left behind, the death of a superior means a step up in rank. Our Regg tonight probably gladly volunteered."

Mary crab-walked her chair over to one of the four desktop computers and started typing. "I think your theory is sound enough to pass along to The Desert," she said without pausing. "At least it couldn't hurt."

"I'll bet more than one of those geeks has already thought of it," Jax snorted.

He was right, the reply—arriving just a matter of minutes after being sent by Mary—confirmed it. The first order of business for The Desert People was to determine if the Regg's fighter's auto destruct had been purposely disarmed or if Jax's USLAP shot had done it. They'd be in touch.

Chapter 110

At ten-forty-five the next night, the Regg fighter lifted out from the top of its daughter ship, which had just completed its four hundred and twenty-mile journey from Lake Champlain, Illinois. Undetected by the armory's radar and ground acoustic microphones, the fighter dropped straight down from an altitude of three thousand feet to hover only two feet off the ground in front of the first of the two main air intakes, well hidden by huge boulders above and on both sides.

Raising its canopy, the co-pilot tossed out a cylinder the size and shape of a Pringles can with a discreet LED green light blinking in the center of a small black box on one end. The craft then just as silently drifted over to the second intake vent four blocks to the north. Another canister was lobbed in front of the similar grated shaft.

Ascending just high enough to see both vents via the fighter's green, night-vision camera, the copilot flicked a switch on the transmitter he was holding, and both cylinders fired with a soft hiss. Clouds of thick, white smoke belched out, immediately being sucked directly into the two air vents. Assured things were working as planned, the ship continued its ascent back to three thousand feet and held its position beside the larger craft to wait, scan, and guard.

From their computer models and decades of testing on humans, they knew ten minutes was enough time for the sleeping gas to neutralize all personnel throughout the U. S. Army's armory, sequestered deep inside the limestone bluffs of Missouri's Ozark Mountains. Given the all-clear, the daughter ship the size of a football field dropped out of the sky and centered itself a few feet above the wide, asphalt driveway leading directly into the underground compound. From a safe, yet effective distance of two hundred feet, it commenced to blowing the two-foot-thick, one hundred-foot-wide steel door right off its tracks with one super-charged blast from its sonic cannon. Along with the door went the adjacent guard shack in one corner. The sleeping corporal on duty never knew what hit him. The ship then moved in closer and fired another round to dismantle the secondary steel door at the back of the garage, taking six halftracks and about a dozen flatbed trucks with it. One final left-to-right spray of ultrasound waves swept all the debris out of the way as slick as a leaf-blower cleaning an autumn sidewalk.

The craft then backed out, pivoted one-eighty degrees, and set down as light as a feather on the driveway. The back end opened from bottom to top, and out raced six, twenty-ton boom trucks, just stolen an hour ago from MacAnich sales lot of new and used heavy equipment outside St. Louis. Each carried two Reggs in the cab and two in the back, all wearing black jumpsuits and gasmasks.

Amid the blaring alarm and spinning red lights, they drove through both busted doorways and down a quarter-mile long ramp to the second level where five-hundred-pound, bunker-buster bombs were stored on wooden pallets. A variety of other armaments, including nuclear weapons, were farther down on Level Three, but the Reggs were interested only in loading one bunker-buster on each truck. With heavy claws holding the bombs in place, the six trucks drove back up the ramp and into the daughter ship.

The rear end closed up and the spacecraft began to lift off in exactly the fifteen minutes their computers had calculated would be enough time before vehicles arrived from the local army base and the F-15 Eagles could fly in from Whiteman Air Force Base seventy miles southeast of Kansas City. Unfortunately, a local squad car was already coming up the road to investigate the reported bangs and flashing lights coming from the limestone bluffs. The car inexplicitly flew backwards three hundred feet and rolled countless times in the adjacent field. The lone officer did not survive.

In the days that followed, the official press release would offer that the main door to the armory was being taken down and replaced with a stronger, more modern one, and that Officer Simpson had apparently left the road to avoid hitting a deer. Not many in the local rumor mill bought either story.

There was nothing to read, believe, or dispute, however, in any of the local or national media about the next two incidents that night. One started fifteen minutes later hundreds of miles to the west in a remote part of a desert with no name.

Chapter 111

At eleven-twenty that same night, Alan and Mary were in the communications room, running diagnostics on the rebuilt silo's newly installed radars, cameras, and parabolic audio dish. The discreet crew of fifteen—consisting of brick masons, construction workers, welders and geeks—had the building back up in only nine hours. Those who weren't part-Mejan were married to one. The talent, expertise, and intelligence working diligently around the farm that day were surpassed only by the loyalty and love of a free, safe planet.

Everything seemed in perfect working order, and the upgrades were fantastic. The radars' range and sensitivity were almost doubled. The cameras now had 4K resolution, four times that of the old 1081p. And the parabolic reflector could pick up a mouse fart from across County Road 34.

But what had Alan giggling like a school boy with his first Daisy B-B gun and Mary shaking her head were the new targeting system and power upgrade for the *Ultra Sonic Laser Assisted Pulse* (USLAP) cannon on the turret high atop the silo's new dome. Two boulders four hundred yards out in the north pasture had already been reduced to gray chunks and dust, and a third was clearly in the crosshairs of its eighty-power scope.

Alan was almost wishing another Regg attack would come. With USLAP's stronger punch and quicker-than-ever locating and target-locking system, one of the black-blooded bastards' fighters would fold up like a pheasant in a full-choke pattern of six-shot. The same would certainly happen with the beefed-up cannons and software installed on the two fighters. True, there hadn't been time to test them yet, having just been installed a few hours ago by their technical guru, Kevin, from the university's College of Astrophysics. But conceptually a Regg fighter wouldn't have a chance.

"I wish our paranoid Desert People would finally say enough is enough with these upgrades," Kevin huffed to Alan and Mary, tossing his tool belt into the trunk of his white Ford Focus right at sunset. "You are already hunting mice with elephant guns, for Christ's sake!" Mary pointed out nothing was too extreme when it came to protecting mother Earth from godless invaders, and Kevin pulled away with a stand-corrected nod.

Before Alan could pull the trigger on the third boulder, one of the large flat screens on the north wall behind him suddenly dumped the Bill

O'Reilly repeat on Fox News in favor of Colonel Joshua Middleton's sweaty face and frantic voice.

"Brookfields," he practically yelled, "we've been hit. Hard."

"What?!" gasped Alan and Mary simultaneously.

"They took out at least two of our upper level hangars and lower level storage and testing areas."

"My God," replied Mary. "Are you alright?"

"Oh, we're safe down here," Joshua said, looking right and left at whatever was drawing his attention at the moment. The background was alive with audio reports walking all over each other. "We're a thousand feet under....er...we're down deep enough that we only lost a coffee pot and one PC monitor from the vibrations. First guess says it might have been something on the order of bunker-buster bombs, three of them, one right after the other...and quite possibly from our own arsenals."

"Terrorists?" queried Alan. "Some air force pilot gone postal?"

"Don't think so," said the colonel, waving off the suggestion. "All signs point toward the Reggs. Just fifteen minutes before the attack we got a red flag signal from our arsenal in Missouri showing the main door had been breached. But no follow up communique, so we weren't sure what had happened. Then just before they hit us here, our radar didn't show any aircraft, which meant super stealth, of course, like only we and the Reggs have. But it did track the bombs on their way down. And each came from the same static location and altitude."

"It would have to be a Regg daughter craft or larger," offered Alan. "Their fighters are too small to carry even one of those bombs."

"Agreed," nodded the colonel. "And speaking of which, guess what got blown to the moon here...dead center, down on level two."

"The daughter ship," winced Mary.

"Kablooie," said Joshua, through gritted teeth. "That Regg fighter you captured last night must have had a homing signal on it somewhere that our instruments couldn't pick up. We had it parked right next to the daughter. It led them straight to us. We should have known that lame attack on your farm was a goddamn setup. We haven't been able to assess the damage, but it's probably extensive. No doubt that was their main objective."

The colonel's attention suddenly cranked hard to his right. He listened intently to a new collage of reports just coming in, and then turned back to the camera, his red face now fading toward pale. "The sonsabitches just hit Area 51."

Chapter 112

The communications room at Brookfield Farms fell under an unnerving silence, as Alan and Mary waited along with Colonel Middleton for more information on the Area 51 attack.

"We need to scramble our fighters, honey," Mary suddenly suggested, the fear evident in her whisper.

Alan blinked himself back to reality. "Yes, on it," he said, punching keys on his communicator. He waited impatiently for replies from all six people on the conference call. Louis was the last to answer.

"The Reggs have hit The Desert and just now Area 51," said Alan, as calmly as he could into his phone. "Joshua is okay, but they took out the Regg fighter and daughter ship."

"Fuck!" said someone, more than likely the man who had almost single-handedly captured both of them.

"Jax," barked Alan, "head for Fighter-One and get airborne. I'll be there shortly to take Two. David, Suzy, get down here to the comm to help your mother watch the skies and man the silo cannon. You can brief them, Mary."

She nodded confidently. She'd been watching her husband make a fool of himself, blowing those rocks to pieces. Hell, with that upgraded software, the new cannon basically aimed and fired itself.

"Mike, Louis, Larry, grab your firearms and get into the haymow. Watch for anything coming down our lane. If they knock out our power again, shoot first, ask later."

"Good idea," said the colonel, catching the gist of Alan's orders with one ear. "But don't try coming to help us. You couldn't find us anyway. Stay right there and protect the home front. Who knows what these assholes will do next."

Alan was already out the door, almost colliding with his son and daughter on their way in. Mike, carrying Jax's M16, was right behind his dad, as they ran toward the big red barn. They parted company just inside the door, Mike heading up the stairs to hayloft, Alan toward the tack room.

Back in the communications room, David settled in behind the joystick and monitor of the silo's enhanced Ultra Sonic Laser Assisted Pulse cannon to get a quick briefing from his mother. It was so much like his video games he quickly waved her off and proceeded to blow the hell out of that third rock his dad had already targeted. "Sweet!"

While facing the two green radar screens, Suzy slipped on headphones to monitor any unusual sounds the parabolic dish may pick up, as well as all radio communications to and from everyone, which were also blaring on speakers inside the room.

Mary got herself mentally and physically ready to monitor all six cameras with the superb day-night vision—two in the silo, two on each fighter. Luckily, the new software and higher resolution could pick up something as small as a nighthawk chasing mosquitoes three miles away. If it weren't for the eighty-percent humidity typical of an August night in the Midwest, the range would be closer to six miles.

"Joshua, any more word from Area 51?" asked Mary over her shoulder, keeping her eyes firmly where they needed to be.

"Seems to be basically what happened here," he said, turning temporarily to face her, then going back to profile. "Three bunker-busters in rapid succession. They took out the main hangar, a few buildings on the perimeter, and part of a lower level where mostly old machinery and failed prototypes were kept. Nothing of particular valuable."

"Why would they even bother then," asked Mary?

"Good question," sighed Joshua. "They apparently didn't have a homing device to guide them there. They just hit it at random. It's not even a secret location."

"Maybe that's why," suggested David. "51 is the only *secret base* everyone in the world knows about. It was an easy target. They didn't know where else to…"

"Hold the phone!" interrupted the colonel, leaning in to better view one of his many monitors. "*Regg fighters* are now attacking 51. What the hell? They just took out the top of the airfield's control tower. These fuckers seem to want an all-out war."

Chapter 113

Jax would concur. He wasn't twenty seconds out and ten feet above the pond, when Suzy was in his ear, saying something at two thousand feet and one mile to the southeast was coming on at a surprisingly casual sixty miles per hour. At that speed it would be here in one minute. Why so slow? Tempted to zip out and meet it head-on, both Mary and Suzy agreed he should stay put and cover Alan's exit from Maude. Besides, the silo's cannon was already locked on and ready to fire, if it was indeed a Regg ship.

Within seconds, Alan in Fighter-Two popped out, and the chute reclosed and sank back below the pond's surface. "I hear we have company coming," he said, pulling up beside Jax.

"In less than a minute," replied Jax, a little nervous. "How shall we handle it?"

"Well, as the girls said, the silo is locked on it, so let's let David take the first crack. If it doesn't go down, we can finish it, okay?"

"Sounds like a plan," said Jax. "Let's just make sure we don't fire on each other accidentally."

"Oh, did we forget to tell you…?"

Inside his anti-gravity spacesuit, Jax turned to his immediate left to visually stare at his father-in-law, who was in the process of becoming a Michelin man himself. "Now what?" he said with a forced groan, actually anxious to hear of what was surely another sexy improvement.

"They gave us a software upgrade that prevents us from shooting each other or the silo cannon, and vice versa. It also has a structure recognition module, so we can't even shoot any of our buildings or the neighbor's."

"Oh, this just keeps getting better and better," grinned Jax, swinging his laser cannon's crosshairs over to center on Fighter-Two. On his screen the outline of the craft immediately flashed red with a barely audible warning alarm. He aimed at the red barn. Same thing. Sure enough.

The two fighters spread out, one on each side of the silo about a hundred yards apart, facing the oncoming Regg ship. Both had it clearly zoomed in by one of their day-night vision cameras, while their other cameras were on a rotating, three-sixty-degree, up-down scan in case other Reggs arrived from different directions.

While stopping the enemy ship was job-one, there was also the issue of where the resulting debris would crash to the ground. They didn't want to wait until it was right on top of the farm, for obvious reasons. But knocking it down outside that perimeter meant difficult to explain space junk all over neighboring fields or structures.

Alan did some fast calculating, and relayed it to David. "Son, take it out at five hundred yards. That should drop it into Emhoff's cornfield."

"He won't be happy," sang Mary.

"True," chuckled Jax, "but we can always spray him with the *forget me dew*."

"And his insurance will cover the crop loss," added Alan.

Mary suggested: "We could pay his deductible."

"Emhoff can pay that himself," rebuked Alan with tongue-in-cheek. "It can be his contribution to saving the earth. We're doing everything else around here."

David's voice from the communications room returned the lighter moment to serious. "Locked on," he announced. "He's descending fast and his approach is slowing. Six thousand yards out now, altitude eight hundred feet. Still slowing. Fifty-five hundred yards. Fifty-three, fifty-two, fifty-one. *Firing!*"

All cameras were zoomed in to watch a red puff of smoke suddenly develop on the nose of the Regg scout craft, followed by its almost instantaneous drop from the sky like a folded quail. It crashed hard in the middle of Emhoff's cornfield, its momentum carrying it another hundred and fifty yards. When the dust had settled, there was a twelve-foot-deep furrow through the black soil, taking out six rows of the tall, green stalks.

But no one saw the crash. Alan, Jax and David were all too busy responding to the multiple, automatic warnings from three different cameras that other bogies were coming in from more than one direction.

Chapter 114

"Holy shit!" shouted Jax, glued to his second camera's monitor. "There's another one right above us at a thousand feet and dropping fast."

As Jax was speaking, David was reporting a second Regg craft right behind the one he had just dropped. "Laser locked," he announced like a seasoned, flying ace. "Firing. Got him! Splash two."

That one also took a direct hit in the nose and plummeted to the ground at this end of Emhoff's field. Being much closer, it skidded through his barbwire fence, over the ditch, bounced across the black asphalt road, over the other ditch, and ended up on Brookfield property just a few yards short of the regulation Little League baseball diamond.

At the same time, Alan's cameras were depicting two more Regg ships, both dropping down out of the sky, almost right on top of them. He reported the sighting, and quickly spun Fighter-Two into position to face their approach. At a distance of only three hundred yards his USLAP cannon locked on one of them, and Alan fired immediately. Dead center.

But as that one dropped out of the picture, the second one launched a sonic blast that sent his Fighter-Two flopping around like a Vaudeville clown in a pratfall. Before its gyro could set things right again, a second blast slammed in harder than the first. Fighter-Two was in a death spin and losing altitude fast, which was a problem since it was only a hundred feet up to begin with.

Alan and his fighter hit the ground hard, bounced once, tipped momentarily up onto its nose, then settled with a thud at the southeast edge of the landing zone previously marked off for the C-17. The impact jostled Alan's brain enough to render him temporarily confused. Wisps of acrid smoke rose from the control panel circuitry to encircle his facemask. He and his fighter were dead in the proverbial water. Looking up through half-closed eyes, he watched the Regg ship fly off, ostensibly to help take out that other Mejan fighter. He didn't see the second one sneaking in behind him, barely one foot off the ground.

As Jax was about to lock in on the Regg above him, everybody else was in his helmet warning of the other enemy fighter coming at him from his lower left. He instinctively accelerated, while jamming the joystick backwards to send Fighter-one scooting for the heavens where he could maneuver better. It's a good thing he did, because a sonic bolt from the Regg ship that just took down Alan missed him by just a scant few feet.

As Jax had hoped, the Reggs still didn't seem to have a lock-on mechanism on their weapons, which were just those sonic cannons, sans lasers. They had to have their target steady in their sights for at least a second, and then the blast could travel no faster than the speed of sound. All Jax had to do was keep moving in an unpredictable pattern.

David dropped a third approaching ship somewhere to the east across County Road 34 in William Tucker's soybeans. He then turned his sights upward to help Jax, but his brother-in-law and the two Reggs were too high and out of sight.

"Jax," he yelled, "get your ass back down here, so I can target the bastards. "You're too high."

Jax's adrenalin was pumping so hard, he had no idea how frightened he was supposed to be. In just the last half minute of cat-and-mouse at six thousand feet, he had learned that those poor Reggs were no match for him. His onboard cameras were keeping each enemy craft in the center of their screens, no matter how they tried to maneuver. And as long as Jax kept moving, they couldn't do any more than take a wild shot at where they thought Jax may be in the next second.

"When you're bird hunting," a cocky Jax narrated to his listening audience," you have to lead your quarry a few feet, and hope the steel shot arrives at just the right time in space." He banked Fighter-One hard to the right and down. "So, if ducks and pheasants had any brains at all, they would never fly in a straight line."

"We can do without the color commentary, Mr. Jackson," admonished his wife. "Just do what David said and get back down here. Now!"

"Why should he have all the fun," returned Jax, thoroughly enjoying himself now with a loop-de-loop. He couldn't crash into the ground or one of the Reggs, even if he wanted to, thanks to his craft's built-in avoidance system.

About then a third Regg ship showed up.

His brain still fuzzy and a bloody nose, Alan instinctively opened Fighter-Two's canopy and pushed the button to retract his puffy spacesuit. He took off his helmet and inhaled deeply to clear his head. Before he could look around, he was immediately sprayed in the face by something from somewhere. His surprise turned to a feeling of pleasant relaxation. A nice man wearing a light-blue jumpsuit and silver helmet standing just outside the fighter told him to remove himself from the cockpit, which Alan gladly obeyed. He was also ordered to retrieve his communicator and put it securely in his pocket.

"Are you part Mejan?" the nice man asked, as they stood face to face shield, Alan a few inches taller.

"No," smiled Alan, weaving to a fro, being held up by his new friend.

"Are there any part Mejans here?"

"Yep."

"Who has the most Mejan blood here?

"Helen, my mother-in-law," offered Alan, without hesitation.

"What is she, half Mejan? One quarter?

"Half."

"Very good. She nearby?"

Alan pointed lazily toward the small, mother-in-law cottage across the pasture. "She lives there."

Removing its helmet, the hairy-faced friend told Alan to run quickly with him to that single-story house with a light in the window about a block away.

They entered the front door into a quaint living room furnished with only a matching cloth sofa and padded chair, plus a dimly-lit reading lamp on a wooden end table. It took only a moment to check out the lone bedroom with one, single bed, looking like it had never been slept in. Last stop—the untouched kitchen, with only a token of appliances—confirmed no one was home…if there ever was.

"Certain she live here?" queried the Regg impatiently.

"Yes."

"She here now?"

"I believe so."

"There a hidden part of house?" asked the Regg.

"Yes, downstairs."

"Show."

Alan opened the kitchen's broom closet, and pointed to the back of it. "There's the door."

"Open."

Alan pushed three buttons on his communicator and the door opened to reveal stairs leading downward.

Chapter 115

With both his onboard, day-night vision cameras tracking the movement of the other two Regg ships, Jax had no way of knowing about the new intruder. He and all his targets were too high for the silo's cameras to cut through the hazy night air. So, no one on the ground could offer a verbal warning, either. Fortunately, he could no longer resist taking out one of the enemies. Fighter-One easily locked on, Jax pulled the trigger, and dead Regg craft number four headed for Iowa topsoil well north of the pond.

So, when the monitor that had been showing that particular fighter suddenly revealed another one, Jax's attitude rapidly turned more serious. "Damn," he said to anyone listening. "They're all over the place up here."

"No shit!" replied David in a frenzy. "I just dropped my fourth, and two more are coming. All from the east and southeast. I need you down here to cover my silo, Jax. Now!"

"Copy that," said Jax, whipping the stick downward. "Let me know when you guys have me on screen."

Three seconds later Suzy was in his ear again, "We see you now, baby. And two Reggs are coming down behind you. Keep maneuvering."

Checking his GPS and altitude, Jax saw he had leveled off just fifty feet above the silo. "I'll lead them over to Emhoff's," he said. "That way we can both keep a visual on them and take them out."

"Good idea," shouted a pumped-up David, dropping yet another Regg, number six in total. "Boo-ya! We got ourselves an old fashion turkey shoot going here."

Bobbing and weaving off to the south, Jax lured his two friends over Emhoff's field. He then cut a quick one-eighty, locked on one, and put a quarter-size hole right through the cockpit. A fast maneuver upward caused the sonic blast from the other Regg to miss and mow down a few hundred dollars-worth of mature field corn. Barrel-rolling in behind the surprised Regg fighter, Jax easily blew a laser hole right up its butt. Splash eight.

And then there were none.

"They're buggin' out!" announced David. Silo Cam-1 picked up a flash of two heading northeast and gone, and Cam-2 showed another joining them from the west, going slower than the others. They didn't know it was a little overloaded with three crammed into a two-man craft.

"Everyone alright?" queried Suzy. All but one complied.

"Jax," said Mary, trying to control the concern in her voice, "you need to check on Alan. We haven't heard or seen anything from him for the past few minutes. We're not even picking up the homing signal from his communicator. Please see if you can locate him."

"On it," replied Jax, swinging back toward the pond.

"I've got him on silo camera-one," chirped David. "His fighter is down in the west pasture inside the circle we drew for the C-17. The canopy is open. Nothing is moving. That's about all I can see from this angle."

Jax was already there, hovering twenty feet directly overhead. "Just a few panel lights blinking in the cockpit," he reported, using his own direct vision rather than the onboard night-vision system. "No sign of Alan."

"Everybody scan the area," pleaded Mary. "He must be out there somewhere. He may be hurt."

Thirty minutes of searching with every day-night camera, plus Louis and Larry on foot with night-vision goggles and flashlights, produced no sign of the Brookfield patriarch. And when a close-up of Alan's helmet—plucked from the passenger's side floor of the fighter—revealed a spot of blood on the inside of the face shield, everyone's heart sank.

Chapter 116

The Desert People were facing a public relations nightmare. The main underground headquarters was in a location remote enough that the attack by the three bunker-buster bombs would go unnoticed by all except a few scorpions and one sidewinder snake. But there was no hiding the fact of the other three bombs blowing up sections of Area 51. The tremors rattled windows in Las Vegas, and now the eastern horizon was painted with faint pillars of smoke in the night. The UFO conspiracy theorists already had hard-ons or wet panties.

In some ways, Brookfield Farm's PR nightmare was almost as bad. How do you explain eight smoking alien slabs of melted metal in two-foot-deep holes, littering the country side with Brookfield Farm right on the fringe? The Desert couldn't help, obviously having problems of their own. Even if Louis and Larry were successful in covering them all up before sunrise with the snow blades on their pickups, there would still be the issue of long furrows of destroyed crops, broken fences, and deep scratch marks running perpendicular across the N56 blacktop in front of the Brookfield's. In a few days insurance adjusters would be out evaluating the crop damage. Then would come the nosy press. Sooner or later they'd have their own UFO junkies arrive with cameras, Geiger counters and metal detectors. There wasn't nearly enough amnesia juice in the storehouse to neutralize them all.

While Louis and Larry worked feverishly with the literal cover-up, no one else wanted to leave the communications room in case some word was received about Alan. Everyone stayed huddled around Mary, doing their best to console her, while keeping close vigilance on all televisions, PC monitors, and radio receivers. She seemed to be doing fairly well under the circumstances. All forty-three years of her life had been filled with subterfuge, deception, fear, joy, love. And now violence and loss. Every time her husband went up in a fighter or even out to bulldoze something, Mary worried for his safety. Now he was gone, disappeared, possibly being held by the Reggs. Her heart might be ripping apart inside her chest, but she was determined to keep her mind positive and focused.

Suzy was certainly her mother's daughter, also remaining calm, positive and attentive. She was more fortunate, however, in that she had Jax's comforting arms wrapped around her. It could just as easily be her husband that went missing. Having it be her father was heart-wrenching enough.

"He's alive," stated Jax firmly, breaking a long silence in the comm.

"I think so, too," said Mary. Suzy nodded. David and Mike just sat with their eyes glued to the various electronics.

"I wouldn't be surprised if this entire attack was to kidnap one of us," continued the logical Jax. "They diverted our attention by coming in waves from the east and southeast, while a few of them came in from above or the west. They gladly sacrificed eight ships to knock down one of ours. And while we were busy fighting them off, they slipped in and snatched Alan."

Everyone let the concept sink in…with a shudder.

"Makes sense," said Suzy after a moment. "The Reggs are desperate. After we captured their daughter ship, they fear we know a lot about them now, while they still know next to nothing about us. They were willing to sacrifice eight ships and at least that many men just to get one of us."

"They are also pretty clever," added Jax. "I'll bet they hit Area 51 at the same time just to draw off any Desert crafts protecting us, making it easier to slip in and nab Alan."

"Now you see why The Desert doesn't let us in on much," said Mary. "They can spray Alan with a gallon of that truth serum, but they won't get much out of him, because he doesn't know much."

Before everyone's stomach could nauseate with the thought of what they would probably do to Alan once finished interrogating him, Mary deflected the attention to her mother, Helen.

"Has anyone checked on Grandma?"

Chapter 117

The lower half of Colonel Joshua Middleton's face was uncharacteristically tense. Even though his eyes were hidden behind his prescription flight glasses, his crow's feet confessed their sadness and dread. It was eleven-thirty the next night. He had finally answered the Brookfield's frantic calls—launched every hour on the hour for the past twenty—asking him to contact them immediately.

"We already know what you have to report," he said, shaking his bowed head.

"You already know?" asked a crestfallen Mary, Alan's wife, Helen's daughter. Her query quickly turned to a demand. *"How* do you *already know?"*

The colonel couldn't answer right away. He seemed to be choking back tears. "God damn it all to hell," he finally mumbled, sweeping his hand through the air in a feeble gesture of surrender. "Watch your screen, folks. Here's what we just got thirty minutes ago. I'm so sorry!"

Joshua's face faded out, replaced by an equally-sharp image of Alan and Helen sitting on chairs, facing the camera, their eyes half shut, a silly smile on Alan's face, the gasmask on Helen's. Mary's scream expressed both terror and relief. Standing behind them with a hand on each shoulder was a wolf-faced Regg, wearing a dark-green jumpsuit with a gold insignia on the left breast and a matching baseball cap, gold markings on the bill. He or she was also smiling with a sinister show of incisors and extended canines. Its yellow eyes with the horizontal catlike pupils seemed to flash with flippancy.

"Hello, humans and half-breeds," it said with a dusky timber. "I am Raquerter Benztick. I am military. My rank would be like your full colonels. Since you may not understand our language, I speak in English. You may call me *Commander.*" He smirked at his clever use of the word. He indeed saw himself completely in command.

"I believe you know these two," he said, bending down to pat them both on the side of their shoulder. "We having nice talk with them. They very cooperative." The commander tapped Alan on the top of his head. "What your name?"

"Alan Brookfield," he replied, like a sleepy five-year-old.

"And where you live?"

"On my farm northwest of Iowa City about five miles.

"And what your name?" he asked, tapping Helen's head.

"Ursalu," she mumbled through the gasmask, in the same state as Alan.

"What your Earth name?"

"Helen."

"How much of you Mejan?"

"One half."

Raquerter Benztick turned his attention back to Alan. "Do you have spaceship on your farm?"

"Yes," grinned Alan.

"Where it on your farm?"

"In the ground under our pond," answered Alan, almost proudly.

"Where its mother ship?" asked the Regg.

Alan scrunched his face. "I don't know," he said, sad that he couldn't help with that one.

"Do you know where mother ship hides, Helen?"

"No, I don't," she replied through her gasmask, also in frustration.

"So, as you can see, Mister Colonel Joshua Middleton," grinned the self-proclaimed commander, reading from his communicator, "and all the rest of you at *The Desert* and *Brookfield Farm*, we have chatterboxes here, who tell us many interesting things about you. We know you recently acquired laser cannons with range of one mile. This how you destroyed many of our fighters. We not expect that.

"Alan was happy to tell us about his farm and underground facilities and silo loaded with technology. We know codes to open all secret doors. We very careful only Alan touch his communicator, because it self-destruct if we do. As you can see, we also know how to connect to special frequency you use to communicate, because we on it right now, thanks to Alan and his communicator. It even serving as the camera we using to make this video.

"I could go on for hours telling all we learned from these two nice creatures," sighed the commander with exaggerated boredom, "but I think you *get the picture*, as your televisions like to say. What most importance to you right now is fate of your two friends here. We know you know we are not opposed to slicing their heads off without slightest hesitation. But not need to happen."

Still from behind, the ugly Regg placed his hairy fingers gently around Alan and Helen's throats. "In one hour...one a.m. Central Daylight Time," he said more directly, full of himself in having been selected to present this official warning, "we contact you again on this frequency. We have small list of demands. If you agree, we release Alan and Helen unharmed. If you do not, well..."

Raquerter Benztick smiled, showing even more of his pearly whites. He then said quite pleasantly, "Alan, pick up your communicator and turn off broadcast."

Everyone watched a sleepy, half-smiling Alan rise from his chair, take one step forward, and reach out with his hand that grew so large it covered the frame. A close up of the lines in his palm shook a little as he searched for the *off* button.

The screen went blank.

Chapter 118

For what seemed like years, no one from either end of the desert-to-farm link said anything. Suzy was in Jax's lap, firmly wrapped in his arms. He held her head against his chest to absorb her quaking and tears. His jaw muscles rippled. That adrenalin of abject abhorrence he felt surge into his mind, heart and body when those bastards were coming at Suzy with that mile-long needle was beginning to rekindle. He envisioned beating their faces to a pulp. David and Mike looked at each other with welling eyes and clenched fists. David brought one of his down hard on the table, causing everyone to jump. Mary just stared emptily beyond the large screen. Her face was pale and expressionless.

Joshua's bowed head had already faded back in. It could just as well have been a snapshot, because he didn't move for a full minute. He finally did when an off-camera voice drew his attention, followed by someone handing him a cell phone. The colonel's profile mostly listened and nodded to the instructions on the other end, with an occasional *yes sir* and *okay*. Clicking off, Joshua turned to face the Brookfield group.

"We aren't going to do anything until hearing their demands," he said flatly, repeating the orders he had just received. "Which will be in…" he looked at his watch, "…in just three minutes. But the general wants me to assure you we will do everything we can to make sure no harm comes to Alan and Helen, even if it means agreeing to all their conditions. We may be military, but we do hold life precious, especially the life of our friends."

Mary broke into tears. "Thank you, Colonel," she blubbered. *"Thank you."*

Her gratitude was shared by all. But so was a sick feeling in the pit of their stomachs. This was a no-win scenario. Everyone knew the Regg's demands would be ridiculous. The world as they knew it would never be the same. For Jax, it was the second upheaval of sensibility in three months.

They didn't have long to wait. At precisely one hour past midnight Colonel Joshua Middleton's face was replaced by the back of a black leather chair—framed in the monitor from headrest to pedestal. It was typical of those found in any executive office…no doubt exactly from where it was appropriated. The background of the inner sanctum consisted only of a dark-green curtain, a la terrorists who want to give away nothing of their location. After waiting a few seconds for obvious dramatic effect, the chair slowly turned to face the camera...presumably again utilizing the one on Alan's communicator.

The first things that stuck out about the seated creature with legs crossed were ankle-high, red, velvet booties that resembled slippers more than shoes. Unlike any of its minions, nothing adorned its head, just combed-back gray hair in multiple shades of light to dark. In between the head and feet was the most noticeable part of the ensemble: a loose-fitting, flowing, black silk pajama-like two-piece with gold trim on all four cuffs, the high collar, and the seam running down the middle of the chest. All in all, he, she, or it seemed more ready for bed than to deliver ultimatums to an enemy.

Back in the Brookfield comm, with a straight face and the tone of a news reporter leading into an exposé, Jax said into his pretend microphone, "Somewhere in a tacky Chinese brothel, the sheets are missing." It was a good thing none of this reached the Regg high command. Colonel Middleton had told the Brookfields to stay completely incommunicado.

"I won't bore you with my name," said Jul Colcack, the Regg's supreme ruler, matter-of-factly in a gruff, but articulate and obviously educated voice. "You would not remember it anyway. So, you may call me *Khan*. Yes, *that* Khan, from the Star Trek movie. I chose it because like that Khan, I have demonstrated the superior intellect. Oh, maybe not in terms of your so-called intelligence quotient rating system. You Mejans can have that honor. But what are brains without cunning and logic? I have outsmarted you. We have captured two of your compadres. We have learned all we need to bring you and your superior firepower, your superior numbers, and your no-longer-superior *intellect* to your knees. Have we not?"

Chapter 119

Khan leaned back in his chair and crossed his skinny legs, dark hair now showing from under one flaring pant leg. "Our demand is quite simple," he continued, with the self-satisfaction of finally being in complete control of the Mejans, the United States military, The Desert, and every Earthling's destiny. "You will give us your technology to build the same weapons you have used on us. This will allow us to achieve a balance of power. Mutually assured destruction works well for Earth's world powers. It will work well for us, do you think not? Yes, you have nuclear weapons, and yes, we could secure some of them as easily as we did six of your bunker-buster bombs. But we all know neither of us would ever use them. If there is one objective we have in common, it is the preservation of the earth. You want to live on it, we want to live off of it.

"Once we are equal in weaponry," he continued, "we want half the earth. The exact territories and boundaries to be determined later. We know you wish to eventually be assimilated, blended, if you will, into the human race. We grant you that. Maybe we will give you, say, all the Americas, while we control Europe and Asia. Maybe vice versa. You must understand, it is our nature to conquer and rule. It is the way of our ancestors."

One of Khan's minions suddenly crossed into camera view and bent down to whisper in his leader's ear. Apparently something had come up: a small fishing vessel had moved in close to their satellite dish. Unhappy with the intrusion, Khan wiggled his dangling foot impatiently as he listened with a scowl. When the messenger had finished, Khan pondered a brief moment, said something decisively to the officer, and waved him away.

Still pensive, the supreme ruler of the Reggs named Jul Colcack but arrogantly calling himself Star Trek's *Khan*, rose and walked slowly behind his chair, coming to lean on the top of the headrest with folded arms.

"Of course, if you do not agree to this simple term," he continued with the same cold-blooded tone, "not only will we execute Alan and Helen, we will begin a campaign of killing off much of the world's population with a plague so black you can only imagine. While you have spent your days and years developing military prototypes, we have been perfecting biological weapons capable of killing humans and Mejans en masse. Our chemistry is far more deadly than your physics. So unless you don't mind spending the rest of your lives hunkered down in your deep bunkers, wearing gasmasks, and listening to the agonizing cries of the dying, I suggest you strongly consider this simple condition."

Khan strutted back to the front of the chair and sat down. "We will await your answer. Consult with your officers and experts, and report back to us on this same channel exactly forty-eight hours from now. Any earlier attempt to contact us will not be received."

Khan pointed at the camera. "We are done. Alan Brookfield, turn off your communicator."

As before, there was a slight jostling of the picture, then the live feed went blank.

Colonel Middleton's head and shoulders were visible once again. For the first time ever, he was not wearing his signature flight sunglasses. His eyes were big and round with hazel-green irises. His face was flushed and stern.

"Needless to say," he began quite pointedly, "since they have Alan's device, all our communications from here on are far from private."

It took only a brief moment for that unsavory prospect to sink in, and all nodded without speaking.

"Kinda makes you long for the old days of landlines, huh?" said the Colonel, his eyes narrowing slightly.

Again silence. But it was suddenly broken by Mike blurting, "But we..."

David's hand was over his brother's mouth in a flash.

"Doesn't really matter," continued Joshua, sadly. "I'm sure we will be agreeing to their demands. Losing Alan and Helen is one thing, but the slaughter of millions of innocent people is unconscionable and to be avoided at all costs." More nodding. "So, let's sign off. *Both of us. Now.* We'll be in touch. God bless all of you."

Chapter 120

"Jesus, Mike," hissed David, "What the fuck?"

"Sorry," sighed Mike. "I wasn't thinking."

Just then the cordless phone somewhere behind one of the computers was chirping for the first times in maybe years, certainly months. David located and answered it. "It's Colonel Middleton," he announced, like the foregone conclusion it was. "He wants to talk to either Mary or Jax."

"Take it, Jax," said Mary. "You're the man of the house for now."

So Jax wouldn't have to leave his seat or Suzy leave his lap, David tossed the phone over.

"Hello, Colonel," Jax said pointedly. "Can't we track those bastards' location somehow?"

"Is the link to us and Alan's phone completely shut down?" asked Joshua, momentarily averting Jax's question..

Jax looked around to verify what he already knew. The screen was blank. "Yes."

"Then put me on speaker."

Jax located and pushed the button on the handset appropriately labeled *Speaker*. He'd forgotten how simple life used to be in the dark ages. "You're on," he said.

"I wish we could," said the Colonel. "But the video chat we just had, or any chat we ever have, for that matter, is over a highly-secure frequency through the cloud and encrypted in a special server…just like with Skype. Even with proxy no one can trace where the transmissions are coming from."

"What about tracking Alan's phone?" asked Jax. "It has a built in homing signal that operates even if the unit is turned off."

"True," sighed Middleton, "but its range is only about fifteen miles. And since it's obviously inside their spaceship, we wouldn't get any signal at all."

"Do you think they're in their mothership?" said Jax, telling more than asking.

"Probably," replied Joshua. "That pompous ass would never lower himself to be anyplace else."

"Any idea where that ship is?"

"Not really," signed the colonel. "Logic and a higher than normal volume of unconfirmed UFO sightings over the years suggest they might be in the Pacific Ocean somewhere off the coast of Oregon."

"Well....?" probed Jax.

"Well, what?" barked Colonel Middleton, his nerves as frayed as everyone's. "The Pacific Ocean isn't exactly your friggin' pond, Jax. It took them seventy years to find the Titanic, for Christ's sake. And they knew where to look, and it wasn't cloaked in stealth, and it couldn't change its location in a blink." The colonel took a deep breath and composed himself. "Sorry, son, but we have no chance in hell of locating that goddamn ship in a thousand years, let alone forty-eight hours."

Defeated, Jax just stared at the handset's speaker a moment, before quietly asking, "So, what are we going to do?"

"I don't know," confessed the half-Mejan colonel in the United States Air Force. "All us brass will be meeting soon to decide. But my guess is we will have to comply."

Chapter 121

Captain Gregory "Cinch" Kelly put the Bic's flame to the tip of his Winston cigarette, sucked hard, and took in a lungful. The expelled smoke plumed from his puckered lips and blossomed across the unfurled navigation chart hanging from the wheelhouse's ceiling. A quick glance down at his Lowrance Elite-5 sonar showed he was still over the Astoria Canyon in six hundred feet of water. Any minute now his charter boat should be entering shallower water. That's where he hoped to find some nests of squid eggs, a favorite of the halibut he and his regular customers from San Francisco would be fishing for tomorrow at first light.

Cinch checked his digital watch: *10:52 p.m.* He'd been out here for about an hour now. If he didn't locate some squid eggs soon, a nap was starting to sound like a good plan B. Those rich guys from San Fran would be waiting for him at the marina in about six hours.

A splashing noise off the starboard bow pulled his attention to the open window on his right. Paring his eyes, he couldn't see anything in the dark. He flipped on the spotlight mounted above him on the cabin's roof and turned it in the direction of the sound. But the light fog lifting off the relatively calm ocean threw the brightness back in his face.

Something else caught his eye. The depth-finder, which always displayed the ocean's bottom and anything in between in graphic, chromatic detail, was suddenly showing nothing except the thin red line at the very top of the screen denoting the surface of the water. Cinch tapped it lightly on the top of its casing. Nothing changed. Then a little harder. Still nothing.

"C'mon you piece of shit," he snapped, slapping its side. "I just bought you a few months ago." Then he noticed the built-in GPS was still functioning. "That's strange. Must be something wrong with the transducer."

Now off the port side he heard a whirring sound, like something mechanical or electronic adjusting itself. He hit the spotlight again and spun it toward the sound. He panned the area with light, still being almost blinded by the flashback. Then the beam caught one of the last objects one would expect to find sticking out of the water ten miles off the Oregon coast. A satellite dish...of sorts.

"What the hell..." breathed Captain Kelly, squinting to better see the oddly shaped object. It was parabolic and solid, about six feet high, seemingly covered in a dark, scaly substance shiny enough to reflect some of the spotlight.

Not wanting to get too close, Cinch pulled back on the throttle, putting the twin Honda outboards into slow reverse. That's when something beside the dish, something like a deck cannon, turned and seemed to point at him. Fear welling up inside, Clinch instinctively reached for the handset of his VHF radio. It was already set on channel 16, the emergency band to reach the Coast Guard.

"This is the Fish Hawk out of Astoria," he yelled into the microphone.

"This is the Coast Guard," came the quick reply. "What can we do for you, Cinch?"

"There's a goddamn satellite dish sticking out of the water right beside me here," he said with a nervous laugh. "I know it sounds crazy, but there's also what looks like a cannon pointing right at me."

"Are they floating or attached to something?" queried the ensign on night duty.

"Seem to be attached," said Cinch, craning his neck. "They aren't moving in the waves."

"What are your coordinates?"

Captain Kelly glanced down at his Lowrance. "Forty-six degrees, seventeen minutes north, one hundred and twenty-four degrees, twenty-one minutes west."

"Got it," said the ensign. "How deep are you?"

"My depth-finder doesn't seem to be working. Last I knew I was in about six hundred..."

The blast from the sonic cannon blew the thirty-two-foot Fish Hawk into a million pieces of metal and wood and muscle and bone.

Chapter 122

It was the longest two days anyone at Brookfield Farms had ever gone through. They felt so helpless. And for all the anguish, it was made even worse thinking about poor Alan and Helen being held captive there in an enemy spacecraft. Hopefully the Reggs were keeping them well medicated, so they would have less sense of their surroundings, peril, and the dragging hours.

Chores still needed to be done, so that kept the boys and hired hands busy. Mary, Suzy and Jax pretty much lived in the communications room, even though there was virtually nothing to watch for. Surely the Reggs would not be attacking. Why would they? They already had exactly what they wanted: a human, a Mejan, and all the aces.

It was assumed The Desert People were going through the same foot-twitching, coffee-drinking, waiting-for-the-clock-to-strike agony. What little there was to decide had undoubtedly been done long ago. They would give the Reggs the blueprints to the USLAP technology in exchange for Alan and Helen. The question was whether those hairy bastards would then honor the agreement and release their hostages.

"Let's give them one of our actual cannons rigged to blow up in their faces the second they try to use it," Jax had facetiously suggested earlier. "Or rig it with a strong homing device, so we could track it to their mothership and nuke 'em!" Of course, no one would do anything to jeopardize getting Alan and Helen back unharmed. But it was fun to fantasize. Still one of Jax's fortes.

Mary kept busy scanning the media for recent reports of UFOs around Johnson County. Just this morning she had hacked into the State Farm Insurance network after an agent had popped up at Emhoff's to inspect the strange loss of crops. That was expected. Now if no vans full of electronic gear, metal detectors and drooling fanatics showed up, the events of two nights ago may blow over.

Suzy took care of the meals, figuring she needed to broaden her culinary horizons, what with the baby due in six and a half months. It helped keep her mind off things. She'd already planned the *Welcome Home* banquet for her dad and grandmother: filet mignon and lobster with twice-baked potatoes, Iowa sweet corn on the cob, sourdough rolls with real butter, and for desert: strawberry shortcake with whipped cream. Oh, and a case of the most expensive wine Jax's money could buy at *The Vino Chalet* in Cedar Rapids.

Jax was half asleep, trying to maintain semi vigilance of the east wall's array of radars and satellite feeds, when the cordless phone chirped. He flew out of the office chair and picked it up on the second ring. As Mary and Suzy gathered around, he put the receiver on Speaker.

"Hello, Colonel?" queried an anxious Jax. He didn't know who else it would be, and there seemed no reason to be calling unless it was important.

"You folks sitting down?" the colonel asked, his tone giving away nothing.

"No," all three said in unison.

"Good," he replied evenly, just before cutting loose, almost shouting, "because we found the Regg mothership and we have the fucker surrounded!"

Chapter 123

The next two hours in the Brookfield communications room were filled with hugging, kissing, dancing, crying, praying, and laughing. By the third hour things had tempered to exhaustion and cautious optimism, while the fourth and final hour leading up to the video-conference call with his majesty, Lord Khan, seemed to drag on slower than a mail-in rebate.

The colonel couldn't and didn't give many details, as some elements were not yet finalized. But he did explain how a charter boat captain off the coast of Oregon had stumbled onto the mothership as it had partially surfaced to deliver that sanctimonious monologue by the pretentious, self-labeled *Khan* two nights ago. The captain, rest his beautiful and conscientious soul, had managed to radio his exact longitude and latitude to the Coast Guard just before the murderous Reggs blew him out of the water. When communication with the boat was lost, the Coast Guard ensign immediately reported to his superior, who reported to his superior, who *just happened* to be part Mejan and well connected to The Desert.

Joshua said a Coast Guard cutter was quickly dispatched to scan the area with sonar and try to take readings of the Regg spacecraft, which presumably would have gone back down to the bottom in over six hundred feet of water. The Reggs would easily detect the sonar signals, but they would assume the cutter was just looking for the missing boat and captain.

To applaud Jax's earlier suggestion, the colonel explained that yes, the spaceship's stealth would just absorb and deflect the sonar pulses, causing no return. And that is exactly what would reveal the size and shape of the craft: while over it, no bottom reading; while not over it, a signal would chart the ocean's bottom. After just a few passes they had a clear outline of the mothership. It was slightly elliptical, generally rounded on top, over two miles long, and a mile and a half wide. For perspective, Joshua reminded Jax and Suzy that the friendly craft used to rescue them that night eleven days ago, Little Sister, was about one-eighth that size.

As they spoke, many forces were being brought to bear on the Regg mothership, all remaining *out of sight* until the appropriate time. It was a concerted effort, involving west coast Army, Navy, and Air Force contingencies, all, of course, directly under the auspices of The Desert. Jax was beginning to wonder how many people and factions in this country were *not*.

Finally, while the upcoming video-conference call with the Reggs would be a back-and-forth dialogue using Alan's communicator and frequency again, Colonel Middleton wanted to make sure the Brookfield camera and microphone were again not a part of it. *Shut down.* They could watch and listen, but there needed to be no transmissions from anyone but The Desert for obvious reasons.

Joshua thought if everything went right, they could have Helen and Alan safe and sound within an hour.

Chapter 124

Buzzing like nervous bees around the communications room were Mary, Jax, Suzy, David, Mike, Larry, Louis, and Joyce. Karen drew the short straw and had to remain topside to babysit the children; they were too young to know about such goings-on under the dirt at Brookfield Farm. Bowls of popcorn and beers were everywhere. The mood was festive, yet apprehensive. You'd think the Rocky Horror Picture Show was five minutes late in starting and these were first-time attendees.

But at precisely 11:00 p.m. Central Daylight Time on August 21, 2015, the main fifty-five-inch screen on the north wall sprang to life. It was a split-screen, vertically down the middle. On the left side in his high-back leather chair, wearing the same outrageous outfit as forty-eight hours ago, was the self-proclaimed *Khan*, looking quite smug, as far as one could tell on a wolfen face full of shiny gray hair. On the right were the head and broad shoulders of some white-haired, square-jawed, marine-looking brass in desert fatigues they had never seen before. Probably a general. Probably *the* general: The Desert's big kahuna. It didn't matter. He looked exactly how you'd want your spokesman to look in this particular war room situation.

"Greetings," began the black-nosed Regg, who thought he held the upper hand. "And who do we have here? A new face. Your name, please."

Without so much as a blink or hesitation, one side of the general's thin lips cracked open just enough to say, "Let's not bother with my real name either, *Khan*. You probably wouldn't remember it anyway. Just call me *Kirk*."

The Regg's yellow, cat eyes began fluttering, apparently making the Star Trek connection. A short smile spread across his mouth, and it looked like he was going to make a snide remark. Then he thought better. "So, *Kirk*," he said with a short bow, "I trust your people have decided to accept our terms and deliver to us the specifications for your USLAP weaponry."

"Before we get to that," said the general, "there is something we feel you should be aware of."

"And what might that be?" sighed Khan impatiently, but with mild interest.

"You are surrounded," stated the general flatly.

"Surrounded?" snorted Khan with a dismissive grin. "By what? My stupid officers?" He laughed, looking to his right. "Of that I cannot argue."

"By six, stealth, Blackhawk attack helicopters," said Kirk, now reading from a clipboard, "closing in on you as we speak, armed with Hellfire missiles. By one of our stealth battleships with its sixteen-inch guns and cruise missiles already locked on you. And in case you consider making a dive, by three, stealth, nuclear submarines under the surface, torpedo tubes loaded and locked on your two-mile-long mothership. They seldom miss something that big and that close."

Khan was already looking back again to his right, speaking softly in his native tongue, trying to get verification from his officers. When there apparently was none, he turned back to the camera and spat, "Bullshit, Kirk! You are bluffing. And only delaying the inevitable. You can't possibly know our location."

"The next sound you hear, Khan," said Kirk, "will be three sonar pings, one from each of the subs." The general looked to his left and gave a short nod.

The Regg's command chamber suddenly chimed with three, almost simultaneous *PINGS*.

More from disbelief than pain, Khan threw his hands up over his ears hidden beneath all that hair. When the echoing had stopped, he shook his head and said defiantly, "That could have been anything. I don't know what game you're playing, Kirk, but it will get you nowhere, except the death of our hostages, if you persist."

Chapter 125

"No game, Khan," said the general evenly. "Your ship with its parabolic-shaped satellite dish, sticking six feet out of the water ten-point-three miles off the Oregon coast at forty-six degrees north latitude, one hundred and twenty-four degrees west longitude is completely surrounded. If you turn on your night-vision infrared cameras and point them ten degrees up in any direction, I believe you'll see our Blackhawks with their Hellfire missiles coming into view. And any time you'd like another ping serenade, just say so."

The head Regg began squirming in his seat. He barked something to his right again, and started to get up.

"I strongly suggest you remain in your seat, Khan," quickly warned Kirk. "At any given moment you and your craft are one second away from total obliteration." To emphasize the point, a quick nod brought three more simultaneous pings echoing through the chamber. "Pretend those are six torpedoes hitting your hull."

Khan settled back down, frustrated, showing clear signs of comprehending his precarious new situation.

"Do you need me to provide you with any more proof, Khan?"

"No. No. That's okay," conceded the Regg supreme commander, a nervous smirk spread across his thin, blue lips. "You had me at *Hellfire*."

All the movie buffs at Brookfield couldn't help but laugh in surprise. They caught the *Jerry Maguire* reference. They had to admire Khan's little stab at humor in the face of certain defeat. The Reggs obviously liked Hollywood movies as much as humans did.

Returning to seriousness, Khan's grin faded as he challenged the general, "You would sacrifice your two people so carelessly?"

"To stop you from murdering billions of innocent people?" replied Kirk. "In a heartbeat!"

"I don't understand," mumbled Khan.

"You dogfaces obviously are Star Trek fans" explained Kirk, "so I'm sure you recall Spock's dying words, '*the needs of the many outweigh the needs of the few*.' Besides, I don't even know your hostages. They mean little to me."

"So, what do you want, *Captain James T. Kirk*, or whatever your name is?" hissed the leader of the Reggs, now trying to appear defiant and save some face in front of his officers.

The general paused for effect. His face remained stoic. "The first thing you are going to do is set up one of your own audio-visual units, so we can continue this conversation on a different frequency and without using Alan Brookfield's communicator. We are sending you that highly-secure megahertz setting now. Tell me when your computer has received it."

This seemed easy enough. Khan looked over to his right, waited for confirmation, and then turned back. He nodded.

"And let me know when your A-V unit is set up," said the general.

It took only a minute of off-camera bustling before Khan faced forwards again to relay it was up and functioning. The switch in channels was made with only a split-second blackout, and Khan's hairy presence was back in frame, this time farther away and with a poorer resolution. Besides inferior weaponry, the Reggs clearly lacked in other technical areas, as well.

"You are doing well so far, Khan," said the general with a patronizing tone. "And just in case you are considering making a vertical run for it into outer space, where our subs and choppers can't follow, may I suggest you train one of your external cameras straight up." He waited while Khan sighed deeply and gave the order to do so. "Do you see that big hole in the stars directly above you?" Khan checked a monitor somewhere behind the A/V unit. His jaw and face dropped. "That's *Little Sister*," said the general proudly. "She's a bit smaller than your craft, but she's much more agile. And oh so deadly." The general paused a moment, then added with a smirk, "Remember when your daughter ship disappeared from the Coralville Reservoir, Khan? It was Little Sister. She ate her!"

Khan stared at the image on the screen a moment longer, then returned a defeated gaze back to the camera. "I assume that's where you presently are, *Captain Kirk*," he sneered.

"Let's just say I'm close by and will continue to be," said the white-haired marine. "What is more important to you is that Little Sister is locked and loaded to blow your ass in eight directions across the Pacific. Or if you prefer, she can zap you with a negative electromagnetic pulse through your satellite dish, fry all your circuits, and send you to the bottom of the ocean to live out your few remaining days in total darkness and choking agony. Your call, Khan."

Chapter 126

"Okay," conceded Khan, with both hands extended to his sides, palms out. "You've made your point. What is it you want?"

"First, show us Alan and Helen," said the general. "Don't turn the camera. Just bring them into view beside you."

That was accomplished quite readily, since Alan had already been in the room to operate his communicator for the earlier part of the conference. Helen was in an adjacent room, and was promptly brought to Alan's side. Behind her gasmask she seemed still under the usual chemical influence. It was more obvious with Alan, whose goofy look and sleepy eyes signaled he had been sprayed with at least one of the controlling mists not too long ago. That was to be expected and could easily be worked around.

"We want them back immediately," said the general. "You will bring your craft up a few feet so the top of the hull is approximately three feet above the ocean's surface. You will then get Alan and Helen topside, along with his communicator. But before they leave this room, you will tell him that once up there, Alan is to call us on the usual channel. You will also tell him that he is to obey any human who speaks to him from then on and ignore all Regg attempts to control him and Helen. One of our Blackhawks will land and pick them up. If you understand this sequence of events, bark twice."

That had everyone at Brookfield howling with laughter, especially Jax and Suzy.

Ignoring the sarcastic jab, Khan slowly, sadly nodded in compliance, and the wheels to free Helen and Alan were set in motion. One of the controls, who had been interrogating Alan throughout his stay, slipped into the picture to relay to him the specific instructions outlined by the general, and both hostages were led away off camera. Khan remained, as ordered.

"Once you have them back," he asked, noticeably defeated, "what do you plan to do? Without them here as a bargaining chip, we have no shield. What would stop you from destroying us?"

"A fair question," Khan," grinned Kirk. "But it might be possible that we don't think the way you Reggs do. We are basically peace-loving and non-vindictive. If you don't try to make a run for it, if you keep your satellite dish up, if you cooperate with the rest of our plan, we will consider sparing your lives and your spacecraft."

"And what might *that* plan be?" sighed Khan, thinking death might be the favored alternative.

"We will discuss it as soon as Alan and Helen are safely away," said the general. "In the meantime, I suggest you start the process of establishing communications with all of your daughter ships around the world. Tell them it's time to come home to momma."

Chapter 127

When Colonel Joshua Middleton called on the landline to inform the farm Helen and Alan were safe and sound aboard a Blackhawk helicopter, the air was filled with cries of joy and popcorn. Mike already had Kool & The Gang celebrating *good times, come on!"* cued up and echoing off the walls from his iPod connected to a Bose speaker. Suzy dirty-danced with Jax. Mary taught David the twist and the mashed potato. Mike twerked with Larry's wife, Joyce, then with Larry. Louis was already in a drunken stupor in the corner, blabbing the good news into his smart phone to his wife, Karen, back at their cottage.

Life was good again. The earth was back to spinning evenly on its axis. God was smiling. The corn was growing.

It was difficult to settle down, but the picture show off the coast of Oregon was resuming. Intermission was over.

"Little Sister, one mile above you," stated the general, "will escort you to outer space, one thousand miles above the earth. Follow her. Set your ascension speed to seven hundred miles per hour to avoid a sonic boom, and do not deviate from the zero degree climb. Remember, Little Sister has you locked on and can outmaneuver you in every aspect. If you attempt any deceptive action, if you even try lowering your dish, you will immediately be destroyed with extreme prejudice. If you understand the words I am speaking to you, begin following Little Sister's lead now."

The self-proclaimed Star Trek villain nodded in compliance and growled a series of commands to his officers. The fifty-five-inch screen in the Brookfield communications room suddenly switched from the two Star Trek characters to two different angles of the enormous, two-mile-long Regg mothership, lifting out of the Pacific Ocean and climbing straight up, slowly at first, then gaining speed.

For as long as possible, the left side of the split-screen showed the Regg ship in profile and pulling away, the text at the bottom reading, "Blackhawk Forward Cam 2." The right side was labeled "Sister Belly Cam 5," showing a virtual static shot of the top of the alien craft with its most distinguishing feature: an omega-shaped, raised portion comprised largely of some type of translucent glass on most of its sections. This presumably was the bridge, command center, observation decks, and any other onboard area requiring a live view.

With both the Blackhawk and Little Sister having the advanced night-vision capability, the Regg ship appeared to be in broad daylight, belying the actual one-thirty a.m. darkness encasing it.

Within minutes the Blackhawk helicopter couldn't follow the Regg craft any farther, and the split-screen dissolved back to just the bird's eye view from Little Sister.

"Begin contacting all your daughter ships now," continued Kirk. "Have them as soon as possible leave their positions at the exact same speed and trajectory as you. Once they are at the thousand-mile threshold, have them proceed at maximum speed along a lateral course to join with you."

"I guess I should thank you for this gesture, Kirk," said Khan cautiously, not sure of its basis. "We will comply. But most of our Eastern Hemisphere ships are incommunicado and will not have their satellite dishes exposed to receive our signal for many hours yet. And the hour has already passed when all of our Western Hemisphere daughters report in. Plus there is the issue of needing time to prepare for such a takeoff. Most have not been mobile for months or years. And once ready, they may not have a clear exit, due to human activity nearby."

"We are aware of these conditions, Khan," said the general. "We will both stay in the earth's shadow at one thousand miles for as long as it takes to retrieve all your daughters, even if it is more than twenty-four hours. Time is no longer a critical issue."

Chapter 128

It did take the full twenty-four hours plus another one for the mother to gather in her children, all one hundred and ten of them. At first it was exciting for the Brookfield bunch to watch the smaller, hundred-yard-long spaceships with their dark-gray, angular outlines being swallowed up in the gaping portals lining the thirty-story side of the Regg mothership. But like a marathon baseball game going into the twenty-third inning still tied, it became impossible for all to stay awake for the duration. All but Jax. His writer's curiosity didn't want to miss a minute of something he was among the chosen few to witness and would never see again. After all, there was that book he hoped to write when all this was over.

Suzy had crashed after four hours, her head on his lap, his ass asleep on the floor, his back leaning against a large throw pillow propped up against a cabinet under the computer table. David and Mike, both getting to experience their first drunken binge—chaperoned by adults, anyway— were passed out on sleeping bags and blow-up mattresses Mary had brought in for the occasion. She herself snoozed until noon on her own bedding, then went upstairs and fixed brunch for everyone. Conscientious farmhands they were, Larry and Louis, while quite hung over, completed the bulk of their chores, and then hit the sheets in their respective houses around two in the afternoon.

Most were back in the communications room after supper, but just drinking coffee or Cokes and chatting excitedly, waiting for word of when Alan and Helen would be arriving. Mary and Suzy had the *Welcome Home* banner already hung across the foyer and plenty of Pontet-Canet Bordeaux on ice, although the prospect of more alcohol didn't appeal to anyone at this juncture.

When Colonel Joshua Middleton called on Jax's smart phone at nine o'clock that night, it was expected to be news about the missing Brookfields. In part, it was: they should be home by this time tomorrow. A little disappointment was detected in the cheers, of course, wishing the arrival could be sooner. But on the bright side, this would give everyone even more time to flush the aftereffects from last night's pre-celebration out of their systems and be in better shape to start all over again.

The other reason for the phone call was to invite Jax and Suzy to join the colonel on Little Sister and witness firsthand the Regg send-off. The colonel explained that once they escorted the mothership more than a few

311

thousand miles from Earth, the current video signal coming into Brookfield would degrade and eventually be lost. The only way to see the Reggs final departure into the great spans of space would be from Little Sister.

The surprise invitation was received with one of Jax's wittier responses: "Say what?"

"The brass figured you two have earned it," said the colonel. "None of this would be possible, if not for all you've done."

In the proceeding seconds of stunned silence, the events of the past months—good and bad—flash before Jax's eyes. He had locked up like a stone pony when he was supposed to shoot a Regg with his M16. *Bad.* He had taken out the entire crew of a daughter ship and flown it into the belly of Little Sister. *Good and good.* He had failed to protect Alan when the Reggs shot him down and kidnapped him and Helen. *Bad.* He had personally splashed three Regg fighters during that same Regg raid. *Good.* And ever since, he had done little more than sit here in the safety of the Brookfield communications room, watching the dramatic events of the past twenty hours unfold on a fifty-five-inch window. *Eh.*

Coming back to the reality, Jax's legs started shaking. "Baby," he gasped, wobbling to where she had been monitoring the networks for any news or rumor of UFO activity, "you and I are invited to join them on Little Sister."

Suzy pulled out her ear buds and turned to face her husband. "Did you say something, hon?"

Still in disbelief himself, Jax shook his head and repeated the good news.

"Oh, my God," Suzy chirped, spinning around in her office chair. "When?"

"When?" Jax asked into his communicator. Listening, his eyes got almost as large and round as his wife's. "Right now."

Chapter 129

Half an hour later, Fighter-One was shooting straight upward into the night sky. Obeying its preprogrammed flight plan, it built steadily to just below Mach 1. As always, regulations required not scaring the shit out of the sleeping populace below with a sonic boom.

Once well into the thermosphere two hundred miles up, the craft automatically arced to an angle of eighty degrees and edged up its speed, topping out two minutes later at ten thousand miles per hour. No worries of sonic booms up here in air too thin and rarefied to carry sound waves back to Earth.

The dark, foreboding profile of the Regg mothership—being chaperoned by the smaller, but deadlier Little Sister hanging directly above it—came into view, still holding clandestinely in Earth's shadow. The actual three dimensional panorama of the subdued blues and browns of Earth, shrouded in intermittent, dark-gray clouds below, had been utterly breathtaking, even in the backlight. The gently curved outline of post-sunset on the distant western horizon glowed a bright orange against the backdrop of a billion stars peeking through the black velvet of outer space.

"Look at all the lights," exclaimed Jax, glancing down at the clusters of city and urban lights sprinkled across their planet's nighttime surface. "Each dot is all the street lights of an entire metro area. It doesn't seem real."

"I know," sighed Suzy with wonder. "I wish we could stay up here forever. It's so heavenly quiet, and even the Regg ship seems serene and part of God's handiwork." Quintessential Suzy.

Jax had done no flying or navigating since leaving the hole in the pond. And so it continued, as Fighter-One's programming slowed it to a crawl to enter the belly of Little Sister. For Jax it was déjà vu all over again, only this time he was in his own craft and entering through a much smaller hatch employing an airlock system.

They were greeted and helped out of the spacecraft by four accommodating corporals—two men and two women—all in the usual brown and tan, desert camouflage fatigues. A short introduction was made to a young female staff sergeant named Lopez, who quickly led them through a series of halls and elevators to a platinum placard reading *Lounge* in black letters. Her code key open the portal to reveal the smell and ambience of what reminded Jax of the interior of the plush, Gulfstream

G650 private jet he and his dad had once taken on a fishing trip to Mexico. But upon visual inspection, that's where the resemblance ended. This room had square corners, not rounded. It was four times wider, had an eight-foot ceiling, brilliant blue carpeting, and no windows. It was actually what Jax had imaged a break room might look like at the CIA or NSA or the mysterious Desert itself.

Rising to his feet to meet them was a most-familiar face belonging to one Colonel Joshua Middleton. His grin and stature were even larger than witnessed during those many video chats between The Desert and Brookfield Farms. And so were his eyes, because those signature flight glasses were presently folded and hanging on the top button of his desert fatigues. With extended hand the crew-cut colonel stepped up to shake Jax's hand. Jax had the one quarter-Mejan officer by two inches and thirty pounds.

"Good to finally see you in three dimensions, Colonel" quipped Jax, pumping the hand. "You look *rounder*."

"And you, Mr. Jackson," replied Joshua, squelching a smile. "You seem considerably bigger than on tee-vee." He turned to petite Suzy and bent over to give her a modest hug. "Suzy Brookfield Jackson," he said softly into her ear. "You are even prettier in the flesh. Welcome to outer space."

Chapter 130

All twelve of the cream-colored, over-stuffed leather chairs were anchored firmly to the floor, forming two sets of three on both sides of the room. Each had a broad tray that swung easily down and out of the way. The colonel had already claimed the aisle seat of the three nearest the front on the port side, so Suzy took the middle and Jax the wall. The Jacksons habitually looked for seatbelts, but were told by the colonel that wouldn't be necessary. Not just yet, anyway.

Directly in front of them on the forward bulkhead were four wide-screen, closed circuit monitors. The upper left one was a bird's eye view from one of Little Sister's belly cameras, peering down on the Regg mothership. The most noticeable feature of the hostage craft was that large omega shape, covering the center half of the ship's topside.

The upper-right screen was presently blank. The screen in the lower-left was a wide angle vista of the dark side of the earth, whose shadow they remained in, keeping it between them and the sun. Joshua explained this was to avoid reflecting flashes of sunlight back to the UFO conspirators, tabloid investigators, and some seven billion other no-need-to-know people below.

The three occupants of the Lounge had no trouble finding things to talk about, which was a good thing because the most boring screen of all—the one on the lower-right—revealed what all the folks back at Brookfield, The Desert, and Lord only knows how many other secret bases had been seeing throughout this entire ordeal: the black leather, executive chair inside of the chamber of his highness, *Emperor* Khan. He was still there, as ordered. But judging from the angle showing mostly the soles of his red boots, he was supine and fast asleep.

Jax was in the middle of retelling the night he and Suzy were kidnapped, when Monitor 1—previously showing just the top of the Regg mothership—suddenly switched to the now-familiar face of alias James T. Kirk. His real name, according to Colonel Middleton, was Theodore A. Cherry, a four-star Army general and commander-in-chief of The Desert. He was clearly a *10*—a one-hundred percent, all-American, card-carrying, Denver Broncos fan, human.

"Hello again, everyone," he began, in his usual low-key, no bull demeanor. "I'm happy to inform you that all the Regg daughter crafts are present and accounted for, at least according to their mothership's computer data files, which we have been aggressively downloading for the past twenty-five hours. While we still have much of the text to translate, fortunately their numbers are our numbers. Mathematics is indeed the universal language."

General Cherry paused to look with a curious brow at something slightly off-camera. "Wake up, Khan!" he abruptly yelled, obviously seeing the same image of Regg feet everyone else was. It took a rousting by a subordinate officer before Khan woke and slowly righted himself in the recliner. He growled something in his own language at the officer, who quickly pointed out the image of Kirk on the screen. Reality set in. The single, derogatory word needed no translating.

Chapter 131

With a subtle, yet contemptuous shaking of his head at the amateurish antics of his counterpart, General Cherry temporarily cut the transmission to the Reggs in order to address only his own countrymen. "In just a few minutes," he began, "we will be leaving Earth orbit to escort the Regg ship out of the solar system. By the time we are bidding them farewell, most of you in the Americas will have rotated to the other side of the planet and be unable to receive our signal. So, we are going to shut down all communications. We apologize, but we are sure you understand. We will, of course, be recording everything from now on, for your perusal at the earliest possible date.

"So, let me take this final moment to say a heartfelt thanks to all of you down there for all you've done to bring about this victory. And a victory it is, like none other. In the history of mankind it is the first victory to be shared by *all* nations of the planet Earth, not just a few. Yet, ironically, ninety-nine percent of its inhabitants will never know of it." He paused, and then added almost as in prayer, "As it always has been and always must be."

"Shit!" Jax said under his breath. There went the last of what was only a snowball's chance anyway of ever being allowed to publish his book.

"So, to those of you who are leaving us now," said General Cherry with a smile, "good bye and God speed. We'll be in touch soon." He gave a salute, nodded to someone off camera, and the feed to Earth was cut.

"To those of you onboard Little Sister," continued the general with the slightest tick of mirth in one corner of his mouth, "please fasten your seatbelts and return your seats to their upright positions. We will be taking off shortly. And to you, Khan, and all your fellow aliens, do whatever you usually do for blast off. As we've already uploaded the sequence to your navigation computers, we will be gradually building to the half-light speed of three hundred million miles per hour."

"You that anxious to get rid of us, Kirk?" sneered Khan.

"You have no idea," returned the general, turning to his right and giving someone the *go* signal with a short nod.

As in the fighters, flipping up a protective cover and pushing a button made their seats slowly and completely engulf Joshua, Jax and Suzy with the high-tech, anti-gravity spacesuits that were themselves connected directly into the ship's own anti-gravity system. Detecting a degree of anxiety from Suzy, Colonel Middleton reached over and tapped her on the inflated white shoulder. She turned her head forty degrees inside her helmet and looked at him through the transparent shield. Her eyes were even bigger than big.

"It's just like in a fighter," he reassured her. "Even at the half-speed of light, you'll think you're floating in water."

Suzy nodded with a weak smile. She then turned to the other way to look at Jax, seated on her left. "Piece of cake, Suzy Q," he grinned. "Just think of what we are going to see."

That took some of the edge off. This was, after all, an extraordinary adventure they were lucky enough to experience. But it did bring up an interesting question. "Just what *are* we going to see?" she asked innocently.

That threw Jax for a loop. "I don't know," he confessed. He leaned forward to look at Joshua. "What *are* we going to see?"

"Hell, I don't know," said the colonel with a shrug that was hardly noticeable inside his Michelin Man spacesuit. "Maybe a planet. Mars? Jupiter? The asteroid belt. I don't know. Shit, I'm no astronomer. Ask the general."

Chapter 132

As advertised, the moderate acceleration to half the speed of light was accomplished in ten minutes and was hardly noticeable. The anti-gravity pressure suit squeezed evenly around Suzy like it was gently taking her blood pressure from head to foot. She found the sensation quite similar to flying in one of the fighters at only a fraction of this speed: kind of exciting, kind of erotic. She had asked and was assured by the colonel it would have no ill effects on her unborn baby. Jax then asked just how many controlled tests on a pregnant woman in a spacesuit leaving Earth at half the speed of light that conclusion was based on. Joshua just snorted.

Once their speed leveled off, the pressure suits deflated, retracted, and our three passengers were told over the PA system they were *now free to move about the cabin.* They could even smoke, if they wished. Joshua went to the wet bar. Suzy hit the head. Jax walked over to see what there was to eat in the galley.

At this juncture there wasn't much to watch on the forward bulkhead screens. All were dark, except the upper left one showing the huge, Regg mothership about ten clicks in front of them, appearing to go nowhere into a massive wash of bright stars, none ever drawing closer. But before anyone could even consider settling into the typical humdrum of a long flight, one particular bright light directly ahead was indeed growing larger. Within a few minutes the telltale blue and gray striations—one of which owned the famous Great Red Spot—foretold they were approaching the solar system's largest gas giant: Jupiter.

Suddenly, the other three screens flashed to life. The one in the upper right rekindled Khan in his usual black silk pajamas in his usual high-back chair. Elbow on armrest, hairy cheek on hairy fist, he made sure everyone knew he was bored with having to stay in his chair.

In the lower left screen were again the head and shoulders of General Cherry, alias Captain Kirk, more of a determined look in his steely eyes, as he kept glancing down at something in his hands.

The lower right screen was apparently a shot of Little Sister's bridge looking forward from behind. Beyond the massive panel of chromatic buttons and lights and dials and switches—manned by two seated, inanimate officers, ostensibly waiting for something to do—was the full-crescent windshield, revealing the Regg craft in the flesh at a distance of ten miles, but still filling the view. Above that windshield was a large television screen, magnifying the same image to the power of four. During acceleration, the eight circular engines on the Regg's broader rear end had been glowing orange from the surging power source. They were now quiet and dark-gray, like the rest of the mothership, as it cruised along at three hundred million miles per hour…Jupiter growing larger.

"Better get your little butt off the pot and in here, baby," called Jax, rapping on the restroom door. "The general appears ready to say something."

"Out in a minute," she said, the sound of water running in a sink.

At the well-stocked wet bar Joshua hurriedly put the final touches on three goblets of his specialty, Planter's Punch. Out of courtesy, one went to Jax. Out of concern for the unborn child, none for Suzy. Out of necessity, Joshua kept two for himself. Jax assumed the colonel was preparing for a long, boring trip, feeling he might as well get half-smashed during it. He was probably long overdue for a vacation anyway. But that's not why Joshua felt the need for alcohol. A lot of alchohol.

Chapter 133

"Before sending you on your way, Khan," said the general straight forwardly, "there is one more thing you need to do."

"And what might that be?" queried the irritated leader of his clan, not moving from his previous position of childish apathy.

"Have one of your officers bring a utility belt over to you, one with the three spray bottles you folks are so fond of using on humans and Mejans."

"What for?" hissed Khan.

"May I remind you," said Cherry with no uncertainty in his tone, "that with the push of one button your craft is at the very least permanently dysfunctional...and at worst no longer part of this universe?"

Two yellow eyes rolled and Khan growled something to someone on his right. The utility belt was produced shortly.

"Show me the gray bottle," said the general.

With a huff the gray bottle—known to make the recipient a relaxed, obedient puppy—was plucked from its slot on the belt and held up for viewing.

"Very good," said Cherry. "Now take off the cap and spray yourself full in the face."

A string of undecipherable verbiage was followed by the English equivalent of go forth and have auto-manipulated sexual intercourse.

"Ready the missile," shouted the general to his right.

"All right, all right!" said Khan, his left hand in the stop position. "Just tell me why."

"Fair enough," said Cherry. "Spray yourself and I'll tell you."

Khan said something so softly it was hard to tell if it was in Reggese or English. He uncapped the bottle, pointed the nozzle at his face from as far away as his arm could stretch, and pushed down the plunger. The narrow mist crossed the three feet span and fell gently on Khan's scrunched up face. When he could hold his breath no longer, he exhaled hard and had no choice but to inhale. Within seconds a relaxed grin spread across his blue lips and his yellow eyes closed halfway.

"Good stuff, huh, Maynard?" teased General Cherry.

"It is kind of nice," slurred Khan. "Very relaxing."

"Yes, it is. Now spray yourself once more for good measure."

This time Khan did so gladly and without hesitation.

"From this moment on," the general continued quickly before anyone near Khan could interfere, "you are to obey only me. You will not hear anything but my voice. Do you understand?"

Khan nodded pleasantly.

"And tell your crew that the same applies to them that applied to you: if your ship does anything but stay on its present course and speed, it will be blown to Regg hell. Tell them now in English and in Reggese."

While Khan did as instructed, back in the VIP lounge Jax asked out loud, "What do you suppose the general is up to?"

"Don't worry," said Colonel Middleton, taking a big gulp, "it's part of the game plan."

"It makes sense," commented Suzy. "It's a good way to keep a leash on Khan until sent on his way."

Jax took a healthy pull on his Planter's Punch and scrunched his tanned brow. "I just thought of something," he said pensively, swirling the ice cubes in the half-full, tall glass. "What's to keep Khan from turning around in a day or week or month or even a year and coming back to Earth? With that ship covered in stealth the way it is, he could easily slip in some night, sink to the bottom of some ocean, and take up right where he left off."

"That is a good question," said Joshua quietly to himself. He took another drink, this time draining cup number one.

"Apparently, the general has been thinking the same thing," offered Suzy. "Let's see what he does here."

Chapter 134

"Very good," said Cherry, when Khan turned back to face his new master. "You did that so well, in fact, I'm now going to give you the pleasure of spraying your face with the blue bottle. Do it now."

Again without hesitation, the Regg leader—calling himself *Khan*, after Ricardo Montalban's character in *Star Trek 2, The Wrath of Khan*—pumped the spray bottle with the *be true blue* mixture full in his face, this time from only a bent arm away. If his goofy expression changed any, no one could tell.

The general waited a few seconds to let the chemical take full effect, then began the pre-listed series of questions, which Khan would be forced to answer truthfully.

"Are all your daughter ships and fighter crafts and members of the Regg nation now inside your mothership?"

"Yes.

"No others out there? Or another mothership?"

"No. We are all there is."

General Cherry looked back down at his notes. "We show your power source is currently off, and you are cruising at a speed of three hundred million miles per hour. Is this correct, Khan?"

"Yes," he said, still smiling drunkenly.

"Do you intend to stay on this course and speed as long as we are behind you?"

"Yes."

"If you were to start your engines again, how long would it take before you could maneuver your craft?"

Khan looked to his right, presumably for verification from his engineers in the know. "About one minute," he replied, almost laughing.

"Thank you. That's about what we gathered from downloading the data in your ship's computers." General Cherry looked down again. "After we leave you," he continued evenly, "do you plan to come back to Earth?"

"Yes," replied Khan, as if telling a waitress she got his breakfast order right.

There was a buzz of verbal activity off screen inside the Regg's command center. The words were unintelligible, but their frantic nature was unmistakable.

"Holy Leptos!" gasped Suzy.

"I knew it!" hissed Jax.

"Shh, listen," said the colonel, pointing at the screen.

"How soon do you plan on returning?" asked Cherry. "A day? A week? A year?"

"Maybe a week," replied Khan matter-of-factly. "We will need to scout out a good new location."

"You will return, even when you know we outgun you and have superior technology in all respects?"

"Yes. We will stay out of sight until our engineers can devise weaponry like yours." He smiled wide. "Balance of power, you know."

The increase in disturbances and volume by the Regg officers in the background prompted another warning from the general. Any change in course or speed would mean immediate annihilation.

"If and when you do achieve this balance," pursued the general, "will you continue with your plan to conquer and colonize the earth?"

"Of course."

"Why?" asked Cherry.

"Because it is what we do," Khan replied methodically with a grin. "It is the way of our ancestors. It is our nature."

A silence fell on the dialogue. Everyone in the VIP lounge was holding their collective breath.

General Cherry slowly looked to his left and gave a *come here* motion with his head. He turned back to the camera and said, "I'd like you to meet someone, Khan."

Chapter 135

The camera zoomed out. An elderly Mejan shuffled into view to stand beside General Cherry. This was not a half Mejan. This was a pure Mejan. Only five foot tall and maybe ninety pounds. He was in his mid-eighties with light gray skin wrinkled like a dried white raisin. His thin gray hair hung straight down from the crown of the shiny bald spot atop his bulbous head. The two, old, sad eyes were the size of tennis balls and black as night. His nose and ears were almost nonexistent, and his button mouth seemed permanently puckered in a kiss. He was hunched over from age, and carried the characteristic Mejan swayback.

"This is *Drutali*," said the general proudly, "more affectionately known around here as *Pappy*. He's one of the originals, only fifteen-years-old when the Mejans arrived on Earth seventy years ago." General Cherry handed him some kind of silver remote device about half the size of the standard issue communicator. It had a round, red button in its center. "We have Pappy to thank for more innovations than I could list in half an hour. But one of his main accomplishments is the very anti-gravity energy source powering Little Sister here and most of our crafts."

As Khan sat in his chair like a half-asleep, uninterested blob of black silk, Cherry put an arm around the thin shoulders of Pappy and gave him a gentle tug. "There is one more thing you should know about this fine being," said the general. "He is the father of the woman named Maggie Connors you Reggs kidnapped and tortured and let die slowly in your foul prison for two years, before grinding her up and feeding her to the fish."

Khan's eyes opened a little wider. He knew of this woman, even though it was from another time and place in the Regg history on Earth. Her information had been most helpful in learning about the Mejans, back when the Reggs didn't know they even existed. So, this was her father, huh? Khan's expression yawned, *So what?*

"Here is what's going to happen now, Khan," said The Desert's commander-in-chief with pursing lips. "Pappy is going to push this button and launch a 220-megaton Cruise missile right up your ass. It is powerful enough to level New York City, so there will be nothing left of you but space debris."

"You kid me," laughed Khan, with no fear in his voice, sitting up straighter.

"I'm sorry," replied Cherry. "I do not."

"But that's murder," said Khan calmly, able to grasp the concept of what was about to happen, but not really caring.

Judging from the off-camera screams and howls, the rest of his crew certainly *did* care. One of them jumped into view and shouted in pure panic, "You kill us all in cold blood? It sassination!"

On the overhead screen on Little Sister's bridge, a soft, orange glow suddenly appeared on the rear end of the Regg spaceship. They were firing their main engines. In one minute they would be able to make a run for it. Not enough time. Not by a long shot.

"Not *sassination*," mimicked Pappy with a frail, scratchy voice. "*Extermination...*" he held the device up toward the camera and pushed the red button. "...of Earth's longtime *infestation*."

The Cruise missile launched from a forward tube somewhere underneath Little Sister and streaked toward its target ten miles away. It was locked dead center on the mothership's huge posterior. There was nothing the Reggs could do to avoid it.

Chapter 136

"Don your suits everybody," warned the general, "and brace yourselves. We're going to be braking in five seconds."

The three in the VIP lounge were already in their anti-gravity spacesuits, thanks to the forewarning from Colonel Middleton, who obviously had been in on this from the get-go. For all Jax and Suzy knew, he might even have been the mastermind.

Three, two, one. Little Sister's retrograde rockets quietly and gently fired for only a second, slowing itself down from half the speed of light to a scant two hundred and ninety million miles per hour. It was enough to send occupants of Little Sister thrusting forward in their seats, and enough to instantly put a few hundred miles between them and the Regg ship as the Cruise missile reached its target.

Beginning to pixelate just before impact, the upper left screen in the VIP lounge was showing the back of some Regg officer in a dark-green jumpsuit, straddling Khan in his chair, pummeling him with relentless right and left blows. It then flashed and went dark with a high pitched tone that lasted only a nanosecond.

Simultaneously, in the vacuum of space, a silent nuclear explosion far off in the distance etched across the upper-right screen with a blinding blossom. In the middle was a thin, horizontal line of white light stretching from one side of the frame to the other.

The shock wave and its accompanying new space debris—the center of it still traveling at its same sub-light speed at the time of the explosion—would never reach Little Sister, which was slowly and steadily continuing to decrease in speed, now some two thousand miles away and subtracting by the second. But even the back edge of that ever-expanding disk of debris would eventually fall victim to Jupiter's gravitational pull, adding the new category of *Regg space junk* to its list of objects being disintegrated in its hot, gaseous atmosphere thousands of miles thick.

At first it didn't seem real to anybody; it was only a sci-fi movie or a bad dream. After all, it was on *television*. Then the reality…the finality…the genocide of an entire race began to seer into people's minds. Still in her voluminous silver and white spacesuit, Suzy passed out, slumping to her left onto Jax's back, as he was bent over vomiting all over the floor between his boots, barely getting his helmet off in time. Colonel

Joshua Middleton sat slumped inside his suit, unmoving, unblinking, expressionless, numb.

On the bridge, Pappy's legs gave out, slumping into the arms of General Cherry. The most non-violent being on or above the earth had just done the most violent act in its or Meja's civilized history.

It was abhorrent. It was genocide of an entire species. But it had to be done. They had no choice. The Reggs sealed their own fate with their unwillingness to compromise, their incapacity to change, their propensity for mindless murder. Earth was saved from God only knows what may have eventually transpired, if the Reggs had been allowed to return.

It was indeed an extermination of an infestation.

Epilogue

Chapter 137

After the short debriefing aboard the Blackhawk, followed by complete mental and physical evaluations at Travis Air Force base near San Francisco, it was determined the best thing was for Alan and Helen to get back home to loved ones and a stable environment as soon as possible. Unfortunately, it was already daybreak, which meant sending a Desert spacecraft for them would violate the strictest restrictions of daytime missions. So, with a most pleasant, one-eighth Mejan, female major from Travis to accompany them, Alan and Helen were given some brand-new carry-on luggage with an odd assortment of clothing and toiletries for filler, and put in first-class seating aboard the morning's first flight out of San Francisco International Airport on a Delta Airlines 737.

To hide Helen's significant Mejan features, her large head was covered with a bouffant-type, brunette wig flowing over her shoulders. A white, air-pollution mask graced her small nose and mouth (allergies, you know). To provide the extra nitrogen she needed in regular, ten minute intervals, a small tank mislabeled as Oxygen (emphysema, you know) was attached to her hip by a white belt. And her large green eyes were hidden behind the pair of oversized, wrap-around sunglasses. Most people onboard just assumed she was a San Francisco native, so she didn't stand out all that much.

They had a short layover in Minneapolis, and then onto Cedar Rapids, Iowa, where they were almost bowled over by Mary, David and Mike at the foot of the airport's down escalator. In conservative Iowa, Helen did look a little peculiar.

Back at Brookfield Farm the celebration began, but the champagne stayed on ice until Jax and Suzy were home safe and sound as well. Fortunately, they didn't have long to wait, as the Jacksons set Fighter-One down inside Maude just a couple hours later. Inside the downstairs recreation room emotions ran the gamut…from pure joy for all being reunited again…to thankfulness for no one being much worse for the wear…from exaltation for being rid of the Reggs…to uncertainty what life would be like from now on without the constant threat of being scanned and kidnapped by a heartless alien race.

Both Helen and Alan had to admit that thanks to the *gray to obey* chemical being sprayed in their faces every four hours during their captivity, they didn't have any bad memories of the experience. It was almost like being on a relaxing, carefree vacation in the Twilight Zone. The residual effects, however, seemed to hang on somewhat into their trip back to Iowa, as the flight attendants became increasingly apprehensive about asking the odd couple if they needed anything. That simple question was continually met with lengthy spiels involving every sexual, culinary, and materialistic desire Helen and Alan could think of. It was a good thing they were never asked anything more personal.

What everyone most wanted to hear about was Jax and Suzy's adventure aboard Little Sister and the Regg departure from our solar system. The pair was embarrassed to admit they had apparently fallen asleep for a couple hours on the way out there, but were awakened in time to see Khan—under the influence of the truth spray—testify that the Reggs would never come back. The mothership was then released to find its way past Jupiter and on out of the solar system.

Both Suzy and Jax had forgotten about the strange taste in the back of their throats upon awaking from their short naps. Jax had experience the *gray to obey* spray and its aftertaste, and Suzy knew of that one, too, plus the *blue be true*. But neither had been hit in the face with the *amnesia* spray that Colonel Middleton had administered to them one hour after the Cruise missile impacted the Regg mothership. Its actual fate was to be kept top secret from everyone except the small, hand-picked crew aboard Little Sister. And any of them who found the experience too horrible to carry for the rest of their lives were granted the amnesia spray, as well.

So, thanks to the expertly-doctored video footage they thought was live, as far as the rest of the people at The Desert, Brookfield Farm, and all the secret bases around the world knew, Khan had sprayed himself with the obey and truth chemicals, vowed never to come back, and took himself and a couple thousand fellow aliens off into the Regg sunset.

Chapter 138

Our solar system was an interesting place in the following days. Jupiter's immense gravitational field continued to draw in various-sized pieces of maraging steel, chromium, silicon, poly-carbonate, manganese, plastic, flesh, hair, bone, and teeth. Any of these elements previously launched in the opposite direction by the nuclear explosion wouldn't arrive right away, of course. But regardless of how far or near they had to travel, all eventually either disappeared with a brief flame-out in the gas giant's thick, hot atmosphere, or simply settled into an orbit around any one of Jupiter's known sixty-three moons.

Meanwhile on Mars, the rover *Curiosity* was on its way to a new quadrant inside Gale Crater…once more to dig into the Martian soil in what was becoming a two-year-long futile attempt to find evidence of water or life—ancient or otherwise—on the Red Planet.

Earth was her usual busy sphere. People went about their daily lives, while repairs were well underway on The Desert's secret location, as well as Area 51, both damaged by the Regg attacks with the bunker buster bombs. Colonel Joshua Middleton had resumed his duties, and Little Sister was back in her crib, deep inside some nonexistent secret facility in a desert not on any map. Due to too much partying, combined with too little sleep and stamina, the celebrating at Brookfield Farms was winding down to crooked smiles and slurred words.

Past the earth a quarter of a million miles, even our dead moon held something of interest, if you looked real close. Just inside the western horizon of its so-called *dark* side—the hemisphere that never faces the earth—is the four hundred and sixty miles wide, three miles deep, *Crisium Basin*. Resting on its bottom inside a trough is an elliptical object, slightly rounded on top, over two miles long, a mile and a half wide. Spanning almost the entire breadth of its topside hull is the tale-telling embossment in the shape of the last letter of the Greek alphabet: omega.

Khan had told the truth. Under the drugs he had no choice. He honestly believed his mothership, with all one hundred and ten daughter crafts, all two hundred and nine scouts vessels, all four thousand and thirty-two fellow countrymen, women, and children were the extent of the Regg presence in this part of the Milky Way Galaxy. He was never told differently.

Consequently, no one on Earth—from human to Mejan to Regg—knew the crew of another Regg mothership had been monitoring all radio and television transmission from the blue marble for well over two years. They had learned a lot. They knew many of the errors their careless brethren had made in trying to colonize Earth. They would not make the same mistakes. They would wait until the time was right and the plan was foolproof.

They had even cracked Suzy Brookfield's algorithm for keeping all communications between The Desert and her family secure. In fact, they had heard every conversation and witnessed every video relay for the past eight months. In tribute to this recent technological breakthrough, posted on one wall inside that very communications room inside the Regg spacecraft is the phrase spoken more than once by Colonel Joshua Middleton:

"Those sonsabitches are indeed the sneakiest, most paranoid bastards in the Universe."

He had no idea.

With a literary career spanning decades and hundreds of feature articles, non-fiction books, and novels, Richard Douglas Taylor's subject matter has ranged from astrophysics to aliens. His imaginative storylines have the right touch of humor to make them a joy to read and difficult to put down.

Books by Richard Douglas Taylor:

Novels—
The Brookfield Daughter
The Brookfield Daughter—Sanctuary
Earth-Two
Earth-Two—Game-Changers

Non-Fiction—
Under the Solar/Lunar Influence
How to Know When to Go
Making Sense of It All

Web site: www.primetimes2.com/books.html
Email: rdtaylor@mediacombb.net